MURDER
MOST
FREQUENT

Roger Keevil

GW00499006

MURDER MOST FREQUENT

Three Inspector Constable murder mystery stories

by

Roger Keevil

Printed by CreateSpace, an Amazon.com company
Available on Kindle and other devices

In homage to some of the great ladies of detective fiction – Agatha Christie, Ngaio Marsh, Dorothy L. Sayers, Ellis Peters, Lindsey Davis ...

MURDER ON THE ROCKS

Dave Copper cleared his throat. "Guv ..."

Detective Inspector Andy Constable glanced up from the report before him. "Mmmm?"

"Is it okay by you if I dump this lot for now and carry on with it tomorrow?"

Constable looked at the clock on the wall above his junior colleague's desk. Ten past six. "Don't see why not. I can't see that the wheels of justice will grind to a halt if a few time sheets don't make it upstairs until then. Why? Got plans?"

"Er ... as it happens, yes, guv."

In the pause that followed, Andy Constable focussed his attention more closely on his colleague and raised a single interrogative eyebrow. "Oh yes?"

Detective Sergeant Copper coloured faintly under his superior's gaze. "Yes, sir. I'm going out for a meal."

Constable put down his pen, swung round in his chair, stretched his long legs out in front of him, and smiled. "Come along, Copper. You don't expect to get away with it as easily as that, do you? I'm guessing that this is not going to be a burger and chips out of a cardboard box, eaten in solitary splendour at a plastic table under a neon strip light. I know you too well. So come on, out with it – who is she? Let's have the how, where and when."

Copper sighed quietly. "Her name's Molly, guv."

"Further and better particulars, if you please, sergeant. As far as I was aware, you devote all your waking hours to the pursuit of your police career, leaving no time at all for frivolities like a social life. So where on earth did you get the chance to meet this young lady?"

Dave Copper grinned. "As it happens, sir, it actually was in the pursuit of my police career. Do you remember that guy who jumped through a window when we went to arrest him, and cut himself to bits? Well, I was the one who got to escort the quite literally bloody idiot to hospital to get himself patched up before we could bung him in a cell - that's where I met Molly. We got chatting – she's a nurse in A & E."

"Couldn't resist a girl in uniform, is that it?"

"Something like that, guv," admitted Copper.

"So you've only known her a couple of weeks, then," deduced Constable.

"Yes. And we've met up for a drink once or twice, but you know what it's like with shift work, sir, so when she said she had tonight off, I thought I'd give it a go on a proper date. And it's her birthday."

"This sounds serious. Where are you taking her?"

"One of the guys was telling me about this restaurant he knew called the 'Palais de Glace'. Sounds a bit poncy, I know, but he said it's a bit unusual and the food's really good. It's up on The Rocks."

"Where?"

"Sydney Street, guv. There's an Aussie pub called the Captain Cook along there, and a few more bars round the corner in Botany Bay Lane, so people have started calling it The Rocks after the place by Sydney Harbour."

"Very whimsical. So will they be serving you kangaroo steaks and tinnies at this place? It doesn't sound too Australian to me."

"I think it's supposed to be more classic French, guv." Copper sneaked a glance at his watch. "And it's a set time for dining – everybody's supposed to get there at seven-thirty, for some reason. So if I can ..."

Constable chuckled indulgently. "Go on, push off. Go and make yourself irresistible for this poor girl, who probably hasn't the faintest idea of what she's letting herself in for. I'll see you on Monday, and I want a full report."

"Guv?"

"On the meal, dolt! Go!"

Constable's face bore a smile as he watched his colleague's brisk exit. He saw a young man in his late twenties, medium height with an unruly shock of light brown hair. In the relatively short time that the two had been working together, and despite the age gap of less than twenty years between them, he had come to feel almost parentally fond of Copper, although the sergeant's irreverent take on the business of policing and his occasionally incongruous sense of humour amused and exasperated him in varying measures. But the younger man's occasional sudden

6

insights into the baffling aspects of certain cases, and his dogged determination never to let anything get on top of him, were qualities that the inspector admired, probably unaware that he saw much of his own younger self in Dave Copper's character.

With a faint sigh, Andy Constable turned his attention to the documents before him. Paperwork – his unfavourite part of the job. And so often the enemy of thought, he mused to himself. He ran his fingers through his dark hair, blessedly thicker than that of many of his contemporaries, although with an increasing sprinkling of grey which he tried not to think too hard about, and settled with determination to his study of the latest demands from the top brass for an improvement on clear-up rates. Oh well, tomorrow is another day, he thought – with luck, something will turn up, and I can stop being a paper-pusher and go and be a proper policeman.

*

At quarter past ten that morning, Giuseppe Roni gave a slight start as he was greeted by a sudden gruff 'Morning, Pepe!' as he entered the apparently deserted kitchen. A head of badly-permed grizzled red hair, held back off the face with a knotted headscarf, popped into view above the burners of a large gas range.

"Oh, Vi! You make me jump. I don't know nobody was there."

Violet Leader rose to her feet, puffing slightly as she did so, and peeled off her rubber gloves. Overall-clad, plump and motherly, she gave the young chef a smile. "Don't you worry about that, young Pepe," she replied in her surprisingly low-pitched Midlands accent. "I'm not going to be here long. And the butcher's just been – he's put all the meat over there where I'd already done the worktop. I was just finishing off this oven – I'm running a bit late because it was all mucky inside. Somebody," she added accusingly, "has been letting their casseroles overflow."

"Don't look to me," said Pepe. "This week I am doing the puddings. You should be telling Oleg."

"What, complain to old Lego?" chuckled Violet. "I've got better things to do with my time than have him start on me. Anyway, he's in a bad enough mood as it is. He's out front with Miss D., so I'm keeping out of his way. Soon as he's back in here, I'm off out there to get on with the dining room."

As if on cue, the door from the bar crashed open, and a grim-looking man in his forties, dressed in chef's whites, burst through it. Oleg Lamb's forehead was deeply etched with frown lines, and his eyes flashed with annoyance.

"You still in here, Violet?" he barked. "You should be gone by now."

"Just finishing now, Oleg, dear," replied Violet, apparently unruffled by the abruptness of the greeting. "But I'll be back later to do your veg prep. You just let me know how much you want." The reply was no more than a grunt of acknowledgement, and Violet picked up her tub of cleaning sprays and cloths. "I'm out front if anyone wants me." She made for the rear door of the kitchen, almost colliding in the doorway with a short man carrying a case of wine. "Whoops-a-daisy!" she cried, as the two sidestepped each other in a vain attempt to pass through. "Shall we dance?"

"Oh, stop it, Violet," responded the newcomer in a rather downtrodden nasal voice. "I haven't got time to mess about. This is heavy, you know." Alan Key looked to be in his early sixties, with a thin wiry frame and thick heavy-rimmed glasses. His hair, such as it was, was greased down unattractively from a centre parting. He deposited the box on an adjacent worktop and juggled with a large bunch of keys hanging from his belt, before selecting one and unlocking a door next to the entrance through which he had just arrived.

"Do you want any help?" asked Violet.

"No thank you," said Alan primly. "I've got my job to do, you've got yours."

"Please yourself, dear," said Violet. "Just thought I'd offer. Well, I'll get on, then." She vanished into the corridor, where a brisk and purposeful clatter soon arose from the direction of the utility room.

"Everything okay, Alan?" asked Pepe hesitantly.

"Not really, Pepe, no," replied Alan. "The delivery lorry was late, and then the driver wouldn't bring the wines round the side because he said he didn't have time, so he just dumped everything on the pavement and was off like a shot before I had time to check everything. So I've had to carry it all round to the back yard myself, and now I'm just starting to check it, and I bet it's not all here. I shall be having a word with Miss Delaroche about those wine people, make no mistake. Anyway, I can't stand here chatting all day. I've got work to do." He turned, picked up the wine case, and disappeared into the wine store to the sound of ripping cardboard and the clinking of glass.

"Talking of work, Pepe," remarked Oleg, jamming his chef's toque on to his head and selecting a fearsome-looking knife from the magnetic rack on the wall, "do you propose to join me, or do you expect the food to cook itself today?" He donned a chain-mail glove, reached for a large plastic-wrapped beef rib joint on the tray in front of him and began to tear off its covering.

"Sorry, chef," apologised Pepe. "I go out and change straight now. I won't be long." He shrugged off his backpack and was already removing his coat as he exited into the corridor on his way to the staff shed in the rear yard.

*

Angelique Delaroche looked around the deserted dining room of the 'Palais de Glace'. It had been, she reflected, quite an achievement, even though it never looked its best by daylight. The heavy crimson velvet curtains had been pulled back from the large windows, and the light fell unforgivingly on the scatter of tables, naked except for their covering of pink plastic oilcloth, which yet looked so stylish when dressed with lace tablecloths and silver cutlery. The figured wallpaper in a rich purple, highly effective in offsetting the gold frames of the many pictures adorning the walls, made the room gloomy on the brightest days, even when – or perhaps because – the harsh fluorescent working lights shed their featureless glare over everything.

Angelique gathered together the papers spread over the table in front of her into a neat pile, rose from her seat and, with a quiet sigh of impatience, crossed the room to straighten one of the paintings which had become slightly askew. Her walk, even in those few steps, had an elegance and confidence which consorted well with her whole appearance. Blonde hair drawn back into a chignon enhanced the shape of her oval face, with large grey eyes and shapely, naturally dark but artistically plucked, eyebrows. Her complexion was pale, with subtle touches of blusher and eye-shadow in shades of bronze, toning well with an almost copper-coloured lipstick. Her slim figure, small feet, and hands with immaculately-manicured nails whose polish matched her lipstick perfectly, contributed to an almost agelessly chic image, and nobody meeting her for the first time would have guessed that she was in her early forties.

The rattle of the letterbox in the front door interrupted her reverie. Crossing to the small lobby, she bent down to collect the mail, and leafed through it as she returned to her seat. The usual mixture – junk mail with the latest offers from an ever-increasing number of broadband providers, and brochures from cruise companies who, for no discernible reason, had added the restaurant's address to their mailing list and who now laid out a tempting selection of destinations at almost irresistible prices. If only, thought Angelique. A few hand-written envelopes which looked as if they contained welcome deposit cheques for party bookings – Carey can deal with those, decided Angelique, placing them in the reservations book which lay open before her and closing it with a slight grimace. She tore open the envelope from the bank and cast her eye down the monthly statement of the restaurant's finances before laying it aside to be scrutinised later. The final item of mail was a heavy cream envelope bearing the discreetly-embossed logo of a prestigious London firm. Intrigued, she slit it open and, with steadily widening eyes, began to read the contents.

*

In the flat above the restaurant, Toby Rockard folded the spare towel neatly and placed it on top of the other sports kit in his backpack. As he glanced around the bedroom, he caught sight of his reflection in the range of floor-to-ceiling mirrored wardrobe doors and, automatically tensing without even being aware of the fact, allowed himself a moment of quiet self-approval.

A little over medium height, Toby had the broad shoulders of a swimmer, tapering to a waist which bore not even the slightest trace of the beginnings of the spare tyre which so many of his anguished thirty-ish contemporaries at the gym were beginning to notice in themselves. That the body was well-toned was obvious, but without the over-defined musculature which betrayed the fanatic, although a sculptor would probably have used discretion in fining down the particularly sturdy calves, whose presence was doubtless accounted for by the lycra cycle-shorts their owner wore. The face was good-looking, well-proportioned in an unremarkable way, with deep-set almost black eyes looking out from beneath a heavy flop of dark brown hair. Toby reached for the tee-shirt lying on the foot of the bed and pulled it on.

Moving into the living room of the flat, Toby opened the heavy velvet drapes to their widest extent to let more of the mid-morning light flood into the room, pushed aside a jumble of brocade cushions, and sprawled on the sofa. Not for the first time, he gave a little snort of impatience. All this stuff is all very well in the restaurant, he thought, but I wish Angie had left it downstairs instead of cluttering this place up with it as well. He picked up his diary from the coffee table before him and began to leaf through it to review his appointments. Just one client for this morning, and two for this afternoon. Good job I checked, he thought – I'd forgotten that Karen cancelled for this evening. I'd have looked a right fool if I'd turned up on her doorstep in the middle of her dinner party. And I must remember to call the community centre to see exactly when they want me to start those spinning classes. He consulted his large, ostentatious, and extremely expensive sports watch. Time to go. He returned to the bedroom, laced on his trainers, hefted his backpack on to his shoulders, collected his phone, keys, and cycle helmet from the table by the front door, and clattered down the stairs towards the restaurant rear entrance.

*

As Candida Peel returned to her desk at the InterCounties Media Group offices, her colleague at the adjacent work station looked up.

"You've just missed a call. Greg wants a word. Can you call him back, please."

"Well, he'll just have to wait," responded Candida airily. "I can't do everything at once. If I don't get this review proofed within the next half hour, I shall miss the print deadline for next month's county mag, and then I shall have the editor down on me like a ton of bricks. Perhaps Greg would like to have to explain that to him! Oh no ... wait a minute," she laughed. "Greg *is* the editor. So he can hold his horses until I've finished." She tucked her hair behind her ears, put her glasses back on, and leaning forward, prepared to give her attention to the screen in front of her.

Candida Peel's striking looks were the envy of several of

her journalistic colleagues, who suspected that they were often the reason why she was chosen for a particularly plum assignment interviewing an awkward local politician or a visiting celebrity. Her generous tumble of auburn curls, entirely natural in colour, offset a pair of dazzlingly bright green eyes which occasionally hid behind a pair of heavy-rimmed designer glasses. The glasses were mostly an affectation – in truth, they were only necessary for reading the smallest of small print, but Candida found them useful in helping to dispel the prejudice, particularly among some of her older and more hidebound interviewees, that beauty and brains did not go together. Her figure, generous without being plump, was a marked contrast to the models who graced the fashion pages of the magazines in which her articles appeared.

"You know, I feel sorry for you sometimes, C." Her colleague rose and came to look over her shoulder. "It must be a terribly hard life, getting paid to go out and enjoy yourself."

"It's a dirty job, Paula," smiled Candida in agreement, "but somebody's got to do it."

"So which restaurant was this?" asked Paula. "Go on, give me all the gruesome details so that I can be really jealous." The questioner's ample proportions were an indication that the subject of food was of some interest to her.

"Bistro just opened over at Camford," replied Candida. "New old-fashioned sort of place, done up a bit like a French wine cellar with half-barrels for tables, loads of naked brick walls, and racks and racks of wine bottles – sadly, most of them empty."

"Never mind about the décor," interrupted Paula. "Get to the bit about the food. That's what they send you to write about."

"Quite good, actually. Sort of Creole-peasant fusion." Candida noticed the time display on her screen. "Look, I would love to take you through the meal course by course, but if I don't get this done soon, I really will be for the chop. You can read all about it and drool over the photos when the article comes out next month."

Paula was reluctant to be dismissed. "I still don't see how you can enjoy a meal properly when you're on your own. And you're out again tonight, aren't you? I think Greg said that's what he wanted to talk about. You know, you ought to take someone else along for a second opinion. Somebody like me, for instance," she hinted with a heavy lack of subtlety. And when Candida refused to rise to the bait, "Anyway, that place must have been all right." Paula took a final look at the screen before returning to her own desk. "You've given it four-and-a-half stars."

Candida's face wore a quiet private smile. "That's because I'm a generous woman."

*

Carey Agnew finished shaving carefully, wiped the residue of foam from his chin, and splashed his face with cold water. He surveyed the result in the mirror, opened the bathroom cabinet, took out a diminutive pair of scissors, and trimmed a couple of errant hairs in his pencil moustache. Satisfied with the outcome, he returned to the bedroom and donned an immaculate white shirt, before turning his attention to the selection of a tie.

Carey was a dapper middle-aged man, slim and almost six feet tall, with an air which hinted at the possibility of some sort of military background. His silvery grey hair was neatly brushed back with a flawlessly precise parting, and the carefully-judged sideburns were not too short, not too long. His manner was that of a perfect gentleman – an air of charm, friendly without being over-familiar, and a beautifully modulated voice with the faintest hint of a Scots burr, made him the perfect choice to deal with the clientele of an elegant restaurant. And so when the opportunity had arisen some few years before to become the visible face of the 'Palais de Glace', he had seemed the ideal candidate. In his tailored blazer with accompanying regimentally-striped tie at lunchtimes, or formal ensemble of black jacket and striped trousers for evening service, he trod a carefully choreographed path, welcoming guests to the restaurant and escorting them to their tables, offering information and gentle advice as to the menu, while preserving a discreet but firm discipline over the waiting staff and a cordial relationship with the kitchen.

The clock on the mantelpiece in the living room of Carey's small but smart garden flat showed that there was plenty of time in hand, and he poured himself a whisky before settling down in an armchair by the window which overlooked the tiny tree-shaded green plot at the rear of the Edwardian house. He picked up the morning's paper and began to peruse the contents, leafing swiftly over the latest depressing news about the international situation, the current medical scandal, and lingering briefly on one or two of the more interesting crime stories, before folding the paper, reaching for a pen, and preparing to tackle the crossword, his cat purring contentedly on his lap. After three quarters of an hour, and with three clues still stubbornly refusing to elucidate themselves, he looked again at the clock, rose to his feet, brushed off the thankfully few cat hairs from his trousers, put down a fresh saucer of milk in the kitchenette, donned his jacket and, quietly humming, set out on the short walk to the restaurant.

*

"May I have a moment to consult my client for further instructions, madam?"

"By all means, Miss Hancart." The magistrate's voice held a tone of dry reserve. "I'm sure that would prove extremely helpful to the court."

Eleanor Eagle turned to the young man, shiny-faced and smartly-suited, seated by her. She lowered her voice to a barely audible whisper. "I really think you have no choice now. You've done what your insurers asked, but in the face of the police officer's evidence and the footage from the traffic camera, it's pointless to carry on with a 'not guilty' plea. If you change now, I may be able to persuade the magistrates to let you off with a smaller fine. Agreed?" The response was the nod of a nervous rabbit.

Eleanor rose to her feet once again. "Madam, my client has reflected on his position and has instructed me, with the court's permission, to amend his plea to 'guilty'."

Some five minutes later, justice briskly executed, Eleanor gathered up her papers and made her way out of the courtroom, through the lofty pillared hall, and down the steps of the civic building, prior to crossing the busy road towards her office. As she approached the porch of the former Georgian gentleman's town house, one of an elegant terrace which curved away to the left, she once again experienced the familiar pleasure at the sight of the brass plate which read 'Griffin, Lyon, Peregrine and Hancart'. Even after ten years, the tiny warm glow of triumph still manifested itself.

Eleanor Eagle was a woman who did not stand out in a crowd. Of medium height and build, and with brown hair in a neat businesslike bob, she was smartly dressed in a tailored charcoal grey jacket over an unfussy white blouse, with a slim black skirt and black patent court shoes. Her only concession to flamboyance was her briefcase – maroon alligator leather, and clearly extremely expensive. But she felt that by now she had earned a small amount of self-indulgence. A long process of studying law at an unfashionable establishment, followed by a struggle to find a place in a practice at a time when many attitudes among legal circles still looked down on the attempts of women to make their way in the profession, and an unconscionably-long period made up of the drudgery of note-taking and conveyancing, had eventually culminated in the desired breakthrough. After the death of the extremely hidebound senior partner in the practice, a welcome change in atmosphere had led to the offer of a partnership, and Eleanor's maiden name, which she had determinedly retained in her professional work despite a brief marriage to a motor company executive, had been proudly emblazoned on the firm's letterhead. Her reputation as an advocate had grown. And these days it was well known among the lesser criminal classes of the area that if you were faced with a charge in the magistrates' court, you went straight to Eleanor Hancart.

"Morning, Elle!" came the cheery greeting from one of Eleanor's young colleagues as he clattered down the steps from the front door. "How'd it go?"

"Same old same old," said Eleanor with a mock grimace. "As Oscar Wilde said, the good ended happily and the bad unhappily."

"Well, it all pays the bills," replied her colleague. "See you later." He climbed into his car as Eleanor pushed open the front door and entered the building.

"Any messages, Glenda?" she enquired of the smart young woman behind the reception desk.

"I've left them on your desk, Miss," said the receptionist. "Oh, and Miss Ladyman rang. She wanted to know if you were free this evening. She said she was just going out, but she'd call you again later."

"Thank you, Glenda." Eleanor headed for her office, closed the door behind her, dropped her briefcase with a quiet groan, and seated herself at her desk.

*

15

At Mallory's Gallery in a narrow lane off the High Street, Georgina Ladyman closed the door behind the exiting customer with a practised professional smile and an inner sigh. Yet another time-waster.

With short thick iron-grey hair brushed back attractively from a strong-featured face, loose-fitting fawn slacks teamed with an open-necked blouse in a soft blue stripe, and a casually-knotted blue scarf around her neck, Georgie had the look of the sort of artist who would have been found working at her canvas around the harbour of St. Ives in the 1930s. Whether the look was a deliberate nod to the expectations of those who visited her gallery in search of an unusual piece of art work for their house or office, or whether it was simply a personal style with which she felt comfortable, was impossible to say.

She walked slowly from room to room in what had been, before its conversion into a small but stylish gallery ten years earlier, an ordinary terraced workman's cottage, and surveyed the collection of items with quiet approval. Though she said it as shouldn't, she thought, she did have pretty good taste. In few cases was there anything so vulgar as a sale price on display – most items bore a small coloured sticker which indicated that there was a discussion to be had. Tiny but exquisite watercolours of Indian rajahs in the midst of a tiger-hunt rubbed shoulders with pencil sketches of human hands or animals which, for those who could not afford an actual Albrecht Dürer work, were a very acceptable substitute. Bronzes of wildfowl in flight stood alongside delicate oriental ceramics in subtle shades of blue and pink. Heavily-textured abstract canvases of swirls and geometric shapes kept uneasy company with fragile antique ivory carvings. And the pale faces and solemn eyes of sixteenth-century notables gazed across the room at oil paintings of the country estates of their eighteenth-century descendants on the opposite wall. Quite a journey, she felt, for the girl who started with nothing, from a very ordinary family on a nondescript estate. But a talent for art had been spotted by a perceptive teacher during her schooldays, and the pursuit of a degree course in the history of art had opened doors into the world of auction houses and galleries. With a few years of the routine of house-clearance valuations behind her, and with a belief that her apprenticeship had been served, Georgie had taken a position as assistant administrator of a small

16

municipal art gallery but, with the aid of an unexpected windfall from the will of a distant relative, had achieved the ambition of creating her own modest business. Mallory's Gallery, named in honour of the beneficent great-aunt, had at its inception received quiet acclaim from the art establishment, and had even garnered an approving mention or two in the more intellectual Sunday papers as a source for the tastefully unusual.

Georgie reached for the telephone to make a brief but unsuccessful call. Glancing at the face of her large unfussy watch with its plain dial and robust numbers, she seemed to reach a decision, slung her sturdy leather bag over her shoulder, put up the 'Closed' sign on the front door and, locking it behind her, headed for the High Street.

*

Oleg Lamb, had he been given to moments of introspection, which he most emphatically was not, would have readily admitted that he was not the easiest person in the world to get on with. But then, with his background, he had never really been in a position to refine his social skills.

With his roots in an Italian family which had moved to Scotland as part of a wave of twentieth-century migration, the most notorious result of which had been the Glaswegian ice cream wars of the 1980s, Oleg had grown up in a world where a talent for football had provided an enticing opportunity to escape from a grimy world and even less appealing prospects. Named for his grandfather, a Russian sailor who survived the Arctic convoys and settled in Clydebank after the Second World War, Oleg was spotted by a scout from a local team in one of the lower divisions, but his natural ability soon had him heading upwards into loftier regions among the English game. Sadly, what promised to be an exciting career was cut short by a knee injury following one of his trademark aggressive tackles, and in his twenties, he was forced to look for another path in life.

What had looked like a disaster, however, turned out to be a happy accident, and it seemed as if the apple had not fallen very far from the tree when a temporary job helping out in the kitchens of a friend's hotel revealed an obviously innate, but hitherto unsuspected, skill in cooking. The intriguing qualities of the story had provided an amusing topic for the media, and soon Oleg had achieved some degree of celebrity as his talents and

17

reputation blossomed. An appearance on the television programme 'Cooking Up A Storm' had done his reputation no harm at all, despite his often prickly reactions to the efforts of others, presenters and contributors alike, and he was even contemplating opening his own restaurant when, one day, he received a telephone call from Angelique Delaroche. The offer was persuasive – a woman with ambitions for her restaurant was seeking a chef with ambitions for his own career, and soon the deal was concluded. Neither had so far had cause to regret the arrangement – Oleg had been given a virtual free hand to exercise his talents within the restaurant's terms, and Angelique had seen the reputation of her establishment soar, following the breathtakingly-swift award of a prestigious Pirelli Diamond accolade not long after Oleg's arrival.

Oleg placed the prepared beef joints in the meat refrigerator and looked across the kitchen to where Pepe was beating a batch of egg whites in the food processor. He raised his voice above the whine of the machine.

"Have you thought about what you're going to do for the ice carving tonight, Pepe?"

Pepe switched off the machine and turned to face the head chef. "Only a bit. Somebody tell me that today is Shakespeare's birthday, so I think maybe I do something for that. Perhaps I do a bust of Shakespeare, or maybe some characters, like Romeo and Juliet."

"How about Lady Macbeth?" muttered Oleg, half to himself.

"Excuse me, Pepe," said Alan Key, emerging from the wine store. "I couldn't help overhearing. I suppose, being a foreigner, you wouldn't know that the twenty-third of April is also St. George's Day, would you? Why don't you do something nice and English like St. George and the Dragon?" he suggested in his prim voice.

"Yeah," agreed Oleg. "Do a dragon. That'd be perfect." With a snort, he turned back to the worktop where several brace of pheasants awaited his attention.

*

Of all his dining experiences, mused Dave Copper, this was probably the most memorable, but the one he would most like to forget.

The evening started well. Copper collected Molly from her

flat sharp at seven-twenty – the young nurse looked even prettier than on their previous encounters, with her dark hair caught back to show off her elfin features to their best advantage, and a dress in some sort of floating fabric in shades merging from lilac to plum. A thin gold chain with a single diamond pendant adorned her throat. An uncharacteristically slightly nervous Copper felt glad that he had chosen his newest and smartest shirt.

"Good evening, sir – madam," oozed Carey as they entered the restaurant in the wake of the small group of people who had passed through as the doors opened just before the couple arrived. "Welcome to the 'Palais de Glace'. Mr. ...? Copper? This is your table here. Please be seated – here is your waitress with your glass of champagne, compliments of the house, and I shall be with you shortly."

"Free champagne?" giggled Molly. "They're pushing the boat out, aren't they?"

"I think I may have mentioned that it was your birthday," confessed Copper. "So, many happy returns."

As the two sipped their drinks, Copper took the opportunity to survey the dining room of the Palais de Glace. Palatial was indeed the first word that sprang to his mind. Everywhere was the sparkle of crystal, with twinkling chandeliers overhead and wall lights with cascades of faceted drops scattering a myriad of tiny points of light all around the room, echoing the reflections from the cut-glass wine goblets on the tables. Silver cutlery and silver candelabra bearing crimson candles gave a more muted gleam, forming an elegant accompaniment to the dull gold glow of the picture frames ranged around the walls. And presiding over all, in pride of place opposite the entrance, a grand portrait of a young woman in extravagant eighteenth-century court dress, her silver-grey hair adorned with ostrich plumes, and her piercing blue eyes perfectly offset by an exquisite necklace of diamonds nestling on her immaculate white bosom.

The meal did full justice to the setting. A procession of ever-more enticing dishes was paraded around the tables for the visual delight of the guests, before being served by the waitress, a middle-aged woman with a quietly competent air. The bottle of wine suggested by Carey proved to be the perfect accompaniment. And as the evening progressed, the young couple

19

grew steadily more at ease in one another's presence as they learned more about one another, the conversation ranging over topics as varied as childhood anecdotes, holiday destinations, and favourite television programmes, with all the while an unspoken agreement to avoid the subject of their work. And it was with faint surprise that Copper noticed that several of the other guests were beginning to rise from their tables to leave.

"I had no idea it was that time already," he said. "I suppose we ought to think about going, or we'll be the last ones here. I hope I haven't talked you to death."

"Of course you haven't, Dave," smiled Molly in reply, reaching across the table and placing her hand on his. "It's been really nice. And we're not in any hurry, are we? I'd love a coffee."

"Oh. Right. Sure. Er … excuse me." Copper put out a hand to attract the attention of Carey Agnew, who was just returning from the front door after seeing two women off the premises amid a flurry of smiles and cries of 'Thank you' and 'It's been lovely'. "May we have some coffee please?"

"Certainly, sir," replied Carey smoothly. "I'll bring it to you straight away." He passed through to the kitchen. "Coffee for two for Table 6, please," he said to Oleg Lamb, "and I'd better take Her Majesty's through to the office as well. Actually, I'll do them. If you're going out front, you'd better get a move on – people are going."

"If I must," grunted Oleg in surly tones. "Better get a fresh apron, hadn't I?" He stamped out through the rear door of the kitchen.

Carey busied himself preparing a tray with coffee cups and a Georgian-style silver coffee pot, before delivering it to Copper's table. "Will there be anything else, sir?"

"Just the bill, I suppose. When you're ready."

"Of course, sir." Carey disappeared back towards the kitchen.

As Copper and Molly began to sip their coffee, their eyes caught one another's, and they smiled.

"Could we …?" They both began to speak simultaneously, and laughed.

"Go on, you first," smiled Molly.

"I was just going to say," said Copper, "I've really enjoyed tonight. Could we do it again some time?"

"I'd like that, Dave" was the welcome response. "It's been a lovely change from – well, you know, all the reality of every day – you know, work, and so on."

"Tell me about it," agreed Copper. "It's a treat to be able to escape once in a while."

The crash of breaking crockery and the muted cry were faint, but all Dave Copper's senses were nevertheless immediately on the alert. "What on earth ...?"

He did not have to wait long for an explanation, as a shaken-looking Carey Agnew appeared in the entrance to the rear hallway of the restaurant. "Somebody, please ... there's been a horrible accident."

"What's the matter?" Copper sprang to his feet.

"Someone had better call an ambulance," spluttered Carey. "It's awful."

Copper took control. "Look, sir – I'm a police officer, and this young lady is a nurse. What exactly has happened?"

Carey seemed to make an effort to pull himself together. "Thank goodness. You'd better come through and see. I think ... I think she may be dead!"

*

"So where were you last night, guv?"

"Badger-watching."

"Eh?"

"There is no need to sound so surprised, sergeant." Inspector Constable's voice was terse. "And you can also close your mouth – the slack-jawed look does nothing for your image as an intelligent police officer."

"Sorry, sir." Dave Copper kept his tone carefully neutral, as the two detectives stood in the dining room of the 'Palais de Glace'. "So, badger-watching, eh? And this would be why we couldn't reach you?"

"Evidently."

"Ah. Right." A pause. "You know, guv, I had no idea that you were interested in that sort of thing. You never mentioned yesterday."

Andy Constable sighed. Obviously an explanation of some kind would need to be volunteered. "My life is not the open book you evidently assume it to be, sergeant. I do do other things from time to time. And as it happens, one of the chaps in uniform is

21

very into wildlife. We got talking in the canteen the other day, he said their group was going on a badger-watch because they thought that one of the setts might have a litter of cubs, and would I like to go along? Better than the endless murder mystery repeats on TV, I thought. Long story short, we all went out into the Forest last night, miles from anywhere, and I didn't get back until about three this morning."

"I did try your mobile, sir."

"Which I had switched off. Piercing ringtones and badgers do not mix particularly well. And I didn't switch it back on until this morning, which of course is when all the voice-mails popped up. Now, will that be all, sergeant, or are there any further details of the cavortings of said badgers you would like me to describe?"

"No, sir. Sorry, sir." Dave Copper sounded abashed.

"Good. In which case, perhaps you would like to bring me up to speed. Who, what, where, when?"

Copper consulted his notebook. "The dead woman is Angelique Delaroche, sir. Age forty-one. Owner of the restaurant, or at least part-owner."

"And what exactly happened?"

"It was about ten past ten last night. We ... Molly and I ... we were having coffee, and another few minutes and we would have been gone ..."

"How very fortunate that you were here on the spot, sergeant," remarked Constable drily.

"Hmmm." Copper did not sound at all convinced. "Not sure I agree with you, sir. And I know Molly wouldn't."

"Put a bit of a dampener on the evening, did it?"

"It's not funny, sir," objected Copper. "I had to get her to come and look, just to confirm that the woman was dead. It's not what you'd call the perfect end to a date, is it?"

"Probably not," confessed Constable. "So what happened next?"

"I got them to call a taxi for her and sent her home, sir. You can talk to her later if you want, but she was with me the whole evening, so there's probably not a lot she could tell you that I can't."

"You may well be right. But just in case we do need to speak to the young lady, I presume you have an address for this Miss ...?"

"Codling, sir. Yes, I have."

"Good. And so much for mixing business with pleasure. Right - to work. Where did all this happen?"

"Through here in the office, guv." Copper led the way out of the dining room and along the short rear corridor towards the office. "It's here at the end on the right."

"And what are these?" asked Constable, indicating the other doors in the corridor.

"The ones here on the right are the loos, and the third one is a sort of storage and utility room," explained Copper. "The one on the left goes through to the kitchen. And that's the back door straight ahead."

"Is that the only way in?"

"Apart from the front door, yes, sir."

In Angelique Delaroche's office two ghostly figures flitted, white-overalled Scene-Of-Crime investigators who stepped aside deferentially as the detectives entered. The room was bare, devoid of the opulent furnishings of the restaurant's public rooms, with a workmanlike L-shaped desk incorporating a computer work-station, two plain metal-and-plastic upright chairs in front of the desk, an ordinary grey steel filing cabinet, and a wall chart which seemed to serve as a combined calendar and work schedule. The sole concession to any form of comfort was a deeply-upholstered swivel armchair in rich burgundy leather behind the desk. On the desk were scattered the usual array of items – a telephone, a holder for pens, paper-clips and reminder notes, a brass art-nouveau letter-opener, and a flexible-necked desk lamp. And immediately in front of where the user would sit, a large A2-sized tear-off pad, bearing the name of a well-known wine wholesaler, which served as a combined calendar and jotter, in the centre of whose otherwise unmarked white paper was a pale red stain.

"That's where we found her, sir." Copper pointed to the armchair. "She was sitting there, slumped forward over the desk. And we had to sit her up in the chair, guv, to check on her, and that was when we could see that she'd been stabbed in the chest. That's where that stain came from – it must have leaked out from the wound."

"Who found her?"

"Chap called Carey Agnew - that's the one who let you in

23

this morning. He's the restaurant's head waiter. It was just after he'd brought us our coffee – he told me he normally took Miss Delaroche a coffee in her office around ten-ish, and apparently he walked in and found her in the state I saw. I heard a yelp and a crash where he dropped the coffee tray – you can see the mark from the coffee on the floor there, sir – and then he came rushing out to the dining room, and I was in here in seconds after that."

"So, being the man on the scene, you took charge?"

"Well, I sort of felt I had to, sir. Obviously, I did try to get in touch with you ..."

"Don't worry, sergeant. I'm not criticising. I think it was extremely resourceful of you. Showing some initiative is going to do your prospects of promotion no harm at all." Constable smiled. "At some point in the very distant future, of course. You're far too useful to me to let you take flight just yet."

Copper looked at his superior in surprise. "Did I hear right, sir? Was that actually a compliment?"

The inspector cleared his throat. "Don't get too used to it. And you might have started, but you haven't finished – so keep talking."

"Right, guv." Copper took another look at his notebook. "I reckon I did everything according to procedure, sir. I phoned it in – got SOCO here as soon as I could – the doc came and took a look at the victim and confirmed that she was officially dead, and he's had her taken away for autopsy, which he says he'll be doing this morning – that's about it, really. SOCO were here at the crack of, but they've mostly gone now, apart from these two."

"Just finishing off now, sir," intervened the shorter of the two, her face protruding from the surrounding white hood like the moulded face of a child's teddy. "We'll be out of your hair in a minute."

"Fine. Anything else, sergeant?"

"I think that's everything, sir," said Copper. "Oh, and I've got a list of all the relevant people who were here at the time, of course."

"I wondered when you were going to get around to that," said Constable. "So, shall we take a seat out in the restaurant, and you can give me the lowdown on who's who." The pair made their way back to the dining room and, guided by Copper, seated themselves at the table he had occupied the previous evening.

"There's quite a few on the list, sir," began Copper, "but fortunately we can pretty much rule out any of last night's customers because most of them went nowhere near the back corridor. But there are a couple that I'm sure we'll want to talk to, according to Mr. Agnew."

"Such as?"

"There were two women here, who I gather are old friends or colleagues of Miss Delaroche's. In fact, I noticed her join them at their table for part of the meal, but I wasn't really paying that much attention, to be honest."

"Understandable. And who are these women?"

"There's a Miss Ladyman – I gather she owns some sort of gallery. And the other one is a Mrs. Eagle. She's a solicitor."

"Eagle? Eagle?" mused Constable. "Can't say I recognise the name. Anyone else?"

"One other woman, sir – a journalist by the name of Candida Peel, who apparently was here to do some sort of review of the restaurant. But here's an interesting snippet, sir. She wasn't eating alone. She was dining in the company of Miss Delaroche's boyfriend, a chap called Toby Rockard."

"Oh yes?" Constable was intrigued.

"But it was all above board, according to Carey Agnew," explained Copper. "In fact, I understand it was all arranged by Miss Delaroche herself."

"How very generous of her. Well, we shall have to speak to the young lady for verification. I take it she is a young lady, sergeant?"

"Yes, sir."

"And attractive?"

Copper hesitated. "Honestly couldn't say, guv."

"Hmmm. I'll take that as a yes. And I'm assuming you have contact details for all these people?"

"Yes, sir." Copper checked his notes again. "Addresses, and I've got all their mobile numbers. The gallery and the offices of the other ladies are here in town. I've had a quick word on the phone with all of them. And Mr. Rockard lives in Miss Delaroche's flat over the restaurant. I've checked – he's up there now. I said we'd want to speak to him this morning, so he said he'd wait in for us."

"Is that the lot? Surely not."

25

"Oh no, guv – I've got several more. There's the head chef, a chap by the name of Lamb – he's out in the staff shed at the back at the moment – and there's his sidekick, who was in last night, although he was out of the restaurant by the time it all kicked off. He's due in a bit later – Italian, I'm told. There's also a maintenance bloke, Mr. Key, who wasn't actually here at the time of the murder, but he turned up later in the midst of all the kerfuffle, and he might be useful for some background. And last but not least, there's the washer-up, who was here during the whole thing."

"And who's he?"

"She, sir. Lady by the name of Violet Leader." Copper permitted himself a small smile. "I think you'll like her, guv – she's quite a character."

Constable was uncertain how to interpret his junior colleague's amusement. "Yes, well, I shall look forward to that. I think."

"I'm afraid you'll have to wait a while for the pleasure, guv. Mr. Agnew seems to have taken it on himself to call her and tell her not to come in today, so she won't be here until Monday morning."

"Right, then – we'd better make a start with what we've got." The inspector got to his feet. "Any suggestions?"

"I reckon it might be politic to start with the chef, guv. Senior man, and all that. Plus I get the impression that he's got something of a short fuse, so he might not appreciate hanging about."

"Well, Sergeant Copper, since you have so far been the de facto senior investigating officer, I shall bow to your superior knowledge. So, where is this staff shed?"

*

The detectives both jumped as the restaurant back door closed behind them with a slam. Andy Constable tapped on the wooden door in front of him and, in response to the ungracious 'What?' which followed, entered the staff shed in the rear yard of the 'Palais de Glace'. The shed was of the unremarkable type found in many a suburban garden, but furnished with a couple of rather shabby old-fashioned fireside chairs, a small table and some slightly battered dining chairs which had obviously been seconded from the restaurant, and a row of metal lockers evidently intended to hold staff personal belongings.

Oleg Lamb looked up from his hunched position in one of the armchairs. "And who the hell are you?"

Constable declined to be intimidated. "My name is Detective Inspector Constable, sir – I am the officer in charge of this case." He proffered his identification. "I believe you have already met my colleague, Detective Sergeant Copper. And as I'm sure you must be aware, we need to speak to you about the events of last night."

Oleg grunted. "Look, if you think I'm going to waste my time answering a load of fu... a load of damn stupid questions, you must be joking. I've got a kitchen to run."

The inspector smiled bleakly. "Not, I'm afraid, this morning, sir. I think you have to put out of your mind any thoughts of operating the restaurant normally today, in the light of the circumstances. After all, we have Miss Delaroche's murder on our hands. And the sooner we can get on with our job, the sooner we will be able to allow you to get on with yours. Does that sound reasonable?"

In the face of Constable's evident quiet determination, Oleg gave a sigh of resignation. "Okay. What do you want to know?"

"Sergeant, perhaps you'd like to take a few details from Mr. ... it's Mr. Lamb, isn't it?"

"That's right."

"First name, sir?" enquired Copper.

"Oleg."

Copper raised his eyebrows. "Would that be O,L,E,G, sir?" A nod in confirmation. "That's a bit unusual, isn't it?"

"Named after my grandfather, if you must know, sergeant."

"I see. Foreign gentleman, was he?"

Oleg began to show increasing signs of impatience. "Yes, Russian, as it happens. Look, what does this have to do with anything? Do you think you're investigating some sort of international plot? Do you want my grandmother's maiden name? How about shoe size?"

"No, that's all fine, sir." Copper conducted a swift retreat in the face of Oleg's belligerence. "And Lamb's as English as can be, isn't it, so I don't think we've got any worries there." A level stare was the only reply. Copper cleared his throat. "So, sir, just to fill in some details, you're the head chef here at the restaurant, I believe. And that's been since when?"

"Four years, give or take." Oleg reflected for a moment. "Yeah, about that. Four years I've been building up the reputation of this place, which is why we've got a Pirelli Diamond, which they didn't have when that idiot who was here before me ran it."

"That certainly is quite an impressive accolade, Mr. Lamb," intervened Andy Constable. "These things aren't easily given out. You must have been very proud."

"Well, yeah, I suppose." Oleg seemed ill at ease with the compliment. His demeanour became almost humble. "But good food … well, it's important, isn't it? I mean, it's … it's what I do."

"And I dare say Miss Delaroche was equally proud. She must have been delighted at your achievement."

"You'd think."

"And so I assume that relations between yourself as the man in charge of the, what shall we say, artistic side of things, and Miss Delaroche as proprietor of the business, were perfectly cordial. No problems in that quarter?"

"No. None at all."

"I'm delighted to hear it, Mr. Lamb. One hears horror stories sometimes about wars between the kitchen and the front-of-house in restaurants. Good to know there was nothing of that sort going on here." Constable turned to Copper. "Sorry, sergeant, I interrupted you, I think. Back to you."

"I was just wanting to know a bit more about last night, sir," resumed Copper. "Can you tell me, Mr. Lamb, when you last saw Miss Delaroche?"

Oleg frowned. "I can't remember exactly when I saw Angelique. Sometime last night, obviously, because she had this habit of coming in and out of my kitchen all the time during service, no matter how often I threw her out. Drove me mad. It breaks the concentration – I don't suppose you'd understand. And sometimes the timings can be absolutely critical."

"Tell me about it," murmured Copper to himself. "But you can't pin it down to an exact time? Well, perhaps one of your colleagues will be able to help us with that. And you yourself – did you spend the entire evening in the kitchen?"

"Yes."

"You didn't leave it at all?"

"No. I don't have time to go prancing off round the place

when we're in the middle of getting food out."

Constable took a guess. "So at what stage, Mr. Lamb, did you go, as you say, prancing off around the place?"

Oleg sighed. "Right at the end of the evening. In fact ..." Oleg took a closer look at Copper. "You ... you were in last night, weren't you? I remember now, you were on table 6, weren't you? And I was just coming over to your table when Carey came out and said Angelique had been killed."

"So what you appear to be saying, Mr. Lamb," said Constable, "is that Sergeant Copper here is your alibi for the murder."

*

"It's not that funny, guv," protested Dave Copper, as the two detectives re-entered the restaurant.

Andy Constable continued to chuckle quietly. "You'll have to forgive me, sergeant. We don't often get anything to amuse us in these cases. It just tickled me, that's all."

"Shall I just carry on with the investigation while you're having a good time, then, sir?" Copper sounded a touch huffy.

Constable took pity on his colleague. "Right, then, Copper. Back to serious. And your remark about timings was not lost on me. I think if we can get the time-line right, quite a lot of things will start to fall into place. So let's ask some more questions. Who's first?"

"The head waiter chap is probably closest to hand, guv. I think he was fiddling around in the bar when I last saw him."

"Then we shall hasten thither and seek him out."

Copper gave his superior a sideways look. "I swear if I told the guys at the station some of the things you come out with, guv, they'd have us both put away."

"The curse of a grammar school education, lad," replied Constable airily. "I shall probably be quoting Keats at you before the case is finished."

Carey Agnew gave a start of surprise as the two officers materialised in the entrance to the small bar situated between the restaurant's dining room and the entrance to the kitchen. "Gracious, you almost had me jumping out of my skin there!" He carefully put down the glass of dark amber fluid he was holding. "We nearly had tawny port all over the place."

"Particularly fine vintage, is it, sir?" enquired Constable

29

amiably.

"To be honest, not especially ... inspector, I think, isn't it? But good enough to charge a bit extra for. The thing is, once the bottle's opened, the ports and so on do oxidise after a little while, so I keep an eye on them to make sure they haven't gone off."

"Well, I apologise for dragging you away from your duties, sir, but we do need to have a talk about last night. Shall we sit down?" Constable led the way to a nearby table, seated himself on the banquette along the wall, and gestured to Carey to take a chair opposite, as Copper attempted to fade discreetly into the background behind him. "So, sir, you know who we are, and my sergeant has told me who you are – Mr. Carey Agnew, if I remember aright."

"That's correct, inspector."

"And you are the head waiter of the 'Palais de Glace'?"

Carey bridled slightly. "I am Miss Delaroche's *Maître d'Hôtel*, inspector. I prefer not to use the term 'head waiter' – it really does not create the right impression for an establishment like ours. I mean, hers. I mean ..." Carey stopped in some confusion. "Oh dear ... I don't really know what I mean. I don't suppose any of us know what will happen now, do we?"

"I'm afraid speculation of that sort is rather outside our remit, Mr. Agnew," replied Constable. "What I'm more concerned about is gathering a clearer picture of the people who are involved with the restaurant, and the exact circumstances of last night. So if you can give us an idea of precisely where you fit into the scheme of things ...?"

"I suppose you would probably say that I am the principal public face of the 'Palais de Glace', inspector," said Carey. "I greet the guests when they arrive – once they've settled in, I go to each of the tables to tell them about the supper menu that we shall be offering them, and then I will usually assist them with their choice of wine and act as *sommelier*. Of course, I also supervise the waiting staff."

"Of whom there are many?"

"That all depends on the number of guests we have." There was a hint of evasion in Carey's voice.

"And last night?" persisted Constable.

"Just one waitress last night – Edna. Edna Cloud. She's one of our most experienced staff. As Mr. Copper here will recall, the

30

restaurant was not exactly at capacity last night. But I had let her leave just before ten as there was so little left to do, so she had left the premises before ..." Carey seemed to be searching for words.

"Before the discovery of the body." Constable was blunt.

"Yes. So I don't see that she could have had anything to do with it."

"We'll want her details in case we need to check anything with her – perhaps you could let Sergeant Copper have those. So, to summarise, you are the man in charge of the operation out in the dining room."

"I suppose you would have to say that, inspector," said Carey. "My chief responsibility is to make sure that we keep up the traditional standards of the very best restaurants. I did spend some time working in France – I'm sure you're familiar with 'Maxim's'. Paris, of course."

"You've worked at 'Maxim's'?" Constable could not keep the surprise out of his voice. "Now that is very impressive, sir. Miss Delaroche must have been extremely pleased to have secured your services. How did that come about?"

"Well, you know how it is," replied Carey. "The restaurant business can be a very small world, and sometimes it is a matter of friends of friends, and personal recommendation."

"And on the subject of Miss Delaroche, how much did you see of her last night? I'm assuming that for the vast majority of the time, you would have been out here in the dining room."

"That's so, inspector," assented Carey. "Of course, I have to go into the kitchen from time to time, but not for any protracted period. But in fact Miss Delaroche spent a large part of last evening in the restaurant. If there happened to be friends of hers dining here she would often join them for at least part of the meal, and then work later in her office."

"Which is where you found her dead body."

Carey gulped at the sudden brutality of the remark. "Yes. I normally took a tray of coffee through to her around ten o'clock every evening, so I did so last night, just as usual, but then ..." He broke off, seemingly unnerved at the recollection.

"And I've already told Inspector Constable what happened at that point, Mr. Agnew," intervened Dave Copper, "so I think we're fairly clear on events from then on."

31

Carey's hands were trembling. "I think, if you don't mind, inspector, I'd rather like a brandy. This is all very upsetting."

"Of course, Mr. Agnew. I quite understand. And we can easily continue this later." With a nod of thanks, Carey disappeared back towards the bar, where the clink of glass was soon heard.

Dave Copper took the vacated chair opposite his superior. "First to see her dead – last to see her alive, guv?" he murmured. "We've heard that often enough."

"Stranger things have happened," replied Constable in similarly lowered tones. "Although we have not a sniff of 'why?', so no reason to think it. File him in 'pending', and we'll move on."

*

"Right." Constable rubbed his hands together. "The boyfriend next, I think, before we go charging off anywhere else. You did say he was somewhere on the premises, I believe."

"That's right, guv. There's a flat over the shop, so to speak."

"Accessible from in here?"

"No, sir. There's a separate door to the staircase round in the side passage."

"Well, lead on, then."

In response to Copper's brisk knock, Toby Rockard opened the flat door and gave a small nod of recognition to the sergeant. His manner was subdued.

"This is my senior officer, Detective Inspector Constable, sir," explained Copper. "He's in charge of the case, and he needs to ask you some questions."

"Yes. You said. Look, is this going to take long? Only I've got an appointment this morning."

"In that case, we'll try not to keep you longer than we must, sir," said Constable with quiet insistence.

"I suppose you'd better come in then." Toby stood aside to allow the two to enter, and threw himself down in his customary sprawl on the sofa. "Sit down if you want to."

"Thank you, sir." The detectives took the accompanying armchairs. "So, it's Mr. Toby Rockard, I understand from my colleague here," began the inspector.

"That's right."

"And you are ...?"

"I'm a freelance fitness instructor and personal trainer."

"No, Mr. Rockard, you misunderstand me. I mean that I gather that you and Miss Delaroche were … friends. In which case, of course, please accept my condolences."

"Thank you." Toby did not seem disposed to be particularly forthcoming.

Constable persisted. "And have you been friends for long?"

Toby considered. "I suppose I first met Angie a couple of years ago, and I've been working with her ever since. As a client, that is. She was put on to me by some friend of hers – the usual thing that a lot of people do when they get to fortyish. Wanted to get a bit fitter, didn't have the time to get to the gym regularly, so the sort of as-and-when arrangement I can do suits them."

"So you became friends. And, may I assume, increasingly close friends?"

Toby gave a snort. "Look, you don't have to beat about the bush. If you want to put it that way, I've been working out full-time with Angie for a year, okay?"

Constable blinked slightly at the change of tone. "And it would be at that point that you moved into her flat to live with her?"

"Yes."

Constable settled back into the comfort of the armchair. "Thank you for clarifying that, Mr. Rockard. I'm sorry if these questions seem intrusive, but we do need to get the complete picture. So, if I read the situation aright, we have a scene of very comfortable domestic bliss. Now, can we move on to the matter of yesterday evening. You were actually in the restaurant last night, I'm given to understand. Tell me, was this a regular occurrence?"

"Not really, no. Quite often I'm working in the evenings. A lot of my clients have got full-time jobs, so the only way they can find time for a session is during the evening, plus of course, with Angie usually down here for at least some of the time, there's no point in me sitting around on my own up here like some sort of spare part."

"So how did last night differ, then, sir?" enquired Constable.

"I'd had a cancellation," said Toby, "and it so happened that there was someone from the press coming in to do a review of the restaurant, and so Angie said would I have dinner with this journalist woman. I suppose the idea was to make the meal a bit more of a social occasion so that she'd enjoy it more, rather than just work."

"A Miss Peel, I gather from my colleague here. Miss Candida Peel, I think, sergeant?"

"That's correct, sir," confirmed Copper.

"And you spent the entire evening in her company, Mr. Rockard? And she in yours?"

"Yes. Well, until we finished. And then she left to go home, and I came back up here."

"So you left the restaurant separately. I see. Tell me, sir, had you met Miss Peel before?" enquired Constable blandly.

"Er, yes ... once or twice, I think," said Toby. "Why?"

"No particular reason, sir. But it must have been that little bit easier if you knew the lady beforehand. Conversation-wise, I mean. I'm guessing you must have touched on the matter of the article she had been commissioned to write."

"Well, yes, I suppose we did. Not that I know a thing about food," confessed Toby, "but I don't suppose that mattered too much."

The inspector looked Toby up and down. "No, sir. I don't imagine it did."

*

As the detectives emerged once more at the foot of the stairs, they became aware of a voice raised in protest at the end of the side passage which gave on to the street.

"Oh, this is ridiculous. Why can't I go in? Look, I've got a job to do, you know."

"I'm sorry, sir," was the reply from the uniformed officer standing guard at the alley entrance. "So have I. I have my orders, and nobody is allowed in except authorised persons."

At a nod from the inspector, Copper went to investigate. "What's the problem, constable?"

"Gentleman here says he needs to come in, sergeant. I've told him he can't."

The new arrival looked up at Copper. "Oh, it's you. Look, can you tell this chap I've got every right to come in. I've got work to get on with. Life doesn't stop just because there's been a murder, you know."

Copper looked over his shoulder at his superior, almost managing to suppress a grin as he did so at the man's choice of words. "This is Mr. Key, sir. I mentioned him to you."

"Of course," acknowledged Constable. He took in the newcomer's waterproof jacket with its slightly over-tightened belt, the rumpled brown trousers, and the owner's rather prominent front teeth. "Well, I think under the circumstances, we'd better have him in. Let him through, officer. I'm Detective Inspector Constable, Mr. Key, and I'm conducting this investigation. So if you'd like to follow me, sir, we'll have a little chat inside." He made his way in through the rear door of the restaurant.

"Oh, by the way," added Copper in an afterthought to the P.C., "there's another chef due in, name of Roni. We'll want to talk to him as well, so you can let him in when he turns up."

"Will do, sarge."

"Take a seat, Mr. Key," said Andy Constable, resuming his former position in the dining room, as Dave Copper caught up with the two and seated himself alongside the inspector. "I believe from what Sergeant Copper has told me that you weren't actually present in the restaurant at the time of Miss Delaroche's death, but that you may be able to provide us with some helpful background information. Is that correct?"

"Yes, inspector, that is so."

"And so I'm sure you'll be quite happy for my sergeant to make some notes."

"Oh yes. Anything I can do to help." There was a note of eagerness in the nasal voice.

"So, first things first. Mr. Key … and your first name is …?"

"Alan, inspector. That's with just the one 'L' – it's so annoying when people spell it with two, but so many of them do, you know."

Constable resisted the urge to turn his eyes heavenwards. "And your job at the restaurant, Mr. Key?"

"I do all the maintenance work around here. I would have thought your young man would have told you all this."

"He mentioned something of the sort, Mr. Key, but there wasn't really time to go into detail."

"Oh, it's a very important job," preened Alan. "There's a lot to it – nobody appreciates how much goes into it. I mean, look at all the lights, for a start." He waved an arm. "I have to check all the bulbs in them every single day, because Miss Delaroche wouldn't like it if any of them weren't working, and let me tell you, it's no easy job getting up to that big chandelier there. And then there's scuffs on the wallpaper and chips on the paintwork – it all has to be checked, you know, to make sure that everything is just so. And some of the things I could tell you about what I have to do to keep the loos up to scratch after we have hen parties in ..."

"Yes, well, I don't think we need to go into too much detail in that respect," interrupted Constable hastily. "Suffice to say that you have considerable responsibilities. And have you been working at the restaurant long?"

"I've been here ever since it opened, about eight years ago. Of course, before that it was an old-fashioned draper's shop. I remember my mother used to come here to buy her knitting wool when I was a boy. That's years ago now, of course. Sometimes she used to bring me along, and I can still recall that funny sort of smell it had from all the different fabrics, and there was one of those compressed-air tube systems from the tills up to the office ..."

"It's really rather more the present day that we're interested in, Mr. Key." Constable sought to bring Alan back to the subject in hand. "You say you've worked for Miss Delaroche for eight years?"

"Oh no," contradicted Alan. "No, when it first opened as a restaurant it was started by a chap named O'Reilly. 'Colcannon's', it was called then. Irish themed, it was – something about thirty-seven different ways to serve potato." He sniffed dismissively. "It never really took off. Went bust in a year. But then Miss Delaroche bought the place, and she just absolutely transformed it, what with the pictures and the Edwardian furniture and the velvet curtains and the crystal chandeliers and so on. I think that's where the new name came from – you know, 'Palais de Glace'. It's French for 'Palace of Crystal' ... or is it 'Ice' ... both, I think."

Constable took a look around. "I think I can see what you mean, Mr. Key. I imagine under the right conditions, the décor would be very impressive."

"Fabulous, some of the pictures are," said Alan, warming to his theme. "Of course, they're all reproductions. Everyone likes that one of Marie Antoinette opposite the entrance." He pointed to the large court portrait hanging on the wall which masked the bar area, directly opposite the front door. "'*The Queen's Diamonds*', it's called."

"Nice rocks," commented Dave Copper. "The necklace, guv," he added in swift response to Constable's quizzically-raised eyebrow.

"Ooh, now that's very famous," continued Alan. "Apparently there was a big scandal about it, and they say it was one of the things that led to the French Revolution. You see, one of the ladies-in-waiting was accused of stealing it, and then ..."

The inspector felt it was time to come to the heart of the enquiry. "Be that as it may, I'm afraid the question of historical thefts is going to have to wait for another day. We need to talk about yesterday, Mr. Key. I'm aware that you weren't at the restaurant at the time of the murder, but I'd like to get a sense of the people concerned and the workings of the establishment. So tell me, what would your movements have been during the course of the day?"

Alan sat up a little straighter on his upright chair, his knees together, his hands in his lap, rather like a schoolboy about to recite a lesson. "I was in just after nine yesterday morning. We usually get a wine delivery on Fridays, so I have to check all that and put it away in the wine store. That's just off the kitchen, you see."

"And were you alone on the premises at that time?" asked Constable.

"No. Violet the cleaner was in the kitchen. She always starts in there first, before the chefs get in. And then Miss Delaroche came down from the flat – that would have been just before ten, I suppose, because she had her meeting with Oleg."

"Oh yes, sir?" Constable's interest was aroused. "What meeting would that be?"

"That's another thing that usually happens on a Friday. Miss Delaroche and Oleg always have a talk about the menus for the following week. Say what you like about Oleg, he does care about his food, but Miss Delaroche didn't always see things his way, so these meetings weren't always a lot of fun."

"We have met Mr. Lamb, sir," said Constable with a smile.

"Well then, you know what he's like," said Alan. "He doesn't take kindly to having his menus mucked about. I say 'mucked' - that's not exactly the work he uses, but you know what I mean. I

37

usually keep out of the way. But I know he wasn't exactly full of the joys of spring when he came back through to the kitchen afterwards."

"Hmmm." Constable filed the information away quietly in his mind. "So can you tell us who else was around the restaurant during the course of the morning?"

Alan thought for a moment. "I know Toby Rockard was down here sometime yesterday morning – that's right, it must have been some time after eleven, because Miss Delaroche asked me to make a note that Miss Peel's booking had to be changed to a table for two, because Toby would be joining her."

"Yes, we have been informed that Mr. Rockard was dining with Candida Peel in the restaurant last night."

Alan looked around and unconsciously lowered his voice. He leaned forward confidentially towards the inspector. "Actually, I don't like telling tales out of school, but Miss Delaroche and Toby had a bit of a row after that. I couldn't help overhearing, because I got trapped behind the bar because I was refilling the sherry decanters, and Oleg doesn't like me going through the food prep area during the mornings, so I couldn't get past without them seeing me."

"And what exactly did you overhear?" asked Constable.

"It was something about Toby having to be nice to Miss Peel, and Toby said he wasn't going to be used like some sort of gigolo, and then Miss Delaroche said that it wouldn't be the first time he'd played around, and it wasn't too much to ask to get a decent write-up. It all got very heated, and then he stormed off."

Constable exchanged glances with Copper. "And that was the last you saw of him?"

"In the morning, yes."

"And how about Miss Delaroche? When would have been the last time you saw her?"

"Ooh, now let me see." Alan paused in reflection. "I think ... no, I'm sure that was just before we opened at seven-thirty yesterday. That's when I go off for the evening. Yes, I'd done my usual, helping Pepe the chef get the ice carving through here ..."

"Sorry, sir?" Constable halted the flow. "What ice carving? I've not heard about this. Copper, what's this about?"

"Sorry, guv," said Dave Copper. "Didn't think it worth the mention. No, when we got here last night, there was some sort of an ice sculpture on a trolley just there." He pointed in the direction of the bar.

"That was one of Miss Delaroche's ideas," explained Alan. "Ice, you see – 'Palais de Glace', and all that. All part of the image. You want to ask Pepe about it – he can tell you all the ins and outs."

"Never fear, sir, we shall. But you were telling us about Miss Delaroche's movements last night."

"Well, I don't think I can tell you very much, actually, inspector, because I wasn't here, was I? No, as I say, Pepe and I came though, and Miss Delaroche was doing what she usually did just before opening, which was going round the tables making sure that the cutlery settings and the glasses were all perfectly aligned – she was a great stickler for everything being just so. You know, making sure that all the ornaments on the shelves were lined up and all the pictures were straight, and so on. Of course, everybody knew what she was like, so they always make sure that everything's spot on ... oh, except for that picture I was talking about earlier on." He gestured towards '*The Queen's Diamonds*'. "That's the one that always has to be straightened up these days, ever since Miss Ladyman had it cleaned. That's the other lady who owns the restaurant," he added in parentheses. "She's an expert on art and what-have-you – got her own gallery – and the picture was looking a bit grubby, so she arranged for it to be sent away to be cleaned. And we had to put up some big picture of a flower arrangement in its place. Horrible! But it was all worth it, because when the picture came back, it looked absolutely beautiful. All bright and fresh, and you could see all the little sparkles on the queen's necklace just like they must have been when it was first painted. The only trouble was, I think the cleaners must have messed about with the frame, because it's never been right since. It sort of drops to one side, and it never used to. I said to Miss Delaroche that I could easily put a little screw into the frame and run a bit of wire to stop it happening, but she wouldn't let me – didn't want me spoiling it, because the frame itself is an actual antique. Well, she's the boss ... was, I should say."

"Indeed, sir," agreed Constable heavily. "So, you saw Miss Delaroche doing some sort of last minute inspection, and then what?"

"That was it, really, inspector. They were just about to open the front door, and I never stay around when the customers are here, so I got my anorak and I went home. And then I came back at about eleven to see the last of the staff off so that I can lock up and set the alarms, and I found your lot here."

"I see. Well, Mr. Key, I'm sure that what you've told us will be extremely useful, so I think that about wraps it up."

"Oh good." Alan got to his feet. "So can I get on with my work now?"

The inspector shook his head. "I'm afraid not, sir. We can't allow any further disturbance to what is, after all, a crime scene."

"But what about tonight?"

"The restaurant will not be opening tonight, sir. So I suggest you make the most of the opportunity to take a day off."

"Oh. Right. I will then." Alan seemed at something of a loss. "If you're quite sure ...?"

"Quite sure, sir." The two detectives watched the disconsolate form of the maintenance man as he slowly made his way towards the exit.

*

"Interesting little morsel, that, guv," remarked Dave Copper.

"And precisely which morsel are we talking about?" enquired Andy Constable.

"That bit about Toby Rockard and Candida Peel. He's acting a bit offhand about her, and now it sounds as if the dead woman, with whom he's supposed to be having a relationship, is pulling some rather grubby strings. She wanted him to jump, so to speak, and it doesn't seem as if he was just prepared to say 'how high?'."

"Reading between the lines, I think we know precisely how high Angelique Delaroche wanted him to jump. My question is, to what degree was this reluctance genuine? I have an odd feeling that our Mr. Rockard, despite what he said, may be better acquainted with La Peel than he's letting on."

"But maybe there's a sniff of a motive there, guv," Copper pointed out. "Macho bloke, maybe being told to perform to order – that's not necessarily going to go down too well ... oh hell, you know what I mean!" he protested in response to the inspector's amused sideways glance.

"I suggest our best source of information on that little matter will be the lady herself," said Constable. "So, if we've run out of people on the premises, let's go and have a nice cosy chat with her. You did say you'd got an address?"

"Yes, guv. I phoned her earlier. Apparently she's at her office this morning."

"Working on a Saturday?" exclaimed Constable. "Now that shows dedication, wouldn't you say, sergeant?"

"Absolutely, sir," assented Copper with an outwardly cheerful smile. "Be nice to have the choice sometimes," he muttered rebelliously under his breath.

As the detectives emerged from the restaurant's rear door into the yard, their ears were assailed by the sound of an operatic aria, sung enthusiastically if not entirely accurately, coming from the staff shed.

"And that, if I'm not much mistaken, is probably the sound of our missing Italian chef," deduced Constable. "Bit of a national cliché, wouldn't you say? Although I have to say that I've never heard that particular piece of music murdered with such determined *brio*."

"Why? What is it, guv?"

"It's 'The Blacksmith's Chorus' from '*Il Trovatore*', sergeant, if you're really that interested. Can't say I've ever detected a particular fascination with opera in you before."

"No, sir, but you're always telling me that odd bits of information never go to waste. Anyway, as he's here, do you reckon we ought to grab him while we've got the chance." Copper paused elaborately. "Strike while the iron's hot, as it were?"

Constable gave his junior a long slow look, then chuckled reluctantly. "Sergeant, you are either remarkably clever, or remarkably annoying. One day, I shall make up my mind which. Come on, get your notebook out." He rapped sharply on the shed door and walked straight in, to find the young chef, clad in white jacket and black-and-white check trousers, adjusting his neckerchief in the mirror as the detectives entered. The inspector swiftly introduced himself and his colleague. "I'm surprised to find you getting ready for work, sir," he commented. "Under the circumstances."

"I know. Is terrible about Miss Delaroche," replied the chef. "Your policeman outside tell me, and I think maybe I should not

41

come in, but he said you want to see me. And I don't have nothing else to do, so when I get here, Chef said that I should get on and prepare as much as I can from today's food delivery, because then we can freeze a lot of things and then they don't go to waste. That's what he's doing."

"Good thinking, sir," approved Constable. "But I'm sure he won't mind if we keep you from that for just a few minutes to answer a few questions."

"No. It's okay. And I like Miss Delaroche a lot – she is a nice lady – so whatever you want, you ask."

"Might as well talk in comfort." Constable took a seat in one of the armchairs and waved the young cook to the other, while Copper positioned himself at the table, pad at the ready. "So, let's start with the basics, sir. Name?"

"My name is Giuseppe Roni, but everybody calls me Pepe. I am the Second Chef here."

"And have you been working at the restaurant a long time, Mr. Roni?"

"I been here about two and a half years now," said Pepe. "I started out before at the Dorchester House Hotel in London, and then I was on the *Queen Alexandra* for a couple of years."

"A cruise ship, eh? That must have been interesting, working for Cunard." Constable gave an irritated glance over his shoulder at the sudden inexplicable snort from Copper.

"Sorry, guv ... bit of a sneeze."

"You hear a lot of stories about all the food they do on these big liners," resumed Constable. "High standards, and so on. I dare say that made it easy to get a job at a good restaurant like this one." He snapped his fingers. "That reminds me! Somebody mentioned ice-carvings, which is the sort of thing they do on these cruise ships, isn't it?"

Pepe was eager to explain. "Yes, that's where I learn to do it, on the *Alex*. We always used to do a lot of ice sculptures for the formal nights and for the special midnight buffets when she was cruising, and I was mostly on the desserts station, and my boss, he was the expert, so he taught me so I could help him out. It was great – I got really into it, and they gave me my own special kit – you know, the hammer and the chisel and the ice-pick and all those. I still got it."

"And I gather you still use it."

"Yes. When I come here, Miss Delaroche, she said it would add a special thing to the restaurant for me to do the sculptures, what with the name – you know, 'Palace of Ice' – so every day I do the different carving, and it goes in the cold room until we put it out in the restaurant at the start of the evening."

"Right then, Mr. Roni." Constable marshalled his thoughts. "Let's retrace our steps, if we may. I'm wanting to build up a picture of the events of yesterday. What sort of time do you usually start work in the restaurant?"

Pepe glanced at his watch. "This sort of time, really. I normally get in somewhere between ten and eleven in the morning, but it all depends on what I'm doing that week – you know, starters or puddings or whatever."

"And were you working on your own yesterday morning?"

"No. Oleg, he came into the kitchen just after I get here, and he was in a big temper. But this is not so unusual with him, to speak the truth. It is because he had just had his Friday menu meeting with boss lady. He was going on about cuts in his budget, and he said that if she thought he was going to risk losing his Pirelli Diamond, she would soon be finding out about the cuts."

"But I presume Miss Delaroche was not with him at that time?"

"No, she was not there then. She was in the kitchen at some times later, but not for long – just to and fro like normal. I don't remember exactly when."

"How about other people around the place?" enquired Constable. "Staff, visitors, that sort of thing."

"I remember I saw that Toby Rockard, he came in through the back door just after I got here, so that must have been about eleven o'clock, I think, but he didn't come into the kitchen, and he went off in a rush about a quarter of an hour later. He didn't speak to me – I don't really have much to do with him. I think he is a bit of a … what is it they say, 'meat-head'?"

Constable managed to keep a smile off his face. "Yes, Mr. Roni, that's what they say, all right. So, anyone else?"

"Miss Ladyman was here – she's a friend of Miss Delaroche, and I think partner too. She comes to the restaurant quite a lot. And she dropped into the kitchen just to say '*ciao*' at about midday, I think."

"Was that all?"

43

"Well, I know she make a phone call to someone after that, because I could overhear it when I go out to the bar to get some liqueur to put in the gateau."

"Do you have any idea what the call was about?"

Pepe thought for a moment. "I did not hear all of it. I remember she speak about 'dissolving things', and then she said something about someone 'having to help because, after all, once a solicitor ...', and then she laugh. And then she said 'I will see you later', but then I went back to the kitchen, so I don't hear no more."

"Okay." The inspector pondered briefly. "That would take us up to lunchtime. Then, I presume, you were busy for a while with service."

"Yes," nodded Pepe, "although yesterday it was not too much."

"How about after lunch? Do you carry on working right through?"

"No, because I go home afternoons because of working in the night. And I was just about to leave, because I had done all my *mise-en-place* for the evening ..."

"Excuse me, sir," interrupted Dave Copper, pencil hovering. "Could you spell that? I didn't quite get it. What is it – some kind of pudding, like tiramisu?"

Andy Constable concealed a smile as Pepe explained. "No, sorry – is chef-talk. It means I had got everything ready for later ..."

"I think you'd better carry on with telling us what happened, Mr. Roni," said Constable, "rather than attempting at this stage to translate the entire contents of the '*Larousse Gastronomique*'. You say you were about to leave. Evidently something occurred to stop you."

"Well, sort of, although it was not to do with me. I was just going past the office to come out here to change, and I could hear Miss Delaroche, and she was tearing the strip off Carey – is that right?"

"Close enough, sir. And this was because ...?"

"He had poured wine all over one of the lady customers at lunch, and the lady, she make one hell of a fuss because it was a designer dress, and Miss Delaroche was saying about 'too much alcohol', and she say 'drinks are supposed to be for the guests to drink', and she told Carey it was the last time he would get away with it, and she didn't care who he was. I know I should not listen," admitted Pepe, "but I was little bit worried, because we all work together, and it is all one big family."

"So you were concerned?" asked Constable.

"Yes. I pop back into the kitchen and say to Oleg, 'Boss lady, she is off again. I think you better talk to Carey', and then I went home. I think that must be about a quarter to three. Yes, that is it, because I see Violet just coming down the road."

"And you returned to the restaurant at what time?"

"I got back about seven o'clock, and then I finish off some bits and pieces, and then Alan and I put the ice carving on its trolley and took it out into the restaurant just before we opened. You know, I think it was one of my best. Alan, he suggest the idea, because it was St. George's Day, so I did the group of St. George and the Dragon, with St. George standing with the sword raised just about to kill the monster. And Oleg, he made the joke, and said it was the best way to deal with dragons."

"Actually, guv, I remember it now," butted in Copper. "It was pretty impressive."

"It is a shame you could not see it, inspector," continued Pepe, "but of course, it has all melted now."

"Rather like Hamlet's '*too too solid flesh*'," remarked Constable, to the evident surprise of the other two. "You know the quote - '*Melt, thaw, and resolve itself into a dew*' – no?" He cleared his throat self-consciously. "Well, no matter. Anyway, you were saying, you took this sculpture out into the dining room."

"Yes. We always put them under the diamonds painting at the start of the evening, and then we bring them back through a couple hours later, before they have melted too much."

"And can you tell us, was there anyone other than staff around at the start of the evening?"

"No, it was just Carey, and the waitress, Edna, out in the dining room before the guests started to arrive. Miss Delaroche had come back through into her office then, I think, but I did see Toby – he was hanging about in the back corridor, and Miss Delaroche came out and was talking to him. I think it was all a bit angry, from what I could see, but then Carey came to fetch him because he say Miss Peel has arrived."

"So I assume those two would have gone out into the

restaurant?"

"No," contradicted Pepe. "It was all three of them, because I think Miss Delaroche was waiting for some friends to arrive also."

" And how about your own movements during the rest of the evening?" asked Constable.

"I was in the kitchen all the time, until I bring the ice carving through into the back hallway on its trolley at a quarter to ten. This was just after Miss Delaroche come into the kitchen to say that she was in the office if anybody want her. And then Edna, she came in and said she was going home early because Carey had said he could manage without her, and Uncle Oleg tell me I can go too, because we had finished everything, and he was just about to do his rounds out front."

"I think he mentioned something about that when we spoke to him, didn't he, sergeant?"

"That's right, sir. Said he was on his way to my table when everything kicked off."

"Mr. Roni?"

"Yes, he did it every evening. It was Miss Delaroche's idea. Oleg would go round some tables at the end of the evening to talk to the customers – you know, 'did you enjoy the meal?', 'did you have a favourite dish?', that sort of thing. He hates to do it, but Miss Delaroche, she insist. Calls it 'P.R.'. So he was going to do that, and Edna said if I was going she would give me a lift, so we came out here and I change quick and then we both go. This was ten o'clock, because it was the news on her car radio. And that's all I know until this morning."

*

"You promised me Keats, guv," remarked Dave Copper, as the detectives headed for Andy Constable's car. "You never said anything about Shakespeare."

"I would have thought by now, sergeant," responded the inspector with a smile, "that you would have got used to the ceaseless flow of intellectual enrichment resulting from my impressive classical education."

"Absolutely, guv," Copper grinned in agreement. "It's like having Wackypedia on legs. So, I assume it's a case of continuing with Plan A and nipping off to see Candida Peel?"

"Correct. And I for one shall be quite interested to learn a little more about the nature of her relationship with our Mr.

46

Rockard."

"Toby or not Toby, is that the question, guv?"

Copper was rewarded with another long slow stare from his superior. "I suppose somebody had to say it eventually," he sighed. "Get in the car. And for that, you can drive."

The offices of the InterCounties Media Group were slightly less impressive than the name might suggest. Occupying the top two floors of a modest red-brick office block, enhanced with bright blue window-frames, which also housed on its lower levels the local branch of a nationally well-known firm of accountants and the headquarters of a house-building company, the group included three local radio stations, whose studios lurked in gloomy nooks dotted around the third floor, and the editorial and advertising operations of a surprisingly long list of print titles.

"Doesn't look much for a big press organisation, sir," commented Copper as the detectives emerged from the car in the sparsely-populated car park, alongside a sign with bore the names of numerous regional newspapers and magazines. "I was expecting something a bit more industrial."

"You're thinking of the old days, sergeant," said Constable. "You've been watching too many old films. Printer's devils and thundering presses, and Fleet Street lined with the palaces of the national press. Long gone, I'm afraid. These days, all someone needs to produce a magazine or a newspaper is a computer and a link to a printing company which, like as not, is sitting in Cornwall or Aberdeen or Malaga. That's if they bother to go to print at all, and don't just publish everything online. Apparently it's called progress. '*Où sont les neiges d'antan*', eh?"

"'*Où?*' indeed, sir," replied Copper, who had been caught out by this comment before and had taken the precaution of looking it up. He surveyed the row of bell-pushes alongside the loudspeaker mounted adjacent to the locked front door. "Ring the bell, shall I?"

"Can I help you?" came the unenthusiastic tinny-voiced response.

"Police," said Copper shortly. "We're here to see Miss Candida Peel."

"Top floor. Lift's on the right." Buzz.

Emerging from the lift, the detectives were greeted, if that was the right word, by a stick-thin girl, bright green streaks in her

47

hair, who looked to be barely into her mid-teens, pecking at a computer keyboard in a desultory fashion. Eyes fixed on the screen before her, she gave a flick of the head and a mumbled 'She's through there'.

"Thanks for your help," said Constable, keeping as much irony as he could manage out of his voice, as he made for the door indicated.

Candida Peel was seated at her desk, apparently consulting a smart-phone as she translated the contents into the document she was creating on-screen. She took off her glasses and stood. "Sergeant Copper, is it?"

"That's me, miss," said Copper. "I'm the one you spoke to on the phone earlier. And this is Detective Inspector Constable." Candida held out her hand with a welcoming smile. "He needs to ask you some questions about the murder of Miss Delaroche."

"Of course. And do please sit down, gentlemen. Coffee?"

"Not at the moment, miss, thank you," replied Andy Constable, as the three seated themselves. "I'm afraid our time's not entirely our own, so I think we'd better press on."

"So it is definitely murder then, inspector?" asked Candida, wide-eyed. She casually played with a lock of her hair. "All I was told was that it was a sudden death."

"Definitely murder, I'm afraid, miss. And I'm given to understand that not only were you acquainted with Miss Delaroche, but you were on the premises yesterday evening."

"Yes, I was, although trust me not to be around at the crucial moment." Candida smiled ruefully. "My editor is never going to forgive me. Not that I'm normally involved with the crime stuff that goes into the locals, of course – I'm not that kind of journalist."

"So what kind of journalist are you, Miss Peel, if I may ask?"

"Features, mostly," said Candida. "Pretty much anything that's of interest to readers in our catchment area, from local authors, commemorations of historic events, society weddings – you name it, I'm there with my little phone to record things." A toss of the auburn hair and a laugh, in which Constable thought he could discern a touch of nervousness. "And restaurants, of course. I write the restaurant review column for the county magazine, and if it's somewhere really special, my stuff sometimes gets picked up by the nationals, which is rather nice."

"And last night, you went to the 'Palais de Glace' for a meal."

"Yes. Quite by chance, really. My editor wanted a piece on the restaurant, so that was all arranged – in fact, I had a quick chat with Angelique yesterday morning, and she very kindly laid Toby on as an escort for me for the evening, which I thought was sweet." She broke off. "Toby Rockard – that's her partner. Did you know?"

"We have spoken to Mr. Rockard already, Miss Peel," replied Constable. He decided to try a shot in the dark. "You're quite good friends, I believe."

"I ... I don't quite see what you mean, inspector." The hint of nervousness reappeared in Candida's voice.

"I mean that you and Miss Delaroche were friendly," explained the inspector comfortably. "I'm assuming that, with your journalistic activities connected with the restaurant trade, it would have been unusual if your paths hadn't crossed at some time. And I think Mr. Rockard and Miss Delaroche had been together for quite some little while, so I assume you knew him as well. Which, of course, brings us very conveniently to the matter of your presence in the restaurant last night. Now, to what extent did your path cross with that of Miss Delaroche during the course of the evening?"

"Oh, hardly at all," said Candida. "She came and said hello when I arrived, but of course after that I was with Toby all evening. I remember seeing her on and off, but I dare say she was busy, and it's not really the done thing for the restaurateur to come and hover over me when I'm supposed to be doing an unbiased review. I remember she was sitting with two other women for part of the time – friends of hers, I think Toby said. But I was paying more attention to the food – and to Toby, naturally." She smiled artlessly.

"Naturally," said Constable. "So that was all you saw of Miss Delaroche?"

"Well, no, I popped out to her office to thank her for the meal, and then I left. And I suppose that would have been about ten to ten."

"And you left alone?"

"Yes, of course I did," snapped Candida in a sudden burst of irritation. "Inspector, you seem to be getting at something, and

49

I'm not sure what."

Constable smiled. "Miss Peel, I'm sure you're not a stupid woman. I think you know exactly what I'm getting at. I'm wondering whether the friendship, relationship, call it what you will, between yourself and Miss Delaroche and Mr. Rockard could possibly contain the seeds of tension which might have a bearing on Miss Delaroche's murder. We've already spoken to one person whose information indicates that possibility, so a little more plain speaking might help us both out."

Candida paused for a few moments in thought, and then seemed to make a decision. "Okay, inspector. Here's a bit more information for you. You want some plain speaking? Fine. I like Toby, and I think he's wasted on Angelique. For a start," she continued with the brutality of youth, "she's far too old for him. Was, I mean. But that's got nothing to do with anything. Do you seriously imagine that I would go killing Angelique in order to get my hands on Toby? The idea's absurd!"

"Stranger things have happened, Miss Peel," countered Constable.

The reply was a snort of ridicule. "Look, inspector, I've no more idea than you seem to have as to who would have wanted to kill Angie. But here's something for free. I'm a journalist, so I meet a lot of people, and I get to hear a lot of things. And one of the rumours that's been floating around of late is that the 'Palais de Glace' is on the rocks financially. That doesn't mean that the food's not great – far from it. In fact, you can only admire Oleg for what he's done in the kitchen, but let's face it, the kitchen isn't everything if you aren't getting people in through the door. Why on earth do you think restaurants are so keen to get good reviews in the media?"

"Obviously, to promote the business."

"Exactly. And Angie was a realistic businesswoman, and she knew that in business you've got to have a bit of give and take, if you know what I mean. She was only too well aware what can happen if the bad word gets around."

"Which, I assume, given what you've said in praise of the restaurant, was in no danger of happening in this case, Miss Peel?"

"Naturally." Candida gave a quiet cat-like smile.

Constable's returning smile was enigmatic. "And who said

there's no such thing as a free lunch?"

*

"I'm just asking myself exactly how far I could throw her, guv," remarked Dave Copper as the detectives returned to their car.

"Considerably further than you could trust her, sergeant," agreed Andy Constable. "So, not blinded by the lady's slightly obvious charms?"

Copper thought it best to ignore the remark. "The thing is, sir," he persisted, "she's dropping hints left, right, and centre about the state of the restaurant and the people involved, but you can't help wondering if this is just some diversionary tactic. Could she be hiding the tree in the middle of the forest? Could it really be as simple as the fact that, like she said, she wanted to kill Angelique Delaroche so that she could get her hands on Toby Rockard?" He gave a dismissive laugh. "And even as I say it, guv, I'm thinking that it's just as ridiculous as she said it was."

"And as I said," replied the inspector, "murders have been committed for less. Let's not discount the theory too prematurely. Motives are funny things. So on that subject, I think we ought to delve a little deeper into the *cui bono* aspect of the case."

"Guv, you're doing it again," protested Copper. "I know you see it as your mission in life to expand my education, but the language options at my school never went much further than French, and I've already had today's French lesson. Is this another one of your legal Latinisms?"

"Well spotted, sergeant. We'll make a detective of you yet. So here's another one for your collection."

"Great," muttered Copper under his breath. "Move over, *locus in quo* and *habeas corpus.*"

"*Cui bono*," continued Constable as if his junior had not spoken, "is the legalese for 'to whose benefit?'. In other words, who profits, in whatever way, from a crime?"

"Or for ordinary dull-witted foot-soldiers such as me, what's the motive?"

"Exactly."

"Well, we've already got a hint of one or two, haven't we, guv?" Copper chuckled. "And I wouldn't mind betting that, if Candida Peel had given Oleg Lamb a bad write-up, she'd probably have found herself on the wrong end of a carving knife."

51

"What a relief that we've just got the one dead body to deal with, sergeant," said Constable. "Let's concentrate on the case we have. Miss Peel seemed quite anxious to draw our attention to a certain amount of financial iffyness in the air, so I think our next port of call ought to be the other partner in the business. Remind me ...?"

"Miss Ladyman, sir. Owns a gallery just off the High Street."

"And you have the address?"

Copper leafed quickly through his notebook. "Yes, guv."

"In which case, sergeant, as the song says, get in and drive."

At the jingling of the old-fashioned bell over the entrance to Mallory's Gallery, Georgina Ladyman looked up from behind the counter. "Yes, gentlemen? Can I help you?"

"Would you be Miss Ladyman?" enquired the inspector.

"That's right. Georgina Ladyman, but everyone calls me Georgie."

Constable and Copper proffered their identifications. "We're making enquiries into the death last night of Miss Angelique Delaroche. I believe my sergeant here has already had a brief word with you."

"That's right, inspector. And in fact, he's probably already told you, I was actually in the restaurant last night. Not at the time, of course. I'd left by the time it happened. But is it true – was she actually murdered?"

"I'm afraid so, miss."

Georgie paused a moment in apparent shock, and her hand went to her mouth. "Oh, that's awful. I didn't really want to believe it." After a few seconds, she seemed to gather herself together. "So, how can I help you?"

"Is there somewhere a little more private we should go?" suggested Constable. "I wouldn't want to disrupt your business."

"Oh, that's all right," said Georgie. "I haven't got any customers in at the moment. In fact," she added, moving to the front door, "I'll put the 'Closed' sign up, and then we shan't be disturbed." She did so, and turned back to the detectives with a businesslike air. "So, inspector, what would you like to ask?"

"I really wanted a little more information about your relationship with Miss Delaroche."

"Angie and I?" Georgie gave a wistful smile. "We go back years, ever since we were art students in London together. Of course, she wasn't Angelique Delaroche then – that was just the professional name. She wasn't French at all – no, she was just plain Angela Stone when we were together at college. And we've stayed friends over the years."

"No, actually, it was rather more your business relationship that I was interested in," said Constable in clarification. "I understand that you were a partner in the 'Palais de Glace' restaurant."

"Oh yes, that's true," said Georgie. "Yes, we've been partners in the place ever since she had the chance of buying a restaurant about five years ago. She'd always had this dream, even while she'd been doing other things. She gave up quite a high-powered job in advertising to start it up, too. And she sank a fortune into it. I think she probably mortgaged everything she had, but I suppose when the chance to realise a dream comes along, you seize it with both hands, don't you?" The wistful smile reappeared. "And it worked. The 'Palais' was a great success. That's when she changed her name, of course – I think she probably thought it would add just a little touch more credibility to the place if the owner of a French restaurant sounded French. Silly, I know, but sometimes image matters."

"And the success continues, I assume? Given the restaurant's reputation?"

"Ah." A hint of unease crept into Georgie's voice. "Well, of course, inspector, given the way the economy is at the moment, people tend to have rather less to spend on the luxuries of life. I mean, look around you." She assayed a light laugh, which did not ring entirely true. "I'm not exactly overrun with customers this morning, am I? But that's the way of business – it goes up and down."

"Even a restaurant with an award for the excellence of its food?" queried Constable.

"The Pirelli Diamond? Oh yes, we're all very proud of that. I have to say, Angie did very well when she chose Oleg to be the new head chef when his predecessor left. He is such a talented man, once you get past the rather discouraging exterior."

"We've spoken to Mr. Lamb, madam," put in Dave Copper with a smile. "We know what you mean."

Georgie gave a small frown of puzzlement. "Sergeant, am I right? Have we met? Your face seems familiar somehow."

"Not exactly met, madam," returned Copper. "You probably recognise me because I happened to be at the restaurant last night. As, of course, were you."

"Which brings us back rather neatly to the matter in hand, Miss Ladyman," resumed Constable. "You were dining at the 'Palais de Glace' last night with a friend, I believe, and I think I'm right in saying that Miss Delaroche spent part of the evening with you."

"Yes, that's quite right," said Georgie. "Angie came and joined us for part of the meal, and then of course she had things to do, so she went back to her office."

"On her own?"

"You mean, did I go with her? Oh no – in fact, I don't think I left the table during the whole of the evening. There was some business we had to discuss, and I know that everybody says one should never mix business with pleasure, but the food really is excellent, so if you're going to mix the two, I suppose there's nowhere better to do it than in your own restaurant."

"And your dinner companion will confirm all this, no doubt?" said Constable. "Sergeant, you did mention the lady's name ..."

"Mrs. Eagle, sir."

"Elle? Yes, I'm sure she will," replied Georgie. "I expect you probably know her, inspector, or at least know of her. Elle Eagle – she's our solicitor. You must have seen her pop up in court at some time or another."

"I don't know the name, Miss Ladyman."

Georgie smiled. "Of course – you would probably have run across her when she's been using the professional name. She's with quite a prominent practice in town - Eleanor Hancart, part of Griffin, Lyon, Peregrine and Hancart. But I think she uses her married name in her private life to avoid any intrusions into that from any of her, let's say, more disreputable contacts."

"I can quite understand that," said Constable. "Yes, of course I'm aware of the lady, although I don't think our paths have ever crossed. A fact which, unfortunately, is going to have to be remedied because of Miss Delaroche's death." Constable paused for a moment. "Can I come back to something we touched on earlier? One of the people we've already spoken to gave me to understand that, as you yourself said, the current economic situation is not of the best. Particularly with regard to your own restaurant. Do you have any thoughts on what they might have meant?"

Georgie gave the inspector a look of consideration, and then seemed to make up her mind. "Well, since you already appear to know something about it, I suppose I might as well be candid. Yes, I think you're probably right. It's perfectly possible that Angie had financial worries, but that really has nothing to do with me, and in case you're wondering, that's certainly not what we were talking about last night. In fact, I've got next to no money tied up in the 'Palais de Glace' anyway – only enough to cover a nominal shareholding for the initial set-up of the company."

"So where exactly did you come in then, Miss Ladyman?" asked Constable.

Georgie gestured around the gallery. "Specialist knowledge, inspector," she said simply. "I know art. Angie was always more of a dilettante. She needed me for my expertise – you know, valuing the antiques and keeping the insurances current and so on. There are actually some quite nice pieces dotted about on the shelves, amongst all the other set-dressing, as you might say. So that's how I became a partner." She broke off as if a thought had just struck her. "Partnership – it's a very flexible thing, wouldn't you agree, inspector? Things can change so much over time, and none of us is the same person we once were." Her tone, which had become reflective, reverted to its previous briskness. "But of course, I'm talking about years ago. We were all very different then."

"Sorry, miss … all?"

"Oh yes, all three of us." And at Constable's continued look of puzzlement, "Angie, Elle, and I. We were all students at the same time. Sorry, I thought I'd said. Yes, we all shared a house in London."

"No, I wasn't aware of that, Miss Ladyman. So would Mrs. Eagle have been at the same art school as you? Surely not."

"Of course not, inspector. She was studying law." Georgie smiled. "No, the only thing all three of us had in common was that we were all as poor as church mice." She chuckled. "We'd do almost anything to earn some extra money. I remember, Angie and I used to do the most awful daubs, and then go and try to sell them to the tourists in Piccadilly on a Sunday morning."

"But not Mrs. Eagle, I gather."

A wary expression came over Georgie's face. "Not exactly, inspector. Elle had to use her talents in other directions. She was a much more ... social person. And, after all, there is more than one way to finance your way through Law School. But I don't imagine that Elle would have wanted Angie to tell too many of her clients about her old, what shall we say, evening job."

Constable, after only a moment's reflection, realised the import of Georgie's hints. "And do you believe that there would have been any danger of Miss Delaroche revealing any ... let's call it 'privileged information' concerning Mrs. Eagle?"

"I really couldn't say, inspector," answered Georgie. "There was certainly nothing of the sort mentioned last night, if that's what you're getting at. Surely the best thing would be for you to ask Elle direct."

"We intend to do exactly that, Miss Ladyman," said Constable, as the sound of sudden knocking came from the shop door. Beyond the glass, a middle-aged couple were seen mouthing and gesticulating. "And it seems that we are keeping you away from your customers."

"Heavens, yes," said Georgie. "It's some people who came in during the week. They were looking at one of the pictures - rather an expensive one, actually - and they said they'd go away and think about it. I never expected them to come back."

"Then you must on no account let them escape again," smiled Constable. "We'll leave you to it."

*

"Wow!" said Dave Copper. "Did I just hear what I thought I heard?"

"Meaning?"

"What did she say – Mrs. Eagle used to be a 'social person'?" Copper pulled a face. "I know what that sounds like to me."

"Judge not, that ye be not judged, young David," intoned Andy Constable. "There's more than one interpretation you could put on those words. You ought to know by now, there is a great deal of networking goes on in and around the legal profession. It's probably the best way to get on. And Miss Ladyman could easily have meant nothing more untoward than that."

"And I'm Queen Marie of Romania!" retorted Copper. And

in response to his superior's look of astonishment, "It's a quote from a poem by Dorothy Parker, guv. Expressing incredulity. You're not the only one who can quote things, you know." With a slightly huffy air, he unlocked the car door and took his place behind the wheel.

Constable chuckled as he took his place beside him. "Sergeant, you are full of surprises. And much as I would enjoy a discussion on the writings of Dorothy Parker, I'm afraid we have work to do. And since by happy coincidence Mrs. Eagle is next on your list, if I remember correctly, we can go and assess the lady for ourselves. Drive on."

The offices of Griffin, Lyon, Peregrine and Hancart appeared deserted, with blinds down and a firmly-closed front door.

"She did say she'd be here, guv," said Dave Copper, pressing his finger on the old-fashioned brass bell-push alongside the classically-proportioned Georgian front door. After only a few seconds, the sound of approaching footsteps was faintly audible from inside, and the door swung open to reveal a woman dressed in rumpled jeans and a loose-fitting sweater, hair tucked behind her ears, and several bulging files in her arms. "Excuse me, we're looking for Mrs. Eagle," explained the sergeant.

"Well, you've found her," was the slightly unexpected response. "And I assume you're the police officer who spoke to me earlier. You'd better come through to my office. Just close the door behind you, would you?" Without waiting for a reply, Elle turned and led the way up the stairs towards her room overlooking the rear gardens. "You'll have to excuse the informal rig, gentlemen," she remarked over her shoulder. "The weekend is the one time I can leave off the strait-jacket the profession demands and actually dress to please myself. Even if I still have to come into work on a Saturday morning to keep abreast of the paperwork," she added with a rueful smile. She pushed open her office door, added the files to the already teetering heap on her desk, and waved an arm towards a leather chesterfield alongside the fireplace. "Do take a seat, Mr. ... Copper, do I remember correctly?"

"That's correct, madam. And this is Detective Inspector Constable."

"Mr. Constable," nodded Elle, shaking the inspector's hand.

57

"I thought I recognised you. I'm sure I've seen you around the courts at some time or another."

"I dare say you have, Mrs. Eagle. I certainly remember being told you were a very persuasive advocate for some of the individuals which my colleagues send up to meet the magistrates from time to time. Sometimes a little too persuasive for our liking," said Constable good-humouredly. "It was just that I didn't recognise your married name when I first heard it in connection with this particular case."

Elle's face assumed a serious expression. "Of course." She sat. "This awful business about Angie. I really only know the briefest outline, from what your sergeant here has told me."

"The briefest outline is all we have at the moment, Mrs. Eagle ... or do you prefer 'Miss Hancart'?"

"I suppose that, as we're not actually speaking in my professional capacity, inspector, it had better be the personal name. Sergeant, I imagine you're about to make a note of this conversation ..."

Copper hastily produced his notebook from a pocket.

"... so the full name is Eleanor Eagle, although everybody calls me Elle – age, forty-two – marital status, divorced – profession, solicitor."

"Which is what, I think, brings you into this matter, Mrs. Eagle," ventured Constable. "As Miss Delaroche's solicitor."

"Well, yes and no, inspector," replied Elle. "It's true, I am ... was ... Angie's solicitor, but we were also very long-standing friends. Rather longer than I care to remember, if I'm honest."

"And I believe the same applies to the other partner in the restaurant, Miss Georgina Ladyman?"

"That's right. Lord," Elle remarked reflectively, "to think we've all known each other over twenty years." She shook her head. "You wonder where the time goes."

"And it was, I understand, this fact of being both friends and business associates which led to your presence at the 'Palais de Glace' last night."

"Yes. Georgie and I had some business matters to discuss – oh, nothing to do with the restaurant, in case you were wondering. But being Georgie's solicitor as well, sometimes I also have to get involved with the occasional piece of legal work for her. All very mundane stuff, I assure you – matters to do with the lease on her business premises, or affidavits regarding the provenance of some of the works of art she supplies – that type of thing. To be honest, I usually delegate that sort of work to one of our juniors, but one likes to preserve the facade of personal attention." She turned to Copper. "And for goodness sake, sergeant, please don't put that in your notes! But yes, to come back to the point, I was at the restaurant yesterday evening to have dinner with Georgie. And I know everybody says that mixing business with pleasure is a very bad idea, but I have to say, I'm a firm believer in it. Especially where Oleg's food is concerned. But you're not here to talk about that, inspector, are you?"

"Sadly not, Mrs. Eagle. I'm more interested to know what you can tell us about when and where you saw Miss Delaroche last night, and what if anything you can tell us which may have some bearing on why somebody might wish to kill her."

Elle's face took on a bewildered expression. "I cannot imagine. Personality-wise, she was always perfectly pleasant to everyone as far as I was aware, but then, in the customer service business, I should think being pleasant is very much part of the stock-in-trade. Certainly I wasn't aware of any enemies." She stopped short and gave an odd half-smile. "And even to hear myself say it, it sounds absurd. Who on earth has enemies these days?"

Constable shook his head sadly. "I'm afraid the world can sometimes be nowhere near as nice as we might wish it to be, Mrs. Eagle. Certainly in our particular profession, we tend to come across more instances of that than most. And surely in yours too, I would have thought. But as far as Miss Delaroche was concerned, enemy or not, somebody evidently felt sufficient animus against her to wish her dead."

"Of course, inspector," acknowledged Elle. "And you haven't come here to ask philosophical questions. So what would you like to know?"

"The mechanics of the evening – who was where and when, who had dealings with whom – in fact, nice ordinary witness-box evidence. I'm sure you can relate to that."

Elle paused for a moment's thought. "Very well. In fact, it was a perfectly typical 'Palais de Glace' evening. Georgie and I met outside just as they were opening, so not long after seven-thirty, I suppose. Carey came round to our table to tell us all the usual things about the menu, and Angie came by for a second, just to say hello."

"She didn't join you?"

"Not at that point, no. And then the food started to arrive – we had a couple of glasses of wine with the meal – and after that, everything was just as normal."

"But I think Miss Delaroche did join you later, didn't she?"

"Oh yes, but there was nothing unusual about that. Yes, she came and sat down with us and had something to eat while we were having our main courses, but she didn't stay for any great length of time after that. As ever, she had things to do, so she left us somewhere around half-past nine, I suppose."

"And did you notice anything about her manner while she was with you?" asked Constable.

"Not really, no," said Elle. "She was always a little distracted under those circumstances, because she always had half an eye on what was going on around her. One of the disadvantages of owning the business, I suppose. But I can't say I noticed anything in particular. We always try to keep off anything to do with business whenever all three of us dine together – usually the conversation ends up talking about the old student days. I do remember Angie made some remark about wanting to speak to Georgie about something or other, but that was all."

"And after Miss Delaroche left your table, you saw no more of her?"

"No."

"And neither of you two ladies left the table during the course of the evening?"

"No. Well, that's to say – I did pop out to the loo just before the main courses arrived, but apart from that, no. And at the end of the evening, Angie was nowhere to be seen, so Georgie and I asked Carey to say our goodbyes for us, and then we left."

"Together?"

"Yes, except of course that she was parked in one direction and I was round the corner the other way, so we said goodnight on the doorstep. After which, the next thing I knew about what had happened was when I received the call from Mr. Copper."

"Thank you, Mrs. Eagle – I think that's all perfectly clear. I take it you have all that, sergeant?" A nod from Dave Copper in response. Andy Constable gathered himself together as if to rise,

60

but then paused. "Oh, just one thought that occurs to me, Mrs. Eagle. The question of what happens to the restaurant now. If, as I assume, Miss Delaroche was single, there would be no obvious inheritor. But of course, she did have a business partner, and I cannot imagine that, as her legal advisor, you would not have ensured that she made a will. Can you help me out with that? Without compromising your professional ethics, of course."

Elle smiled. "How very delicately you put things, inspector. Yes, I'm sure I probably can help you, although not straight away. But your assumptions are correct – I can certainly confirm, without breaking any client confidences, that I handled matters when the business was set up, and I was responsible for drawing up the original partnership agreement. And Angie did have a will – in fact, she made a new one only last year. The thing is that, of course, I couldn't let you have sight of those documents, even if I wished to, because everything of that nature is locked away in our strongroom, and the earliest I could get access to that would be Monday morning."

"How extremely disappointing, Mrs. Eagle." The look on the inspector's face clearly indicated that he was hoping for more.

Elle's expression softened. "But perhaps, under the circumstances, I could refresh my memory on Monday, and then see my way to letting you have some helpful indications."

Constable held out his hand as he stood. "That's very kind of you. And now we'll leave you with your mountain of papers. Come along, sergeant – we also have things to do."

*

"And these things would be ...?" enquired Dave Copper as the two detectives resumed their seats in the car.

"Many and varied," replied Constable. "In fact, altogether too many to think of at once. My head's buzzing." He reflected for a moment. "Right. First thing, get on to the mortuary and see if the doctor has any results from the post-mortem. That may help us along the way."

A few minutes later, Copper switched off his phone with a discouraging look. "No luck, guv. The doc's been called away – some sort of family crisis, apparently – so the p-m's not going to get done until Monday morning."

"How about SOCO?"

Copper pulled a face. "Doubt it, guv. They've only had

whatever they might have found for five minutes, plus have you ever tried to get any sense out of them over the weekend? That might have to be another thing for Monday."

"Try them anyway."

"... Oh, hello – it's D.S. Copper, on the Delaroche case ... I didn't expect to find anyone there ... well, that's good ... if you have got something for us, that's great ... the D.I. and I will be there straight away. Give us ten." Copper pressed the off button. "There's a turn-up. SOCO seems to be a hive of activity, sir."

"And what's brought that on, I wonder."

"That new broom in charge, guv. Only took over this week, and it looks as if she's making them jump about a bit."

Constable snapped his fingers in recollection. "Of course – I remember now. It was in one of those emails from the top floor which I love to read. Doctor ... oh, what's the woman's name ...?"

"Can't think how you would have forgotten it, guv," laughed Copper. "Dr. Sicke. I thought it was a joke when I heard, but I checked. It's a real name – there's actually one in the phone book. Good job she went into the scientific side of things instead of medicine. Can you imagine turning up at the surgery and being told who your appointment was with?"

"Be that as it may, if they've got some results already, let's go and find out what they are. And no dreadful jokes about the lady's name when we get there, sergeant, or there will be trouble."

Copper adopted his most innocent expression. "Me crack bad jokes, guv? As if." He started the car.

Under the harsh glare of neon lights in the windowless laboratory, several individuals were poring over computer screens and peering into microscopes as the detectives pushed open the door at the foot of the basement stairs. In the glass-walled office to one side of the door, a competent-looking woman in her forties, wearing heavy-rimmed glasses and a white lab-coat, rose from behind a desk and advanced to meet them.

"Good morning, gentlemen." A glance at her watch. "Make that afternoon. If there's one thing we need to have around here, it's accuracy. I take it you're Sergeant Copper."

"That's me, ma'am. And this is my guv'nor, D.I. Constable."

"Pleased to meet you, Detective Inspector." The woman held out her hand.

Constable smiled as he shook it. "And I assume you're Dr. Sicke."

"For my sins, yes," smiled the woman in reply. "It's the cross I bear. So shall we make it easy on ourselves by saying that all the jokes have already been made a thousand times, but if you can come up with a new one, fire away."

Constable turned to his junior. "Copper … anything?"

"Not a dickybird, sir."

"Excellent," responded the woman. "I can see that we shall be friends. And since my friends all call me Fran, short for Francesca, why don't you do the same?"

"In which case, please call me Andy."

"Short for Andrew?"

"Short for nothing in particular," said Constable hastily. "And sometimes I soften into calling this young lout David, but you'd better stick to 'sergeant' for him, or else he'll be getting ideas above his station."

"But as we're in the basement, guv, …" remarked Copper with a grin. And at a look from his superior, "I'll just shut up, shall I?"

"Ignoring the mutterings of the lower ranks, Fran," said Constable, "I gather you have some information for us."

"Some," agreed Fran. "But I shouldn't get too excited at this stage – it's early days. But you may as well come and take a look."

"And all this whatever-it-is came from the premises of the 'Palais de Glace'?" asked Constable, as he followed the scientist to a bench at one side of the lab.

"Yes," said Fran. "The bins, mostly. Amazingly fruitful source of forensic material, bins. People seem to think that throwing something away is the same as obliterating its existence. Fortunately for us, they couldn't be more wrong. So, here's our haul." She indicated a group of items encased in clear plastic evidence bags.

"And what exactly do we have?"

"There's a knife." Fran held up a bag containing what looked like a sturdy all-purpose kitchen knife with a steel blade and a wooden handle.

"Which, considering we seem to have a stabbing on our hands, is a very good start." Constable looked more closely. "Those look like initials stamped on the blade. Am I right? Looks

63

like 'something … L'. Is that first letter a G or an O? Copper, what do you think?"

Copper peered at the knife. "Difficult to tell, sir. Could be either. It's not easy to see with all that muck on the knife." He looked enquiringly at Fran. "Where did it come from?"

"It was in the waste food bin in the wash-up area of the restaurant kitchen."

"Any chance that it could be the murder weapon?"

"That," said Fran, "is going to be very difficult to tell. Not knowing the nature of the wound, I couldn't express an opinion. And with all the food residues on it, we are going to find it extremely challenging to isolate any possible DNA traces from the victim, even if there are any."

"Fine." Andy Constable grimaced. "So far, so bad. What else?"

"A pair of rubber gloves." The yellow household gloves were held up in turn for inspection.

"And these were where?"

"Discarded behind one of the dustbins in the rear yard."

"Could have been used by the murderer to hold the knife to avoid fingerprints, sir," theorised Dave Copper. "And then chucked in the bin on the way out afterwards – except that someone didn't have a very good aim, and missed."

"Not impossible," agreed Constable. "Except that surely the dimmest criminal knows these days that the fingerprint is not everything, and we'll get much better identification from the DNA which is bound to be found on the inside of the gloves."

"I can see you've done this kind of thing before, Andy," said Fran with a smile. "And you're absolutely right. As long, of course, as they haven't been worn by more than one person. That will complicate your job, no doubt. We'll be getting on to that as quickly as we can. And if there's any relevance, we'll know soon enough."

"That's rather better news. So, moving right along, what's exhibit C?"

A large plastic-encased sheet of paper was produced.

"I recognise that, guv," said Copper.

"As do I, sergeant," said Constable. "The top sheet of the blotter pad from Angelique Delaroche's desk. Complete with bloodstain."

64

"Quite," said Fran, "but it's not quite as simple as that. Yes, it looks like a bloodstain, except that there's something not quite right about it." She frowned. "Can't tell you exactly what at the moment, but something. Anyway, there's probably nothing to stop us confirming that it's the victim's blood, once we've had a chance to do an analysis. Not that there's any reason to suppose it isn't, I assume. But it's another thing I'm going to have to let you know."

"Okay." Constable sighed gustily. "Any better news on the next one?"

"That's rather more straightforward, you'll be pleased to hear," replied Fran. She handed across the next bag. "And in apparently pristine condition too, apart from the fact that it's been neatly torn in half, which may make matters less perplexing."

The plastic bag contained a cheque, evidently drawn on the business account for the 'Palais de Glace' at the Sydney Street branch of Barcloyds Bank, just across the road from the restaurant. The cheque was signed, a bold flowing signature clearly legible as 'Angelique Delaroche', and the amount inserted in both words and figures was 'One Thousand Pounds', ostensibly in the same handwriting. Just one detail remained blank – the name of the payee.

"And this was discovered where?" asked Constable.

"In the waste-paper basket underneath the owner's desk in the office, I'm told."

"Dated yesterday, guv," observed Copper. "But not made out to anyone. And then chucked away unused. Why would that be, I wonder?"

"Could be any one of several reasons," surmised Constable. "Change of mind as to whether the payment ought to be made or not, or maybe the amount was wrong and Miss Delaroche didn't want to make a mess by altering this one, so she wrote a substitute." He looked enquiringly at Fran. "Do we have the chequebook?"

"Not here, I'm afraid," answered Fran. "I assume my people saw no reason to take it."

"Pity," said the inspector. "Because it would tell us if she did make out a replacement, or if this was the last cheque she wrote. In which case, it might be significant. I'd love to know who

65

it was intended for."

"We could take another look in the office next time we're at the restaurant, guv," suggested Copper. "You'd think she'd keep the chequebook handy around the office somewhere, so it shouldn't be too hard to find. Unless something funny's going on, that is. Because if there is a replacement cheque, surely the payee's name will be on that."

"Excellent point, sergeant. We'll do exactly that. And I for one have a little idea whose name it might be. But for now, we'll carry on with what we have here. And it looks as if we're coming to the end of the trail."

"We are, Andy," said Fran. "Just one thing left. And I'm afraid I've saved the worst until last." She proffered a bag which held a quantity of tiny square scraps of cream paper.

"And what on earth is that?" asked Constable.

"That," explained the scientist, "represents the contents of the shredder bin in the victim's office. The good news is that, as far as we can tell, it is the product of a single sheet of paper. A business letter, to judge from the colour and quality of the stationery. But the bad news is that, unfortunately, Miss Delaroche had invested in an extremely efficient cross-cut shredder, so instead of a series of strips of paper which any two-year-old could reconstruct in about five minutes, we have a delightfully complicated mosaic job on our hands. It's likely to take quite a while to reconstitute."

"But are we sure it's relevant?" asked Copper. "It might have nothing to do with the murder."

"You're absolutely right, sergeant," agreed Fran. "We have no way of knowing. But I prefer to proceed on the assumption that anything inexplicable found within three feet of a murder victim may have something to do with that murder, so we shall simply have to grit our teeth and check it out. I'll put one of the team on to it straight away."

"Do you have provision for extra staff overtime in exceptionally urgent cases?" enquired Constable with a smile.

"All requests required in triplicate, countersigned by the Police and Crime Commissioner," responded Fran in similar fashion. "Don't worry, Andy – we shan't be dragging our heels. I'll let you know the minute I have something."

"Then we'd better get out of your way," said Constable.

"Come on, sergeant – let's let these people do their job."

"And I expect we shall be seeing more of each other in future," said Fran, shaking the inspector's hand in farewell. "As long as you can keep providing us with interesting items to analyse. I shall look forward to it." There was no mistaking the warmth in her words.

"Er … yes … me too." As Andy Constable turned to leave the laboratory, Copper was sure he could detect a faint reddening at the back of the inspector's neck. He decided that it would probably be wisest to refrain from comment.

"Well, that's that." Outside, Constable's words were brisk and purposeful.

"I reckon you're right, guv," said the sergeant. "I don't know there's a lot more we can do at the moment. We've had a word with everyone we can get hold of so far, and forensics and the body shop aren't going to come up with anything soon. Looks like we're stymied."

Constable drew a long deep breath and came to a conclusion. "Right. Drop me back at my car at the restaurant. You and I are going to take the rest of the weekend off, and come back to the whole thing, refreshed and reinvigorated, first thing on Monday morning."

"You're convinced of this, are you, guv?" grinned Copper, climbing into the car.

"Absolutely. And the first thing I'm going to do when I get home is get out of this suit, into some scruffy jeans and a pair of sturdy boots, and head back out to the country for a long walk. Clear my head."

"Never had you down as a country boy, guv."

"Maybe I've acquired a taste for it."

"More badgers, then, is it?"

"Not at this time of day. But maybe the odd pint of Badger's Ale. Don't just sit there doing nothing – drive."

*

On Monday morning, Andy Constable was faintly surprised to find that Dave Copper had beaten him to the office.

"What's this, then, sergeant? Unusually eager, aren't we?"

"Woke up early, sir. Couldn't get back to sleep, what with all sorts of things charging round in my head about this Angelique Delaroche business, so I thought I might as well come in. Just as

67

well I did – there's a fistful of messages."

"Do tell."

"For a start, they want to get the post-mortem under way, but for some reason they want you to take a look at the victim first. Soon as you can, is the request. Oh, and it's not the normal doctor either. Apparently he's still off fielding his daughter who's having an attack of the hysterical habdabs at being away from home for the first time at university, so they've drafted in his old predecessor as a stand-in. Dr. Mortice, they said."

"What, old 'Rigor' Mortice?" laughed the inspector. "Oh good lord! You're in for a treat, sergeant. I don't think you ever met him, did you?"

"No, sir. He must have gone by the time I came here. I only know our usual chap. What's the matter with this Doctor Mortice?"

"Oh, merely the fact that he takes the existence of every corpse as a personal affront to his professional dignity," explained Constable. "Not exactly what you'd call the caring approach to his clients. As you will discover. We'll get over there now. What else was there?"

"Your new friend at the forensics lab called, guv." There was a hint of a smile on Copper's face.

"I'm assuming you are referring to Dr. Sicke, sergeant," enquired the inspector with a touch of ice in his tone.

"Er ... that's right, sir. She just wanted to let you know that they're making some progress, and she hopes to let you have some more details later this morning. Oh, and there was a call from Mrs. Eagle, and would you ring her back at her office."

"I'll do that when we've found out what the score is with the late Miss Delaroche. Anything else?"

"Miss Peel has been on. She says her editor wants her to cover the story for the local rag as she was more or less on the spot, and she wonders if there's any chance of an interview."

"Journalists!" tutted Constable. "They can't even wait until the body is cold. I've got much better things to do at the moment than talk to the press. She can go to the bottom of the pile. Is that the lot?"

"Just one other thing, guv. I took it upon myself to get in touch with the cleaner from the restaurant, as she was the one person we haven't had a chance to talk to yet, and she's going to come in to the restaurant this morning. I hope that's okay."

"Very resourceful, sergeant," said Constable. "She can be number 2 on the list. In the meantime, let's get over to the mortuary and see what's exercising Rigor."

Dr. Mortice inhabited a world of brilliant white lighting, gleaming stainless steel, and the sharp glint of a fearsome array of surgical instruments, all to a gentle background music of steadily trickling water. As the detectives, swathed in the obligatory white overalls and footwear which the department rules dictated, entered the laboratory, the doctor greeted Andy Constable with a loud bark of recognition.

"Constable! There you are! Heard you were in charge of this case. Last time I saw you, you were a rather diffident sergeant who kept apologising for the number of corpses you were always turning up for me to sort out. I see nothing's changed now they've promoted you to inspector. And now you're here, we can actually get on. Not before time!"

"The promotion or the examination, doctor?" enquired Constable, exchanging a quiet smile with Copper.

"Bit of both," replied Mortice. "Right, come and take a look at this woman who's been stupid enough to get herself murdered. At least she's reasonably fresh – if there's one thing I could never stand, it's cold cases where I had to delve around in human mush."

"It's very good of you to stand in like this, doctor."

"Oh, needs must when duty calls, laddie," boomed the doctor. "And I don't suppose it's a bad thing to do the odd p-m from time to time – keeps my hand in!" He chortled at the remark as he snapped on a pair of thin blue latex gloves. "She's over here." Portly but brisk in his movements, and with a shock of white hair and a bushy moustache which lent him a unsettling resemblance to Albert Einstein, he turned and headed for the bench in the centre of the room where the outline of a sheet-draped body lay.

"I understand you wanted me to take a look at the body before you made a start, doctor," said Constable. "Any special reason?"

"Course there is," responded Mortice. "No point in wasting your time or mine otherwise. I could have had her spread around the room in bits by now if I hadn't been cooling my heels waiting for you to turn up. You know the score – No. 1 scalpel at the ready, a nice big Y-incision, and then it's in with my little circular saw and away we go." Dave Copper, in the background, began to look faintly nauseous. "Don't worry – the reason I haven't made a start yet was that I wanted you to have a look at this." He drew back the sheet, to reveal the features of the corpse.

Constable stood looking at the face for a moment. "So that's Angelique Delaroche."

"That's right, sir," confirmed Copper quietly.

"I never saw her," explained Constable to the doctor. "She was long gone before I arrived on the scene."

"So I gathered," said Mortice. "Which is why I wanted you to see this." He pulled the sheet lower, exposing the stab wound in the centre of the chest. "Initial visual examination indicates a single blow which has disrupted one or other of the vital organs – can't confirm exactly which until I get a closer look."

"I'm still not sure why you needed me to see this, doctor. I've already been told she was stabbed. What else is there to know?"

"Nature of the wound, dear boy," replied the doctor. "Not just your ordinary knife-blade. Thicker, and it looks to have had a slightly odd shape. Can't be more precise at the moment. But I thought you ought to take a look, because as soon as I start making incisions, all that lot will be gone. We'll have photographs, of course, but it's never the same."

"Excuse me, doc," piped up Copper from the background. "I was just wondering – have you cleaned her up at all?"

The doctor frowned. "What an extraordinary question. Of course we haven't. Why on earth do you ask?"

"Oh … it's just that …" stammered Copper, intimidated.

"Go on, sergeant," said Constable. "If you've got a question, ask it. As the doctor will tell you from my own dealings with him in the past, it's the only way to learn."

"Well, it's just the blood around the wound, sir," said Copper. "It looks as if somebody has tried to wash it away."

"If they have, it's nothing to do with us," stated Mortice firmly. "So if there's nothing else …" He pulled the sheet back up to the body's chin.

"We'll be on our way," said Constable, swiftly picking up his cue. He lingered for a moment, his eyes fixed on the calm features of Angelique Delaroche, oddly serene and still beautiful in their waxy pallor. "'*Thou wast not born for death*'," he murmured absently.

"Keats, guv, by any chance?" asked Dave Copper softly, alongside him.

"Keats," confirmed Constable. He shook himself slightly and turned back to the doctor. "'*Cover her face*'." He sighed. "Come along, sergeant – we have a murderer to catch. And in case you're wondering – Webster." He led the way swiftly from the room.

*

Andy Constable still seemed subdued as the detectives resumed their seats in the car.

"So what next, guv?" asked Dave Copper tentatively, starting the engine.

"Onwards and upwards, I suppose," replied the inspector. "We obviously know more than we did ten minutes ago, even if we're not sure what it is. So let us see what other nuggets of information we can mine in the hope that they will all coalesce into something helpful. Remind me, who's on our list?"

"There's the cleaner at the restaurant, guv," suggested Copper. "She should be there by now. Should we head over there?" At his superior's nod, he let in the clutch.

At the 'Palais de Glace', the front door was opened by a nervous-looking Carey Agnew.

"Mr. Agnew," Constable greeted him. "I'm surprised to find you here today."

"What else can I do, inspector?" asked Carey. "Nobody knows what is happening, and somebody has to answer the phone and get in touch with our customers to let them know we aren't open tonight, but then they ask why not, and when we shall be open again, and I really don't know what to say."

"I hope we shall have some answers for you before too long," Constable reassured him. "And in fact I've come to have a word with one of your colleagues – your cleaner, I believe."

"Oh, yes," said Carey. "She's waiting for you over there." He pointed to a shadowy corner. "I'll ... er ... I'll carry on then, in Miss Dela... in the office." He sidled away towards the bar, as the detectives made for the table where their target sat waiting. They saw a dumpy woman bundled up in a tweed coat, her frizzy red perm crowned with a shapeless knitted hat, a string bag clutched

71

in her hand.

"This is the lady I told you about, sir," said Copper.

"Of course." Constable gave his most charming smile, the one he usually selected to put ladies of a certain age at their ease. "I'm Detective Inspector Constable, madam – I'm the officer in charge of this investigation. I think you've already met my young colleague here, Sergeant Copper, who will be taking a few notes for me." Copper hastily produced his notebook and made ready to comply. "And you are ...?"

"Violet Leader, dear." The woman seemed in no way intimidated by the forces of law and order ranged before her. "But you can call me Vi if you like – everyone does."

"So, you're Vi Leader, and I'm given to understand that you're responsible for the cleaning."

"That's right, dear."

"Well, I hope you don't mind, but I have to ask you some questions about this very unpleasant murder, Mrs. Leader."

"Miss!"

"Sorry – Miss Leader."

"Don't worry about it, dear. But I know this nice young man of yours will want to get everything right in that little book of his. And do call me Vi, otherwise I shall think I've done something wrong."

"Er ... very well – Vi it is." Constable found himself slightly disconcerted by Vi's approach to the interview, as Copper sought, almost completely successfully, to conceal a smirk. "Now, about the events of Friday ..."

"You ask me anything you want, dear," said Vi comfortably. "I'm here practically twenty-four hours a day, so if I didn't see it, it probably didn't happen."

"Well, that's very helpful, Miss ... Vi. But twenty-four hours a day sounds rather excessive." A thought struck him. "You don't live on the premises, do you?"

"Course not, dear." Vi smiled at the thought. "Far too posh around here for me. I live up on the estate. But I've got the two jobs, see – I come in in the mornings to do the cleaning, plus a bit of tidying up after lunch, and then I'm back in the evening three nights a week to do the washing-up."

Constable raised his eyebrows appreciatively. "Sounds quite a task. And you do all that on your own?"

"No," scoffed Vi. "Well, not the washing up, anyway. The cleaning's all mine, because between you and me, I wouldn't trust anybody else to make a proper job of it, and some girls these days, they don't know what a bit of spit and polish is, but as for the washing-up, normally I've got young Michael with me in the evenings. He's a student, so he's doing it to earn a bit of extra money, except that on Friday he didn't turn up, so I had to do the whole evening on my own. And let me tell you, I shall be having a few words with that young man the next time I see him. Whenever that may be," she added.

"Whenever that may be," echoed Constable, "considering the uncertainties of the situation. So, just to give me a clearer picture of the running of the restaurant, what would your daily routine be normally?"

"I usually start about nine in the morning in the kitchen," explained Vi. "You see, the chefs clean their own worktops and equipment, because Oleg is very particular about the hygiene regulations." She leaned forward confidentially. "Apparently, one place he used to be, they had the Rat Man in once – I know they're supposed to be called the Health Inspector or some such, but everyone calls them the Rat Man – and he found so many things wrong, he closed the whole place down for a month. Lego said he's not having anything like that happening to him, what with his precious Pirelli Diamond thing. So he and Pepe do their stuff, and I have to do the floors and the tiles and the cookers. Then I start out in the dining room around ten when Lego comes in."

"Sorry," interrupted Constable. "Lego?"

"Oh, that's just what I call him," chuckled Vi. "Just my bit of a joke because of the name, see – Oleg Lamb, Lego Lamb! And I never bother with the rest of it, but he never uses it anyway. Now on Friday, I got a bit held up in the kitchen because of a mucky oven, but as it happened it didn't really matter because he had his usual Friday meeting with Miss Delaroche about menus."

"I think we've already heard about that, haven't we, sergeant?" asked Constable.

"That's right, sir," confirmed Copper. "Mr. Key mentioned it."

"Not that I usually pay much attention," continued Vi, "even if I'm around at the time, which I wasn't. So when I'd finished in the kitchen, I went off out to do the dining room, and

73

then everyone seemed to disappear off somewhere, because I had to open the front door to Miss Peel. That must have been about eleven."

"Ah, so you were responsible for admitting Candida Peel to the premises during the morning?"

"Nothing wrong with that, is there, dear?" said Vi, a touch defensively. "And it's not as if I left her on her own or anything. She said it was something to do with coming for a meal. Anyway, just then, that Toby Rockard came in through the back, so I left her with him." She giggled at the memory. "I think she quite fancies him, from the way she was going on. I thought to myself, 'Whoops! You'd better watch yourself there, dear'. But then I went through to the office to tell Miss Delaroche that she was here."

"Anything else that springs to mind about the events of the morning that you think we ought to know?"

Vi considered. "Not really, dear. Apart from the fact that everybody kept disappearing. Oh, I do remember, I did have to go searching for the reservations book for Miss Ladyman. I found it eventually – it had slipped down the side of a chair where Carey must have been sitting checking through the bookings, but it took me ages, and Miss Ladyman was hanging on the phone in the bar all the time. That's where it normally lives, by the extension there, because usually Carey or Alan or myself is somewhere within earshot if it rings with someone wanting to book a table, and you can never be sure Miss D is going to be around her office."

"So why did Miss Ladyman need the book? And how come she was in the restaurant?"

"Oh, no particular reason that I know of, dear. She quite often pops in to say hello if she's passing. But she said it was to book a table for Mrs. Eagle."

"I see," mused Constable. "So, we've got you cleaning the restaurant in the morning. What about the afternoon?"

"I came back about a quarter to three," said Vi. "I didn't actually see anyone then, but when I came in through the back door, I did hear Miss Delaroche having a go at Carey about something when I came past her office. Poor man, it sounded as if she'd been going on at him for quite a while, but I don't like to eavesdrop, and I had things to get on with, so I never found out what that was about. I thought to myself, I dare say if it's

74

important, somebody will tell me, because you can't really keep secrets in a place like this. Anyway, I wasn't here too long because we weren't that busy on Friday lunchtime – we never seem to be, these days – so I was quite quick giving the dining room the once-over for the evening."

"How about the washing up?" enquired the inspector.

"Oh no, dear," replied Vi. "Like I said, there's never very much at lunchtimes, so that gets left in my little wash-up, and I do it first thing when I get in for the evening."

"And how about the evening part of your job?" asked Constable, with a quick glance at Copper to make sure that the sergeant's frantic scribbling was keeping up with the narrative.

"I got back at half past seven to wash up. No point in coming in any earlier, dear – I'd only get in the chefs' way when they're running about, and they just pile the stuff in my wash-up, and I get on with it as soon as I arrive. It's not too bad – in fact, it's quite cosy in there."

"Rather claustrophobic, I would have thought," said Constable, recalling the cramped area alongside the door from the kitchen to the rear corridor.

"Ah, well that's just where you're wrong, dear," said Vi. "I've got a window in there above my sinks which overlooks the back passage, so I usually see anyone who goes past – that is, unless I'm loading the glass machine or clearing the food waste bin out."

"So does this mean that anyone in that corridor can see through into the kitchen? I know some restaurants like to do that."

"Ah. No. Now that's where it was quite clever, you see, and it was all Alan's idea. He does have them sometimes, you know, for all that he's a funny old stick. He thought of putting one-way glass in there, and having a frame around it in the passage, so that I can see out, but from the other side, it just looks like a mirror. And you should see what some people get up to," chortled Vi. "Women tarting up their hair when they come out of the loos and pulling faces to try and make themselves look more attractive - so they think. And some of the men are just as bad. Disgusting habits, some men have got."

"Yes, well, we won't go into that," interrupted Constable, eager to forestall any further irrelevant detail. "What I'm rather more interested in is whether there was much in the way of to-ing and fro-ing during the course of Friday evening."

Vi laughed at the recollection. "Oh, it was like Piccadilly Circus out there that night. Mind you, I don't keep a list of everyone who goes to the loo, you know. And most of the customers I've never seen before, so I wouldn't know who was who."

"That's not really what concerns me," said Constable. "It's rather more the members of staff, plus one or two of the guests who were in. Mrs. Eagle and Miss Ladyman, for example, and of course Miss Peel."

"Now I do remember her," said Vi eagerly. "Yes, I saw her come by and go into Miss Delaroche's office at about ten to ten, but she was only there a minute or two, and she came out looking pretty grim. I thought to myself, 'Hello, there goes someone who doesn't look as if they've had a very good time. We'd better brace ourselves if she gives old Lego a bad write-up'. She went off back towards the restaurant."

"And how about anyone else?"

"Toby," announced Vi. "He was out there a couple of minutes after that. I glanced up, and there he was. I thought, 'What's he up to, just hanging about out there?'. Good-looking boy and all that usually, although he's not as good-looking as he thinks he is, if you want my opinion, but you wouldn't have said so if you could have seen the expression on his face. He and that Miss Peel made a right pair. Anyway, I got on with my pans, and I'm almost sure he went out of the back door towards the flat. He always rushes everywhere."

Constable seized on the slight uncertainly in Vi's voice. "Now what makes you think that Mr. Rockard left the restaurant at that point?"

"Because that back door always makes such a racket," explained the cleaner. "If you don't close it just so, it makes a hell of a crash. Many's the time old Lego's had me jumping out of my skin when he's come through like a whirlwind. Now Pepe, he's different – he always tries to close it properly, like he did when he and Edna went home. But the door went again about ten minutes after that, but I don't know who that was, because I was juggling with a full tray of glasses out of the machine, so I never saw."

"You're certain about the time?"

76

"As certain as I can be, dear," replied Vi. "I'm not one of those who's always watching the clock every five minutes. But it was just after Carey came into the kitchen and told Oleg that Miss Ladyman and Mrs. Eagle had left, thank goodness."

"Why would he have said 'thank goodness'?" wondered Constable.

"Search me, dear. Old friends of Miss D?" hazarded Vi. "And she was with them at the table for some of the time that evening, so he said. And that Miss Ladyman is one of the owners too, so I suppose he thinks he has to dance around them. Anyway, he said to Oleg, should he tell Miss D what had been going on, although he'd rather avoid her if he could, and Oleg said 'Not after this afternoon. Leave it – I'll sort it.' And I'm not one to be nosy, but you like to know what's going on around you, don't you, but before I got a chance to ask him what that was all about – you know, subtle-like – he'd disappeared. And the next thing that happened was Carey saying that he'd better take Miss D her coffee, and five minutes after that, all hell broke loose."

"Got all that, Copper?" Constable turned to his assistant.

"Pretty much, sir," replied the sergeant. "All I've got to do is dovetail everything with all my other notes, plus what I know from then on." He did not look enthralled at the prospect.

"Is that it, then, dear?" enquired Vi. "Only if you've finished with me, I could do with getting on. I'm meeting my sister down at the Monday market to pick up some fresh veg," - she brandished her string bag in corroboration - "only I don't usually get the chance to go this early on account of normally I'm in here working, and by the time I get there, all the best stuff's gone, so I thought I'd take the opportunity, seeing as how I can't do anything in here today with all this going on. Oh well, you know what they say – every cloud, and so on." She broke off and laughed. "Here, that's quite funny, isn't it?" She was rewarded with blank looks. "Oh well." A thought occurred to her as she got to her feet. "I don't suppose you know what's going to happen with the restaurant, do you, dear? Only my sister and I need to know where we stand."

"Your sister?" Constable was puzzled.

"Yes, dear. My sister Edna – she works here as well."

Light dawned for Copper. "Edna the waitress! Of course! She was the one who served me on Friday, sir – Edna Cloud. I

77

mentioned her, but she was gone before … well, before anything happened."

"Yes, she went off early," said Vi a touch grumpily, "so I never got my lift home."

"I hadn't realised you and she were related," said Copper.

"Oh yes," replied Vi. "That's the thing about this place – it's a proper family concern."

*

As Vi bustled purposefully towards the back door, Copper's mobile rang.

"Yes?"

"*This is Glenda Neare from Griffin Lyon. I have Miss Hancart for Inspector Constable,*" came the voice at the other end.

"Miss …? Oh, right. Hold on a second." Copper held out the phone towards the inspector. "It's Mrs. Eagle's office again, sir," he mouthed. "Wants to talk to you."

"The lady seems very persistent," replied Constable in similar fashion, taking the phone. "Obviously there is something important afoot. Yes?" He continued aloud. "Oh, hello, Mrs. Eagle … yes, I'm sorry I wasn't able to get back to you sooner, but we have been rather preoccupied … ah, now that is good news, because I'm getting questions which I can't answer … and how long do you imagine this appointment is going to take you? … in that case, do you suppose you would be able to be here at the restaurant in …" He consulted his watch. "… about an hour? … Good. That will give me time to make sure that all the relevant people are here. If you'll contact Miss Ladyman? … Good. I shall see you later." He handed the phone back to Copper.

"What was that all about, guv?"

"Progress of a sort, sergeant. The lady has been rooting around among the relevant papers, and she's got some information from the will and so on about what happens to the restaurant in the event of Angelique Delaroche's death. Apparently she's got an appointment with a client now, which is why she called in the hope of catching us before she got tied up with that. But she's going to come over here afterwards."

"Which is why you wanted her to get Miss Ladyman in on the meeting," surmised Copper.

"Of course. She's part owner – all this affects her as well as the staff. So … just let me think for a moment." A slow smile lit up

78

the inspector's face. "What a very convenient thing it would be if Candida Peel were able to be here in her reporting capacity. Why don't you call her and offer her the interview with me that she was wanting – just don't let on that there will be anybody else here."

"Isn't that just the tiniest bit devious, sir?"

"Of course it is, sergeant. I didn't get where I am today, and so on, and so on. Softly, softly, catchee murderer. Right, you get on with that, and I shall sit here quietly for a second and marshal my thoughts."

"Righty-ho, guv." Copper disappeared round the corner into the bar, where the sound of muttered conversation arose shortly afterwards.

Constable's reflections were brought to a close by the sergeant's reappearance.

"Sorted, guv," declared Copper. "She'll be here in time for Mrs. Eagle's meeting, but she thinks she's just coming to talk to you. So, what next?"

"I have a mental list," said Constable. "I want to go back on one or two things people have said to us, but I think the first thing I want to do is verify this matter of the company cheque-book."

"Check up on the cheque, eh?"

"Precisely."

The detectives made their way along the rear corridor towards the office, but were surprised to hear the murmuring of voices and the clatter of utensils coming from the kitchen. Constable poked his head through the door.

"Mr. Lamb," he exclaimed. "And Mr. Roni." The chefs looked up, equally surprised at the police officers' appearance. "I didn't expect to find you at work today. You do realise, the restaurant can't open until our investigations have reached some sort of conclusion, don't you, Mr. Lamb?"

"Of course I do," snapped Oleg. "I'm not stupid. But in case you hadn't noticed, since you wouldn't let Violet in here on Saturday morning, nobody cleaned up the kitchen after Friday night, so unless I want the place crawling with cockroaches, somebody has to do it properly for the time when, if ever, you decide to let us open again. And since Pepe and I have got nothing better to do, we're getting on with it. If that's all right by you, of course, inspector?" The irony in his voice was manifest.

79

"That's absolutely fine, Mr. Lamb," said Constable mildly. "In fact, I'm rather glad you're here, for two reasons. Firstly, it saves having to get in touch with you, because Mrs. Eagle and Miss Ladyman will be coming in this morning with some news regarding the restaurant's future. And secondly, I wanted a quiet word with you, in fact on that very topic."

Oleg gave a look of consideration to the inspector. "Pepe," he said abruptly, "go and lose yourself for five minutes."

"Okay, *zio*," said Pepe, climbing to his feet from where he had been cleaning the surface beneath a set of gas burners. "What you want I should go?"

"I don't know," replied Oleg irritably. "Go and count the blocks of ice in the freezer or something."

"Okay, chef." Pepe disappeared towards the back door.

"So? What?" The old belligerence had returned to Oleg's voice.

"Mr. Lamb," began Constable, "I've been wondering if you've been completely straight with me. When we spoke before, you told me that there were no sources of tension between yourself and Miss Delaroche. But when I listen to other people, I find that that isn't entirely accurate. I think you had concerns about the way the restaurant was being run. I think you were troubled by the fact that business has been on the decline of late. And I think that you were afraid that all this might jeopardise your Pirelli Diamond, and you might well have thought that something should be done about the situation. Any comments on that?"

Oleg sighed and leaned against a worktop. "Wouldn't you, in my place? Okay, I know we haven't been doing so well lately, but that's not the fault of my kitchen, and Angelique should have known that. I've worked hard to get that Pirelli Diamond, and I was damned if I was going to let her lose it for me."

"So, what? Drastic action to sort out the problem?"

"Don't be ridiculous, inspector," scoffed Oleg. "Murder isn't going to do the place's reputation any good, is it? I want people to come and eat my food, not frighten them away. And the last thing I needed was a bad write-up from Candida Peel all over the press. We all know how she operates. I talk to other chefs – I know what goes on. And I don't care if the money is tight or not – if it took a little special treatment to keep that Peel woman sweet, Angelique should have done it."

"But you think she didn't?" suggested Constable.

"Weren't we just on our way to find out exactly that, sir?" murmured Copper in his ear.

"We were," said Constable. A thought struck him. "Hold on a moment." He delved frantically through his memory. "Didn't Pepe Roni just call you '*zio*'?"

"So?"

"Just a minute." Scraps of recollections of a distant childhood holiday in Italy arose in Constable's mind. "Isn't '*zio*' Italian for 'uncle'? And when we were talking to him, Pepe referred to you at one point as 'Uncle Oleg' – you remember, Copper?"

"Yes, sir. But I thought it was just some chef thing."

"Is it, Mr. Lamb? Or are you and Pepe actually related?"

Oleg shrugged. "So – what if we are? That's not a crime, is it?

"Hang on, guv – I've got a note that Mr. Lamb told us he was Russian." Copper sounded increasingly bewildered.

"And I thought that, when you asked us if we wanted your grandmother's maiden name, you were having a little joke with us, Mr. Lamb," said Constable drily. "So, just to set my obviously confused sergeant's mind at ease, could you oblige with a little more detail? Where does the Italian link come in? Are you Mr. Roni's uncle?"

Oleg looked skywards in irritation and sighed. "Cousin, actually, inspector. Or second cousin, or something like that. We're all Italian from way back. Pepe's grandmother was my father's sister – she went back to Italy when she got married to her husband Giuseppe, and my father stayed in Scotland and married Grandpa Oleg's daughter. Is that clear enough for you and your sergeant? Although exactly how this is relevant to your job in finding out who killed Angelique is a mystery to me."

"And that is obviously what Vi Leader was meaning when she said that this whole place was a proper family concern," persisted Constable. "I assume that when Pepe wanted a job after his stint on the cruise ships, the first thing he did was contact his relation in a smart restaurant." A nod. "And I've just had another thought. Miss Leader also said that you may use the name Lamb, but that isn't the whole thing. So is Lamb your actual name, sir?

81

Doesn't sound too Italian."

Oleg glared. "This is actually getting ridiculous. What the hell has that got do with anything?" And as it became clear that the inspector was intending to wait until he obtained an answer, Oleg capitulated. "Lambrusconi, if you must know. Not exactly a name you'd associate with the highest levels of cuisine, is it? 'The Pirelli Diamond is awarded to Oleg Lambrusconi'? I don't think so. So I dropped it as soon as I could. Now, is there anything else you want, inspector, because my patience is wearing extremely thin, and I'd like to get on." Oleg's hackles were clearly rising again.

"I think that gives us quite enough to go on with, sir," said Constable calmly. "For the moment. And I wouldn't want to hold you up longer than necessary – of course you must get on." He made to leave, but paused. "But I hope you'll be able to spare some time when Mrs. Eagle arrives. No doubt what she has to say will affect everyone." He stepped though the door to the corridor, Dave Copper at his heels.

*

"Bit of a turn-up, that, guv," remarked Copper in lowered tones. "Who knew? Not that I suppose the fact that he's Pepe's uncle or whatever-it-is has anything to do with anything. Nothing unusual in giving a job to a member of the family."

"And after all, the Italians did invent nepotism," commented Constable.

"Do you suppose there's any mileage in the Italian connection, guv?" wondered Copper. "You know, hot Latin blood feuds, and so on. And our Mr. Lamb is not what you'd call the calmest of characters. Maybe it all got too much for him, and he grabbed that knife Forensics have got and did the dirty deed in a fit of fury. It's all a bit clichéd, I know."

"Far too clichéd for my liking," agreed Constable. "Plus, if what Dr. Mortice told us is right, that knife doesn't fit the bill as the murder weapon."

"So what's it doing getting chucked away, sir?"

"Another question we shall have to ponder. In the meantime, shall we do what we set out to do, and see if that chequebook is anywhere to be found." Constable tapped on the office door and, in response to the reply, entered, to find Carey Agnew at the desk, the reservations book lying open before him, a half-full brandy glass at his elbow. The head waiter regarded the detectives nervously.

"Sorry to interrupt you, Mr. Agnew," said Constable, taking a seat across the desk from Carey. "There was just one item we wanted to take a look at, if that's possible. Do you happen to know if Miss Delaroche kept the company chequebook here in the office?"

"I believe so, inspector," said Carey. "Just a moment." He began to open the drawers of the desk. "It should be … yes, here it is." He held it out to Constable. "Were you … I mean, did you want it for any special reason?"

"No, nothing special at all, Mr. Agnew," Constable reassured him blandly. "There was just something I needed to verify." He leafed through the stubs. "Tell me, just as a matter of interest, is this the only chequebook on the account?"

"I really don't know, inspector. But I can't see why there should be another one. Miss Delaroche always took care of paying all the bills personally."

"So was she the only signatory?"

"No, I think Miss Ladyman can also sign the cheques, being one of the partners. But I don't know that she ever did so. Why, is it important?"

"That's the thing, Mr. Agnew," replied Constable. "We can never tell what's important until we have all the facts. One thing I am sure of is that, as of now, we don't have all the facts, so I hope you may be able to fill in some gaps. Two, in particular. Firstly, I gather, from what your colleagues have been saying, that you had something of a run-in with Miss Delaroche on the afternoon of her death."

"Oh, that." Carey licked his lips, and his eyes darted from side to side. "But that was nothing really, inspector. Just a slight misunderstanding over a wine order. Not important at all. What was the other thing?" he hurried on.

"I'm also told," continued Constable, noting the evasion, "that you spent quite a considerable time attending to Miss Delaroche and the other ladies who were dining here on Friday evening. I was just wondering if the conversations between the three ladies might have shed any light on what happened." Constable raised his eyebrows in invitation.

Carey met his look and shifted uneasily in his chair. "Well,

83

of course it's true that you can't help overhearing customers when you're serving them, inspector – it just happens. A well-trained waiter should be all but invisible – people tend to forget he's there."

"How extremely useful," said Constable, a hint of amusement in his tone. "So no doubt this fortuitous cloak of invisibility allows you to hear all manner of things. Such as ..." He waited.

Carey succumbed to the pressure. "I know Miss Ladyman and Mrs Eagle are supposed to be old friends, but it certainly didn't sound like that on Friday night."

"Really, sir? Care to elaborate on that?"

"Of course, I didn't hear all of it – just snippets. But Mrs. Eagle said something about 'things going missing' and 'the Queen not being too happy to lose them'."

"Any inkling as to what they were referring to?"

"I'm afraid not, inspector." Carey now seemed eager to co-operate. "They were keeping their voices quite low, and I couldn't linger, obviously. I did think at the time that it all sounded very tense. But a little while after that, I heard Miss Ladyman make some remark about Mrs. Eagle 'still keeping up the standards of her old profession', and then she said something to the effect of 'just the three of us, but that can easily change'."

"And was Miss Delaroche with the other ladies at this point?" enquired Constable.

"No," said Carey. "That was before she joined them at their table. She didn't sit down until we were about to serve the main courses. But they all seemed very friendly after that."

"Seemed?" The inspector caught a note of uncertainty in Carey's voice.

"I don't know – it just seemed to ring a little untrue." Carey shrugged. "I couldn't say why, but when you've been dealing with the public as long as I have, you pick up these things. And while Miss Delaroche was with them, she quietly said to Miss Ladyman 'We have something to discuss. It's important', and it sounded to me as if it was something she didn't want Mrs. Eagle in on. And I can't remember whether it was then or later, but I do know Miss Delaroche looked across towards where Mr. Rockard and Miss Peel were sitting, and she didn't look happy at all. It was more of a glare, really. I just kept my head down – it usually pays to do that."

"I think that will probably do us for now, Mr. Agnew," said Constable, getting to his feet. "A little more food for thought. Oh, by the way, Mrs. Eagle will be coming in a little later to talk to everyone – I hope you'll be available."

As the detectives left the office, Carey leaned back in his chair with a look of relief, picked up his brandy glass, and downed the remaining contents.

*

"Here's a thought, guv," said Dave Copper, as the two detectives stood outside the entrance to the stairs towards the flat above the restaurant. "What if Angelique Delaroche had got serious about Toby Rockard, and she'd either made him some sort of partner in the restaurant or was planning to do so? She'd need Mrs. Ladyman's okay for that. That might give him a nice financial motive for bumping her off. Although ... no, hang on. That wouldn't work if the place isn't doing too well business-wise. Or ... how about if she'd planned to do that, but then she was having second thoughts because she saw him cosying up to Candida Peel? We know that Miss Peel wouldn't be averse to getting her claws into him." The sergeant reflected for a second. "Damn! That doesn't work either. It's more likely to give Delaroche a motive to kill Rockard rather than the other way round. You know – a woman scorned and all that."

Andy Constable smiled slightly. "I have to say, sergeant, that your wild flights of speculation are a great source of joy to me. I'm sure, if left to yourself, you could come up with a plausible reason for everybody to want to kill everybody else."

"Just trying to inject a bit of sideways thinking into the situation, guv," said Copper, a touch defensively. "Like you're always telling me to."

"I'm not discouraging you, David," said Constable, in an unexpected softening of tone. "The oblique view is very helpful sometimes. And I think you're not wrong in considering the Rockard factor as part of the mix, which is precisely why we're on our way to see him now." He started to climb the stairs. "That is, if he's in."

He was. When Toby Rockard opened the flat's door in response to the inspector's knock, Constable noted the dark shadows under the other's eyes. The stubble seemed a little more

85

prominent, and a little less designer, than before.

"Oh. You again."

"Yes, Mr. Rockard. I'm sorry if we're disturbing you, but we'd like a few words, if it's not inconvenient."

"Yeah, fine," replied Toby. "You'd better come in." He led the way into the sitting room and threw himself down in his customary place on the sofa. "I wasn't doing anything anyway. My morning appointment called to cancel anyway – stupid woman was cooing on about 'tragic loss' and 'she'd quite understand if I couldn't go ahead under the sad circumstances'. I couldn't get off the phone quick enough. So then I thought, to hell with it, and I scrapped the rest of the day."

Constable decided to come straight to the point. "I can appreciate your difficulties, Mr. Rockard. The thing is, I don't believe that some of those difficulties haven't had at least some small contribution from yourself."

"What?" Toby sat up a little straighter. "What on earth are you talking about?"

"Well, to be blunt, sir, the situation regarding Miss Candida Peel. I'm not sure we've had the full story from you. We've spoken to the lady herself, who seems to have one view of the relationship, but on the other hand, other people have given us evidence of an altogether more fraught version of the situation. Hints of coercion of some kind, perhaps?" Constable deliberately kept the references vague, in the hope of drawing Toby out into indiscreet revelations. "So tell us, exactly how did you feel?"

"You want the truth, inspector?"

"Always helpful in my profession, Mr. Rockard."

"Okay then. You're right – yes, I wasn't too happy with Angie over this Candida Peel business, but that's no reason to kill her."

"And by 'Candida Peel business', you're referring to the … arrangements, I suppose is the best way to put it … between yourself and Miss Peel on the night in question. But Miss Delaroche's input wasn't exactly conducive to the sort of loving relationship of two people living together which you indicated to us before, was it, sir? Or did you perhaps impart a little additional shine to that for our benefit?"

"Look, Mr. Constable," said Toby, leaning forward to give his words extra emphasis. "Any time I wanted to get out of this

86

situation, all I had to do was walk. I'm not tied to this place – I haven't been dependent on Angie for support. Okay, it's all been very comfortable, but I've got plenty of people who are only too happy to pay me a lot of money to do what I do. All right – so what if they are mostly women, and what if they are mostly older than me? That's just the way the world works."

"And, of course, wealthy women will always enjoy dining at fine restaurants, won't they, sir?" mused Constable. "I'm wondering if that was ever a consideration."

"You think what you like," riposted Toby. "But I'll tell you one thing – I was worth too much to Angie for her to think about chucking me out or paying me off or whatever."

At that moment, Dave Copper's mobile rang. "Sorry, guv," he apologised, as he fished in his pocket. "Hello … just a sec … it's Dr. Sicke again for you, sir. She's got some more information …"

"Tell her I'll ring her back in two minutes," said Constable, unwilling to hold the conversation in front of a suspect. "So that will be all for now, Mr. Rockard. But please come down to the restaurant in about half an hour, if you would be so good, because I'd like to continue our little chat then." The invitation was clearly more of an instruction. "And don't bother to get up – we'll see ourselves out." He turned and headed for the stairs.

As the detectives rounded the corner of the building, they almost collided with Pepe Roni, who was emerging from a small shed alongside the main staff shed in the rear yard. The young chef was sucking a finger.

"Are you want me again, inspector?"

"No, not at all, Mr. Roni," replied Constable breezily. "I think we've got more than enough information on you and your family to be going on with. Finished your ice-counting, or whatever it was you were doing?"

"Yes," said Pepe. He indicated the shed. "Is the overflow freezer room – we don't have not enough space in the kitchen, so the ice blocks, they live out there. And we got plenty, special if we don't know when we're going to be open again." He looked down ruefully at a smear of blood on his apron. "And they got sharp edges – I should have wear gloves. I better put a plaster on my finger." At Constable's gesture of agreement, he disappeared through the back door and into the restaurant.

"Want me to call Dr. Sicke back for you, guv?" prompted

Dave Copper, as the detectives followed the chef into the building.

"Do that," said Andy Constable. "Let's find a quiet corner and hear what she's got to say." He sat at an empty table and held out his hand for the proffered mobile. "Hello again, doctor ... alright then, hello Fran. I gather you're making progress?"

"*There's a couple of things I thought might help you,*" replied the scientist. "*That shredded letter – we've managed to piece together the letterhead, or at least enough of it to tell us who it was from. And that's Christeby's Auctioneers in London.*"

"Somebody's keeping very elevated company," remarked Constable. "They're in Bond Street or some such, aren't they?"

"*The very same,*" said Fran. "*That's the blessing of an engraved letterhead – the raised characters stand out, which helped us to pick them out from the rest of it. I've got a phone number if you need to call them.*"

"I may have to if you can't reconstruct the rest of it. Any luck there?"

"*Sadly not as yet. Just one word which seems to have jumped together of its own accord, and that's 'court'. Other than that, work still in progress, but I thought knowledge of the sender might be of use.*"

"I'm sure it will be. And you said there was something else?"

"*Well, there is and there isn't. That sheet of paper from the victim's desk with the bloodstain on it ...*"

"What about it?"

"*Nothing really. Just to confirm that it's absolutely consistent with it being her blood – nothing funny going on there. It's just that it's somewhat diluted, and nobody's mentioned a water spillage or given us a glass to look at. Could SOCO have missed something?*"

"I doubt it - they're always pretty thorough," said Constable. "You'll find that out when you get to know them better. So if they haven't passed anything on to you, I can only assume that it's because there was nothing to pass."

"*Just a thought,*" said Fran. "*Well, we'll get back to work. More when we know it.*" The line went dead.

In response to Copper's quizzical look, the inspector swiftly relayed the burden of the conversation. "This mention of 'court', guv," said the sergeant, seizing on one of the facts revealed. "That sounds like something to do with Mrs. Eagle.

88

Although what she would be doing getting letters from posh London auction houses beats me."

"Me too, for the moment," admitted Constable. He glanced at his watch. "However, we shall be in the fortunate position of being able to ask her before too long, provided her appointment doesn't run over." As if in response to his words, there came a crash from the direction of the back door, and Elle Eagle appeared at the end of the corridor.

"Good morning, inspector," she greeted Constable as she deposited her briefcase on a nearby table. "I managed to get away a little sooner than I expected. And I've called Georgie – she'll be here soon. I hope that's not inconvenient."

"Not at all, Mrs. Eagle," replied Constable. "Very much the reverse. It will give us a chance to have a little chat before you get down to business."

"By all means, Mr. Constable," replied Elle, a little uncertainly. "Although I'm not sure what more I can tell you, other than the facts pertaining to the future of the restaurant which I shall be telling everyone else."

"Take a seat, Mrs. Eagle," said Constable, pulling out a chair for her and seating himself across the table. "You see, we can't really talk about the future until we've got a completely clear picture about the past. Because knowledge of the past can throw up some very interesting possibilities regarding people's motives for killing Angelique Delaroche."

Elle looked puzzled. "This is all very mysterious, inspector. I don't suppose you'd care to be a little more specific, would you?"

"I'm not sure that I dare, Mrs. Eagle," smiled Constable. "You being in the position you are. The last thing I would want is to find myself on the wrong end of accusations of defamation. But if, say, someone had told me that a young law student had at one time been financing her education through unconventional means – means of which not everyone might approve, morally speaking – then I would have to look at that in the context of a potential motive for wishing to prevent that knowledge from becoming public. I'm sure that, as a woman well versed in the law, you would understand that. I speak purely hypothetically, you understand."

"I think you are very wise to do so, Mr. Constable," replied

Elle in frigid tones.

"And of course, in the absence of any evidence, I would not expect you to comment."

"We all have things in our past which we'd rather people didn't know about," said Elle, rather to Constable's surprise. "I'd be amazed if you haven't turned up a few of those while you've been pursuing this investigation. Georgie, for example. I assume she's been telling you tales of the old times in London, but I dare say she didn't paint a fully-detailed picture, so to speak. And I wonder if you know all there is to know about Carey."

Constable frowned. "I don't know if you're referring to what we seem to have observed, which is that Mr. Agnew is, shall we say, very familiar with the range of drinks which his bar is offering to the restaurant's customers. But perhaps that is all part and parcel of being a good *sommelier*. He certainly seems to have the background. I was quite impressed by the fact that he'd spent some time at 'Maxim's' in Paris."

Elle gave a snort of derision. "Is that what he told you?" She laughed. "Time at 'Maxim's' indeed! Oh inspector, I do hope that you don't believe all the rubbish some people try to foist on you." The amusement faded from her face. "I'm probably leaving myself wide open here, but I don't think that you'll be too surprised that a woman in my profession has many contacts with the police. Some of them are official – some not exactly so. I have friends in your business – no, don't look interested, because there is no chance that I'm going to name names – but from time to time, they provide me with information. Yes, of course they aren't supposed to, and it would be highly unethical if I were to use it in an inappropriate way. But sometimes it's personal. So when one of my contacts got wind of one particular piece of information, knowing that I had links with Angelique and her restaurant, he put it my way. And the fact is, the only 'time' Carey has served in France was not at 'Maxim's' – it was in a maximum security prison because he used to have a nice little career as a con man and a jewel thief on the French Riviera. Now there's a piece of personal history that I'm sure he wouldn't want revealed."

Constable was slightly taken aback at the waspish note which had entered Elle's voice. "How fortunate for him that this didn't all emerge before he came to join the 'Palais de Glace' family, Mrs. Eagle," he observed.

"I doubt if it would have made any difference," said Elle. "Considering whose family he is."

"Sorry?"

"Oh dear," smiled Elle. "You really don't have all the facts, do you, inspector? Let me see if I can help you out. Agnew - I dare say you did French at school – you might remember enough to know that 'agneau' is French for 'lamb'. Carey's original name is Carlo Agnelli – the drunken fool is Oleg's cousin!" As the detectives regarded her with astonishment, Elle picked up her briefcase and opened it with a snap. "And now, if you will excuse me, inspector, I really think I ought to glance through these papers one last time before the meeting."

Copper's eyebrows rose at the dismissive tone, but his superior seemed in no way ruffled by Elle's words. "Of course, Mrs. Eagle. And the sergeant and I have one or two things to do, so we'll leave you to it." He stood and, followed by Copper, made his way out into the rear yard of the restaurant, and remained for a few moments, silently gazing into space.

Copper thought he recognised that faraway look. 'The guv's cogs are turning,' he thought. "What are we doing out here, guv?" he enquired tentatively.

"Keeping out of range of eavesdroppers, chiefly," replied Constable. "There seems to be far too much of that going on around here as it is."

"What, you mean like the stuff that Carey Agnew overheard at the table between Mrs. Eagle and the others," said Copper. "She very craftily didn't address that, did she? And not only that, but what about all this stuff she's spilling out about him and the others. Do you reckon that's the old trick of chucking accusations around about other people in the hope of diverting suspicion away from yourself?"

"It wouldn't be the first time we've come across that particular tactic," agreed the inspector.

"So what now, guv?"

Constable looked once again at his watch. "Almost time for this famous meeting." He thought for a second. "Right – you can be in charge of getting all our ducks in a row. Go and marshal everybody – get Toby Rockard down from upstairs, make sure Candida Peel is on her way if she hasn't already arrived, and then you can just hover menacingly in the background. That should manage to unsettle them all. I intend to take advantage of this nice quiet staff shed to get my thoughts straight."

At that moment, Copper's mobile bleeped. "Text from Dr. Sicke, sir," he reported on checking the screen. "Just says '*Letter to Ladyman. Still working.*' That's it."

"Another piece of the jigsaw," said Constable.

"So do you reckon everyone's still in the frame, guv? Because it looks to me as if, one way or another, everyone's got some sort of motive. And they were all on the spot, so that rules nobody out. But we still don't know about the knife."

"All these things, sergeant, are what I want to clear up in my own mind. I've got a feeling I know everything I need to know – it's just a question of putting facts together. Let me have your notebook – I want to check over your notes on a couple of things. And then off you go – get everyone sorted."

"Will do, guv." The back door crashed to behind him as Copper re-entered the building.

*

When Andy Constable made his way back into the 'Palais de Glace' dining room some ten minutes later, it was to find Elle Eagle on her feet, a sheaf of papers in her hand with more spread on the table before her. The lights hanging low over the dining tables had been switched on, their Tiffany-style shades shedding a degree of multi-coloured warmth over the scene, and although soft spotlights gave a subtle glow to various points of the décor, they could not dispel the atmosphere of tension which reigned. Alongside and slightly behind Elle sat Georgina Ladyman, her face shaded. On the next table, his features bearing their usual truculent expression, Oleg Lamb was making it very clear that this was the last place he wished to be, while behind him, Pepe Roni hovered uncertainly. On one of the banquettes nearby, Toby Rockard sat hunched, strain evident in his every muscle, while a few feet away, and casting occasional hesitant glances towards him, was Candida Peel. In the background, in the entrance to the bar, stood Carey Agnew, uneasily shifting from foot to foot. And discreetly to one side, his eyes moving constantly over the assembled company, Dave Copper.

"... and so, as is quite normal with this kind of partnership agreement," Elle was saying, "there is provision for the partnership to revert to the surviving partner or partners in the event of the death of one of them. This is of course provisional on there being satisfactory financial arrangements, so these will need to be verified before anything can proceed further. But in theory, there would be nothing to prevent continuation with the business under the revised ownership." She leaned forward and picked up a fresh document. "The situation is made slightly more complex by the question of the will ..."

"Forgive me for interrupting you, Mrs. Eagle." Constable stepped forward. "I hope the rest of you will also forgive me, because I'm sure you are all extremely eager to know what will be happening to this establishment, and to yourselves, in the wake of last Friday's events. But the truth is that nothing can move forward until the death of Angelique Delaroche is satisfactorily resolved. Which is why I have arranged for you all to be here now."

"So we're not here to talk about the future at all?" said Georgina Ladyman.

"Oh no, Miss Ladyman," replied Constable. "Far from it. I'm here to talk about the past. Very much so, because that gives us the key to what has happened here. And Miss Peel," he said, as Candida made to rise, "I really would advise you to sit tight and listen. Isn't that what good journalists should do if there is a possibility of a scoop which would be of enormous interest to their editor?" Candida subsided, a tentative half-smile on her face.

"So what are you saying, inspector?" challenged Oleg. "That somebody here killed Angelique? Bloody ridiculous! Why would any of us do such a thing?"

Constable permitted himself a small dry smile. "Sadly, nowhere near as ridiculous as you appear to think, Mr. Lambrusconi. You don't mind me using the full version of your name, I assume. After all, it seems to be no secret. But no, let's stick to the name you use for professional purposes. As do certain other members of your family." The inspector's words caused several of those present to exchange looks of puzzlement.

"In fact," he continued, "despite Mr. Lamb's professed incredulity, there were plenty of people with good reasons to kill Angelique Delaroche. Or, at least, reasons which might have seemed good enough to them. Elle Eagle and Georgina Ladyman had known her the longest – they had been friends ever since they all shared a flat in London some twenty years ago. That

93

length of time might well give plenty of opportunity for some sort of friction or resentment to arise – friendships can change a lot over twenty years, especially when you know something about someone which they don't want to become public knowledge. Oh, please don't worry, Mrs. Eagle," he said, as Elle seemed to be about to rise to her feet to protest. "I haven't the slightest intention of saying anything on the subject of, what shall we say, certain privileged information. And as for Miss Ladyman, I think I am as capable as anyone of reading between the lines of what you have told me regarding your old relationship with Miss Delaroche, but I don't believe that that is any business of mine. However, it's not necessarily what I believe that matters. Suffice to say that you two were both aware of the extent of Angelique Delaroche's knowledge of yourselves, and it is quite plausible that you could have perceived that as a threat. Not only that, but a whole field of possibilities opens up when we consider that your relationships had moved on from the personal to the professional. And the professional aspect also applies to Candida Peel – if it were to become known that the contents of her articles could be influenced by financial or, let's be blunt, other more personal and intimate considerations, her career as a nationally-known journalist could be threatened."

"Inspector," interrupted Candida, "I was under the impression that I had been invited here to report on a current news story. I wasn't aware that you were intending to make me the target of some sort of wild accusations. And I think my readers would be shocked to learn that the police, instead of doing their proper job of investigating a murder, are instead fabricating ludicrous theories without a shred of actual evidence to back them up. That is, unless you do have some actual evidence, inspector?" Candida subjected Constable to a defiant glare.

Andy Constable declined to respond to the heat in Candida's words. "It's a funny thing, evidence, Miss Peel," he said. "It tends to fall into two categories. There's the sort we can produce in court – the so-called smoking gun, the fingerprint, the DNA trace, the sworn statement – and then there's the other kind – the hint dropped, the words overheard, the gap in the records where something should be but isn't. A lot of my work involves the latter. And many's the time – and I believe this case is one of them – when I have to make bricks without straw, and take a blind leap of faith from one piece of information to another in order to come to a conclusion. So you should all know that, evidentially, we're far from being able to make a watertight case." He smiled faintly. "So to speak. But if it should turn out that any of my thinking aloud is completely wide of the mark, I'm sure you'll tell me." He looked around at the faces before him – nobody seemed disposed to speak up.

"I mentioned threats," he went on. "So far, I've only dealt with the ladies. So let's turn to the gentlemen, because here also we find there is a range of motives at our disposal. Within the restaurant, we can clearly see dangers to the careers of both Carey Agnew and Oleg Lamb. Now, as for you, Mr. Agnew ..."

Carey looked at him with the eyes of a frightened animal, but did not speak.

"You were faced with two hazards, one current, and one historical. As for your present situation, granted, there's many a man or woman who likes an occasional drink to help them through the rigours of the day, but if the drink is more than occasional, and that leads to them not being able to perform their job satisfactorily, with a resultant showdown with the management, who knows what action might ensue? As for your personal history, perhaps the actual facts of the period you spent in France were about to become known to Miss Delaroche. Certainly Mrs. Eagle had very little hesitation in revealing them to us this morning. Maybe she had told Miss Delaroche, or was about to do so. Either way, discovery could well bring a ruined reputation and an end to your cosy and respectable position.

"On the subject of reputation, Mr. Lamb, you also certainly had a great deal to lose. Was your greatest achievement, the celebrated Pirelli Diamond award for your remarkable culinary skills, in danger because a hard-nosed businesswoman set a higher store on finances rather than talent? I know from the conversations we've had how greatly you treasure that accolade, and if it were lost because you weren't allowed to exercise your skills fully on account of cash constraints, you would be doubly damaged. Not only by the simple fact of having your prized award taken away from you, but by the possibility that the word would go round in the restaurant world – 'has Oleg lost his touch?'. Chefs are notoriously volatile – I think you'd probably admit that you are certainly no less so than most – so could a feeling of resentment boil over into drastic and violent action? You have to admit, I must consider that possibility.

"Mr. Rockard – now your relationship with Miss Delaroche was, of course, personal rather than professional. I say that, but it seems that there was a certain blurring of the lines. I think that the way matters stood between yourself, Miss Delaroche, and Miss Peel is convoluted, to say the least. Were you the user in the affair, I wonder, or were you being used? And if the latter, what self-respecting man could put up with being told to – let's say 'perform' - to order, especially when he was more used to playing by his own personal rules?"

"Look, inspector," said Toby, "this is all rubbish. You know what I felt about Angie and me – I told you plainly enough, but I didn't expect you to go blabbing in front of everybody. But whatever the score, we were mostly pretty good together, so why would I kill her?"

"Ah, Mr. Rockard," replied Constable. "If I were to tell you the number of people who are murdered by their own partners, I'm sure you'd be astonished. Or perhaps not. Because, yes, you and I have spoken, and I've gained the impression during those conversations, as well as from what others have told me, that you are as capable of impulsive action as anyone. Is that what happened in this case? Did something suddenly snap?

"So there we have a summary of one of the three main pillars on which I have to build a case – motive. Each of you has one. Granted, some are more obvious than others, but taken in conjunction with other details, each might be sufficient. So then we come on to means. We know the lady was stabbed – that's not a secret. But as yet, we don't have an identifiable murder weapon. There are possible candidates, including a knife discovered by chance, but Forensics are still investigating them, so perhaps I should leave that matter for the moment. Although, on the subject of Forensics, they are in possession of several items, found at or near the scene of the crime, which pose a number of questions, and which perhaps also provide a number of answers. There is, for instance, a cheque for a significant amount of money. Except that that cheque was left incomplete, so we ask ourselves why that might be. If it was of no use, why wasn't it shredded like the business letter which was also found in Miss Delaroche's office?

There are bloodstains – we have questions concerning those. And there were some kitchen gloves, also not where one would expect them to be – I wonder if it is possible to account for the number of gloves used daily in the kitchen of an establishment such as the 'Palais de Glace'? Just some of several so-far-unanswered questions. There are others. Who was most affected by the restaurant's financial uncertainties? Who was most threatened by what Angelique Delaroche knew about them? And finally, what about that extremely noisy door to the back yard? It's made me jump more than once, although I dare say you are all used to it and don't give it a second thought. But somebody was heard to use that door at what might well be the crucial moment on Friday night. The question is, who?

"And that brings me to the third principal question – opportunity. We know all the suspects were in the restaurant at some time during the day on Friday, except for Elle Eagle. At least, we know where she was at midday – at her office taking a call from Miss Ladyman. What she did before arriving at the restaurant in the evening, and who else she spoke to, we have no idea. Not, of course, that it is particularly relevant, because the time we have to consider is the evening. And with the assistance of the notebook of my colleague, Sergeant Copper, I believe I have been able to reconstruct a sequence of events which accounts for all the facts. And this is where the leaps of faith which I spoke of earlier come in. I believe I know the truth. And if you can tell me I'm wrong ... well, let's see about that."

"Inspector," said Georgie Ladyman, leaning forward so that her face moved into the pool of light over her table, "you keep talking about possibilities and considerations and questions, but is this actually getting us anywhere? Do you intend to tell us what these deductions of yours are, or is this all just for dramatic effect, like some final scene in a film?" Her expression held a challenge.

"I wish I could call them deductions, Miss Ladyman," responded Constable. "But deductions are arrived at from provable facts. The best I can offer everybody is abductions – the sort of conclusions which seem to be the only ones to fit the available information. The difference was once explained to me by a very pedantic law lecturer – someone even more pedantic than I am sometimes accused of being." He smiled gently. "And thank you for your use of the word 'dramatic', because we have a situation here which is not unlike a play. We have a backstage area, as well as what some of you call 'front-of-house'. And we have the players, who, to quote Shakespeare, '*have their exits and their entrances*'. So let's take it from the rise of the curtain at seven-thirty on Friday evening, when the restaurant opened as usual. Everything was ready for the guests to arrive – the tables were immaculate, the ice sculpture in pride of place. At quarter to eight, Toby Rockard was seen having heated words with Miss Delaroche. Was she insisting that he adhere to her request, or was he digging his heels in? Did she have a change of heart? We can only speculate. A few minutes later Candida Peel arrived, and she and Mr. Rockard were in full view of everyone in the restaurant until ten to ten. So were Georgina Ladyman and Elle Eagle, who arrived together at around quarter to eight. Miss Delaroche, we know, joined them between eight-thirty and nine-thirty, before going through to her office to work, reminding Miss Ladyman of her wish to speak to her later. Oleg Lamb was of course in the kitchen, working together with Pepe Roni, until at least quarter to ten – at some time after that he was to and fro between the kitchen and the dining room, and his movements cannot be confirmed. And Carey Agnew's duties meant that he could be anywhere at any time.

"So, the last time Angelique Delaroche was verifiably seen alive by more than one person was when she went into her office. At around ten minutes to ten, Candida Peel was witnessed entering Miss Delaroche's office. Was it merely to compliment her on a pleasant evening? I don't think so. I believe that there was a much more business-like intent, judging from what we have been told concerning what we might call the commercial value of her writings. A value of one thousand pounds, apparently, to judge from the cheque which was found in the office. So I think that Miss Peel demanded her payment, either in cash or in kind, in the form of Mr. Rockard's services. But I think Miss Delaroche was in no mood to be bullied – we know that she must have refused to complete the partially-written cheque, instead tearing it defiantly in two, and no doubt threw Miss Peel out with, I imagine, an exchange of harsh words. Perhaps she sought to turn the tables on Miss Peel with the threat to expose her to her editor and finish her career unless she backed off. At any rate, Miss Peel was seen to leave the office with a face like thunder, and she swept through the restaurant and out of the front door, ignoring Mr. Rockard. How many blows to his self-esteem can one man be expected to take during the course of an evening? So it's not surprising that he himself was seen storming out towards the back door, past the ice-carving on its trolley, at five to ten.

Constable briefly consulted the notebook in his hand. "According to my sergeant's notes – and I have to pay tribute to the meticulous way he has compiled these …"

All eyes turned to Dave Copper, with expressions which varied from unease to bewilderment. He ducked his head in a sort of embarrassed half-bow of acknowledgement.

"… the next move in the drama came just before ten o'clock. Carey Agnew entered the kitchen, where he found Oleg Lamb. The two discussed the arguments between Georgina Ladyman and Elle Eagle which Mr. Agnew had overheard at their table, and Mr. Lamb was heard to declare that he would follow the matter up with Miss Delaroche. In his own words, he was intending to 'sort it'. Mr. Agnew returned to the dining room to see Miss Ladyman and Mrs. Eagle out of the front door at ten o'clock, leaving Mr. Lamb alone in the kitchen, having dismissed his colleague Mr. Roni. The two ladies said their goodbyes to one another outside the front door. And so it appears that, one by one, four of our actors have left the stage, with just Mr. Agnew and Mr. Lamb remaining. Except, that is, for one small piece of information. Vi Leader heard the back door crash closed again a few moments later. She didn't see who it was. But in my view, only one person could plausibly have been responsible.

"Miss Peel had left at the end of a conversation at which there was probably very little remaining to be said. Mr. Rockard, in the mood he seemed to be in, would surely not have been minded to return for a renewal of the earlier scene after his swift and noisy exit. Mr. Agnew was busily attending to the remaining customers in the restaurant, and after his earlier contretemps with Miss Delaroche, was probably wisely keeping out of her way. And Mr. Lamb, despite his manifest dislike of the requirement, was engaged in his 'social round' of the dining tables. Which leaves us with just one person - Mrs. Ladyman, with whom Miss Delaroche had expressed a desire to speak further about an important matter."

"Just a moment, inspector," intervened Elle Eagle. "That

can't be right. Georgie didn't leave the table after Angie left us. And you yourself just agreed that Georgie and I left here together."

"But for one thing which you yourself told us," countered Constable. "True, you left together, but you were not together after that. You told us were parked around the corner, so you couldn't witness Miss Ladyman's actions. And this is what I believe them to have been. And no doubt," he said, turning to Georgie, "you'll point out any flaws in my logic." The gallery owner sat stock-still, her face expressionless as she gazed at the inspector.

"You returned to the restaurant via the back door, hoping thereby to remain unseen. And I think at that point, you were careful to close it very softly behind you. Despite the considerable amount of to-ing and fro-ing, you succeeded in entering Angelique Delaroche's office without anybody else being aware of the fact, and were confronted with the revelation that you had feared – a letter addressed to you from Christeby's, the prominent London auction house. It really wasn't particularly clever of you to have given them your address as the restaurant rather than your gallery, but if people who commit crimes didn't make mistakes, my job would be a great deal more difficult. So why should they be writing to you? Well, as the letter has been thoroughly shredded, I do not have the definitive answer to that, but a few pieces of it have been reconstructed so far, and they were enough to start a train of thought. The word 'court' was identified – not, as I immediately thought, a reference to Mrs. Eagle, but a pointer to the identity of a certain painting. One which you recently removed from the restaurant for a time to undergo cleaning, and which has never hung properly since it returned. 'The Queen's Diamonds' – the court portrait of Marie Antoinette in all her finery, which everybody else believed to be a copy. But I think you suspected it might be an original eighteenth-century work by a celebrated artist and, as such, an extremely valuable item. And so you removed it, had a copy made which you placed in the restaurant, and sent the genuine portrait to Christeby's for verification. Tell me, Miss Ladyman, how am I doing so far?"

"It's by Louise Elizabeth Vigée Lebrun," said Georgie calmly. "It was in a job lot I bought at auction when we were setting up the restaurant, with a lot of other thoroughly mundane things. Well, look around you. Nobody thought any of them were anything other than copies, and sometimes not very good ones at that. And in the dim light of a restaurant ..." She tailed off.

"But his one was different?" suggested Constable.

"It was the eyes," said Georgie. "Ever since the 'Palais de Glace' opened, they have followed me – they seemed almost to be pleading to be rescued from anonymity. So I did some research, and in the end there was nothing to do but take the picture itself to be authenticated."

"And that sounds all very noble, Miss Ladyman, but I have an idea that it was not quite as simple as that. Because tied up with all this is the fact that the finances of the restaurant have, for one reason or another, fallen on hard times. You yourself told me that you have next to no money invested in the establishment, but I believe that you thought that was no reason why you shouldn't be able to take a great deal out. An ethical partner would have shared the good fortune with her old friend and colleague – a selfish one would have taken everything for herself. So when you entered Miss Delaroche's office, she confronted you with the letter. I imagine that she would have been furious, considering that she was about to lose everything if the restaurant failed – I'm guessing that she quite possibly threatened you with reporting your actions to the police."

"I begged her not to," said Georgie. "I pleaded with her. We'd been friends for so long. Couldn't she just overlook one stupid error of judgement? We were so close once – so good together. Why not again? But she said that cut no ice with her - she was adamant."

"So you took your fatal decision. 'Hell hath no fury like a woman scorned', was that it?"

"Think what you like, inspector. I'm not responsible to you for the way I live my life."

"No, Miss Ladyman," replied Constable heavily. "But you have to answer for the way you ended Miss Delaroche's life. And here is the closing act of the tragedy. You had reached a dead end as regards your former friend. I think you left the office, boiling with rage and rejection, and came face to face with the ice sculpture in the rear hall. St. George and the Dragon, with the saint's hand raised, holding a still formidable ice lance. And in that tiny window of opportunity you seized the lance, burst back into the office, stabbed the startled Miss Delaroche with a single blow to the heart, shredded the incriminating letter, and fled, slamming the back door behind you, at five past ten."

"Congratulations, inspector," said Georgie wryly. "You paint a very convincing picture. I don't suppose there's any point in attempting to deny what happened – you seem to have covered everything. So what happens now?"

"May I suggest," said Elle Eagle, rising to her feet, "that what happens now is that you do not say another word. Excuse me, inspector, but I am now speaking as Miss Ladyman's legal advisor." She turned to Georgie. "That is, if she'll have me?"

"For old times' sake?" Very quietly, the tears began to flow down Georgina Ladyman's face.

"For old times' sake." agreed Elle. She took Georgie in a prolonged hug, but then resumed a brisk and businesslike attitude, surveying the stunned faces around her. "I hope everyone will agree that any talk regarding the future of the 'Palais de Glace' will have to be put on hold. Georgie, I think we are going to go with the inspector now. Mr. Constable has his duty to do – and I have mine. Will you lead the way, inspector?"

The small procession, Dave Copper bringing up the rear, made its way out of the front door.

*

"So, George really did kill the dragon, then, guv?" The two detectives, mugs of canteen tea in their hands, were taking their seats at their desks at the police station, as Andy Constable prepared for the tedium of putting the case into a written report for his superiors.

"It's a slightly unchivalrous way to describe the late Miss Delaroche, sergeant, but yes."

"Anything you want me to do?"

"Not really. Although ... yes, you can call Dr. Sicke and tell her to put her investigations into that kitchen knife on the back burner for the moment."

"How so, guv?"

"Well, I'm pretty sure, and you can confirm it for me by having a word with Vi Leader and Oleg Lamb, that the knife will turn out to be one of his set. And I bet that chefs spend a fortune replacing their precious knives because the wash-up staff are forever throwing them away in the food waste by accident. And while you're on to Vi, just ask her as a matter of interest how many pairs of yellow gloves she gets through in the average week. I don't think Forensics are going to have to trouble themselves overmuch with those rubber gloves either."

"So no worries about who was wearing them?"

"Supremely irrelevant, sergeant. Who needs to worry about fingerprints when the murder weapon is going to melt away in minutes into a little pool of water?"

"Which is why ..." A smile spread across Copper's face as light dawned. "So that's how you figured it out."

"Exactly. How else were we going to account for what you yourself noticed, which was that the blood around the wound looked as if it had been partly washed away, plus the diluted bloodstain on the blotter where the body had fallen forward. We saw how Pepe Roni cut his finger on an edge of ice, so we knew it could be sharp – and the heat of the dead woman's body effectively removed the evidence."

"And you want me to tell Dr, Sicke all this, guv?" asked Copper. "You know, I think it would be much better if she heard it from you direct. In fact, why don't you go and see her straight away – save her wasting her time. I'm sure she'd be grateful. And I could make a start on your report for you." The sergeant failed completely in his efforts to stop a slow grin from spreading across his face as he spoke.

"David, you wouldn't by any remote chance be indulging your famous sense of humour at my expense, would you?" enquired Constable as he slowly stood, a mock-severe expression on his features. He reached for his coat. "Although maybe you're right. I'll pop over and speak to Fran ... Dr. Sicke ... before I make a start. That's if you're happy to get on with things in my absence."

"Oh, I'm quite happy, guv," said Copper, taking the inspector's place at his desk. And as his superior disappeared along the corridor, he added, "I like everyone to be happy." He looked briefly at the retreating form, gave a little chuckle, and then bent his head to the papers before him.

*   *   *   *   *

DEATH WAITS IN THE WINGS

Few places, thought Detective Inspector Andy Constable as he stood looking at the empty auditorium, are as mournful as a deserted theatre. And the Queen's Theatre at Westsea did nothing to change his opinion.

Built towards the end of the nineteenth century, one of the smaller creations of a celebrated theatre designer, the Queen's was a rare survivor in a world where many of its contemporaries had fallen victim to the successive fashions of cinema, television, bingo, and supermarket shopping. But somehow it continued to cater for a lively local amateur theatrical scene, together with occasional provincial tours of not particularly distinguished drama productions, an annual pantomime, and infrequent concerts by local dance schools, community choirs, and tribute acts for long-defunct rock bands. But it could not be denied that the original glamour was gone, and in the auditorium, lit only by a few naked bulbs, there was no disguising the general air of decaying grandeur. Wall lights with red velvet shades were set at intervals down each side of the gently sloping stalls, but a closer glance revealed the occasional drooping fringe or missing lamp. The upholstery of many of the seats was rubbed down to the base material. A noble central chandelier, its crystal drops defiantly glinting in the little light available, showed signs of tarnish on its gilded frame. Heavy black stage lamps on brutal metal mounts disfigured the otherwise elegant curve of the small balcony. Dusty plaster cherubs pouted down from the front of the boxes, two on each side of the proscenium arch. 'Well, at least there's no Box 5,' thought Constable with a flash of wry humour. 'That should make things easier.'

The massive stage curtain, swagged purple velvet bravely sporting the town's coat of arms in heavy padded embroidery which looked to be in danger of ripping the slightly threadbare elderly fabric, suddenly began to move convulsively as if being beaten from the rear, and the form of Detective Sergeant Dave Copper eventually appeared in the central gap.

"Oh, there you are, guv."

"Do I detect a hint of criticism, sergeant?"

"No, sir, not at all," asserted Copper hastily. "I just thought you'd come in through the stage door round the back. That's where I was waiting."

"Not for too long, I hope. I started out as soon as the phone call came through." Constable thought with regret of the just-poured glass of Sancerre and the immediately-abandoned, and now rapidly congealing, plate of Turbot Veronique from the supermarket Microwave Supreme range now sitting on his dining table.

"It's those road works at the bridge, isn't it, guv?" sympathised Copper as the inspector climbed the steps at the side of the stage to join his colleague. "They always take me ages to get through. It's a good job I was working late on that report on the racehorse business. Only took me a couple of minutes to get here from the station when the theatre people called it in. Anyway, you're here now. And I've got on with a few bits and pieces in the meantime. There's half a dozen or so people who were about at the time, and I've had a word with most of them. They're all waiting downstairs – there's a sort of sitting room under the stage. I don't know if you want to start with them."

"Not until I know a bit more about what we've got – who, where, when, and so on."

"We'd better go up to the dressing rooms then, guv." Copper held back the stage curtain to allow Constable to pass through. "The stairs are back here."

"And you can fill me in on the way."

*

It had been only moments after seven o'clock on the Monday evening when the phone on Dave Copper's desk rang.

"Yes?"

"*Sergeant?*" came a voice from the control room. "*We've just had a call from the Queen's Theatre – sudden death, male, looks like suspicious circumstances ...*"

"I'm on it." Copper was already on his feet, closing down his laptop and reaching for his car keys. "Can I leave it to you to do all the usual – SOCO, the doc, and so on. Oh, and can you call the guv to let him know what's on?"

"*D.I. Constable's actually gone home already?*" laughed the officer at the other end of the line. "*Bit unusual for him, isn't it?*"

"Apparently he does have a life," responded Copper. "News

to me. And if you quote me, you're on traffic duty for the next six months. Right, I've gone." Odd sheets of paper fluttered to the floor in the draught as the door closed behind him.

At the theatre stage door, Copper was greeted by an anxiously-hovering man who looked to be in his seventies - thin, balding, bespectacled, wearing a cardigan.

"Are you the police?"

"Yes, sir. Detective Sergeant Copper." Copper flashed his warrant card. "And you are ...?"

"My name's Peter Castle. I'm the stage doorman. I got my little booth just inside here. And it was me what found him. You see, what happened was, I was..."

"Just a moment, sir." Copper turned his attention to the blue-flashing patrol car which had just pulled up to the rear of his own. "Good timing, guys. You're just the people I need. Mr. Castle, has anyone left the theatre since you called us?"

"Not that I know of. And I would, see, because this is the only way in and out."

"No other access to the theatre?"

"Well, there's the box office at the front, of course," explained Castle. "That's open for ticket sales up to half past seven, but the doors to the auditorium are kept locked when there's no performance on."

"Good." Copper turned back to the two uniformed officers. "Right, one of you stay here, the other one go round to the box office, just in case. Nobody comes in, nobody leaves without my say-so. Oh, except for D.I. Constable – he should be on his way by now. And SOCO, obviously. Okay?"

"Right, sarge." The officers took up their positions as Copper made his way in through the stage door with Peter Castle shuffling in his wake.

Copper produced his notebook. "You'd better give me some details, Mr. Castle," he declared briskly. "All I know so far is that somebody has reported the sudden death. So tell me ..."

"You'd better come and see," said Castle. "He's up in the Number 1 dressing room."

"Lead on, then." The pair mounted the bare concrete staircase to the first floor, where a corridor with doors along one side of it stretched to a further staircase at the far end. Castle held open the first door, its chipped green paint sporting a large chrome figure 1, with beneath it a small metal card-holder containing a piece of paper bearing the words '*MR. NELSON*' in rather wobbly capitals.

The room was sparsely furnished and lit by a single naked overhead bulb, with a bench along one side at worktop height bearing a plastic toolbox containing a variety of items of stage make-up, with boxes of tissues, towels, deodorant spray, pairs of socks, a play script and other oddments scattered about. On the wall above it, a range of mirrors surrounded by light-bulbs. At one end, a washbasin with toothbrush, soap, a wet razor and a can of shaving foam. At the other end, a part-full bottle of undistinguished supermarket whisky and two not particularly clean tumblers, one of them used. A barred window with opaque glass had clearly been painted shut many years ago. Behind the door lurked a sagging elderly armchair upholstered in dingy brown corduroy, piled with discarded clothing, with alongside it a clothes rail whose hangers bore several shirts, pairs of trousers, and a suit. And beyond the rail, in the corner of the room, a shower cubicle, in which was slumped the naked body of a man.

"That's him," said Castle, somewhat unnecessarily.

Copper swiftly knelt to check for a pulse. Nothing. "And who is he exactly?" he asked, rising to his feet.

"His name's Stuart Nelson. He runs the theatre company. Now, that's not the same as running the theatre, you know. No, the way it is, see, ..."

"Yes, all in good time, Mr. Castle," interrupted Copper, sensing an imminent digression. "First things first. You say you're the one who found him? Exactly like this?"

"Yes. After the bang, like. I knew he was dead straight away. I thought I'd seen enough dead men to last me a lifetime. I was in Kenya, you know ..."

Copper ruthlessly overrode Castle's inclination to ramble. "And you've touched nothing?"

"No, not a thing," asserted Castle virtuously. "I know what's right. Well ... that's to say, I did turn off the shower. I mean, I don't know what he was doing taking a shower then anyway. Most people have a shower after the show. But it didn't seem proper to leave it running, somehow, with him lying there and everything."

"But other than that ...?" Castle shook his head in response.

107

"And nobody else has been in here?"

"No," said Castle. "Some of them wanted to, but I wouldn't let them. I made them all go downstairs to the Green Room and then went to dial 999."

"You seem to have taken control of the situation very efficiently, Mr. Castle," said Copper.

"Ex-army," replied the other shortly. "I was a sergeant – bit like yourself, I suppose. You get used to telling people what to do." He puffed himself up slightly. "And being as I'm stage doorman, they all know better than to get on the wrong side of me."

Copper blinked slightly. "I'll bear that in mind, Mr. Castle. So, if you can show me where these other people are …?"

"Like I said, they're all in the Green Room – it's underneath the stage. I'll take you down there." Castle started out of the room and headed back down the stairs.

Copper, in his wake, was struck by a thought. "Better idea, Mr. Castle, is if you just point me in the right direction, and then you can … er … take post at the stage door again. I think it's probably vital that we have someone reliable there to control access. Plus there'll be some of my colleagues arriving very soon, and they'll need to know where to go."

"Oh. Right." Castle drew himself up a little straighter, looking gratified. "Yes, well, you leave it to me, sir … sergeant. I'll take care of that."

Copper suppressed a smile. "Thank you. So, this Green Room is where?"

"Just keep on down the stairs till you get to the bottom. You can't miss it."

*

Dave Copper opened the door at the foot of the stairs, to reveal a large room which evidently stretched the full width of the stage, and which was furnished with a clutter of mismatched armchairs, shabby sofas, a chaise longue apparently recently upholstered in a rather bilious yellow brocade, and a scatter of bentwood chairs and occasional tables. Rugs and carpets of differing sizes in various colours, all showing signs of age, covered the floor in a disordered array. Cupboards, many with padlocked doors, lined one wall, while in one corner was a stack of miscellaneous theatrical paraphernalia – an oriental throne, a

108

giant pumpkin with a cage of rather moth-eaten white mice on top, a stack of medieval weaponry alongside a mannequin wearing a suit of chain-mail which appeared to have been fashioned from knitted string painted silver, and a Victorian lamppost, with a jumbled pile of stage lamps of varying kinds, together with reels of electrical cable. As the sergeant entered, the murmur of subdued conversation inside the room died away, and eight faces turned to him with varying expressions of surprise and enquiry.

"Good evening, ladies and gentlemen. Thank you all for staying put as Mr. Castle asked. I'm Detective Sergeant Copper ..." Once again Copper displayed his warrant card. "... and I shall be needing to ask you some questions."

A burly man who looked to be in his mid-forties stood and approached Copper. "Sergeant, can you tell us what's going on? All we've been told is that Stuart seems to be dead, and the next thing we know is that we're corralled down here without any idea of what's happened. How do we know that it's not natural causes or some horrible accident?"

"We don't, sir," replied Copper bluntly. "What we do know is that there is an unexplained death. And until I'm told otherwise by my superiors or the doctor, we shall be treating it as suspicious. And the first thing I need to find out is, who's involved." Copper produced his notebook. "So let's start with you, sir. You are ...?"

"My name's Don Abbott. I'm the company manager for this tour. Well, I was – I suppose we're all out of work now."

"Sorry, sir, but I'm not exactly clear on the set-up. I'm not really a theatre person. Can you clarify for me, please?"

"Right. Where to start?" Don drew a deep breath. "I suppose the first thing to say is that we're a bit of a dinosaur. The Victory Theatre Company, that is ... that's who we are. Pretty much of a one-man-band – Stuart Nelson was what they used to call an actor-manager. Put together his own company, and we do short tours of plays around small theatres like this one. Not too many of them left these days, but we scrape a living somehow." He smiled faintly. "Stu was directing this production, and he was also playing the lead – well, he always did. And he always managed to pick a play which had a great part for him – funny, that."

"You say funny. What, so it's a comedy?" hazarded Copper.

Don snorted. "'*Playing Away*'? Not so's you'd notice. No, it's one of those miserable psychological things, like the stuff that keeps popping up on television. Ran for about three weeks in the West End a few years ago and then died the death. Just the sort of thing to pack the audiences in." The sarcasm was plain to hear.

"Well, at least it's not a murder mystery," muttered Copper under his breath. "Thank goodness for that."

"Anyway, not my job to choose the plays," Don went on. "I just do what I'm told."

"So what exactly is your job, Mr. Abbott?"

"Allegedly, I'm the one who keeps everything running smoothly. I stage manage the actual performances of the play, and then there's sorting out the transport, doing the wages, making sure that everything's paid for, and so on. Mind you, Stu kept hold of the chequebook – he was a bit of a control freak all round really."

"And you last saw him when?" Copper's pen was poised over his notebook.

"On stage after tech, I think," said Don. "That's technical rehearsal this afternoon, sergeant. It's the last run we do before dress rehearsal." He looked at his watch. "Which we should have been in the middle of now, ahead of tomorrow's first night. Well, that's not going to happen, is it?"

"I'm afraid not, Mr. Abbott." As Don resumed his seat, Copper's attention moved to the woman sitting next to him on the sofa. "And your name, madam?"

"I'm Delia Armstrong," she replied. Looking to be in her early fifties, with short wavy blonde hair liberally mixed with grey, she wore a long loose ethnically-patterned waistcoat over practical grey blouse and trousers. "I'm in charge of props for the play. Properties," she clarified in response to Copper's slight look of puzzlement. "The bits and pieces that the actors handle on stage – bottles and glasses, newspapers or letters, ornaments to dress the set, weapons, fixtures and fittings – that sort of thing. To tell the truth, I'm a bit of a fixture and fitting myself." She gave a small half-smile.

"You've been with the company a long time?"

"Heavens, yes. In fact, I've probably known Stuart longer than anyone here – we were at drama school together thirty

110

years ago. Well, the first year, anyway. But his acting career worked out and mine didn't – that's theatre for you. And then I found my niche doing what I do. And Stuart and I had worked together on and off over the years, but we'd never been that close. But then I came to work for him a while ago, and sort of stuck in place." The small smile reappeared.

"Can you remember where and when you would last have seen him this evening?" asked Copper. He addressed the room in general. "I shall need to ask all of you the same thing, if I'm to build up a picture of what happened."

"I remember very well," said Delia. "The last time I saw Stuart, he was going into his dressing room, and that was about half past six, because I remember thinking, 'Right, that gives me almost an hour before we're due to start'. Because of course I had my props to sort out."

"Thank you for that, madam. And how about you, sir?" continued Copper, addressing the young man in the armchair next to the sofa. On reflection, mused Copper, possibly not quite as young as he'd like people to think. Maybe around late thirties, but with the haircut, complexion, white smile and bright eyes of a man a good ten years younger. Only the beginning of fine lines around the eyes and an incipient lack of tone in the neck gave him away. "Where do you fit into all this?"

"My name's Matthew Edwards," replied the man. "Well, that's my Equity name. I suppose you'll want the real name for your enquiries, or whatever it is they say. It's actually Nigel Clegg, but I changed it – well, you would, wouldn't you? And as for where I fit in, I've got the part of Daniel Allen in 'Playing Away'."

"Sadly, sir, I never got to see the original play in the West End," said Copper, with only a hint of irony detectable. "So would that be one of the leads?"

"Well ... I suppose. It's a sort of secondary rôle to Stu." Matthew seemed to realise that he was not exactly sounding particularly enthusiastic. "I mean, I'm really glad he gave me the part, even though it's not the main character, but of course he always played the lead in his own productions."

"And I assume you worked together quite happily?"

"Yes, of course. And I talked to him at the end of technical rehearsal, but I don't remember seeing him after that."

"And you, miss?" Copper turned to the nervous-looking

111

young woman in a chair alongside that of Matthew, who reached out for her hand and gave it a reassuring squeeze.

"Oh ... um ... yes, Stuart did come into my dressing room around teatime, but that was the last time I saw him. And they wouldn't let anyone go into his room after ... well, you know."

"No, miss, what I meant was, can I just make a note of your name please?" clarified Copper, seeking to soothe the uneasy flutterings.

"Oh. I see." The girl gave a tremulous half-giggle and pushed back her long blonde hair from her face. "Sorry, but I've never been involved in anything like this before." She took a breath and seemed to steady herself. "My name is Jessica Davenport. I'm twenty-nine, and I'm playing Rachel – she's a mental patient who's lost her memory, so she has no idea who she is."

"Sounds quite challenging, miss," remarked Copper.

"It's not really my kind of part," said Jessica. "I'd much rather do comedy, but you can't be choosy in this profession, so when my agent sent me to audition for Stuart, he offered me the part and I took it."

"Yes, well, he would, wouldn't he?" came a muttered growl from a man leaning against the wall opposite Jessica.

Copper swivelled to face the man who had spoken, a tall strongly-built individual with a heavily-lined face and thick iron-grey hair. Late fifties, estimated the sergeant, his senses prickling at the first hint of conflict. "You have some thoughts on the subject, sir?" he asked mildly.

"Just a few," replied the man, heaving himself upright and taking a step towards Copper. "And just so's you know, the first thing anyone will tell you is that Stuart Nelson and I just did not get on. I'm David Winston, by the way – I'm L.X. Sorry, that's tech-speak – I mean I do the lighting."

"What, do you mean for this particular touring production or just for the Queen's Theatre?" Copper sought to clarify.

"Both," said David shortly. "We're all freelance these days – you have to take the work where you can get it."

"Even if it's offered by someone you would not consider a friend?" probed Copper.

David shrugged. "That, or starve. It's just one of those things, and it's not as if I was the only one who ever got on the

112

wrong side of Stuart. He was an arrogant swine who never appreciated anyone else's work, which is why we had that row after tech, but it's not as if I'm going to kill a man just because he said I got my lighting cues wrong. In his opinion! That's the trouble with these actor managers – they all think they wear the mantle of Laurence Olivier, and they think they know everything. Begging your pardon, ma'am," he added, turning to a woman seated quietly at the end of the room, "but that's just the way I feel."

"I don't think there's the need for you to wash quite so much of our dirty linen in public, David dear," reproved the plump middle-aged woman in the chair alongside him. "We've had quite enough of that as it is." Dressed in a sort of smock with several pockets from which protruded various ends of ribbons, scissor handles, and tape measures, her crinkly faded red hair was tied back with a chiffon scarf which trailed down over one shoulder. At her wrist, a kind of bracelet with a foam pad held several pins with coloured heads. "Anyway, that's really rather more my job." She gave a quiet chuckle. "Sorry, sergeant – slightly misplaced black humour, I'm afraid. My name's Angela Bailey. Miss. I'm the company wardrobe mistress, hence the laundry thing. Which reminds me, I've got some things in the tumble dryer up in my room which will be absolutely baked to a frazzle if I don't go and rescue them. Sergeant, would you mind awfully if …?"

Copper registered the implication of her comments. "I shall want to speak to you at some point, but I think that will be all right, Miss Bailey, provided you don't leave the theatre," he replied.

"Leave the theatre, dear?" Angela laughed again. "No chance of that – they'll have to drag me out kicking and screaming. So I'll be up in Wardrobe when you want me. Do come up and have a chat. Just keep on up the stairs until you bump your head on the ceiling, and that's where I am."

"Actually, sergeant, would you mind if I bunk off too?" The individual who spoke wore black from head to foot, with a T-shirt bearing the logo of a celebrated heavy metal rock band, a heavily studded leather belt, biker's boots, long black hair caught back at the nape of the neck, and piercings in ear and nose. Heavy silver rings, variations on the death's-head motif, adorned the fingers of

113

both hands. "The way I left my board, the damn thing's liable to crash if it doesn't get to do something every so often."

"Sorry, sir?" Copper sounded thoroughly confused.

"My F.X. board – the sound board – sound effects for the play," explained the other. Copper began to catch on. "It's all computer controlled, and I was half-way through an update when all this kicked off, and the whole thing gets very temperamental anyway, so can I go and rescue it – please?"

"I suppose if it's essential, Mr ...?"

"Mott – William Mott. Will. I'm the sound technician. Look, I promise I won't run away. And I expect you'll want to talk to me anyway – away from other people, if you see what I mean."

"Er ... yes, by all means, Mr. Mott," said Copper, who was beginning to get a mild sense of loss of control of the situation. "But again, please don't leave the theatre."

"I'll stand surety for him if you like, sergeant," commented Angela brightly. "Come on, Will – you can make yourself useful. Carry this basket of costumes up for me." She pointed to a half-full hamper of garments sitting alongside her chair and headed for the door as Will, shrugging amiably, followed in her wake with his burden. The door closed behind them as Copper turned to the final occupant of the room, the woman who sat calmly, slightly withdrawn from the others, hands clasped in her lap.

"And you, madam?"

The woman regarded him coolly from clear grey eyes. Dark hair in an elegant ageless style framed a face of classic proportions, subtly made up to enhance its natural beauty. Early forties, guessed Copper to himself. Wrapped in a long dressing gown, maroon silk with a dragon motif in dull gold, she exuded an air of quiet self-control. "My name is Elizabeth Hamilton, sergeant. And Stuart Nelson was my husband."

Dave Copper was slightly taken aback by the unsensational nature of the revelation. "Oh ... I'm sorry, madam, but I had no idea. Um ... please accept my condolences for your loss."

"Thank you, sergeant," replied Elizabeth. "You're very kind. And I dare say you'd like some more information from me."

"Well, yes ... that's if you feel up to it, Mrs. ... er ... Miss ..."

"Miss Hamilton will do very well, sergeant," said Elizabeth, taking pity on Copper's unease.

"Only I wouldn't want to cause you any upset at a time like

114

this."

"Please, sergeant, don't worry that, because we're theatre people, we're all going to engage in theatrics. I think we're all a little more grown up than that. Well, some of us are, anyway," commented Elizabeth drily. "So, what would you like to know?"

"You say Mr. Nelson was your husband?"

"Yes. I met him when we were both doing '*Pygmalion*', and we've been together ever since. We married not long after, so that would be ..." A brief pause for reflection. "...twenty-two years ago now. Goodness – as long as that. It's probably something of a record in this profession."

"And have you always been involved with Mr. Nelson's company?"

"Oh, gracious, yes. Ever since he set it up. Stuart enjoyed running his own theatre company – it's probably what he was born to do. He was a very good director – and actor, of course." A sigh. "And now it's all come to an end."

"And can you tell me when you would have seen Mr. Nelson this evening?"

"Stuart came into my dressing room at about a quarter to seven," replied Elizabeth. "I didn't see him after that."

"Then I think I'll leave it there for the moment. If you wouldn't all mind waiting here for a little while longer, I'll just go and check ..." Copper let the sentence fade away as he headed for the door. As he was about to leave the room, he turned back with a final afterthought. "And once again, please accept my sympathy."

*

"... so, now you know as much as I do, guv," said Dave Copper, closing his notebook with a snap.

"And I've got a feeling we're both about to learn a lot more," remarked Andy Constable, as the sound of bluff rumbling tones wafted up the staircase in the wake of the detectives. "Nobody else sounds like that – we are about to be joined by the medical department."

"Evening, Andy ... sergeant," wheezed the man who lumbered into view on the landing. "I do wish sometimes that you could regiment your corpses into appearing during nice civilised hours like nine to five. Either that, or you can be the one who explains to my wife why she is sitting at home in a posh frock on the phone to a rather nice restaurant, cancelling our reservation."

"Sorry about that, doc," replied Constable. "But '*Death will come, soon, too soon*'."

"Don't you start quoting Shelley at me," grumped the doctor. "I did that poem at school too, you know. I did the other one, too - '*I met Murder in the* way'. So, did we? Let's have a look at your dead man, and I'll soon tell you."

"Just through there, doc," said Copper, indicating the Number 1 dressing room.

The doctor knelt at the side of the shower cubicle. "He's a bit untidy, isn't he?" he commented. "Well, let's see what we've got. Middle-aged man, late forties, maybe fifty-ish ... looks well nourished ... reasonable physical condition as far as I can see ... oh, rather nice bruise coming out there on his jaw ... can't see any other obvious wounds on the body, but it's difficult to tell when he's all doubled up like this. There may be something to find when we've got him laid out nice and flat ..."

"And I assume that's when you'll be able to give us a likely time of death," said Constable.

"Oh, we've already got that, guv," interposed Copper. "Just on seven, by what I've been told. The chap down at the stage door said something about a bang, and he came rushing up and found Mr. Nelson like this."

"A bang?" echoed Constable. "What, like a gunshot? But doc, you say there aren't any wounds. As far you can see, obviously."

"Equally obviously, Andy," replied the doctor heavily, "gunshot wounds tend to be associated with a certain amount of blood. Of which we have a distinct lack here."

"So any ideas as to cause of death?"

The doctor took a closer look at the floor of the shower tray. "Far be it from me to tell you how to do your job, gentlemen, but perhaps you should be considering this." Beneath the slumped body was a towelling mat, of the type more likely to be found on the floor outside a shower than inside it. The doctor lifted the corner gingerly. Tucked under the mat, and taped to the plastic of the tray with a sturdy white tape which rendered them virtually invisible to a casual glance, were a pair of wires whose exposed ends lay in the pool of moisture under the waterlogged fabric. "Not, I would suggest, part of the standard fittings of your normal shower."

"Sergeant, see where those wires go," ordered the inspector sharply.

Copper crouched down alongside the doctor and examined the area. "They go just under the corner of the glass door, guv," he reported, "and then they look as if they've been shoved under the edge of the carpet here." He crawled along the floor towards the door. "Yes, they go all along here at the foot of the skirting board, and then out into the corridor ..." He opened the door and looked out. "... and into a wall socket here just outside. Which at present is switched off."

"Well, at a guess, it probably wasn't switched off at the crucial moment," remarked the doctor. "I can do a few tests, once my minions have hauled him away from here when you've finished looking at him, but I'd say that a reasonable working hypothesis would be that your man has been electrocuted. Result, heart failure. And since, as I say, showers do not usually come wired up to the mains, I'd say you have a definite case of murder on your hands."

"Shall I just go back home and have a quiet evening in front of the television?" enquired Constable mildly. "You two seem to have the case pretty much sorted between yourselves."

"Oh, you don't get out of it that easily, Andy," chuckled the doctor. "I, on the other hand, do. I don't think there's anything here which tells me that my professional skills are going to be needed any time before tomorrow morning, so I am going to leave the late lamented in your capable hands and see if I can salvage something out of this evening. You know, it's strange," he continued, as he reached in a pocket for his mobile phone and dialled. "Getting to grips with a dead body always sharpens my appetite. Funny, that. You'll have the report on your desk tomorrow, Andy. Toodle-oo." Before the detectives could react, the doctor was out of the room and disappearing down the corridor. "Hello, darling ... yes, I've managed to escape ... look, why don't you call the restaurant back and see if they've still got that table ..." His voice faded away as he descended the stairs.

*

"That was all a bit short and sweet, wasn't it, guv," commented Copper, still rather taken aback at the speed of the doctor's departure. "So now what?"

117

"Further and better particulars, I suppose, sergeant," responded Constable. He surveyed the rather forlorn spectacle of the dead man lying naked in the shower. "Let's see if we can't have this guy taken care of with a bit more dignity, and then we can have a word with the chap who found the body." He made his way out of the dressing room and down the stairs, to be greeted at the foot by the arrival of a group of overall-clad officers. "Impeccable timing, everyone," he said. "I was just wondering where you lot from SOCO had got to. And you're Sergeant ..." He searched his memory.

"Singleton, sir," the leader replied. "Una Singleton."

"Excellent." Constable turned his attention to two sombrely-clad individuals who had entered in the wake of the SOCO team. "And I assume you two are what the doctor is pleased to call his minions."

"Yes, sir," said one of the new arrivals. "We just caught him before he jumped into his car and zoomed off. Dead man up on the first floor, so he said."

"Dressing Room 1," confirmed Copper.

"Leave him to us, sir."

"Good. And Singleton and the rest of you, make a start in there, but then you'd better move on to the other rooms in that corridor in case there's anything relevant, and then ... oh, to hell with it, you know what to do. See if you can find one and one and make them add up to three. At the moment we have no idea what we're looking for, so just rummage the whole place."

"Very good, sir." The team leader began to issue orders briskly.

"And if I'm not much mistaken, guv, this is where we'll find Mr. Castle," said Copper, tapping on the half-glazed door of a small cubicle just inside the stage door.

The knock was answered by a rather wan-looking Peter Castle. "Oh, it's you, sergeant." He held back the door and admitted the two detectives to the cramped fug of his booth.

"This is my senior officer, D.I. Constable," explained Copper. "We'd like you to tell us what happened in the period running up to Mr. Nelson's death."

"What, the whole day?" asked Castle.

"If you think it will be helpful, sir," said Constable.

"You'd better sit down then." The detectives squeezed on

to two folding chairs which the stage doorman produced from alongside his desk. Castle took a deep breath and seemed to marshal his thoughts. "Now, the first thing I can tell you is that there wasn't anyone else in the theatre today apart from the cast and the technical people. I know that, because they all have to come past me, see – I've got that little hatch there ..." He indicated a sort of glazed serving hatch with a sliding door in the wall overlooking the entrance hall. "... so I can see anyone who goes out or comes in."

"What about the box office people?" interjected Copper, recalling an earlier conversation.

"Oh no, they don't come round here," said Castle. "Like I said, they're all quite separate. We don't mix. They only go in at the front, and all the doors between the foyer and the rest of the theatre are kept locked unless it's a performance."

Constable resumed the questioning. "So, Mr. Castle, tell me about today."

"I always get in about nine-thirty in the morning, because the post and the deliveries come to the stage door. Not that there was anything today – most Mondays there isn't."

"Anyone else from the company in at that point?"

"What, the actors? Fat chance!" snorted Castle. "You won't get an actor anywhere near a theatre before midday. No, the only ones who were here this morning were Stuart, David Winston, and Will Mott. David was going through the lighting plot with Stuart, and Will told me yesterday during get-in that he had some sound effects to sort out, so he came in just before twelve, as far as I can remember. So then I suppose they were busy around the stage after that, because I didn't see anything of them until Stuart and Will went over to the pub for lunch around one o'clock."

"Mr. Winston didn't go with them?"

"No. I don't know what he did."

"So what about the period after lunchtime?" asked Constable.

"The whole company was called for two o'clock for the technical rehearsal at two-thirty."

"Sorry – what exactly is the technical rehearsal?"

"It's where they go through all the technical bits and pieces for the show," explained Castle. "Because, even though they've been here before with other productions, it's always that bit

119

different for every theatre they go to – you know, timing on the lighting or the set changes, cueing the curtain up and down, sound effects and what-have-you. They don't do the whole play – just the bits where something happens." He leaned forward confidentially and lowered his voice. "To be honest, it's always very bitty, and usually ends up a bit of a mess, and that's when the fur starts flying. I stay out here and keep my head down."

Constable stored the thought away in the back of his mind. "So you say everyone came into the theatre at two o'clock?"

"Well, more or less. Delia Armstrong came in a bit earlier, but she usually does if she's got props to lay out ready. And Don Abbott got here just at the same time Stuart and Will came back from the pub, and he grabbed Stuart – said he wanted a quiet word with him. Of course, I was sat here in my little booth with the hatch open, and you can't help overhearing if someone's right outside."

"And the quiet word was ...?" coaxed Constable.

"Something about needing more time to sort the money out, and Stuart told him to get on with it, because he wasn't prepared to wait for ever. Mind you, as far as I know, everything was ready to start the rehearsal on time."

"So all the other people were in by then?"

"No. Miss Hamilton's taxi dropped her off a few moments later, and then Matthew Edwards and Jessica Davenport came in just after that – I think he'd given her a lift. Oh, and Angela Bailey rushed in about five minutes before they were due to start, but that's like her – she's always late for everything. Not that it really mattered, because they weren't using costumes because it wasn't a proper dress rehearsal until this evening."

"So we now have the entire *dramatis personae* on the scene." Constable permitted himself a small quip, but was rewarded only by a slightly odd stare from the stage doorman. "What about after that?"

"I didn't really see anybody much after that," said Castle, "being as they were mostly on and around the stage, and I was here in my booth. I just had my little radio on – actually, there was quite a good play on this afternoon – a nice old-fashioned Dorothy Sayers. Not like some of the modern rubbish they stick on that stage through there." He gestured dismissively. "Mind you, I did hear a few bits and pieces."

"How's that then, sir, if you were here and everyone else was through onstage?"

"There's this loudspeaker system rigged up so that you can hear what's going on onstage when you're in the dressing rooms or in the offices," answered Castle, pointing to a small speaker affixed to the top of the wall opposite his hatch opening. "It's normally on all the time, but generally I just sort of tune out of it. But that's how I heard the row about the lighting."

The inspector's attention was alerted. "And what row would that be, sir?"

"I think that's the one I mentioned to you, sir," murmured Copper.

"I missed the very start of it," continued Castle, "because I wasn't really taking much notice, but then Stuart was going on at David hammer and tongs, and Miss Hamilton was telling him not to be unreasonable, and Jessica was crying, and Don was trying to calm everybody down. That was about five o'clock, when the tech finished. But then I suppose Stuart must have gone off, because it all died down."

"I see." Constable mused for a moment. "And can you tell us anything about Mr. Nelson's movements after that?"

"I did see him about ten to six, because Miss Hamilton was coming down from her room, and he was chasing after her and trying to get her to hang on. But she said, 'Don't you talk to me!', and then she stormed out of the theatre, but I've no idea what that was about. One of their usual rows, I expect – well, you have to expect it with these tempestuous theatricals. It happens all the time, whoever we've got in here. And then Stuart went back up towards the dressing rooms."

"Did you see him after that at all?"

"I did. In fact, it was the last time I did see him – well, alive, that is. It was about quarter past six, and I'd popped down to the Green Room to make myself a cup of tea. I asked Delia if she wanted one but she said no, she was busy, and when I came back up I saw Stuart heading up the stairs. I heard him muttering something about 'the damned electrics' under his breath, so I suppose he was heading up towards the lighting box, but he had a face like thunder, so I just looked the other way."

"The lighting box?" queried Constable. "Wouldn't that normally be out somewhere at the top of the auditorium?"

121

"It is," confirmed Castle, "but at the top of these stairs, there's a pass door and a little corridor which goes through, so's you don't need to go through front-of-house. And the sound room lives up there as well."

"And I'm afraid I interrupted you, Mr. Castle. You were saying about how you saw Mr. Nelson heading in that direction ...?"

"Well, that was it, really. I came back in here with my tea, and I saw Miss Hamilton come in through the stage door just before a quarter to seven. And I was sat here reading my paper, when all of a sudden the lighting started to flicker, and I heard a bang from upstairs, just like I tried to tell your sergeant here, so I ran up to the dressing rooms. Everybody was standing in the corridor, all saying 'what's going on?', except for Stuart, so I knocked on his door, and when there was no answer, I went in and found him. So then I got everyone to wait downstairs while I went and dialled 999."

"Which is where I came in, guv," said Copper.

Constable mused for a moment. "Then I think that will do for the present, Mr. Castle. If I can just ask you to stay here at your post, if you will. I have officers conducting a search of the building, so if they have any queries, perhaps you would assist them as necessary."

"Of course, sir." Castle almost saluted, as the two detectives creaked to their feet from the extremely uncomfortable folding chairs and made their way back into the corridor.

*

"Lighting box? Flickering lights? Any connection, do you suppose, guv?" said Dave Copper.

"Not impossible," replied Andy Constable. "So let's see if we can find our way to this pass door and check it out." He led the way up the stairs.

At the very top, next to an iron ladder set into the wall which appeared to lead to a hatch to the roof, and opposite an ordinary panelled door marked 'Wardrobe' from which emanated the sound of a sewing machine in action, lurked another door, only about five feet in height, which bore a boldly-painted 'KEEP CLOSED' legend.

"This, I take it, is the pass door," said Constable.

"Bit small, isn't it, guv?" observed Copper. "Who's it

designed for – munchkins?" He grasped the handle and pulled. "Blimey – this thing weighs a ton! What's it made of – cast iron?"

"You know, I think you're probably right, sergeant. It's obviously all part of the theatre's fire precautions, like the safety curtain. Time was, in the nineteenth century, they had theatres burning down left, right, and centre because they were all using gas lighting, so they started building them with a fire barrier between the stage and the public areas. That's what this is."

"Well, I suppose it's better to have your arm pulled out of its socket than to get fried," muttered Copper, massaging his shoulder. "After you, guv.'"

Constable crouched to pass through the door and entered the blessedly full-height, but extremely narrow and grimy corridor behind it. Two or three small windows at intervals gave a view down into the auditorium below. Avoiding the selection of dangling cobwebs, the detectives emerged through a conventional door at the far end, to find themselves in a further corridor with two doors off it, marked 'F.X.' and 'L.X.' respectively. Behind the first, which stood open, could be seen the back view of William Mott, leaning on the desk before him and looking out through the windows on to the front of the stalls and the stage curtain. He turned at the sound of the detectives' approach.

"This is Mr. Mott, sir," said Copper. "He's the F.X. man."

"I beg your pardon, sergeant?"

"Sorry, sir – it's just some jargon they use in theatre," replied Copper, with only the tiniest hint of smugness. "Bit of a play on words, so to speak. 'F.X.' - sounds like 'effects', see. It means he does all the sound for the production. It's like 'L.X' next door – 'elecs', short for electrics."

"Yes, well, thank you for the tutorial, sergeant," remarked Constable with a touch of asperity. "So, Mr. Mott, I am what my sergeant here might call the police man – Detective Inspector Constable ..." He produced his warrant card. "... and I'm hoping that you may be able to help me with some information." The swift look up and down at Will Mott's appearance, and the slight flicker in the inspector's expression, hinted at doubts.

"Of course, inspector." Will's cheerful smile, the hand held out for a robust handshake, and the clearly well-educated accent, warned Constable of the perils of judging a book by its cover.

"Ask me anything you like. Mind you," he continued, "if you want the one who killed Stuart Nelson, don't bother to look any further – I'm your man." The shocked look on the faces of both detectives caused him to hurry on before they could respond. "Sorry, joke in very bad taste."

"Would you care to explain the nature of this joke, Mr. Mott?" Constable did not sound remotely amused.

"I'm sorry, inspector." Will was immediately contrite. "You're right – it's not funny at all. No, I was talking about the play. There's this shooting effect during Act Two, you see, and I have to cue it, so I would have been responsible for killing Stuart every night. Except tonight, of course," he added hastily.

"I think you'd better elucidate a little more, sir," said Constable.

"It's actually one of Delia's props," explained Will. "She's brilliant at making that sort of thing. There's a tiny explosive device built into one of Stuart's costumes, so that when someone supposedly shoots at him, a charge goes off in his jacket and it looks as if he's been hit by a bullet. They use them a lot in films."

"I always wondered how they did that," commented Copper, intrigued. "So how exactly does it work, sir?"

"I'll show you," said Will, turning to the bank of switches in front of him. "It's very simple. It's all electronic – Delia's built it so that I hit this button on my sound board here which makes the sound of the shot, and at the same time sends a radio signal to fire the explosion. Of course, Props have to replace it for every performance, and Angela has to sew a new breast pocket on to Stuart's jacket each time, but it looks really good. Great way to kill someone." He shook his head sadly. "All gone to waste now, of course." He stopped in the realisation of what he had said. "Sorry, inspector – that's not what I meant. It just came out wrong."

"So may I take it, sir, that you would have no wish to do Mr. Nelson any harm?"

"Hell, no."

"Good friends, then?"

Will considered for a moment. "Maybe that's going a bit far. I mean, Stuart was all right, I suppose – I never had too much trouble with him, but we all got on the wrong side of him from time to time. Well, except for Jessica, of course."

"Oh? In what way, sir?"

"For some reason, he always seemed to gravitate towards the young actresses. He's actually quite notorious for it around the business – everyone calls it 'The Nelson Touch'. I mean, I don't know that he ever actually did anything he shouldn't," said Will hastily, "but I still think it's a bit creepy, and I don't think Jessica was too keen on it, but sometimes in this business you have to be nice to the boss or you don't get the work."

"So, Mr. Nelson had an eye for the ladies." Constable squirrelled the information away in the back of his mind for further consideration. "Can we come on to practicalities, Mr. Mott. Would you fill us in on the events of the day as you saw them? And sergeant, ..."

"On it, sir," said Copper, producing his notebook.

"I was in this morning sorting out some final details on sound – there's always something that has to be tweaked whichever theatre you're in – and then Stuart asked me if I wanted to go over to the pub for some lunch, so I did. And when we came back, Don Abbott had just come out of the bookies' next door, and he grabbed Stuart as we came in, and I went on down to my control board at the back of the stalls."

"I thought this was your control board," commented Constable.

"Oh, it's the main one," explained Will, "but I've got a sort of temporary one downstairs, just for tech and dress rehearsals, which works in parallel. Otherwise I'd be forever up and down the stairs. Anyway, after that I was all over the place at different times, adjusting equipment. In fact ..." Will paused in thought. "Come to think of it, there was a funny atmosphere about the place all day. Wherever you went, there was someone having a huddled conversation about something, but they always stopped when they saw you."

"So, of course, you would have had no idea of the nature of these conversations?"

"Only the one," said Will. "There was one point when I was in the wings – it was during the interval of tech, so it must have been about quarter past four, I suppose – and it was all quite dark, and Delia was there talking to Elizabeth Hamilton, and I heard Delia say 'I was so shocked! I gave up everything, and now see what's happening'. And then they saw me and shut up quick, so I've no idea what it was about."

125

"And Mr. Nelson himself. I assume you must have had some sort of dealings with him during this afternoon's rehearsal?"

Will shrugged. "Not that much, actually. Except of course when he was barking orders about a cue being half a millisecond off, but that's nothing unusual with directors. You get used to it."

"So when would have been the last time you saw him?" persisted the inspector.

"Just before six o'clock, I think. Yes, that's right. I was on the stairs, and I was just passing the landing that gives on to the dressing room corridor when Stuart came up and knocked on Jessica's door and marched in. And then I heard him say 'What are you doing in here? Out! I want to talk to Jessica', but I was gone before I could see who came out."

"And that's the last thing you can tell us about Mr. Nelson's movements? You don't know anything about his whereabouts after that?"

"Ah! Not so fast, inspector," grinned Will. "I said that was the last time I saw him. I didn't say it was the last I heard of him." He folded his arms and leaned back with an expression of amused self-satisfaction on his face.

"Well, do go on, Mr. Mott," said Constable. "You're evidently dying to tell us something."

"Okay, inspector – you're right," admitted Will. "I have been saving the best bit till last. You see, I was down at my control desk ..."

"The one in the stalls?"

"That's the one."

"And when would this have been?"

"It was about fifteen minutes later, so around quarter past six, I suppose. And I had my cans on ..." A puzzled look from Constable. "... sorry, earphones – I had them on because I'd just been speaking to David Winston up here in lighting control. There's an intercom system with headphones, so that sound and lighting and stage management can all talk to each other during performances. Like these." Will held up a set of earphones with a microphone attached.

"I get the picture, Mr. Mott. And so ...?"

"So, I still had mine on, and David must have taken his off, but his mike was still live, because I heard Stuart go into the lighting box and start going on at David again, and then there was this great crash, and I reckon David must have decked him. Huge fun." Will laughed, but then seemed to recollect the gravity of the situation in response to Constable's lack of amusement.

"And Mr. Nelson's reaction to this?"

"Oh, nothing physical, if that's what you're wondering. No, Stuart obviously picked himself up, and he said something like 'You'll never work in theatre again after this show'. His voice sounded really tight, like he was absolutely furious. Well, he would be, I reckon. And then David said 'Watch out, or I'll put a real bullet in that gun', and then he threw Stuart out. I don't know if anyone else heard. After that, it all went quiet, until ..."

"Until what?"

"Until about seven o'clock – that's the first I knew anything was wrong, when all the lights went mad. And then someone told me that they'd found Stuart dead – must have been Peter Castle, I suppose, because then he got everyone to go down to the Green Room while he phoned the police. And that's it."

"So other than the argument between Mr. Nelson and Mr. Winston, you know of nobody who had any reason to do Mr. Nelson any harm?"

"That's the trouble with being the sound man, inspector," said Will. "I never usually get to hear any of the interesting stuff. Only my boring old sound cues. Sorry."

*

"That must be where Nelson got that bruise from, guv," remarked Dave Copper as the two officers emerged into the corridor.

"One question answered at least," observed Andy Constable. "Let's see if we can find out the answers to a few more in here." He pushed open the door marked 'L.X.', only to find the room deserted. A large and complex-looking board with an array of switches, sliders, and coloured indicator lights was located below a bank of windows which gave a clear view of the stage below, while to one side, a spotlight on a stand was positioned in front of one of the windows which had been slid open. Reels of cables were dotted about, together with boxes of metal slides containing plastic filters in various colours. Tall metal cabinets along one wall spilled out a variety of electrical paraphernalia – plugs, sockets, more bundles of cable, stacks of light bulbs in a bewildering range of sizes and types – while on another wall was mounted a pegboard which held a comprehensive range of tools – hammers, screwdrivers, drills, pliers, and all the requisites of the electrician – each one neatly outlined in bold red marker pen, and each regimented in its place.

"All the what, and none of the who," commented Constable. "I don't know about you, but all this means very little to me without the man who runs it."

"He'll be back downstairs in the Green Room if you want him, sir," said Copper.

"I think I'll be wanting all of them," replied Constable. "You've seen them – I haven't, and I'd quite like to form my own impressions. So we'll head back downstairs and see what else there is to be discovered." As he re-entered the corridor, he noticed a further door, almost hidden in the shadows, at the opposite end to where they had entered. "And where does that go, I wonder."

Copper opened it and poked his head through. "Top of another staircase, sir," he reported, and descended a few steps. "Looks like it's the top of the stairs which the audiences use to get to the circle, but there's a rope barrier at the bottom of this flight to stop them coming up," he called. "Oh, and there's another thing," he said, reappearing in the doorway. "There's a keypad on the lock this side – obviously you need to know the code to get through. Keeps out the unauthorised. Oh, hello!" He bent to pick up a bright yellow item from the dusty corner at the foot of the door. "It's a cable-tie, guv – it looks as if they've put it though these brackets here on the door and the frame to stop the door being opened from outside anyway."

"And," noticed Constable, "two things – first, it's nice and clean, so it doesn't look as if it's been lying down there amongst all the muck for very long, and two, it's very neatly sliced through. Not so much of a security precaution, wouldn't you say? Well, bag it anyway – try not to get too many more of your prints on it, and we'll let SOCO have a look at it, just in case it means something. In the meantime, we'll go back down the way we came and see if there's any progress elsewhere."

As the detectives passed back through the small door at the top of the backstage stairs, the sound of the sewing machine from the wardrobe department had been replaced by a rather shaky soprano warble in a rendering of a song almost recognisable as an Ivor Novello tune.

"Aha! The wardrobe mistress, no doubt," deduced Constable. He listened for a moment. "And by the sound of it, no massive loss to the performance side of the business. But let's take the opportunity to pay her a call. It'll give the SOCO bods a few extra minutes to rootle out anything that may be lying around to be rootled." He tapped on the door.

The singing stopped abruptly. "Yes?"

As Constable entered the room, it was to discover Angela Bailey sitting with an evening dress spread across her lap, busily wielding a needle and thread. Costumes on hangers were dotted about the room on rails, hooks on the wall, or hung over mirrors, while other items were piled haphazardly on chairs and an ironing board. Pairs of shoes, tied together by the laces, littered the floor. A tumble drier, its top stacked with a miscellany of hats, stood in one corner.

"Miss Bailey, isn't it?" Constable introduced himself. "And you've already met Sergeant Copper. And if I gather correctly from what he's told me, you may have some helpful information for us."

"You'd better sit down, gentlemen – if you can find somewhere. Oh, just push some of those on to the floor." Angela waved vaguely in the direction of some of the clothing heaped on chairs. "I'm sorry it's all such a mess in here – it's not usually like this. Normally I take the chance to get everything neatly sorted out and tidied away once everyone's safely on stage for dress rehearsal, but of course, what with all the horrible business of Stuart, I haven't had a chance. And I hope you don't mind, but I absolutely must get on and finish sewing this, or I shan't know where I am."

The detectives obediently removed a pile of shirts and a box of mixed ties and scarves from two rather spindly bentwood chairs which had obviously seen better days, and cautiously lowered themselves on to them. "Now, Miss Bailey," began Constable, "I'd obviously like your help in establishing the events of the day. And I was intrigued by the fact that apparently you mentioned something about 'washing dirty linen in public'. I wonder if you'd care to tell me exactly what you meant."

Angela put a triumphant final stitch into her work and laid

129

the dress aside. "Now the first thing I'll say, inspector, is that you won't get any idle gossip or tittle-tattle from me!" she asserted. "There's far too much of that sort of thing in theatre as it is. Mind you, not that some of them don't deserve it, the way they go on."

"Oh?"

Constable's mild response seemed to encourage Angela to forget her intended discretion. "Now I'm not saying she had anything to do with anything, because you couldn't meet a nicer woman, but I'm surprised Elizabeth didn't put an end to Stuart Nelson years ago. And then there was the way he treated the backstage crew – you'd think they were something he'd stepped in. Even Delia sometimes, and they've known each other for years."

"I remember she mentioned something to that effect, madam," confirmed Copper. "Something about drama school."

"Oh yes," said Angela. "She trained to be an actress, you know, and they say she would have been really good, but for some reason she packed it all in. Heaven knows why. Well, some do. It's not a profession for the faint-hearted."

"I'm rather more interested in the events of today, rather than the distant past, Miss Bailey," commented Constable. "Perhaps you can tell us what you know about those."

"Well, inspector, I can't tell you about the whole day, because I didn't get here until quite late. I got held up because I had to go to the cleaners to get Stuart's jacket. They'd tried out this gunshot business of Delia's yesterday ..." She broke off. "Oh, not a real shot, inspector – don't think that."

"Mr. Mott has already explained to us about the shooting in the play, madam," put in Copper.

"Oh. Good." Angela seemed relieved. "Anyway, I think for some reason they'd put in an explosive charge that was too big, because there were stains all over the jacket front, as well as the pocket being almost blown off. So I had to rush down to the cleaners this morning first thing and get them to express-clean it, and it was all a panic, and they didn't really want to get it done by lunchtime but I managed to persuade them because it was for the theatre, and then I had to put a new pocket on the jacket, and fortunately I'd thought to take a spare with me so I was able to do it at the digs before I came out. But then it wouldn't go right, and I had to take it off and put it on again, so I didn't get here until just

130

before they started technical rehearsal." Angela's slightly breathless narrative created a firm impression of her somewhat chaotic existence.

"So, once you'd arrived at the theatre ..."

"I took the jacket straight up to Stuart's dressing room, and there he was on the stairs with Jessica backed into a corner, and he was saying 'I want you to give me a really good performance', and I thought 'Hmmm. That's not the first time he's used that line'."

"And did Miss Davenport reply?"

"Not that I heard, inspector. She just looked at him. I was telling Don and David about it later, not that I'm one to talk, of course, and I said it's a wonder he doesn't get his face slapped, or worse. Anyway, I just dropped the jacket off in Stuart's room and came on up here to Wardrobe. And they started the tech soon after that."

"Were you present for any of the events of the afternoon?" asked Constable. "I gather there may have been one or two incidents."

"I spent most of the afternoon up here in my room, listening to everything on the loudspeakers while I was doing some odd bits and pieces of sewing," replied Angela. "It's actually quite an easy show for me – not like some of these where I spend half my time in the wings getting people in and out of their costumes in a mad rush for their next entrance. No, there's only one quick change for Elizabeth in Act Two, and this afternoon wasn't a dress rehearsal anyway, so I wasn't going to go traipsing up and down all those stairs if I didn't have to. I just wish someone would tell me why it is they always put the Wardrobe right at the top of the theatre," she remarked, in a slightly grumpy aside.

"So did you remain here the whole time?"

"Well, not the whole time, inspector. I sat up here most of the afternoon, listening with half an ear to what was going on – tech rehearsal isn't really that interesting, because it's mostly people shouting at other people about light and sound cues, or something happening with the scenery. Anyway, I could hear it was coming to an end, so I went down as they were finishing, just in time to catch the big row ..."

"Which we have already heard about from one of your

131

colleagues," said Constable.

"Oh, that's all right then – you won't need me to tell you what went on. But I thought, 'I'm not getting involved with all this nonsense', so I just quietly collected Stuart's jacket and brought it back upstairs to mend, ready for dress rehearsal."

"But I assume you went back downstairs at some point, Miss Bailey?"

"Yes, of course, because I had to take Stuart's jacket back down to his dressing room. Now some people, especially the young ones, although you wouldn't think it, they'd take pity on my poor old bones and come up here and collect their costumes for themselves. Not Stuart Nelson. Oh no – far too grand, my dear." A dismissive sniff. The detectives exchanged surreptitious looks. "Anyway, I went down just before half past six, just as Delia was coming out of the room with all her bits and pieces, which was perfect timing, because she said 'I've just put the new bullet pack in there ready for you', so I found it on Stuart's chair and put it into the jacket and plugged it in to the battery. And as soon as I'd done that, Stuart burst into the room holding the side of his face, and I was about to tell him that I'd sorted his costume out, but I thought 'Whoops! He doesn't look to me as if he's in the mood for a chat', so I nipped off double-quick just as Delia was going into Jessica's room along the corridor."

Constable glanced across at Copper to see him busily scribbling. "Would that have been your last encounter, as it were, with Mr. Nelson?" he enquired.

"No, it wasn't, inspector. The last time I saw him was about a quarter of an hour later."

"So around a quarter to seven?" asked Copper, beginning to look slightly fraught at the relentless flow of information.

"I suppose it must have been, sergeant. You see, I was taking Elizabeth Hamilton's costumes back to her room, because I'd had to do a few little alterations – silly me, really, because I could have taken them down at the same time as Stuart's and saved myself a trip, but you don't always think of these things at the time, do you? Anyway, just as I arrived outside her door, I heard her say 'You are responsible for that child', and then I knocked and she said 'Come in', and in I went and found Stuart standing there. I hadn't realised – I think I thought she was just going through some lines. But then there was a sort of heavy silence, and they were obviously waiting for me to go, so I just hung the costumes up and left."

"And returned here?"

"That's right. And I'd just popped a batch of shirts and whatnot into the dryer about a quarter of an hour later when all the lights went funny, and I went through to David to see what was going on, and then we came downstairs together and found out what had happened. After that, I was down in the Green Room with all the others until you arrived, sergeant."

*

"How's the writer's cramp coming along?" asked Andy Constable with a smile as the two detectives descended the stairs.

"Very nicely, thank you, sir," responded Dave Copper with a mock grimace. "You know, there are times when I could do with being ambidextrous."

"Taking a leaf out of Leonardo de Vinci's book, eh? Mind you, that probably wouldn't be the wisest course of action. He used to do mirror writing as well, and with your scrawl, it's difficult enough to read as it is. If you fell under a bus, it would be downright impossible for the rest of us to fathom out any of your notes."

"I shall take great care crossing the road, sir," grinned Copper. "I wouldn't want to make life any more difficult for you than I already do."

"*For this relief, much thanks*," quoted Constable. And in response to his junior colleague's quizzical look, "Don't worry – it's '*Hamlet*', not The Scottish Play. I'm not trying to jinx the job. But no relief for you, I'm afraid. I think it's about time we caught up with all the other players – so to speak." But his immediate intention was thwarted as, reaching the stage level, he was greeted by the head of the SOCO team who was just emerging through the door to the acting area.

"Oh, great, sir," she said. "I was just coming to find you."

"From which I deduce, Sergeant Singleton, that your time so far has not been wasted."

"Not at all, sir." she replied. "Far from it. In fact, if you'd like to come and take a look at what we've got to date, I've got things spread out on a table through here." The officer led the way on to the stage where, in the wings, a pair of trestle tables stood. The former contents had been cleared into a heap to one end, leaving a clear space which bore several items encased in clear sealed plastic bags. "Apparently it's where the props are usually laid out."

"Very appropriate," commented Constable. "So, what props have been used in this particular drama?"

"We started out in the room where the dead man was found," explained the Scene of Crime Officer. "Obviously, once the body had been cleared, we checked that mat in the shower tray. And it had definitely been rigged to impart an electric shock, so we've gathered up all the elements of that. There's the mat itself that was used to conceal the wiring, the wires themselves, and the plug that ran to the corridor outside. We'll check them all for source and traces of anything unexpected, of course, but to be honest, everything looks thoroughly ordinary to me, so I have my doubts as to whether the materials themselves will tell us anything."

"Prints?" asked Constable, without much hope.

Singleton shook her head. "Nothing, sir. A few smudges on the plug and the socket it was fitted into, and a few fibres which I'm guessing probably came from a pair of electrician's gloves. I'll confirm later. But no sign of any such."

"Fine. Well, so far, so bad. Got anything more encouraging?"

"Oh, I think so, sir," smiled the officer. "I started with the worst first. But we can do much better than that."

"Do tell."

"Very interesting little collection of scraps of paper from the waste-bin in the victim's room. We've roughly placed them in position to reassemble the original in the bag for you to see, but nothing's fixed, so best not touch the bag. There."

Constable leaned over the item indicated. In the bag, and loosely reconstructed, could be seen the torn fragments of a typed I.O.U. "Five thousand quid," remarked the inspector. "Not an inconsiderable sum. And dated about a month ago. And, irritatingly, no names."

"There's the remnant of some sort of scrawled signature, sir," pointed out Singleton. "Just the very tag end of an odd letter – not really enough to make anything of. But the rest of it was nowhere to be found. Trust me, we checked very carefully. Perhaps whoever it was had the wit to take it to avoid any identification."

"Hmmm. Well, we'll see if its existence tallies with any of our other information. Maybe the debt got paid off, and the whole thing is supremely irrelevant. So, moving on, what else do we have?"

"This nice little trinket, sir." The officer held up a bag with a tiny item nestling at the very bottom. "A gold ring. Hallmarked nine carat – not your average Christmas cracker rubbish, so not the sort of thing you'd want to throw away."

"But somebody had?"

"Couldn't say if it had been deliberately discarded, sir, but it was a little odd to find it where we did. One of my chaps was checking along the skirting edge where the wires were tucked away in the corridor, and he noticed it in one of the corners. Anyway, we thought it might be worth looking into. And there's an inscription."

Constable inspected the ring more closely. "A signet ring, by the look of it. Engraved with a '*D*'. And there's a date letter in the hallmark." He read the details aloud. "Google that date letter, Copper. You never know, the age of the ring might turn out to be relevant." He examined the object again. "And there's something engraved inside as well." He squinted at the tiny characters.

"Looks like '*Forever*', sir," said Copper, peering over the inspector's shoulder. "Quite small, though, isn't it? I mean, it wouldn't fit me." He held up a hand in illustration.

"That, sergeant, is because you were born with specially large hands for dropping on to the shoulders of evil-doers as you detain them," commented Constable with a smile. "If you're talking about normal people, the thing could quite easily fit either a man's little finger or a woman's ring finger. Any chance of any prints on this one?"

"Slightly better luck, sir," replied Singleton. "Two partials – one is smudged into unintelligibility, but I have hopes of the other."

"And you will of course be checking everyone in the building?"

A slightly pained look was Constable's reward. "Give us a chance, sir – I don't think we've got on too badly so far. And as it happens, I was just about to despatch Darren here with his cunning little scanning machine to do just that."

135

"Most of the people are downstairs still," Copper told the young officer who stepped forward. "But there are a couple up at the top – one to the left, one to the right."

"Don't worry, sarge – I'll find them." Darren trotted off on his mission.

"And the next object is ...?"

"This." Singleton pointed to a photograph of a young baby.

"And what do we think this has to do with anything?" enquired the inspector.

"I honestly don't know, sir." The SOCO officer shook her head in slight bewilderment. "I just got one of those feelings. You see, it was in the dressing room which I gather belongs to Jessica Davenport, and everything was lying around everywhere, open to the world, apart from one drawer, which was locked. Now if there's one thing which I always enjoy, it's the challenge of a locked drawer. No challenge at all, actually – it was the simplest kind of lock, and inside, there was just this one photo. No valuables, nothing else – just this. No reason, but I just felt it was a bit odd."

"Never disregard that itch in the back of your brain, sergeant," advised Constable. "Nine times out of ten it doesn't mean anything, but there's the odd occasion where it just makes all the difference. But no idea of who or whose this baby is?"

"Not a clue, sir. Nothing written on the back or anything else helpful like that."

"Miss Jessica Davenport's, maybe? Hmmm. Okay." Constable filed the matter away in the back of his mind. "What other treasures did the dressing rooms reveal? Any more itches?"

"Afraid not, sir," smiled Singleton in acknowledgement. "So then we moved on to the stage area. And there's so much clutter and rubbish around here that it could take forever to go through everything."

"Sadly, we do not have forever."

"Ah, well, you might not need it, sir. We've had a couple of things turn up which might interest you."

"Which I imagine are these next two?"

"That's right, sir. Another bit of paper, which they have very kindly neglected to tear up."

"And 'they' would be who?"

"That may be the puzzle, sir." The next plastic bag

136

contained a sheet of paper, apparently torn from a notebook, which had evidently been screwed up, but which had now been smoothed out for inspection. On it was the signature of Stuart Nelson, repeated eight times.

"And this was found where?"

Singleton pointed to the far side of the stage. "Over there in a rubbish skip."

"Do you reckon Stuart Nelson was expecting to be inundated by autograph-hunting fans, guv?" suggested Copper facetiously. "Do you suppose he was practising his signature so's he could avoid writer's cramp like mine?"

"I'm amazed that you have the time to pass witty remarks, given that you are in the middle of making copious and comprehensive notes, Sergeant Copper," responded Constable. "Or so I assume."

"Absolutely, guv," muttered Copper, burying his nose once more in his notebook.

"So," Constable turned back to the forensic officer, "given the absence of fondue sets and cuddly toys, our final object is …?"

"Rather a dinky pair of electrician's pliers," said Singleton with a note of triumph in her voice. "I suppose I ought to have linked these with the wiring and so on at the start, sir, but I thought I'd save them as a *pièce de résistance*."

"Electrical resistance, would that be?" quipped Copper. "Sorry, guv – busily making notes as instructed."

Singleton continued as if there had been no interruption. "And these attracted our attention not so much for what they were, but because they were found where no such pliers had a right to be found – jammed down the back of that fire extinguisher out on the landing." She indicated the piece of equipment which could be seen attached to the wall immediately outside the stage pass door.

"Couldn't have been dropped down there by accident?" queried the inspector.

"Doesn't appear likely from the position they were in," said Singleton. "It looked to me as if there had been a definite attempt to conceal them. Which seemed, at the least, suspicious."

"It's an obvious link to the way Mr. Nelson died, sir," observed Copper. "Is it too obvious to carry that on and link it with the company electrics man? After all, he was heard to make a definite threat against the dead man, according to what Mr. Mott told us."

"Just because a fact is obvious doesn't make it suspect, Copper," said Constable. "If criminals didn't do stupid things along the way, we'd have a much harder time of it. But I agree, it's worth raising the point with Mr. Winston. I suppose there's always the possibility, however remote, that he may break down completely under our ruthless questioning and blurt out a confession, but I shan't be holding my breath." He looked once again enquiringly at Una Singleton. "And that's it so far?"

"So far, sir. But there are areas we haven't yet covered, and you did say go over the whole place."

"Then I won't hold you up from that any longer. Let me know if anything else interesting pops up – I shall be down in the Green Room taking the measure of our band of theatricals. Copper, you're with me – you can introduce me to your friends." Constable gestured to his colleague to take the lead, and the two left the stage and started down the stairs.

*

"Oh, sergeant – you're just in time for a nice cup of tea." On entering the Green Room, Dave Copper came face to face with Delia Armstrong, two steaming mugs in her hands which she swiftly handed to Matthew Edwards and Jessica Davenport, seated nearest the door. "I've just made a big pot, so there's plenty. And I expect you'd like some too, wouldn't you, Mr. ... er ...?"

"This is Detective Inspector Constable, my senior officer, everyone," explained Copper. "He's in charge of this investigation, and he's got some questions for you all. But yes, Miss Armstrong, a cup of tea would be great. You, sir?"

"Not just at the moment, sergeant, thank you." Constable's reply held a note of reserve. He addressed the room. "As Sergeant Copper has said, there are questions which need to be answered. And to confirm what I'm sure you already know, this is definitely a murder investigation. Mr. Nelson has been deliberately killed, and various pieces of information have come to light which need explanation."

"We've just had that young man with his interesting little machine down here taking our fingerprints," twittered Delia, plying the teapot at the table in the rear of the room and handing a mug to Copper alongside her. "So clever – I thought it was all going to be smudgy ink-pads and pressing our thumbs on to pieces of paper, but it was all so quick and easy."

"We've all moved on since the days of Conan Doyle, Miss Armstrong," said Constable with the ghost of a smile. "At least, with technology. Other things, less so."

"You'd better ask us whatever you want, inspector." The man standing nearest the door seemed more prepared to be businesslike. "David Winston, by the way, in case you're wondering," said the electrician. "I know I haven't got anything to hide. I can't answer for the rest."

"Well, no, Mr. Winston," replied Constable, content to take up the offer. "On the face of it, you don't appear to have anything to hide, since I gather your antipathy to Mr. Nelson was extremely well known. You've made no kind of secret of it. And as far as we're aware, you're the only person who took that antipathy as far as physical action."

"Ah. That."

"Yes, sir. That." Constable waited patiently for further reaction.

"I didn't know anyone had seen that."

"Not seen, Mr. Winston – heard. But it amounts to the same thing. We know that you and Mr. Nelson had a violent altercation."

"All right – I admit it. So, yes, I gave Stuart a smack when he came up to my lighting box to carry on having a go at me, but that's because he deserved it. Oh, not just me – he treated everybody like dirt, and I'm not too sorry that he's dead ..." He turned to the woman seated close to him. "Sorry, Elizabeth. I know that's not the sort of thing one says, but this is the time for speaking the truth. I'm sure the inspector here agrees."

"I do, sir. So you'll also agree that you went on to threaten Mr. Nelson."

"What? Oh, you mean that stupid thing about the gun? Oh, for crying out loud, you can't make anything of that. The thing's just a replica – it's plastic. Ask Delia."

"Sorry?" The props supervisor looked up from her lap where her hands were cradling her tea. "Oh yes, inspector – it's not real at all. And anyway, Stuart wasn't shot ... was he?"

"No, that's right," said David. "That fingerprint guy said

something about electrocution because the shower tray was wired up to the mains, or some such."

"Sergeant Copper," said Constable severely, "would you please make a note to remind me to stress to our young colleagues on the SOCO team the virtue of discretion during a murder investigation."

"Will do, sir," muttered Copper. 'Wouldn't like to be in Darren's shoes', he thought, having caught the rough edge of his superior's tongue in the past.

"Oh, I see where this is leading, inspector," said David, voice heavy with sarcasm. "Electrician has row with actor – actor killed with electricity – so obviously, the electrician is the one who killed him."

"Did I say that, sir?"

"No, you didn't, but the implication's obvious, isn't it? Look, I'm a specialist. I can make electricity do all sorts of clever things. But you don't have to be an expert electrician to wire up a shower tray – anybody with a bit of DIY knowledge could do it. Any idiot can change a plug."

"Not everyone would have the equipment to do it," countered Constable. "And one thing which requires explanation is the fact that a pair of electrician's pliers have been found discarded in an extremely odd location. Would you have any idea why that would be?"

"So where are these pliers? Show me!" challenged David. "Have they got yellow tape on the handle?"

Constable thought for a moment. "No, sir," he said slowly. "I don't believe they do."

"Well then," riposted David. "They can't be mine, because all mine have got yellow tape on them, and what's more, all my tools live on a board up in my room. Go and check to see if anything's missing if you like – feel free!"

"Um, sir," intervened Copper hesitantly from the background. "I think he's right, sir. I did notice the board, and there didn't look to be any gaps."

"Thank you, sergeant," responded Constable, the wind slightly taken out of his sails. "But we shall double-check, Mr. Winston," he added. "And it's entirely possible that your own personal items aren't the only tools in the theatre. So, for the moment, we'll move on. And one of the things we're anxious to establish is the precise sequence of Mr. Nelson's movements during his final hours, and who he had dealings with. Now I have details of most of the people he saw and spoke to, and when, but there is one gap in our knowledge. Mr. Nelson visited one of the other performers' dressing rooms, and had a brief altercation with one of the people inside. I wonder, can anyone shed any light on that matter?"

"I suppose you mean me."

"Do I?" Constable turned to the young man seated close by in the circle of chairs facing him. "I'm guessing, from what my sergeant has told me, that you would be Mr. Edwards?"

"Yes, I am ... Matthew Edwards. And if you're talking about Jessica's dressing room, yes, it was me in there when Stuart came in." The actor's hand stole unconsciously into that of the young actress seated alongside him. "About six o'clock, as far as I can remember. I'd gone in because I was worried about her – she'd been a mass of nerves all afternoon, and I wanted to see if there was anything I could do to help."

"I would have thought that attacks of nerves would be all part and parcel of an actor's existence," suggested Constable mildly.

"That's because you haven't spent much time around Stuart Nelson and his damned Victory Theatre Company," retorted Matthew sharply. "You get used to being nervous in the ordinary way of things, but this wasn't like that, and I know it was all bloody Stuart Nelson's fault. He'd been all over Jessica like a rash ever since we started rehearsals. I would have told him to back off before if I hadn't thought it would cost me my job. But the way he was going on today, that was just too much for anyone to put up with."

"So did you decide that you would do something about that?" Constable's voice was quiet and undramatic.

"Yes, I did." Matthew caught his breath as he realised the implication of the inspector's words. "I mean ... no! No, of course not." The words tumbled out in a rush. "You mean, did I kill him? No! I couldn't do anything like that. I wouldn't have a clue how ... I mean, that's not the sort of person I am. Okay, I went to see Jessica, and I did think that somebody had to say something and it probably had to be me, and then suddenly, in walked Stuart. And I was all set to have it out with him ... but then I bottled it." The

141

young man slumped in his chair. "Couldn't get the words out. And he told me to get out, and I just went. That's it – I didn't see him after that."

After a moment's pause, Constable addressed the young woman next to Matthew, her hand still linked with his. "Miss Davenport, I take it?" A mute nod in reply. "You seem to have found yourself in the midst of a very upsetting situation. So how did that make you feel?"

"I ... I really can't talk about it." Jessica's voice quavered, and she cleared her throat before speaking in firmer tones. "But I suppose I must. All this business with Stuart hovering around me ever since we started work on the play. I always felt there was something wrong about it all."

"You are, of course, much younger than he was," said Constable sympathetically.

"I'm twenty-nine," said Jessica. "I didn't mean wrong like that. And of course, he was a married man, but that's not the point. No, it just felt weird right from the start, but of course, then I didn't really understand why. I just felt like my character in the play – a bit bewildered, with nobody to turn to. And I'm adopted too, just like her, so it all got tangled together." She looked towards the young man beside her. "But Matthew has been so lovely to me – he's just like the big brother I never had."

"You're an only child?"

"Yes."

Constable digested the actress's comments for a few seconds. "Miss Davenport raises a rather delicate question," he began. "The fact that Mr. Nelson was a married man."

"You don't have to pussy-foot, inspector." Elizabeth Hamilton spoke up from her position in a rather grand Queen Anne *fauteuil*, slightly distanced from the other occupants of the room. "My husband was not a man of great discretion in any aspect of his life."

"Miss Hamilton, sir." Dave Copper spoke up from the back of the room by way of introduction.

"So I gathered – thank you, sergeant. And my condolences, madam."

"Thank you, inspector." Elizabeth was brief and dismissive. "But please don't imagine that anything you say here will produce any startling revelations. My husband and I had reached a perfectly satisfactory *modus vivendi*. Well, to be honest, perhaps neither quite perfect nor entirely satisfactory. But I've had enough years of putting up with Stuart Nelson's behaviour to have grown used to it."

"So … forgive me … the situation regarding Miss Davenport was not unprecedented?"

"Far from it," replied Elizabeth drily. "Don't think that Jessica Davenport was anything new or anything unusual – although having said that, of course, she was, but I'm the last person you should be speaking to about that." The oblique look she sent in the direction of the young actress was hard to read. "Sometimes it's simply wisest to look the other way. Then again, sometimes not."

"And … forgive me again, but if similar circumstances have arisen in the past, how have they been resolved?"

"Oh, the normal way." Elizabeth gave a bitter laugh. "Which is what I suggested to Stuart when the matter first started to rear its ugly head – again. I told him to pay the wretched girl off and replace her, but he said you needed money to do that, and the way things were financially, he'd be surprised if any of us got our money unless something got sorted out."

"Therefore," said Constable, "if the normal course of action was not available to deal with what looks as if it was becoming an increasingly intolerable situation, one might be forgiven for thinking that abnormal action could be seen as the only solution. In other words, someone took drastic action to free you, and Jessica, and the company as a whole, from the tangle."

"So someone committed murder as a favour to the rest of us? Is that seriously what you are suggesting, Mr. Constable?" enquired Elizabeth. "How extremely altruistic of them."

Constable began to feel that there was little to be gained by pursuing the matter further, given Elizabeth's current attitude, but one of her remarks sparked a fresh train of thought. "I believe that this is the first inkling we've had of any financial difficulties involving the company. Was anyone else aware of these?" A circle of blank expressions was the only response. "Surely you would have something to say on the subject?" he continued, turning to the one remaining man in the room who had not yet spoken. "Since I'm assuming that you would be Mr. Abbott? The company manager, if my sergeant informs me correctly?"

143

"See here, inspector, this is all confidential stuff. And there's nothing wrong with the finances of the company that I can't sort out, given a bit of time," replied Don Abbott.

Beneath the facade of bravado, Constable thought he could detect considerable unease. "So all is well?" he probed. "No unexplained holes in the budget? No unaccountable expenses? Nobody with, for example, any personal financial issues which might impact on the general health of the Victory Theatre Company? No awkward questions from Mr. Nelson? Oh, not that we have any specific knowledge of anything of the sort, Mr. Abbott, I hasten to add. I'm simply seeking to cover all the possibilities." He smiled blandly and waited patiently.

Don moved close to the inspector and lowered his voice. "Look, Stuart was very good to me. All right, he'd made me a bit of a loan because I'd had some bad luck ..."

Constable was quick to respond. "Any particular kind of bad luck, sir?"

"Oh, just ... just a string of bad choices, I suppose," answered Don evasively. "Anyway, that wasn't the point, because I had it all under control. And as for Stuart, he had his finger firmly on the pulse, and all the payments had to go through him anyway. Nothing could ever happen without his signature, so it's not as if he wasn't aware of everything that was going on."

"And, no doubt, no concerns about the future either?" enquired Constable. "A new play – I imagine there must have been a certain interest among the public? Good advance bookings, and so on?"

"So-so, I suppose."

"And although I've heard it said that there's no such thing as bad publicity ..."

Don snorted. "Whoever told you that didn't know what they were talking about. What, a murder in the company? That's just what we needed! Oh my god!" A realisation seemed to hit him. "That means we're going to have to refund all the box office take. But ... we'll never manage it." He turned away and slumped in a chair, gazing unfocussed at the wall.

"Are you sure you wouldn't like that cup of tea now, inspector?" Delia Armstrong materialised unexpectedly at Constable's shoulder. "It'll only get cold otherwise, and you must be parched with all this talking."

"Oh … er, thank you, Miss Armstrong," said Constable, taking the proffered mug.

"And your sergeant said you don't take sugar."

"No, that's right." He sipped.

"Poor Stuart," said Delia into the silence. "I still can't believe he's dead."

"Am I right in thinking that you'd known Mr. Nelson for some time?"

"Oh yes. Since drama school – goodness, we were just eighteen. I wish everyone had known Stuart when I first met him," she said wistfully. "So popular with everyone. He was young and handsome and absolutely charming – he really swept me off my feet." She shook her head. "But of course, that was thirty years ago, and a lot of things can change in that time. You never know what's going to happen in this business. But now I suppose we're all going to have to make a new start. Especially the youngsters."

"Why them in particular?"

"It's never a bed of roses when you're young, inspector. The rest of us, we've all been around long enough to know how to cope. But with Jessica … well, you know the situation there. But she'll be all right, I'm sure of it. Even though nothing is ever easy for a young actress." A faint smile. "I should know."

"I believe you started out as an actress yourself?"

"Oh goodness, yes, but that was long ago, as they say, and in another country, and besides …" She tailed off. "Anyway," she resumed with a bright smile, "that was then, and this is now. I've never really regretted not becoming an actress – you just have to do what you feel is right for you at the time. The theatre can be cruel. And having seen how it changed Stuart, I'm sure I did the right thing."

Constable felt that the personal reminiscences were leading the investigation astray. "There is one thing I would like you to do for me, Miss Armstrong, if you would."

"Of course, inspector."

"We have discovered various items around the theatre which may or may not have some bearing in this case. I'd be grateful if you would come with me up to the table where I understand you keep the items used in the action of the play, and confirm for me whether they are in fact part of your own equipment, or whether we have to look further into them. So if

145

you'd like to go ahead with Sergeant Copper for a moment ..." The other two, Copper ushering Delia before him, headed for the door as Constable held back. "Just one small matter before I go, ladies and gentlemen. I wonder if you'd mind letting me have a look at your hands." A puzzled murmur arose. "If you would just hold them out for me, palms up, then the backs, that would be very helpful." As those present exchanged looks of bafflement, Constable swiftly circled the room, surveying the hands held out for his inspection. "Thank you, everyone. Please remain here – I shall try not to keep you too long." He left the room, closing the door behind him.

*

"Firstly, is there anything missing?"

"It's rather difficult to tell, inspector," replied Delia rather huffily. "Everything's been moved – I like to keep all my props neatly laid out so that everything is in its right place when the actors need it."

"And these all stay here all the time?"

"Mostly. Unless there's anything valuable like ... well, like this necklace, for example." Delia held up a piece of jewellery which sparkled dully in the dim light of the working lamps. "I mean, it's not really worth a great deal, but it looks as if it is, so it might prove a temptation to somebody light-fingered. So that gets locked away between performances in my little den." She pointed to a small dark door a few feet away which, when opened, revealed a small room lined with shelves holding a miscellany of objects and dusty cardboard boxes, and barely furnished with a battered bentwood chair and a small table with a desk lamp. "I go and sit in there sometimes when I'm not needed, or if I've got a little job to do."

"Like the shooting effect?" suggested Copper.

"That's right, sergeant," smiled Delia. "How clever you are."

"But the gun – a replica, you say? So not practical at all?"

"No, sergeant – that's why we don't need to lock it away. But anyway, it's here where it should be."

"But as far as you can tell, there's nothing gone astray?" Andy Constable brought the questioning back to the point.

"Not that I can see, inspector. Why do you ask?"

"Because we are slightly puzzled as to how to account for these things here, Miss Armstrong." Constable indicated the

146

plastic evidence bags. "If they are part and parcel of the action of the play, we need to answer the question of why they were found where they were. If they aren't, then the question is a different one. So are you able to confirm for me that these items do not feature on your list of props?"

Delia examined the bags one by one. Her face held an expression of mild curiosity as she surveyed each in turn, and finally she turned back to the inspector. "No, inspector. Nothing here relates to our play at all. Are all these things really so important?"

"They may well be."

"Then I'm very sorry I can't help you, Mr. Constable."

"Not to worry, Miss Armstrong." Constable appeared to dismiss the matter. "We shall just have to keep thinking. But thank you anyway. And if you'd like to rejoin your colleagues downstairs, I'm sure you'll be more comfortable." The dismissal was subtle and graceful, and Delia turned and made for the stairs without a backward glance.

"So, does that get us any further forward, guv?" enquired Dave Copper.

"It's ruled out some possibilities," said Constable. "That's always helpful."

"And I don't understand that business with the hands, guv. The SOCO chap's going around scanning everyone's prints, and it's not as if you can tell anything from just looking at people's fingers in the raw anyway."

"And that, sergeant, is just where you're wrong. And as it happens, I wasn't interested in the tips of the fingers anyway – more the other end."

"Sorry, sir?"

"Come on, Copper – think it through. We have here, in one of our little bags, a ring. Have you never noticed that, if someone wears a ring for any length of time, it leaves a mark on the finger – a sort of narrowing of the girth where the ring usually sits. Not noticeable usually, of course, because the ring is in place, but when the ring is left off, the mark is plain to see, even after some time."

"Gotcha!" Copper caught on. "So if our mysterious ring was usually worn by one of the company, and had been removed for whatever reason, you would be able to tell."

147

"Exactly."

"Well? Had it?"

"Sadly, not." With a smile, Constable punctured his junior's growing excitement. "No indication at all that any of our participants ever wore a ring. Well, except for Miss Hamilton, who had an engagement ring and a wedding ring safely in place on the appropriate finger."

"So we're nowhere?"

"Again, sergeant, eliminating possibilities is never a bad thing. And remember what Sherlock Holmes said about eliminating the impossible. Don't forget, also, there's a so far unexplained print on this ring. With luck, we will be able to eliminate some people from our list of candidates for handling it. That is, when young Darren has finished his circuit. Which surely he should have done by now. Look, see if you can track him down, would you, and get him to report to me."

"Righty-ho, sir. Will you be here?"

Constable glanced over to the far side of the stage, where a subdued murmur arose as the SOCO team could be seen continuing their work. "No – I fancy another look at where it all happened. Let me have your book – I want to go through your notes to see if anything jumps out. I'm going up to Stuart Nelson's dressing room. Tell Darren to come and find me there."

*

The Number 1 Dressing Room did not live up to its title. As Andy Constable stood in the doorway scanning the room slowly, various things caught his eye. A couple of crumpled tissues stained with make-up lay on the bench in front of the actor's place at the mirror. A pair of brown shoes, polished to a surprising shine, stood neatly placed together in immaculate order, oddly out of kilter with the general dishevelled appearance of the room. A threadbare hand towel had slipped from the back of a nearby chair to lie in an untidy heap on the floor. A cheap paperback crime thriller by an author Constable had never heard of lay open, face-down, its spine cracked at the point where Stuart Nelson had evidently broken off reading. Constable found this last unexpectedly poignant. Well, he thought to himself, he'll never find out whodunnit, will he? The question is, will I?

So, let's go back to basics, he mused – the old mantra of means, motive, and opportunity. Well, the means are pretty self-explanatory. And although the mechanics of the murder tend to point in one obvious direction, the booby-trap could have been set by anyone with even a slight knowledge of do-it-yourself, according to David Winston. Not that that rules him out, of course, but it could easily rule everyone else in. Everyone? Anyone? Does that imply that I could be looking for more than one person, working together?

And the answer to that could lie with the question of motive. Plenty of food for thought there, he reflected. The old tried-and-testeds are all present in one form or another – we've got jealousy, revenge, fear, money all swirling around in the mix. Is any one of those sufficient on its own to provide a motive for murder? Or could it be that two or more of them dovetail together to make something more complex? Plus there's the mystery of the things which SOCO found which nobody seems to know anything about. If something's been hidden, or discarded, or its ownership can't be accounted for, then surely there's a relevance there.

Opportunity? Again, plenty of chances for practically everybody to have seized the moment to put that wiring in place – I don't suppose it would have taken more than a few minutes. And in the period between the end of the technical rehearsal and the scheduled start of the dress rehearsal, everybody seems to have been off in different directions at various times, with nobody fully accounted for all the time. Which make any talk of alibis totally pointless. Typical!, he snorted. Only one thing for it – I shall just have to plough through all Copper's notes and see if any inconsistencies pop up. Constable lowered himself gingerly into the rather creaky armchair, opened his colleague's notebook, and began to browse.

It was some little while later that there came a tap on the door, and Dave Copper poked his head into the room. "Oh, you're still here, sir." He reacted to the fact that his senior officer was sitting relaxed, head back, with his eyes closed. "Sorry, guv … didn't mean to wake you."

"I was not asleep, Sergeant Copper," replied Constable calmly, opening his eyes. "While you have no doubt been charging around, I was reflecting quietly on certain aspects of the case. You should try it – it helps. And you will be pleased to know that many things have made themselves considerably clearer as a result.

Now, I assume you have managed to track down Darren and his fingerprint machine ..." The inspector glanced at his watch. "... after what seems to be an unconscionable length of time."

"Yes, sir. Sorry, sir. He was up with Will Mott talking motor-bikes, and I got sort of drawn in. But he's outside now."

"He's no good to me out there, is he, sergeant?" pointed out Constable as he rose to his feet. "Wheel him in."

A muttered instruction brought the young SOCO officer into the dressing room. "Sorry I've been so long, sir. I got sort of distracted."

"I hope it's been worth the wait. Well, what have you got?"

Darren's face split in a triumphant grin. "A result, sir. At least, I hope it's a result. That partial print on the ring that you were interested in, sir – I've got an identification. Take a look." He held up the device he carried, on whose small green screen was displayed the print in question. "And now this one." He pressed a few keys, and another fingerprint came into view alongside the first. "And if I do this ..." Another button was pressed, and the two prints slid together, coinciding almost perfectly.

"Very impressive," commented Constable. "The miracles of modern technology. And the print belongs to ...?"

"Jessica Davenport, sir."

There was a lengthy pause. Constable took a long deep breath, and then gave a profound sigh of satisfaction. "You know, gentlemen, the ancient Greek tragedians had it right all along. And it's oddly appropriate, seeing that we're in a theatre."

"You what, sir?" Copper struggled to see the relevance of the remark.

"The Romans too," continued Constable. "They called it *deus ex machina*, but the Greeks thought of it first. I can't offhand remember the Greek expression."

"Thank the lord for that," muttered Copper under his breath. And after the two junior officers had exchanged glances of bewilderment, he continued, "Sorry, sir, but I'm afraid you've lost us completely."

The inspector smiled. "And that, gentlemen, is where the benefit of a grammar school education comes in handy. You see," explained Constable patiently, "the expression *deus ex machina* comes from the classical theatre. It means 'the god from the machine'. In Greek and Roman plays, you would very often find

150

yourself with an impossibly tangled problem with no obvious solution. Now, what you couldn't do was leave an inconclusive ending – the audiences wouldn't stand for it, and you'd end up with riots on the streets of Epidauros or wherever. So, in order to resolve the situation, you would suddenly have one of the gods from Mount Olympus come flying in – probably on some monster mechanical crane designed by Archimedes – to provide the metaphorical final piece of the jigsaw. Which is what Darren's useful little device has just done."

"Has it really, sir?" asked Darren, pleased but clearly still slightly confused.

"It has, although I suggest you don't rush off down the stairs crying '*Eureka!*'. Instead, I recommend you report back to Sergeant Singleton – you can give her the glad tidings that, in my opinion, there may not be that much of any relevance left to find, and that I will look forward to reading her report in the wake of the arrest which Sergeant Copper is about to make."

"I am, sir?" Copper was startled.

"You are indeed, sergeant. I always like to let the junior ranks have their moment of glory," responded Constable. "But first, you can go and ask Miss Bailey and Messrs Mott and Castle if they would be good enough to join us in the Green Room. Then we can ring down the final curtain on this particular production." He led the way through the dressing room door.

*

"Ah, inspector." Don Abbott was the first to speak as the two detectives entered the Green Room, followed by the other members of the company, who took seats around the room amidst an exchange of puzzled looks and mute shrugs. "Do you suppose you will be letting us go any time soon?"

"Very shortly, sir," was Constable's brief reply.

"Thank heavens," remarked David Winston. "Many more cups of Delia's tea and I shall explode."

"I'm sorry if you all feel that I have been keeping you waiting, ladies and gentlemen," said Constable. "I assure you, it's been no longer than necessary. And considerably less time than it might have been."

"But you say that we can go soon?" intervened Elizabeth Hamilton.

"Most of you, madam. I'm afraid not all."

151

"So ..." Elizabeth realised the import of Constable's words. "Do you mean that you know who was responsible for the death of my husband?"

"I believe I do, Miss Hamilton. And I am sure that you will agree that it will be in the interests of all of you to understand what happened.

"One of my first considerations was, who had most reason to want Stuart Nelson dead? Right from the start, it seemed that there were plenty of motives. Mr. Abbott, despite your denials, it is clear that you had financial worries, and it surely can't be a coincidence that you came straight out of a betting shop and started talking to Mr. Nelson about money. You mentioned a number of bad choices – I wonder how many of those choices had four legs. Mr. Winston, you had very public differences which had already boiled over into violence, and you had been humiliated in front of the whole company by the dead man. As had you, Miss Armstrong – your old friendship with Stuart Nelson seems to have given you no protection. And as for you, Miss Davenport, we had to ask ourselves whether Mr. Nelson's persistent and unwanted attentions drove you to take drastic action to rid yourself of him. Or did you, Mr. Edwards, carry out the murder to protect the girl you seem so fond of? And finally, Miss Hamilton, one might well wonder if, despite what you yourself said to me, you finally reached breaking point at your own humiliation after years of flagrant infidelities?"

"And did I, inspector?" asked Elizabeth calmly. "Is that the conclusion you have reached?"

"All in good time, Miss Hamilton."

"Here, what about these others?" butted in David Winston. "Will and Angela and so on? You haven't said anything about them."

"For the very good reason, Mr. Winston, that I can see no trace of a motive for any of them," replied Constable. "Granted, Mr. Mott is no doubt completely at home with matters electrical. And I would imagine that, in the various aspects of her job, Miss Bailey has acquired a considerable degree of deftness. As for Mr. Castle, I'm sure that he knows the ins and outs of this theatre probably better than anyone, and would have a very good idea of how to undertake a project such as this which has led to Mr. Nelson's death. But from all that I have gathered from my conversations with all three of them, I can't see a factor which would lead any one of them to commit this crime. Unless you can tell me any different." There was no response. "So it looks as if we are left with just the six of you.

"Now," he continued, "we have the supporting evidence of a number of items which have been discovered around the theatre. There is a discarded piece of paper bearing several versions of Stuart Nelson's signature. Why on earth would he have felt the need to write out his name repeatedly? It is of course a ridiculous question. He would have no need to practice his signature – but somebody else might. So, where might such a signature be required? We've been told that Mr. Nelson kept a very tight hold of the chequebook. But is it beyond the realms of possibility that a person might somehow abstract a cheque from that book, and execute a forgery in order to obtain a substantial amount of money – perhaps for the purpose of paying off a debt to Mr. Nelson himself? We have evidence that such a debt existed, and who knows how many crimes have been committed for financial gain?

"What of the other things? We have a pair of electrical pliers that nobody will admit to owning. There is a photograph which is nothing at all to do with the play. And finally, there is a mysterious gold ring. Small, but valuable – perhaps our most valuable piece of evidence, in all senses. And what does the initial engraved into the ring stand for? 'D' – it could relate to so many of you. Don? David? Delia? Davenport? But let's not forget the rôle which is played by Matthew in the drama – the part of Daniel Allen. No, surely not him – we've been told that the ring does not feature on the properties list for the play. So if it does belong to one of the others, how did they come to lose it? Or was it thrown away? And by whom? Well, we have one possibility, since we have managed to identify a fingerprint on the ring. And that print belongs to Jessica Davenport."

The eyes of every individual in the room were immediately fixed on the young actress. Under their gaze, she seemed to shrink into herself, her lip trembled, and tears started to form. "But I ... Stuart was ... Matthew!" She turned in appeal to her companion, who put his arm protectively around her.

"Inspector, is this bullying tone really necessary?" challenged Matthew. "You can see how upset Jess is."

153

"And I'm sorry for that, Mr. Edwards," replied Constable. "And I assure you, there is no intention to bully. But in my view, the facts seem to point to one inevitable conclusion – the central figure in the whole mystery is Jessica Davenport." The inspector was conscious of a sudden and distinct air of stillness in those around him. "Consider what we know. The 48-year-old Stuart Nelson was paying unwanted attentions to the 29-year-old Jessica. This was not new, but perhaps the situation reached some sort of a climax. Angela Bailey saw Stuart making advances to Jessica before the rehearsal, and later heard Elizabeth Hamilton apparently urging him to take responsibility for his actions. She also mention her puzzlement at Delia Armstrong's abandonment of a promising acting career – I wondered, was Delia the first in a long line of young actresses of which Jessica was just the latest example? Mr. Mott's and Miss Hamilton's words may well have given us the answer to that. And Angela did see Delia going into Jessica's dressing room – was that simply to tell her to take care, or something else?

"Some things we know – others we have to guess at. Among the things we know, thanks to the very careful and comprehensive note-taking by my colleague Sergeant Copper ..." The young officer gave an uneasy half-smile of acknowledgement. "... is the fact that Miss Davenport was already in an upset state during the afternoon, thanks to the testimony of Peter Castle, who also witnessed the argument between Stuart Nelson and Elizabeth Hamilton before Miss Hamilton left the theatre. Was this anything to do with the conversation witnessed by Will Mott between Elizabeth and Delia, in which the latter spoke of 'shock' and having 'given up everything'. Will was very nearly in the right place at another significant moment – he almost witnessed Matthew being evicted from Jessica's room. Matthew, the man to whom Jessica referred as 'the big brother she never had'. Because Jessica was an adopted only child – she never knew who her actual parents were. But she does now – as does Elizabeth, and I believe, before he died, so did Stuart Nelson.

"I said that there are some things we have to guess at. This, I think, is where I have to enter the realms of guesswork, and I hope you will all forgive me if I make what follows sound like the synopsis of a play. But I believe that this is the only logical explanation which brings all our known facts together to make a

154

coherent story.

"Thirty years ago, a young aspiring actress and actor met. They had a relationship, and this relationship led to an unintended consequence, as so many do. The young actress discovered that she was pregnant – for whatever personal reason, she chose not to share this information with the father, nor to remedy the situation, but instead to have the baby at the expense of the abandonment of her career. She left drama school and cut off all her old contacts, but for reasons we can only surmise – lack of support, shunning by family, financial insecurity, who knows? - she found that she was unable to cope with caring for the child. Instead, she made what must have been an agonising decision – she decided to give the baby up for adoption. All she kept was a single photograph, hidden and treasured. And all she could give the child was a signet ring, engraved with her own initial."

"It was an eighteenth birthday present from my own parents," said Delia, quietly but clearly, into the silence. "They died in a car accident the day after my birthday. I could never bear to wear it, but I thought … I don't know … a new life … new hope …" Her voice tailed away.

"Perhaps it did bring new hope," continued Constable kindly after a pause. "The baby was adopted by a couple named Davenport, who named their new daughter Jessica. An oddly prescient choice of name – the daughter of a tragic Shakespearean character. And, perhaps because of the coincidence of the initial of their surname, they evidently decided to keep the ring in trust for the child, although I assume they never revealed its source. And as the child got older, the powerful acting genes she had inherited from both her parents must have come to the fore – it's no surprise that she grew up to become an actress. And at the age of twenty-nine, she was employed by Stuart Nelson.

"Which brings us to the events of today. I'm assuming that, at some stage during the course of the day, Jessica's mother discovered her daughter's identity when she saw Jessica's signet ring and realised with horror that Stuart's latest target for his attentions was his own daughter. She resolved that the situation had to be dealt with. She confided in Stuart's wife – again, Will Mott was almost a witness to the conversation – and Elizabeth confronted her husband – Peter Castle told us about the resultant argument. But, stressed to breaking point, Delia took what I believe to have been a totally uncharacteristic decision – she planned a more permanent solution.

"Using her technical expertise built up over many years in theatre backstage work – and Will Mott gave us an early hint of this when he testified to what he called Delia's brilliance at devising props such as the electronic shooting effect – she rigged the wiring to Stuart's shower. It must have been a risky business, but in one sense she was lucky, in that she took the opportunity between six o'clock and six-thirty when Stuart was either in Jessica's room or up in the lighting control box for his confrontation with David Winston. Nevertheless, she only narrowly escaped being witnessed by Angela Bailey. Delia then went to Jessica, showed her the photograph which she had treasured for some twenty-nine years, and broke the truth about her parentage. We can only imagine the sort of emotions that were involved, particularly for Jessica, who was already in a fragile state."

"But why is the ring so significant, inspector?" intervened Matthew Edwards. "I mean, Jess, you never normally wear a ring, do you? I've never seen it before."

"I usually keep it on a chain round my neck," faltered Jessica. "My parents … I always thought of them as my real parents, even after they told me that they'd adopted me … that's when they gave it to me, when they explained everything. But I've never actually worn it. Until today, that is. And I don't know what made me put it on today. There must have been something …"

"Whatever it was, Miss Davenport," resumed the inspector, "it turned out to be the one tiny detail which set today's events in motion. Because it was the clinching factor in both revelations – to Delia, to provide an answer to a question which must have long haunted her – whatever became of her daughter? - and to Jessica, who must have wondered about her birth mother, and who now also had her own answer, since I imagine that Delia's knowledge of the ring's interior inscription would have proved the matter beyond doubt. So why was the ring no longer in Jessica's possession? I think it's because Jessica probably pressed Delia to accept it back. But perhaps Delia realised that it might incriminate her in some way, and so attempted to dispose of it."

156

"Oh, it was much simpler than that, inspector," said Delia with a watery smile. "I realised that the whole thing had been a shock for Jessica, so I decided to leave her alone in peace to think. But my hands were shaking so much when I left the dressing room that I just fumbled the ring and dropped it in the corridor. It rolled away out of sight, but before I could retrieve it, I heard somebody coming, and I was in such a state that I just ran."

"And then presumably you went up on stage and hid the wire-cutters?"

"Yes." Delia sounded almost relieved to be able to tell the truth. "And then I went and sat in my little room and just … waited. And if I'd had time, perhaps I would have realised how mad the whole thing was, and perhaps I would have gone and dismantled the whole apparatus. We could have worked everything out, I'm sure. There would have been no need for …"

"Quite," said Constable. "But then fate intervened. For some reason, Stuart Nelson decided to take a shower before the dress rehearsal rather than afterwards. And at seven o'clock, the theatre itself killed him."

In the ensuing silence, Elizabeth Hamilton rose and moved to Delia Armstrong, taking her in a totally unexpected embrace. "You and I have a great deal in common, my dear," she said, in that slightly husky voice which had entranced so many audiences. "We both loved Stuart – and we both hated what he had become. But I can't hate you for what you did. This world makes fools of us all."

"Mother …" Jessica also rose. The use of the word came uneasily to her lips.

Delia pressed her back into her seat. "No, darling. You'd better stay here. Matthew, would you …?" The young actor nodded a silent acknowledgement of the unspoken request. "I think I had better be going with the inspector."

"Sergeant Copper, if you would, please …" said Constable, as the junior officer gently took hold of Delia's arm and escorted her towards the door. "As for the rest of you, you are free to leave. We shall be in touch."

As he left the Green Room, Constable heard Elizabeth Hamilton speak once more. "And so it all ends. '*La commedia è finita!*'" The door closed behind him.

*　　　*　　　*　　　*　　　*

157

LAST ORDERS

"Are you coming out for our training run tomorrow, then, Rex?" Penny, the wife of the landlord of the Three Blind Mice, looked up from where she was re-stocking a row of bottles of tonic water on the shelf beneath the bar, and smiled invitingly.

"Oh, dear lord," replied Rex Hope, clutching his brow in mock anguish. "Is it really that time already? Why can't I just have a day of rest like civilised people?"

"Because it's not just an ordinary Sunday, that's why," sparkled Penny. "It's the last chance for us all to get together before the run next week. And you do want to be in the team, don't you?"

"I suppose."

"Well, you should," retorted Penny. "And Sam's coming too, aren't you, Sam?"

"Mmm?" The young barman looked around from where he was replenishing the huge and gleaming coffee machine. "Oh yes … sure. Wouldn't miss it."

"Leaving me to set up the place on my own – again. Thank you very much, everybody." The remark came from the well-built man in his late forties who had just appeared through the door from the cellar as he hefted a crate of beers on to the bar. Bob Farmer stood an impressive six foot four, with broad shoulders and, despite being no longer a youngster, the still-rugged physique of a born athlete, and strong attractive features which drew many admiring glances from his lady customers.

"Oh, Bob, don't be grumpy." His wife draped herself over his shoulder appealingly. "You know we'd all love it if you were part of the team, but you know you can't be. Anyway, teams of three, that's the rule. So it's got to be me and two of the boys. Don't worry, I'll be back in plenty of time to help serve the lunches." Penny looked up at Bob with pleading in her large grey eyes and shook back her long blonde mane. "You do want us to win, don't you?"

To all those who knew the couple, this performance by Penny was a normal part of the stock-in-trade of the attractive wife towards the husband almost twenty years her senior, and they marvelled that it never failed to produce results. Bob sighed. "Of course I do."

"Well then!" Penny smiled triumphantly. "We've got to beat the Dagger boys."

"Girls, isn't it, this year?" queried Sam Booker, as he turned from stacking coffee cups to checking the bottles of liqueurs on the mirrored shelves at the back of the bar.

"Oh, don't worry about them," said Rex. "We can handle them easily." A thought occurred to him. "So, I suppose Mark is coming along tomorrow as well?"

"I haven't asked him yet," replied Penny, "but I'm sure he will. He wouldn't want to miss the chance. And after all, it is between the three of you. Best two out of three." She grinned impishly. "I'm looking forward to it."

*

Each of the villages of the Dammett Vale was famous for having its own distinctive character. Upper Dammett was perhaps the most picturesque. Its single street shared its course with the chuckling waters of the Dammett Brook, and was lined with thatched cottages, many with their cob walls painted in a variety of pale pastel shades, homes to well-heeled commuters who caught the daily train to London from nearby Camford Parkway. Bishop's Dammett, once part of the extensive land-holding of the region's diocese, was graced with an enormous and spectacular fifteenth-century church in the perpendicular style which completely dwarfed and dominated the huddle of houses clustered around its skirts. Dammett Slaughter was popularly believed to have been named after a legendary battle between a heroic Anglo-Saxon king and a band of marauding Vikings, where the Danish invaders had come off considerably worse, and traded for all it was worth on that reputation to the sadly few tourists who passed that way. Any mention of Dammett Worthy still provoked a lowering of the voice and a look over the shoulder, in recollection of the still-vividly-remembered events at the Dammett Hall annual garden fête. And Blaston Dammett, named for the long-extinct Blaisetonne family who had accompanied Duke William in his conquest of 1066 and been rewarded with lands to build their now vanished manor, was celebrated for the rivalry of its inter-pub fun run.

Nobody could quite remember how the run had come into

159

being. Probably initiated at some time during the 1960s, when there had been a great fad for sponsored walks and runs in aid of various local and national charities, it had reached its peak in the 1990s, sometimes attracting thousands of participants decked out in pink wigs and tutus in support of health causes, or bearing the T-shirts of a campaign for the relief of suffering in distant countries. Of late, the event had contracted to become a much more local affair, with the consumption of beer as a prominent theme. From the Three Blind Mice, a stately Georgian coaching inn at one end of Blaston Dammett, which in former times had provided the final change of horses for the long run down into Camford, the mile-long course ran around the back lanes of the village, crossed the churchyard, passed through Blaise Copse, skirted the fields of Manor Farm, and ended after five circuits at the bar of the Sword and Dagger at the opposite end of the village. In early days, participants had been obliged to down a glass of the Sword and Dagger's own home-brewed ale each time they passed the inn – in these more politically-correct times, water or fruit juice was considered an acceptable alternative, although many die-hards regretted the passing of the tradition. And at the end of the race, the arrival of each runner at the Dagger was hailed by the ringing of the bell behind the pub's saloon bar, its strident chimes, accompanied by the traditional cry of 'Last orders, please!', sadly now far less frequently heard in an era of all-day opening hours.

The rivalry between the two hostelries had never been thought of as serious. True, each had its own atmosphere and clientele. The Three Blind Mice, with its mullioned windows and elegant stone porch, had always regarded itself as a cut above its competitor, and attracted tourists as well as residents from the more prim local houses with its continental selection of coffees, its chalked-up wine list, and its small bistro-inspired bar food menu. At the lower end of the village, and catering largely for workers on the surrounding farmland, The Sword and Dagger, named for the old manorial coat of arms, made the most of its heritage as a former row of agricultural labourers' thatched cottages, with its low beams, flag-stoned floors, scrubbed deal tables surrounded by a mismatched miscellany of country-built chairs and settles, and three unique home-brewed ales from the micro-brewery in the old brick out-house. And the fact that the licensees had similar backgrounds might have been thought to make them closer than they actually were, but that would be to disregard the traditional mutual disdain felt between the military and civil arms of the forces of order. Bob Farmer, landlord of the Three Blind Mice, was an ex-sergeant from the military police who had chosen to be invalided out after a helicopter accident left him with an injured leg which he felt made him unable to do the job he loved. And Adelaide Knight, who ran the Sword and Dagger, was a former Metropolitan police officer who had risen through the ranks, joining the political protection unit, and eventually becoming part of the protection detail of a notable woman cabinet minister, before an unguarded exchange of words late one night at the gates of Parliament led to the suggestion that a discreet and graceful retirement on full pension might be advisable.

*

Sunday was a perfect late spring morning. The sun shone, the air felt crisp and clear, and the foliage on the trees was at its freshest and greenest, with only the oaks dotted along the hedgerows displaying their usual tendency to lag behind their fellows. Rex Hope closed the door of Lombard Cottage behind him and started across the green towards the Three Blind Mice, arriving just as Mark Lowe jogged into sight around the corner of School Lane.

"Morning, Mark. You made it, then?"

"Course I did," replied the younger man. "Can't really say 'no' when Penny issues her orders, can we? It's jump to it, or take the consequences."

"You'd better not say that too loudly," cautioned Rex. "You never know, Bob might be listening, and I don't think he'd take it too kindly if he thought you were taking the mickey. You might get a smack."

"Yeah," grinned Mark, "but he'd have to catch me first, and that's not likely, is it? Anyway, where is the lovely team captain? She said half past ten, and ..." Distant chimes wafted on the air. "... there goes the church clock."

As if on cue, the front door of the inn opened, and Penny Farmer emerged, with Sam Booker in tow. In complete contrast to the nondescript T-shirts, loose jogging bottoms, and admittedly grimy trainers of the three men, Penny was decked

161

out in the pristine kit of a participant in an exercise video. Pink stretch fabric accented the generous curves and trim waistline of her figure, purple leg-warmers drew the eye down towards shiny silver shoes bearing an extremely prestigious sporting logo, and her long blonde hair was tamed by a neat matching headband. "Hello, boys," she cried gaily. "Still up for it, are we all?"

"Of course," replied Rex a little stiffly. "In fact, we were just about to start wondering where you were."

"Oh, I was just sorting one or two things out with the kitchen staff for lunchtime," explained Penny airily. "But I'm sure Margaret and Sue will have everything under control. It's only the usual carvery. And then, look, Sam came over a bit early so he could help me finish getting the bar ready so I wouldn't be late. Wasn't that sweet?" She bestowed a beaming smile on the barman, who blushed faintly.

"And speaking of being late, shouldn't we get on?" suggested Mark. "Otherwise it'll be teatime, never mind lunchtime. Now, the thing is, Rex," he continued, with a sideways glance at the other man and a consciously straight face, "do you want the rest of us to give you a bit of a head start? Being the much older guy, and all that."

"Bloody cheek," retorted Rex. "I'd back my 40-odd against your 30-odd any day. All you do is sit around all the time teaching boring subjects to a load of truculent school-kids. At least I go down to the gym after work every day."

"Yes, well, you'd need to," smiled Mark. "I can imagine the tremendous strain it must be on your muscles, lifting millions of pounds from one account to another, or whatever it is you do in that City tower of yours. I bet the shareholders of your bank think it's money well spent."

"Come on, boys, enough of that," chided Penny. "We're all meant to be on the same team – well, three of us will be, anyway. Let's see what happens. Now, what I suggest is, we do a couple of gentle circuits to warm up, then we'll take a little break to see how we feel, and then we'll go really seriously at the last three. How does that sound?"

"Fine by me," said Mark.

"Sam?"

"Yes, that sounds okay to me." Sam shrugged his way into his small backpack. "Oh ... hang on. I forgot to top up my water bottle. Shan't be a sec." He darted back into the building.

"Well, whatever we do, I reckon we ought to get on with it," proposed Rex. "Because don't look now, but Bob is starting to glare at us out of the window." Surreptitious glances proved the truth of his words. "So if you're all ready – catch me if you can!" As Sam re-emerged from the inn, Rex started off at a vigorous pace, leaving the other three scampering to catch up.

On the picnic benches on the flower-tub-decked forecourt of the Sword and Dagger, the four sat gently allowing their breathing to return to normal, Rex making strenuous efforts to disguise the fact that for him the process was taking markedly longer than for his companions.

"Half-way, boys," said Penny. "How are we feeling?" She was greeted with a chorus of 'fine' and 'couldn't be better'. "Good. Then let's make it a real race for the second half. Otherwise I just don't know how I'm supposed to choose between you. So, let's say that the first two back to the Mice are in the team, and the last one can be the reserve. Is that fair?" She smiled winningly at the three men.

"Brilliant idea," said Rex, just as a young woman appeared at the door of the Sword and Dagger. "Ah ... Anna! Perfect timing. You're just the girl I need. Who says there's never a gorgeous barmaid about when you want one?"

"Good morning, everyone," said the new arrival. She looked to be around twenty, with elfin features and long dark hair. "Did you want something?"

"That's the sort of question can get a girl into trouble," smiled Rex. "Now, as you can see from this extremely flattering rig I'm wearing, Penny has got us all in training for this run next week. And I don't know about the others, but I for one could do with a shot of caffeine to fortify me for the rigours to come. How about the rest of you? My treat." He reached into his bum-bag for his wallet.

Anna looked at her watch. "I shouldn't really," she said. "We don't actually open until eleven."

"Oh, come on," coaxed Rex. "It's almost that now. I'm sure Addy would stretch a point. Where is she, anyway?"

"Out the back checking on the latest batch of Old Foozler."

"Well then ... what the eye doesn't see, and all that. We'll be gone before she knows it. So, double espresso for me – what

163

about you, Penny?"

"I don't know … we really ought to get on. And I do have to get back to Bob, because … you know …"

"We do," chuckled Rex. "Mark?"

"Thanks, but I'm with Penny. And I'm not really an elevenses person."

"I expect you'll have one though, won't you, Sam?" asked Anna, smiling shyly at the young barman.

"Er … thanks, Anna, but not for me. I'll just stick to my water." Colouring slightly, he fumbled with the fastenings on his backpack and busied himself extracting a water bottle from it.

"Just me, then," shrugged Rex. "Look, don't worry if the three of you want to get on. I'll just have my coffee, and then I bet I'll catch the rest of you up easily. You know, hare and tortoise stuff. Anyway," he lowered his voice conspiratorially, "I want to pick Anna's brains on the sly about team tactics." He winked. "I dare say you're on the Dagger's team for the run, aren't you, Anna?"

"That's right. Addy, me, and Barbara."

"Bloody hell! You've got the real professionals, haven't you?" groaned Rex. "I can see I'm going to have to worm my way into your confidence in the hope of nobbling your whole enterprise." He turned to Penny. "I hope you appreciate the sacrifices I'm prepared to make on your behalf, captain. I shall expect my reward, you know."

Mark, impatient, got to his feet. "Look, you can muck about all you want. I'm more interested in winning this thing. So shall we make a move, before we all seize up completely?"

Rex waved a hand. "Go. You never know, I may still be here next time you come past. And I bet I'll still beat you to the prize." There seemed to be an underlying challenge in his words. "Oh, don't worry – I'm kidding. I'll be along like a rocket as soon as I've gulped down my coffee."

"All right then." Penny stood briskly. "We'll see you in a minute." She set off up the lane alongside the pub towards the church tower, the other two men in her wake, as Anna made her way into the bar, leaving Rex lounging on his bench. After a moment, he rose to follow Anna.

*

The body lay sprawled on its face in the undergrowth just

164

at the side of the path, some hundred yards into the wood. Vividly-striped plastic tape ran from tree to tree, cordoning off the area where the police doctor crouched, watched by his two detective colleagues.

"No mystery here, gentlemen," said the doctor. "Neatly stabbed in the back. One blow. Largeish blade with a single edge, as far as I can judge – I'll let you have best estimate of dimensions once I've had a chance to rootle about inside him back at the lab, just in case you find it's relevant. Not much blood, and from the position of the wound, the knife looks as if it went straight to the heart of the matter, so to speak. Probably dead before he hit the ground."

"And left to lie where he fell, by the look of it," commented Detective Inspector Andy Constable.

"No drag marks, guv," confirmed Detective Sergeant Dave Copper. "I noticed that when I got here. And that's exactly how he was found, according to Mrs. Farmer – that's the woman who found him." He nodded in the direction of a tree some twenty yards away, where Penny Farmer stood wrapped in a blanket, a tearful expression on her face, with Mark Lowe and Sam Booker in uneasy attendance. "Tripped over him, by all accounts."

"And do we know who he is?"

"We do, sir. Gentleman named Rex Hope, resident of Blaston Dammett, according to the driving licence in his wallet. But those three knew him anyway. Apparently they were all out on some sort of training run together. Something to do with the village pub – she's the landlord's wife."

"Right." Constable rubbed his hands together, thought for a moment, and then began to issue brisk orders. "Doc, feel free to take the late Mr. Hope away and do your necessary. SOCO, by the look of it, have their search of the area well in hand." He glanced towards the several overalled individuals who were carefully picking their way through the undergrowth within and beyond the cordoned area, some on their hands and knees as they examined the contents of the leaf litter. "And I'll have a word with Mrs. Farmer and the others – although on reflection, perhaps here is not the best place to do it."

"Her pub, sir?" suggested Copper hopefully. "It's just at the top end of the village."

"Know it, do you?"

"I've been there once or twice. Not for ages, though."

"Good plan. Okay, so if you can pour those three into your car and take them up there, I'll follow behind you."

"Righty-ho, guv." Copper headed towards the disconsolate group of runners as Constable stood for a few moments gazing at Rex Hope's body reflectively, before turning and following in his junior's footsteps.

The car park of the Three Blind Mice was already fairly busy as the detectives parked their cars alongside one another. Bob Farmer appeared almost immediately in the doorway and hurried down the steps to take his wife into an enveloping embrace.

"Penny, are you all right? I've been worried to death. You were gone forever, and then when I heard the sirens go past I thought something terrible had happened."

His wife looked up at him, a tremulous attempt at a smile on her face as she blinked away returning tears. "I'm fine, Bob. It's not me – it's Rex. He's dead."

"What! Why, what happened?"

Andy Constable intervened. "That is what we're here to find out, sir. Do I take it that you're Mrs. Farmer's husband?"

"That's right. Bob Farmer."

The inspector delved into a pocket for his warrant card. "I'm Detective Inspector Constable, sir – this is my colleague Detective Sergeant Copper. And yes, I'm afraid that what your wife says is true – Mr. Rex Hope is dead."

"You mean ... some sort of an accident?"

"I'm afraid not, sir. He was killed."

"Oh my god. And ... what ... Penny, you were there?"

"No, Bob. But I was the one who found him. It was awful ..." Penny seemed disposed to dissolve into tears once more.

Constable took control. "Mr. Farmer, this is probably not the best place for this discussion. If I might suggest, is there somewhere more suitable indoors where we might continue ...?"

"Of course." His arm still around his wife's shoulder, Bob climbed the steps and pushed open the door. A hum of conversation and the clink of cutlery could be heard from the bars on either side. "We'd better go upstairs. Our flat's up there – it'll be quieter." He led the way up and into a spacious sitting room overlooking the car park and the fields at the rear of the property, followed by the two detectives who ushered Mark and Sam ahead of them. As the party seated themselves, Bob remained standing, shifting uneasily from foot to foot. "Inspector, I know it may sound bad, but do you need me for the moment? Only I've got nobody looking after the bar downstairs. What with my barman being involved, by the look of things." The glance he gave to Sam Booker was not altogether friendly. "That's if you're all right, darling?" He bent down to Penny with a concerned look on his face.

"I'll be fine, Bob," she reassured him. "It was just … just the shock. But you go. I'm okay … honestly."

"Well … if you're sure." With some reluctance, Bob left the room.

As Dave Copper produced his notebook in response to a signal from his colleague, Andy Constable took a second to focus his thoughts. "Right, Mrs. Farmer. If you can tell me exactly what happened."

"All four of us were out for a run," began Penny.

"The four of you being …?" intervened Copper.

"Myself, Rex, Mark, and Sam."

Copper looked interrogatively at the two men seated alongside one another on a sofa.

"I'm Mark Lowe. I teach in the local school."

"I'm Sam Booker. Like Bob said, I work here as a barman."

"Full time?"

"Yes."

"Thank you, gentlemen. Sorry to interrupt, sir. Do carry on."

"Thank you, sergeant. Most kind," replied Constable, one eyebrow raised in gentle reproof. "Mrs. Farmer, you said you were out for a run …?"

"Yes. We're training for the village fun run next week – and there's always a sort of competition between the two pubs."

"So you aren't the only pub in the village?"

"Oh no. There's Addy's place, the Sword and Dagger, down at the other end."

"I'm sorry, I butted in. Please go on."

"The four of us started out, but there can only be three per team, so I decided that we would make today a sort of trials to see who else would be on the team with me."

167

"So you are part of the team?"

"Yes. It's supposed to be the landlord, but Bob can't run since his accident, so I take his place. Anyway, we started out, and everything was fine, and we stopped for a little break outside the Dagger, halfway round, and then we carried on, but ... but Rex said he wanted a quick coffee, and we decided not to wait and ... he said he'd catch us up but ..." Penny's hand went to her mouth, and her voice shook. "But he didn't. And then the three of us carried on together, and when we came past the Dagger again there was no sign of him, and then I put a bit of a spurt on just as I was coming into the woods so that the boys were a few yards behind me, and then ..." She burst into a flood of tears. "I just tripped over him. His foot was sticking out, and I tripped over him. I thought it must be a root or something. And I fell down, and when I looked ... it was Rex!"

Mark Lowe rose from his place, perched on the arm of Penny's armchair, and put a comforting arm around her. "I can tell you what happened next, inspector. Not that there's much to tell. It was just like Penny said. We weren't far behind her, and we saw her fall, so we sprinted to catch her up, and then saw Rex. I picked her up, and Sam had his phone with him, so he called the police."

"And did you see anyone else during all this?"

"Not really, did we, Sam?"

"No," agreed Sam Booker. "Well, there were people going into church for the morning service, but apart from that, nobody."

"And the three of you were together all the time?"

"Yes."

"Except for when you stopped to have a pee behind a tree," put in Mark.

"Well, yes," said Sam, reddening slightly. "But that was way further on from the place we found Rex. And anyway, I caught you up before you got to the stile at the end of the woods. I could see you ahead of me all the way round."

Constable considered. "Right. I think that'll do for the moment. We'll take statements from you all later." He addressed his junior. "Two things, Copper. First, we need to notify next of kin." He turned back to the other three. "Do any of you know who that might be? Is there a Mrs. Hope?"

"No," answered Mark. "Rex wasn't married."

"Girlfriend? Boyfriend? Anyone special?"

Mark smiled faintly. "No, I don't think so, inspector. Rex liked to spread himself around, as it were. As for family, I've no idea. Penny?"

"No. He never said anything to me, apart from … well, you know what Rex was like."

"Maybe there'll be something at his house, sir," said Copper. "We've got the address. And he had some keys in his bum-bag, so there's probably a house-key amongst them. I could take a look there if you like. What was the other thing?"

"I want to set up an incident room in the village. It'll make it easier for interviewing people, rather than have them traipsing in to the station in town. Mrs. Farmer, I wouldn't want to impose, but is there by any chance a room here we might use – a function room, or something like that?"

Penny shook her head. "Not really, inspector. There's only the skittle alley, and we had a leak last month and all the electrics are still out."

"How about the Old School?" suggested Mark.

"Is that where you teach, sir? Not really suitable to have it in a school, I'm afraid."

Mark hastened to clarify. "No, it's the old village school, inspector. They don't use it as that any more. All the classes got transferred over to County High, which is where I teach. So then they put the village library into one of the old classrooms, and the other one is used for meetings and community stuff. How would that be?"

"Sounds ideal, guv," said Copper. "Do you want me to get on to that?"

"Please do, sergeant."

"You'll need to talk to the librarian, sergeant. Penny, have you got Phyllis's number?"

"Bob'll have it behind the bar somewhere." Penny was sounding increasingly fragile. "Inspector, do you mind if I go and lie down? I'm really not feeling very well."

"Of course, Mrs. Farmer," said Constable kindly. "It's the shock – it happens to everyone in circumstances like these. Get somebody to bring you a cup of tea."

"I'll do it." Sam jumped to his feet. "And then … inspector, would it be okay if I got back to work? Only I'm sure Bob's going

169

to be busy downstairs, what with all the lunchtime customers ..."

"Yes, by all means, Mr. Booker. We'll talk again at a more convenient time."

"Thank you, Sam," murmured Penny, holding out a hand to the barman. "You are a godsend."

"I'll ... er ... I won't be long." Sam bolted from the room.

"Shall I go and see if Bob's got that number for you, sergeant?" asked Mark.

"We'll all go, sir," said Constable. "We'll leave Mrs. Farmer in peace for a while." He stood and led the way downstairs.

*

"Rex Hope's dead?" Phyllis Stein's long thin nose quivered with a mixture of horror and excitement as she unlocked the front door of the Old School. "I still can't believe it! Mind you," she continued in a more subdued tone, "not that I suppose any of us should be surprised, the way he carried on sometimes. But nobody deserves to die, do they? And stabbed, you say? How horrible!" She threw open a door to the right and ushered the detectives into a large room with high arched windows, furnished with a quantity of folding tables, with stacks of plastic chairs at one end. "Will this be suitable for you?"

Andy Constable looked around approvingly. "I think this will do very well, Miss Stein. Plenty of power points – although I don't suppose you have particularly high-speed broadband out here in the sticks, do you?"

"Ah, but we do, inspector," beamed Phyllis. "The council organised it specially when the library was established. Well, I made sure that they did. I couldn't possibly be expected to run a library without all the modern internet access now, could I? And in all modesty, I'm not without influence, so I'm sure there won't be any difficulty in getting in touch with the other users and cancelling their bookings. I'm hall secretary too, you see."

Constable felt faintly intimidated by Phyllis's self-assurance. "That's extremely kind of you, Miss Stein. And we'll square everything with the council from our end. We'll move things in tomorrow morning, if that will be all right with you."

"Perfectly, inspector. And you'd better have a spare key, hadn't you? I think I can trust you with it – not that I give them out to just anyone, you know. I've got one through here in my desk." She led the way into what Constable assumed was the

170

other former classroom, now dotted with fully-laden tall bookcases. "In case you have to be coming and going at all hours. I'm not quite here absolutely all the time, you know." The middle-aged spinster gave an incongruously girlish giggle. "Even though it feels like it sometimes. So if there's ever anything you need, I'm just through here in the library. Oh, by the way, there's a little kitchenette and the ... er ... usual offices through that little door there in the hallway. So, I expect you'll be as snug as a bug in a rug."

"Thank you, Miss Stein," replied Constable, suppressing a smile. "We shall do our best."

"What next then, guv?" enquired Copper, as the two headed back down School Lane towards their cars, the sound of jingling keys fading behind them as Phyllis relocked the Old School front door.

"Let's see what more we can find out about the dead man," said Constable. "You never know, the old adage 'know the man and you know his killer' may be true in this case. You said you've got the address and some keys."

"Right here, guv. 'Lombard Cottage, The Green, Blaston Dammett', according to his driving licence, so if I'm any kind of detective, it should be somewhere around here." The bottom of the lane opened out into a large open space, one side dominated by the lofty presence of the Three Blind Mice, the centre grassed, with a reed-fringed duckpond alongside a modest stone war memorial, and the other sides lined with houses and cottages in various styles. "Left or right, guv?"

"Whichever way we go, it'll no doubt be the last place we get to," smiled Constable. "Left." He set out to follow the road which encircled the Green.

As it turned out, he was unduly pessimistic. Lombard Cottage stood almost exactly halfway round the circuit, its whitewashed frontage shielded from the road by only a white picket fence and a small front garden, mostly gravelled, with a few evergreen shrubs in tastefully disposed terracotta pots. The double Georgian frontage, sash windows arranged in perfect symmetry about the black-painted front door with its gleaming brass dolphin knocker, forsook all attempts at ostentation, yet subtly hinted at a degree of style and elegance within. Copper selected what looked like the appropriate key and opened the

171

door.

The hall had the air of having been recently decorated by a designer with exacting but minimalist tastes. A white-painted staircase rose straight ahead, its treads bearing the same carpet in some sort of woven plant material as that which covered the floor of the hall. Walls painted in the palest of creams displayed two or three large framed prints of architect's drawings of buildings in the Palladian style, while a small sofa table in a light wood under a wall mirror was adorned with nothing other than a stylised wooden sculpture of a seagull and a large ceramic charger with a motif of cream and brown swirls. A door to the left led through to a sitting room which stretched the full depth of the house, furnished with a pair of large cream leather sofas artistically dotted with cushions in shades of caramel and chocolate, a large flat-screen television in the recess to one side of the evidently original marble fireplace, and a mahogany Georgian bureau in the other. Small tables bore lamps of a modernist design. The hall carpet was carried through to the french windows at the rear, which gave a glimpse of the garden beyond.

"Not exactly what you'd call characterful, is it, sir?" remarked Copper. "It feels more like a hotel than anything."

"My thoughts precisely," agreed Constable. "Doesn't tell us a lot about the man, does it? Let's see if the rest of the place is any more forthcoming."

It wasn't. The dining room on the opposite side of the hall was furnished with table and chairs of Scandinavian design, with on the walls a sprinkling of monochrome prints of birch forests in the snow to reinforce the image. The kitchen, with glass-fronted wall cupboards and black granite worktops, resembled that of a show house. Upstairs, the main bedroom was again a study in white, with a deep carpet, a king-size bed with a scatter of cushions in amber and ochre, and one wall lined with mirror-fronted wardrobes which, when opened, revealed an immaculate array of suits and shirts, shelves with neatly-stowed jumpers and underwear, and a full-height rack of shoes. The en-suite bathroom was just as unrevealing – a white claw-foot bath, an obviously expensive suite of fittings, and a cabinet of toiletries from an extremely prestigious shop in London's Burlington Arcade. The other two bedrooms were simply furnished, with a single bed in each together with wardrobes and cabinets of plain

172

design but good quality, and seemed to be unused.

"Don't know what to make of him, guv," said Copper, as the detectives descended the stairs. "Obviously, loads of money but a real ..."

"Conundrum," broke in Constable. "There has to be something about him, otherwise what is he doing lying murdered in a wood?"

"I suppose it could have just been random," said Copper. "Kid with a knife, hanging about to mug somebody – something went wrong, and our bloke ends up dead."

"Not actually likely, though, is it, sergeant?" said Constable. "For a start, look at the location. It's not exactly somewhere where you're going to get a lot of passing traffic, is it? Plus stabbing in the back? That's not really classic mugging, is it? And you said there was a bum-bag?"

"Yes, guv. That's where I snaffled the keys from. SOCO have got it now."

"Together with the rest of the contents, no doubt. Like the wallet that the chap's driving licence was in. A phone, maybe?"

"Oh." Copper was crestfallen. "Of course, you're right, sir. I didn't think it through. Sorry."

"Not to worry, sergeant," responded Constable breezily. "When you've got as little to go on so far as we have, even daft suggestions sometimes bear fruit. I suspect we may get some idea of a motive once we've had a chance to talk to a few people. And ..." His eye lighted on the bureau in the sitting room. "Once we've had a chance to take a look through this." He sat down, dropped the front leaf, and began to browse through the sheaf of papers revealed. "Ah. Well, here's an answer to one of our questions. Now we know where the loads of money come from."

"And where's that, sir?"

"He worked in the City of London." The sound of riffling paper. "Some kind of trader with Morgmann Brothers."

"Never heard of them, sir."

"To be honest, I don't really know that much about them. I've just heard them mentioned on the money programmes on the BBC from time to time. Moving cash, buying investments, that kind of activity – not exactly the sort of thing I'm going to be chucking my pension at when it finally arrives, but I know that some people do. So that's how Mr. Hope managed to finance this

173

rather pleasant house with its rather expensive contents."

"So maybe somebody killed him because he was rich. Not everybody loves a banker these days."

"True, but a mite tenuous. Let's see what else we've got. Oho!"

"Oho, sir? Really?" Copper sounded amused.

"Could have been worse," admitted Constable. "I could have said 'hello, hello, what have we here?'."

"And what have we, sir?"

"An address book."

"You what?" Copper was incredulous. "That's all a bit antediluvian, isn't it, guv? Who keeps an address book these days? I've got everything on my phone."

"Hmmm." Constable leafed through the pages. "Phones can fall into the wrong hands. And sometimes you might want to keep a little book for a particular reason."

"Such as ...?"

"That I don't know. But I'll tell you one thing that strikes me. All the names in here are women, Penny Farmer among them. And ... oh look ... one of them has the Sword and Dagger as her address. One Adelaide Knight. Or, for short, Addy, as mentioned by Mrs. Farmer. What a coincidence."

"Her pub being the place where Rex Hope was last seen alive, sir."

"Exactly. So, let's follow the trail and go and see the lady. You never know, we may actually be beginning to get somewhere."

*

The car park at the rear of the Sword and Dagger was emptying rapidly as Andy Constable and Dave Copper drove in and parked alongside one another in a corner. Entering the bar, the detectives found it sparsely populated by a straggle of customers who looked as if they were in the throes of polishing off the last of their drinks before heading home for a late Sunday lunch. The smiling young woman behind the bar greeted them brightly.

"Good afternoon, gentlemen. What can I get you?"

"Police." Constable and Copper both proffered their warrant cards. "We're looking for Mrs. Knight. Would that be you?"

"No, I'm Anna. Addy's out in the kitchen. And by the way, it's Miss." Constable and Copper exchanged glances. "Oh … this is about poor Rex, isn't it? I'll get her for you." Anna pushed through the door at the rear of the bar, and a murmur of voices was heard.

"Good afternoon." A woman appeared in the doorway. Mid-forties, Constable guessed. With short dark hair, and dressed in jeans and a check blouse, she exuded confidence. "I thought somebody would be round before too long. I'm Adelaide Knight. I gather you're looking for me."

"We are, Miss Knight. I'm Detective Inspector Constable and this is Detective Sergeant Copper." The two re-presented their identification. "And I'd like to ask you a few questions."

"Good lord, that takes me back," responded Addy unexpectedly. "The number of times I've heard a conversation start with those words."

"I beg your pardon?" Constable sounded puzzled.

Addy laughed. "Sorry, inspector. It's just that we're on the same side. Well, used to be. I'm ex-Met. Used to earn my living in the big city before I came out to live in greener pastures."

"Uniform?"

"Plain-clothes. Actually, extremely plain. I used to be part of one of the protection squads."

Constable was impressed. "Exciting stuff, I should imagine. Can't think why you'd want to give up something like that. Don't you find country life rather dull by comparison?"

Addy shrugged. "Oh, there was a bit of a misunderstanding, and I had the chance to get out early with quite a nice pay-off, so I grabbed it. Just enough to enable me to get this place. Anyway, I expect you're not here to talk about me. And as for dull, if life around here were that dull you wouldn't be standing in my bar."

"True, Miss Knight. Obviously I need to know what you can tell me about the events of this morning." Constable looked around. Just one or two customers remained, but his eye lit on a quiet corner at the far end of the room. "Shall we sit down?"

"Do you want a drink while we talk? We brew a very fine drop of ale here," coaxed Addy. "Three, in fact. Or are you going to stick to the 'not while on duty' mantra?"

"I think we'd better," replied Constable, ignoring Copper's appealing look and faint groan of disappointment. And as the three seated themselves, "Now, I gather that this was the last place Rex Hope was seen alive."

"Not by me," said Addy. "I was out the back in the brewery at the time. My girl Anna saw Penny Farmer and her little trail of hangers-on – you'd better speak to her if you want any information about that."

"We shall. But there are one or two things I'd like to clarify. You knew Rex Hope, I take it?"

"Yes. Everybody knew Rex."

"Well?"

"Not especially. Why?"

"I was just wondering why your name would feature in a little book we found in Mr. Hope's house. Names, addresses, phone numbers – quite a number of ladies."

Addy smiled wryly. "Yes, that sounds like Rex. He was … how shall I put it … always eager to expand his circle of friends."

"Including yourself?"

"He might have wanted to," snorted Addy. "It didn't do him much good!"

"So are you saying he made advances? Unwelcome ones?"

"Nothing I couldn't handle, Mr. Constable." Addy gazed levelly at the inspector.

"Well, that's good to know. How about other people? Can you think of anyone else who might not have felt as capable as yourself? Anyone who might have had something against him?"

"You're talking about enemies, aren't you, inspector?"

"Frankly, yes."

"I couldn't honestly say. I never really had any dealings with him, so he never did me any harm. As for anyone else, they'll have to speak for themselves. Why don't you ask around?" Addy clamped her lips firmly together. Evidently there was a story to be told, but it was clear that she was not prepared to reveal anything further.

Constable elected to leave the matter for the moment. "No doubt that's exactly what we shall be doing, Miss Knight. And if there's nothing more you can tell us about this morning, we'd better speak to your colleague."

"Anna," called Addy. "Can you come over here, please." She stood. "I'll leave her to you."

"Take a seat, Anna," said Constable affably, as the young barmaid approached nervously. "So, it's Miss …?"

176

"Prentiss. Two 's'es."

"And you work here in the bar."

"Only at weekends. I'm a student at Camford. Chemistry."

" I see." Constable smiled. "Must come in handy if you have anything to do with the pub home-brews."

"Er ... yes." Anna nodded uncertainly.

"Now, I understand you may have been the last person to see Mr. Hope alive. Can you tell me what happened?"

"Not much, really. Mr. Hope and the others were out training for the run ..."

"People keep mentioning this 'run'," broke in Constable. "I don't actually know what that's all about."

"It's some sort of village tradition," explained Anna. "I don't really know the history of it – some sort of fun charity thing, I think. And all sorts of teams take part, including two from the two pubs in the village – us and the Three Blind Mice, that is. There's an old rivalry which goes back years, but it's all quite friendly really."

"And are you part of the team from the Dagger?"

"Yes. There's me, Addy, and Barbara."

"Who?"

"Barbara Dwyer. She's one of our customers. She lives just round the corner in Church Lane. Number 8," she added, in response to Copper's interrogative eyebrow as he made notes.

"And Mr. Hope and the others were out for a run ...?" prompted Constable.

"And they stopped off here for a breather, and Mr. Hope said he fancied a coffee, but the others didn't. So they carried on while Mr. Hope came inside and I made him his coffee. He took it back outside, and then he must have gone off after them just a few minutes later."

"And that was the last you saw of him?"

"Yes. I went out to fetch his cup, and he'd gone."

"One thing I notice, Anna," said the inspector. "You refer to Mr. Hope as just that – Mr. Hope. Everyone else calls him Rex. Any special reason?"

Anna seemed slightly flustered by the question. "No. It's just that ... well, he was quite a bit older than me. Not that that seemed to bother him."

"Ah." Constable pounced on the unguarded remark. "Are

177

you saying that Mr. Hope was maybe a little friendlier towards you than you wanted him to be?"

"Maybe. But people say all sorts of things to you when you're serving behind a bar. You get used to it. It doesn't usually mean anything."

"So you had no particular reason to dislike Mr. Hope?"

"No. None at all. Honestly."

"What about other people? His companions this morning – Mr. Lowe and Mr. Booker?"

"I don't really know Mark Lowe," shrugged Anna offhandedly. "He doesn't come in here."

"And Mr. Booker?"

"Sam?" A glow came into Anna's eyes. "Sam's nice. I like him. Of course, we've got a lot in common, with our jobs and so on. And he used to be on the same course as I'm doing. But I don't think he's got a lot of time for me." She sighed. "I don't suppose that helps you, does it?"

"Then I think we'll leave it at that for the time being." Constable rose to his feet, the others following suit. "Thank you," he called in the direction of the bar, where Adelaide was clearing away glasses and rearranging bottles. As he headed towards the door of the now deserted room, his eye was caught by a large glass case mounted on one wall, its sliding doors sheltering an impressive array of weaponry, ranging from basket-handled swords which looked as if they had seen service in the English Civil War, Italian stilettos with intricately-chased handles, Napoleonic vintage bayonets, a native American tomahawk, a Ghurkha kukri, and a cavalryman's dress sabre. Other less notable weapons completed the display.

"That's a fearsome collection of ironmongery you have there, Miss Knight," he remarked.

"Oh, those," replied Adelaide casually, joining the detectives in their inspection of the cabinet. "Just a little hobby of mine, since I took over the pub. I suppose it's a leftover from when I was in the force – I had training in all sorts of combat, armed and unarmed, and it's quite surprising what you have to learn to defend yourself against if some loony decides to come charging towards you. And it's quite appropriate, considering the name of the place, don't you think?"

"Hmmm. Maybe." Constable did not sound altogether

178

convinced. "As long as everything is safely secured in there. I must say, those door locks don't look particularly sturdy."

"Oh, they're mostly fine," said Addy. "We've had one or two bits and pieces pinched occasionally, but nothing valuable. Rusty old junk, usually. Probably just the local lads doing it for a dare when I'm looking the other way. All the good stuff is wired in."

"I'm glad to hear it," replied Constable. "We shan't keep you any longer. Thank you both for your time, ladies." He headed out from the dim interior on to the forecourt, blinking slightly in the late afternoon sunshine.

*

A thought struck Andy Constable. "Copper."

"Guv?"

"Do you by any chance still have about your person that little book of Rex Hope's?"

"I do, sir," said Dave Copper, producing it from a pocket.

"Just for fun, take a little look through it and see if the name Barbara Dwyer features."

"Righty-ho, sir." The sound of flicking pages. "And here it is."

"Gracious me," said Constable in mock astonishment. "Yet another coincidence. Well, as fortune seems to be smiling on us, shall we push our luck a little further and see if the lady is at home to callers? As she seems to live just round the corner."

"Why not, sir?" grinned Copper, as the two set out. "Since she seems to be part of the Rex Hope harem. Because that's what it's starting to look like, isn't it?"

"He certainly does seem to have had a partiality for the ladies. Which of itself is not a crime, but you and I have seen enough cases to know that it can lead to all sorts of trouble."

"Especially if you're involved with someone like Adelaide Knight, sir. After all, she told us herself, she's a woman who knows how to handle a knife."

"The fact had not escaped me, sergeant. Well, let's see what our third lady runner has to add to our sum total of knowledge." He rapped on the door of 8 Church Lane.

The woman who answered the door was slim, slightly taller than average, and looked to be around forty. Her clear complexion, devoid of make-up, her fair hair pulled back off her face, and the light summer dress she wore, all combined to give

179

an impression of glowing well-being.

"Mrs. Dwyer?"

"That's me."

Constable introduced himself and his junior colleague. "I wonder if I might ask you a few questions?"

"This will be about Rex Hope, I suppose. Oh, don't look surprised, inspector – word gets around very fast in a village like this. You'd better come in." Barbara led the way into the kitchen. "I hope you don't mind if I carry on," she said, indicating two tall stools for the detectives to perch on. "I was in the middle of getting my supper sorted out." She took up a knife and resumed the task of chopping vegetables which had obviously been interrupted by her visitors.

"You live alone?" enquired the inspector.

"Thankfully, yes," was the slightly unexpected reply.

"Is there a Mr. Dwyer?" probed Constable.

"There is, inspector, but not here. In fact, he lives a very long way away indeed, in Dubai."

"That is a long way."

"It is. Probably just about far enough." She turned back to Constable. "Sorry, inspector, I don't sound very helpful. But just for the record, my husband and I divorced a few years ago, our son lives with him, and I live here. Not, I imagine, that any of this has anything to do with why you're here."

"That may not be strictly true," said Constable tentatively.

"Oh?"

"Obviously, Mrs. Dwyer, we're trying to find out as much as we can about Mr. Hope with the aim of identifying contacts, any motives anyone might have to wish him ill, that sort of thing, which means we're looking into all his affairs."

Barbara snorted. "Well, you can certainly count me out there. I've had enough of charming forty-something men to last me a lifetime!"

"Not actually the sort of affairs I meant, Mrs. Dwyer," smiled Constable, "but thank you anyway for clarifying the point. We had already been given the impression that Mr. Hope saw himself as quite a ladies' man."

"And I was definitely not one of those ladies. And before you even think it, Rex was not a factor in my divorce."

"Interesting to hear, Mrs. Dwyer. But I'm now slightly

puzzled. Because, you see, we have found what you might describe ... what he might have described ... as Mr. Hope's little black book. Names, addresses and so on of a number of people. Generally ladies. Your name was among them. Which is what has brought us to your door." Constable waited, an enquiring look on his face.

"I can only repeat, inspector, that I had no sort of romantic involvement with Rex Hope. If that's the sort of motive you're looking for here, you won't find it." Barbara's words had a tone of finality.

"Well, it's always useful to be able to rule out certain possibilities," said the inspector, getting to his feet. "Oh, by the way, your name also came up in another context."

"I seem to be very popular," replied Barbara drily. "And what was this?"

"Oh, merely in connection with next week's village run. The Sword and Dagger was the last place Mr. Hope was seen alive, so we had a talk with the landlady there, and we gathered that you're part of the pub's team."

"That's right, inspector." Barbara unbent a little. "In fact, I have been called their secret weapon. I'm not sure whether that's a compliment or not."

"How do you mean?"

"Some people have said that as a professional, I ought not to be eligible."

"Sorry ... professional what?"

"I'm a fitness instructor, inspector. I work at the Blaston Grange Spa and Hydro."

"I know it. Big country house on the Camford Road."

"That's right. I'm senior instructor there. I organise the exercise classes, work out the fitness regimes for our clients, conduct one-on-one training programmes, that sort of thing."

"And just for the avoidance of doubt, Mr. Hope didn't feature in any of these one-on-ones?"

Barbara's features froze. "He did not."

"Ah well, another potential trail we needn't follow," smiled Constable. "We'll just have to keep wondering why Mr. Hope had made a note of your details."

"How unfortunate that you'll never be able to ask him."

"True. And now I think we'll leave you to carry on with

181

your supper while we pursue our enquiries elsewhere. Don't bother to see us out – I'm sure we can find our own way." He beckoned Copper to follow him in the direction of the front door.

Out in the lane, Dave Copper blew out his cheeks in a mock sigh of relief. "That's one tough lady, guv," he remarked, as the two made their way towards their cars. "Definitely a touch of steel under the exterior. She wasn't giving anything away, was she?"

"Which leads me to suppose that there's something to give."

"I reckon you're right, guv. There's some sort of entanglement there. We just need to find out what it was."

Constable looked at his watch. "I think tomorrow will do, sergeant. Get the incident room running, and then we can do some more digging. In the meantime, I shall go home and slump in front of the TV all evening to recharge my brain cells."

*

The former playground of Blaston Dammett village school, now the car park of the library, was already occupied by three cars as Andy Constable drove in just after nine on Monday morning. Standing in the doorway of the old classroom, he nodded with quiet approval as he watched Dave Copper supervising the set-up of the room, as other officers quietly tapped at computer keyboards on trestle tables in the background.

"Morning, guv," Copper greeted his superior, breaking off from his task.

"Good morning, sergeant," rejoined the inspector. "You seem to have everything under control."

"Didn't want to let the grass grow under our feet, guv," replied Copper. "And there looks to be quite a lot of ground to cover, what with this not being a nice tidy locked room mystery like all the best detective stories, plus there's quite a few people in the case, so I'm getting as much background codified as I can." He nodded to his silently working colleagues.

"Good work. And with a bit of luck, we should have some more to go on before today is much older."

"Inspector! I hope everything is satisfactory." The voice of Phyllis Stein, coming unexpectedly from immediately behind him, startled Constable. He whirled round.

"Ah. Miss Stein. I didn't hear you. Yes, everything seems to be fine. I didn't expect to see you quite so soon. I was under the impression that the library didn't open until later."

"It doesn't, inspector. Eleven o'clock, actually. But I thought I'd come in a little earlier today, just to make sure that everything was all right."

"Perfectly, thank you. At the moment we're just in the process of getting together what we know so far."

"I see. So no doubt you'll be wanting to find out as much as you can about the people who might be involved." There was a clear meaning in the look which Phyllis gave the inspector.

Constable was quick to take the cue. "I would imagine, Miss Stein, that someone in a position such as yours would be an invaluable source of background information regarding the people in the village."

"Not, of course, by way of vulgar gossip, you understand," said Phyllis hastily. "One naturally eschews that kind of thing. But if it's a question of duty, and helping the police in the investigation of a crime ..."

"Then naturally, a good citizen would wish to do everything possible to assist," soothed Constable. "So anything you can tell us ..."

"I've just popped the kettle on. Why don't you go through to my library, and I'll bring you some tea in just a minute. Milk? Sugar?"

"God bless the village busybody, guv," said Copper in lowered tones as the two detectives seated themselves in a pair of tub chairs in the library reading corner. "If she's got the dirt on a few people, this'll save a helluva lot of time, plus a few miles-worth of shoe-leather. Notebook at the ready, I take it?"

"Of course," replied Constable. "But you'd better keep it fairly discreet. Let's preserve the fiction that this is just a helpful social conversation instead of somebody evidently dying to spill the beans on everyone."

"Here we are, gentlemen." Phyllis arrived carrying a tray which bore two steaming mugs for the officers, and a dainty bone china cup and saucer for herself. She settled herself comfortably. "Now, how can I help you?"

Constable marshalled his thoughts. "I wonder if you happened to be about yesterday morning ... did you by any

183

chance see Mr. Hope?"

"Actually, inspector, I did. I was on my way to church, and I noticed him outside the Sword and Dagger. Only briefly in passing, I should say. I wanted to make sure I wasn't late for the service. But I shouldn't have worried, because the vicar was still outside greeting people when I arrived. But yes, Rex was there with Penny Farmer and the rest of her usual entourage." Phyllis sniffed dismissively.

"You're not a great fan of Mrs. Farmer?" enquired Constable delicately.

"Oh, I dare say she's a pleasant enough young woman when you get to know her," said Phyllis. "But of course, far too young for that husband of hers."

"Yes, I did notice there was something of an age difference. Why, do you believe it to be relevant?"

"I honestly couldn't say," said Phyllis, lips pursed. "But there is something of a story there. I suppose you know who she used to be?"

"No."

"I'm surprised, inspector. I should have thought most men would be. Of course, she was still Penny Worth then. But perhaps you don't watch that kind of programme."

"I'm not with you, Miss Stein."

"She was the winner of 'Catwalk Star', inspector. On Channel 6. It was a few years ago. It was one of those so-called reality programmes where they were looking for a new top model. And she won it. She was quite famous for a while, but these made-up phenomena never last, do they? Just a nine-days wonder."

"I thought I recognised her, guv," interrupted Copper. "But I couldn't think from where."

"So, it was 'local-girl-made-good', was it?" enquired Constable.

"Oh no, inspector, far from it. She isn't from round here at all. No, the story was, at the height of the celebrity kerfuffle, she was involved in an event in aid of 'Support For Soldiers' – you know, the charity that looks after members of the forces if they've been wounded. Anyway, she was making an appearance, and Bob Farmer was there on account of his injury. Military police, he had been, before the accident. Obviously they must have hit it off, and

184

before anyone could turn round, he'd brought her back here as his new bride. So she now queens it over the bar at the Three Blind Mice, and all the men in the village are running around after her, obviously just as smitten as poor Bob was."

"I see." Constable was intrigued. "And Mr. Hope was one of the runners? But not the only one."

"Certainly not. That poor boy who works at the inn with her is obviously head-over-heels, and then, of course, there's that other one." Another sniff. "Mr. Mark Lowe."

"Mr. Lowe? You don't sound as if you approve of him."

"I've nothing against him at all, inspector," responded Phyllis, a hint of hauteur in her tone. "No doubt he's a very good teacher. Standards have all changed, of course, since I was in the profession. We had no time for personal relationships then."

"By which you mean ...?"

"Oh, I'm sure there was never anything in the rumours about him," said Phyllis stoutly. "Certainly nobody I ever spoke to believed them for a minute. But there was talk – it was never more than that – that Mark Lowe had become a little too interested in one of the girls in the senior year of the school. It was never taken any further, but it just goes to show that some men aren't as careful as they should be in their friendships. Sometimes they can't see the obvious."

"Which brings us back to the question of Mrs. Farmer and her ... admirers. How do you suppose Mr. Farmer felt about all this?"

"I have no idea," said Phyllis. "I know how I'd feel if I were in his shoes. But you must ask him yourself."

"I expect we shall, Miss Stein." Constable sipped his tea reflectively. "For the moment, I'd rather come back to the other pub which features in this matter, and that's the Sword And Dagger. Now, you say you came past there ..."

"That's right. The village's other little private kingdom."

The inspector was surprised by the waspish tone. "You're not fond of Miss Knight and her establishment?"

"I never go there, inspector. Not my kind of clientele at all. But of course some of the locals all flock there for what she offers."

"Yes, she mentioned her house ales when we spoke to her. I gather she was out attending to them when the runners and you

185

came past."

"Yes, busy behind the scenes, I dare say. Always brewing something special, as you might say, inspector." The look which accompanied the words hinted at a deeper meaning. "But I never pry into what goes on behind locked doors."

"Miss Stein, let me see if I understand you correctly. Are you telling us that Miss Knight holds some sort of lock-ins at her pub after hours?"

"That's not for me to say, inspector. I don't have the means to look into these matters. But of course, the local authority would be bound to take an interest if it came to their ears, wouldn't you say?" A grim smile lit Phyllis's features.

"Not," explained Constable, "that such a thing would necessarily be illegal. If the building is not open to the public, and no money is changing hands, Miss Knight is quite at liberty to offer her personal hospitality to her friends, no matter what the hour."

"It depends on what she's offering, surely, inspector. But as I say, that's all really no concern of mine." Having thrown her pebble into the pool, Phyllis seemed quite content to let the ripples spread of their own accord.

"Let's get back to the events of yesterday. You say that you came past the Sword and Dagger on your way to church, but you saw nobody else?"

"Only that Anna girl who works there."

"Of course. She's one of their team for the run. As is Mrs. Dwyer. We've spoken to all three, and as far as we can tell, there seems to be no reason to connect any of the three with Mr. Hope's death."

"Hmph!" Phyllis snorted derisively. "Well, I wouldn't put it past that Barbara Dwyer, for one!"

"Really?" Constable was surprised. "Why, is there something we aren't aware of?"

"I should think there is," retorted Phyllis smugly. "I'm quite amazed it didn't come out in conversation. Of course, I'm sure you know all about Rex Hope."

"We know he was very interested in the ladies," said Constable carefully.

"No, no, no, not that at all," said Phyllis impatiently. "I mean his job."

186

"He worked for some sort of bank or investment house in the City, I believe. Isn't that right, Copper?"

"That's correct, sir. Morgmann Brothers, it was."

"So how is this relevant, Miss Stein?"

"Well, inspector," Phyllis leaned forward and lowered her voice, "it's not exactly a secret, but I don't suppose Barbara would have wanted it known too widely. You see, Rex used to offer a little what you might call professional advice on investments to friends from time to time ..."

"Are we talking insider trading here, Miss Stein?"

"Oh, I don't know about all the technicalities, inspector." Phyllis pushed aside all questions of business ethics. "The point was, Barbara had received a rather large sum as part of a divorce settlement ..."

"Yes, she mentioned that she was divorced from her husband."

"He was something in oil. Out in the Gulf. Ridiculous amounts of money. Anyway, Barbara was awarded a huge quantity of cash, and she went to Rex for investment advice. And I don't know what went wrong, but it all evaporated! I don't know if it was part of the crash, or whether somebody had embezzled it, because I didn't like to pry too closely – I'm not that kind of woman. All I know is, she was left with hardly a bean, and it was apparently all Rex Hope's fault. He must have thrown all her plans into turmoil. There! Wouldn't that be a good reason for her not to be too well disposed towards him?"

*

"That's given us a few things to follow up, hasn't it, guv?" remarked Dave Copper as he perched on the edge of a table in the incident room. "Motives starting to come out of the woodwork in all directions. Jealousy ... revenge ... "

"Oh, I have a horrible feeling we shall discover a few more before this business is over," said Andy Constable. "That's the trouble with these picture-postcard-perfect villages – they look so charming on the surface, but underneath there are all sorts of undercurrents. As we have had occasion to discover not so very far from here."

"True, sir. Well, it looks as if this lot probably isn't going to be sewn up in an afternoon, so where do you want to make a start?"

187

"I think we'll begin with the jealousy angle. Let's follow Miss Stein's suggestion and go and have a little word with Mr. Farmer at the Three Blind Mice."

"Righty-ho, sir. Do you want me to drive?"

"Certainly not, sergeant. We spend far too much time sitting in a car as it is. It's only just round the corner. We'll walk."

"Bloody ridiculous!" said Bob Farmer shortly. Obviously not a man to mince his words, thought Constable. "And if you've been round at the library, I can guess who told you that. Damned woman should keep her long nose stuck in her books instead of poking it into other people's business!"

"So no truth in the suggestion that your wife might be the centre of attentions which you might not be happy about, sir?" persisted Constable mildly.

"I didn't say that, inspector." Bob continued his task of wiping down the copper surface of the Three Blind Mice's lounge bar. "Look, it's obvious. Penny's a pretty girl. Anyone can see that. Probably far too pretty for the likes of me, according to some." A wry smile suddenly transformed a face which had previously been set in an unprepossessing scowl into one which showed the rugged good looks of a mature and attractive soldier. "They can think what they like. She gave a lot up for me, and we're happy together. And in a pub like this, you're going to get people coming in, seeing a beautiful woman behind the bar, and they're going to try it on. Not seriously – it's just a traditional game. Flirting. Everybody does it, but nobody makes anything of it. Least of all my wife. Or me. So if you're looking for a motive to kill Rex because of jealousy regarding Penny, you're going to have to look somewhere else."

"Well, I think that's clear enough, Mr. Farmer," said Constable. "But since I gather you used to be in the same line of work as ourselves, perhaps you'll let us know if any helpful thoughts strike you," he continued with a smile.

"Yes, used to be," said Bob. "Not for a while. Not since the accident."

"Do you mind if I ask what happened?"

"Chinook," replied Bob succinctly. "They're not supposed to crash. Well, this one did. Could have been worse. At least everyone walked away … more or less. In my case, less. But it left me with no kneecap and one leg an inch shorter than the other.

Not too clever when it comes to the business end of policing a bunch of squaddies who decide to get a bit playful. I could have stayed on behind a desk, but it wasn't for me, so I took the Queen's very large cheque and opted for a change of scenery. And here I am running a pub."

"But not running on its behalf, sir. Sorry, that was a joke in extremely poor taste. I apologise."

"No need, inspector. I've heard worse. You should hear some of the cracks the locals make involving my beer and the word 'limp'. Water off a duck's back. Actually, none of it's as bad as what some of them say about Addy's beers down at the Dagger. It's all in fun. She does brew some pretty fine ales, but for goodness sake don't let anyone know I said that." Bob chuckled.

"But seriously, Mr. Farmer, the fact that you weren't able to take part in the run, and your wife was, could be relevant to our enquiries. She was after all one of the last to see Mr. Hope alive."

"Well, at least you can be certain she wasn't responsible. She was with Sam and Mark all the time. They'll confirm that, surely."

"We intend to give them every chance to do so, sir. In fact, now might be a useful opportunity to do just that. Are your wife and Mr. Booker around?"

"Penny's lying down," said Bob. "She's still a bit shaken up after finding Rex yesterday. But Sam's about somewhere, if you want to talk to him. I'll give him a shout." He opened the door at the rear of the bar and let out a resounding bellow of 'Sam!'.

A few moments later, the amiable features of Sam Booker appeared in the doorway. "Sorry, I was down in the cellar checking stock for the next order. Did you want me?"

"I don't, but these gentlemen do," replied Bob. "They want to ask you about yesterday. I'll leave you to it, inspector. If anyone wants me, I'm in the kitchen doing the paninis." He looked at his watch. "Should just about get them done by twelve. I haven't got the kitchen staff in today – they only do Sunday lunches, which is what I was also doing yesterday, just in case you wondered - and somebody has to keep this place going." He vanished through the door.

"Shall we sit down, Sam?" said Constable pleasantly. "That's if you've got time. I don't want to drag you away from your work."

189

"No, that's all right, inspector. What is it you want to know?"

"Just wanting to confirm a few things we didn't really have a chance to cover yesterday. Understandably, considering the circumstances. Now, to begin with, you obviously knew Mr. Hope."

"Of course. Ever since I started work here."

"And you were friends?"

"I suppose so, yes."

"And rivals, of course."

"Sorry. I ... I don't understand."

"The race. You were both rivals for a place on the pub team, I gather."

"Oh, that. Yes, of course."

"Now, coming back to yesterday, the four of you were out for some sort of training for the run proper next Sunday. Can you remember whose idea this was?"

"Penny's, I think. Mrs. Farmer's, I mean. She obviously wanted us to be at our best because she was determined to beat the Dagger's team. Me too, of course."

"Oh?" Constable raised an eyebrow.

"Yes. I used to work there, before I came here."

"With Miss Prentiss?"

"Anna? Oh, just for a bit. Not long."

"But now there's this friendly rivalry between the two pubs?" said the inspector. "Nothing wrong in that, I suppose, as long as nothing gets out of hand. Unfortunately, yesterday, something did. So take me back, please, to the time when you left the Sword and Dagger to continue your training. Mr. Hope stayed behind, didn't he?"

"He was just having a quick coffee. But he said he'd catch us up."

"But he didn't."

"No. We ran on ... Penny was ahead of us, with Mark and me a bit behind ... and Rex was nowhere to be seen. Mark cracked some gag about the old bloke not being able to keep up with us younger guys, but that was all. I don't think anybody gave Rex much thought, until we came back round into the wood and Penny found him."

"But still within sight of you when she did so," clarified

190

Constable. "She was slightly ahead of you at that point."

"Oh yes," confirmed Sam. "She screamed. She was really upset. She couldn't have had anything to do with it."

"You seem eager to exonerate her," observed Constable.

"Of course I am," said Sam. "She's not the kind of person who'd do something like that. She's just ... well ... nice to everyone."

"So not the kind of woman to take offence at any attempt by somebody like Rex Hope to, shall we say, go beyond the bounds of normal friendship?" probed the inspector.

"Of course not," said Sam hotly. "I mean, Rex was a bit of a sleaze, but Penny didn't take any notice really. She was used to it. She's pretty good at handling people. Like some others I could mention."

"Oh yes?" Constable's interest was aroused. "Please don't leave us in suspense, Mr. Booker. Go ahead and mention them."

"Well, there's Adelaide Knight," replied Sam.

Constable felt slightly deflated. "We've already had words with Miss Knight. We know that Mr. Hope might have made advances to her, but she told us that they were rebuffed."

"I bet she didn't say how. She was telling everyone she was sick of him making remarks and suggestions when she'd told him he was wasting his time, and in the end, she got so fed up with him that one night, just at closing time in the Dagger, she gave him a good seeing to. Thumped the living daylights out of him, from what I heard. I wasn't there at the time, of course, but the next time I saw him, he had a cut lip and a pretty spectacular black eye. But then, she's the kind of woman you don't want to get on the wrong side of."

The inspector mused for a moment. "Thank you for that, Mr. Booker. No, that particular snippet of information hadn't come our way. Was there anybody else who might have had any sort of grudge against Mr. Hope?"

"Not that I can think of."

"Mr. Lowe?"

"I don't see why. He's never said anything to me."

"And you're good friends with him?"

"I ... I guess. I mean, not specially, but we talk."

"And he'll confirm everything you've told us about the events of yesterday?"

191

"Should do."

"Fine." Constable turned to his junior colleague. "Copper, can you arrange to do just that. You've got his mobile number, haven't you?" A nod from the sergeant. "He's probably tied up at school now, so send him a text and ask him if he can come in to the library as soon as possible."

"On it, sir." The sergeant took out his phone and started tapping the screen.

Constable rose to his feet. "I suppose, just for the sake of form, I ought to ask you whether you had anything against Mr. Hope yourself, Sam?"

"Me? No. Why should I?"

"Good. Oh, just one thing. Is there by any chance a plan of the route of the race? It might be useful to know the details."

"Yes, of course, inspector. We've got some behind the bar somewhere. We have them for the race teams who don't come from the local area. Saves them getting lost in the village back lanes. Hang on, I'll get you one." Sam dived beneath the counter, produced a sheaf of photocopies, and handed one over. "See, the route's marked with a dotted line."

"That all seems clear enough. I'll take another, if I may. And then we'll let you get on. I dare say Mr. Farmer could do with your help. Tell him we'll be in touch."

*

Back out in the Three Blind Mice car park, Dave Copper's phone bleeped. "Reply from Mark Lowe, guv," he reported.

"That was quick. Obviously teachers aren't as busy as I thought they were."

"Says he's got a couple of free periods tomorrow morning. He could come in at half-past nine if that would be convenient."

"Highly. Get back to him and confirm. And then I want you to go back to the incident room and bring everything up to date. Take this copy of the route. You can mark it up – see if you can get pictures of all the relevant people and plot where they were at the relevant times – oh, all the usual stuff. And you can write up your notes so far and let me have a copy to browse through. That should keep you busy for a little while."

"How about you, sir? What are you going to do?"

"I, sergeant, am going to enjoy a nice healthful walk in the fresh country air."

192

"Sir?"

"I'm going to follow this little map and walk the route of the run. A bit of old-fashioned boots-on-the-ground plod-work. It might be helpful to have an idea of the general setting. You never know what thoughts may pop up. So I will see you back at the school in due course."

"Righty-ho, sir."

As Constable strolled down the main street of Blaston Dammett, taking a left turn into a tiny side-road which led between two terraces of thatched cottages towards an imposing brick wall, pierced by an equally imposing pair of wrought-iron gates which obviously led to a house of some substance lurking behind a screen of trees, he reflected on the new information which had come his way.

Adelaide Knight's reported clash with Rex Hope presented an intriguing question. Surely if he had been on the receiving end of a beating from her – and having met her and heard of her background, Constable could quite easily visualise the situation – then that would be more likely to give him a motive against her, rather than the other way around. Unless, of course, she considered the job only half-done. Then there was the matter of Bob Farmer – he had lightly brushed aside any considerations of jealousy, but he also had the sort of military background where actions sometimes replaced words when it came to resolving problems. And whereas he had been occupied in the kitchen today, that didn't seem to have been the case on the day of the murder. So did that free him up to be elsewhere? The question of an alibi was still to be resolved there.

The lane twisted and turned, sometimes between randomly-scattered cottages surrounded by chocolate-box country gardens, sometimes past tall hedges which seemed intent on guarding the privacy of residents, sometimes with a vista of open fields to one side, with apparent dead ends unexpectedly resolving themselves into passages between houses which led on to the next road. Eventually Constable found himself emerging back on to the main street through a narrow alley, with on one side an old-fashioned shop, its frontage all plate glass, gilded lettering, and currently empty slabs of white marble which proudly proclaimed itself as a 'Traditional Family Butcher', and on the other a more mysterious establishment calling itself 'New

Age Solutions', its windows draped in mauve voile and featuring a small group of white plastic bottles bearing product names in an unreadable cursive purple script, posed among an artistically-arranged collection of large smooth grey pebbles. Across the road, on the corner of Church Lane, lay the Sword and Dagger, where Adelaide Knight could be seen, watering-can in hand, attending to the tubs of flowers on the forecourt.

"Miss Knight. This is very convenient. I wonder if we might have another word? One or two things have come up."

Addy put down the can and faced Constable with a somewhat wary expression. "Certainly, inspector." She waved him to one of the benches. "Now, as you're here with no witnesses, are you sure I can't persuade you to try a drop of one of our own special beers?"

"It's tempting, Miss Knight. I've heard them well spoken of."

"We've got three – there's Hare's Breath, which is the lightest, then we have Ferret's Firkin, which is a bit chewier, but most people's favourite is Old Foozler."

"Foozler?"

"Yes," smiled Addy. "It started out as Old Methuselah, but by the time someone's got a couple of pints down them, they tend to start falling over their tongue ordering the next one. Thoroughly foozled, as they say round here. So the name got changed."

"I think I'll resist the temptation," said Constable. "Under the circumstances, being foozled is the last thing I need." His face grew serious. "I have questions."

"So I gather, inspector." Addy's tone matched the detective's as she took her place on the seat opposite him. "You'd better ask them, hadn't you?"

Constable came straight to the point. "I don't think you've been completely candid with me, Miss Knight. When we last spoke, I asked you about the situation between yourself and Mr. Hope, and you said that it was nothing you couldn't handle. I now learn that the way you handled it seems to have been by giving him a beating. You told me you didn't have dealings with him. That sounds very much like dealings to me."

Addy sighed. "You've based yourselves up at the library, haven't you? Well, I can guess where that particular piece of

194

information has come from. Delivered with glee, I have no doubt."

"Funnily enough, it wasn't Miss Stein who told us, if that's who you're referring to. No ... someone else entirely. But the point is, is it true?"

"Yes, of course it's true," retorted Addy. "The man was a pest, and he made one remark too far, and it got under my skin, so I taught him a lesson. And I'll tell you one thing ... it certainly made him change his ways. Around me, anyway. I can't answer for other people. But he was as nice as pie to me after that, and I haven't time to hold grudges, so as far as I was concerned, that was that."

"You didn't regard it as unfinished business?"

"What? You mean, did I take it a step further and chase off up the lane and stab him in the back?" Addy snorted in derision. "Think about it, inspector. With my training, I've got more ways to kill a man than you can shake a stick at. If I'd wanted Rex Hope dead, I could have made a much tidier job of it."

Constable was slightly taken aback at the offhand nature of the comment. "I dare say you could, Miss Knight." He paused. "Oh, there was one other thing. I've had it mentioned to me that the hospitality of your establishment sometimes extends beyond what some might call conventional limits. Any comments on that?"

"So who's doing their best to drop me in it?" asked Addy, tight-lipped. "If it's not Phyllis, which I doubt, seeing she's got the longest nose and the biggest mouth in the village."

"I really can't reveal the source of any information."

Addy thought. "In that case, I bet it was Sam Booker."

"Was he working here at the time of the incident with Mr. Hope?" enquired Constable neutrally.

"Was. Isn't any more."

"No, he works for Mr. Farmer up at the Three Blind Mice now, doesn't he? We've certainly had a talk with him about the events of yesterday."

"Hmmm," grunted Addy. She stood abruptly. "Well, if that's all you have to ask me, inspector, I really ought to get on. A pub doesn't run itself. I have things to attend to at the back."

"Then of course you must do so, Miss Knight," said Constable, rising. "Just one thing before I go. All this talk of your own special ales – I'd be fascinated to take a look at where you

195

make them."

"Oh." Addy seemed momentarily disconcerted. "Right. It's round here." She led the way round into the pub's rear yard, and opened the door of one of the outbuildings. "Here we are. It's actually the old brewhouse. Most pubs used to brew their own before the big breweries came in and took everything over, so we've just brought it back to its original use."

Alongside a large wooden tub, evidently of considerable age, stood a tall vessel in gleaming stainless steel, with associated pipes, funnels and tubes forming a complex set of equipment. "Very impressive," remarked Constable. "Not that I'm really a beer man myself – that's more my sergeant, so you could quite easily talk of mash tuns and wort and baffle me completely." He smiled. "Or foozle, I suppose I should say." He caught sight through a half-open door of the shining copper coils and containers of what seemed to be a further installation. "And what's in there?"

"Oh, just another bunch of spare equipment," said Addy. "Not very interesting really. All the beer-making goes on in here." She pulled the door to.

"And I expect you're eager to get back to it. I'll be off. And if I have any further questions for you, I shall know where to find you, shan't I?" The inspector smiled pleasantly and set off back round the building in the direction of Church Lane, leaving Addy gazing after him, a speculative look on her face.

As Constable passed the churchyard, his eye was caught by a sturdy middle-aged woman, dungaree-clad, who was busily demolishing the particularly vigorous weed growth around an impressive Victorian tomb which was surmounted by a weeping angel.

She looked up, and hailed him with a cheery greeting. "Good afternoon. Beautiful day, isn't it? Just the sort of weather these blasted weeds like. Have to keep them under control, or they take over the place. Whoever said the devil makes work for idle hands certainly knew what he was talking about!"

A thought struck the inspector. He made his way into the churchyard. "I wonder, might it be possible to have a word with the vicar?"

"Nothing easier," said the woman.

"Can you tell me where I might find him?"

"You've found her," responded the woman, removing a gardening glove and extending a still rather grubby hand. "Reverend Salter. How can I help you?"

Constable introduced himself.

The vicar nodded understandingly. "Of course. You'll be looking into this dreadful business of Rex Hope."

"I am, vicar. And I'm hoping that, as I gather you were about at the time, you may have seen something that might be relevant."

"Come and take a seat in the porch," suggested the vicar. "My aching back could do with a rest, so I shall gladly use you as an excuse to salve my conscience." She made for the nearby entrance to the church and lowered herself on to an ancient-looking bench with a slight groan.

Constable took his place beside her. "Have you been in this parish long?" he began.

"About eight years," replied the vicar. "Which is long enough to get to know pretty much everybody around here, if that's what you're fishing for."

The inspector smiled, acknowledging the other's acuity. "You're very sharp, vicar. That was exactly my train of thought. I was wondering if you knew Mr. Hope."

"Not well. He wasn't one of my regular worshippers. Rather better acquainted with Mammon than with God, I should say. But of course I knew him slightly through my husband."

"Oh? In what way, may I ask?"

"They worked together. Well, not together, but for the same organisation. They used to catch the same train up to London most days."

"Morgmann Brothers in the City, I believe."

"That's right. My husband's in the legal department – Rex Hope was somewhere on the money side. But I'm not quite sure how this relates to what happened yesterday, inspector."

"To be frank, Mrs. Salter, neither am I," admitted Constable. "But at the moment I'm building as complete a picture of the victim as I can. Now, as regards yesterday, no doubt you'll be aware that the running team from the Three Blind Mice came past your church several times."

"Yes."

"I gather that you may have been outside at the crucial

197

moment. Did you by any chance see any of those involved?"

"Yes, I was out here, as usual. I like to greet my parishioners as they're arriving for the service as well as when they leave. You know, a little like the reporter on the aircraft carrier in the Falklands - 'I count them all in, and I count them all back out again'."

"Including Miss Stein."

"Ah yes. Phyllis. One of the more assiduous members of my flock. Always keenly involved in the affairs of the parish."

"I believe she likes to know everything that is happening locally, Mrs. Salter," said Constable solemnly.

"I think we understand one another, inspector." The vicar's eyes sparkled, but she maintained an admirably straight face.

"And Miss Stein tells us that she witnessed the runners. I'm wondering if you did the same."

"Well, yes and no. Of course, I was in the throes of welcoming the arrivals, but I did notice Penny Farmer. Mind you, it would have been hard not to, given the particularly lurid shade of pink she was wearing. Yes, she skipped past on her own at quite a rate of knots, and then I was speaking to someone, so my attention was distracted. Oh, I did see that young man who works for her ..."

"Sam Booker?"

"That's the one."

"And Mr. Hope?"

"Sorry, no. That was after she'd gone by, though, and I wasn't really paying attention. But I'm afraid that's all. The service began shortly after that, and of course when we emerged, it was to find quite a scene of activity. I don't know I can tell you anything beyond that."

"Then I'll be on my way, and leave you to tackle your weeds." Constable got to his feet. "I would offer to help ..."

"... but you have other pernicious growths to deal with," smiled the vicar. "Don't worry, inspector. A little hard work never did anybody any harm. In fact, this morning has given me an idea for my next sermon. I think I shall spend the rest of my weeding time composing a text on the parable of the wheat and the tares. I'm sure sorting out the two is a task you're familiar with in your job. Not, I imagine, that you can wait until the day of judgement to resolve matters."

"No, vicar," replied Constable. "The mills of God may grind exceeding slow, but I try to work a little faster."

*

Andy Constable turned out of the churchyard and carried on up Church Lane. After a little while, the houses petered out, and he soon came to a gate which gave on to the path which continued ahead through Blaise Copse. He paused for a moment. The sense of peacefulness was almost palpable – a slight breeze stirred the leaves of the trees into the faintest rustling, and distant birdsong was the only other thing to disturb the silence. A very different atmosphere from that of only twenty-four hours earlier, he mused.

The path continued straight ahead for a while, but then began to writhe in a series of curves and bends as he penetrated deeper into the wood. Constable halted briefly to survey the spot, still cordoned off with police tape, where the body of Rex Hope had been discovered, and then proceeded on his way. Huge craggy-featured oaks flanked the path, intermingled with the smooth grey-green bark of beech trees, while occasional flashes of the silver-grey of birch lit up the more distant depths of the wood. Overall, the light faded to a dim watery green, with shafts of sunlight making an occasional foray through the canopy as far as the leaf litter underfoot. The path continued its convoluted circuit – once or twice, the inspector felt obliged to check his map to make sure that he was following the correct route as the path forked – but eventually, he found himself emerging at the end of the gigantic loop at a stile which led him once more on to the road. Contentedly, he drank in the view. Over the hedge to his left stretched farmland – nearby lay a field green with the foliage of some root crop whose identity the inspector did not feel qualified to guess at, while further away he recognised the distinctive yellow blossoms of oilseed rape making their bright splash on an area of rising ground. On the skyline, its growl muted to a soft murmur by distance, a tractor went about its business.

The chime of the church clock recalled him to himself, and he checked his watch. Good grief, he thought, where's the time gone? He carried on along the road, his route clear as he passed a group of modest but still spacious brick-built cottages, probably constructed in the early years of the twentieth century for agricultural workers on the surrounding estates. Lines of washing flapped in the breeze, the sound of high-pitched laughter came from a garden where a child's tricycle had been casually abandoned in the gateway, and neat vegetable plots peered out from behind businesslike wooden sheds. After only a couple of minutes the road resolved itself into School Lane and, with the chimneys of the Three Blind Mice visible over the roof of the library, Constable turned into the car park of the former school.

"Hello, guv." Dave Copper looked up from the table where he was seated typing on a laptop. "I was just starting to wonder where you'd got to."

"Getting a feel for the place, sergeant," replied Constable. "It never does any harm to understand the ground you're covering, so I've done the full circular tour of the village. Including the spot where Mr. Hope was killed."

"Our old friend, the *locus in quo*, eh, guv?" grinned Copper.

"The very same. And I've had one or two interesting conversations."

"Oh yes?"

"One was with our former colleague, if you can call her that, Adelaide Knight. I tackled her on the subject of the beating she dealt out to Rex Hope, and she didn't deny it. In fact, she seemed rather proud of the fact that she'd sorted him out, so as far as motives go, hers seems to be past its sell-by date. But then I met the vicar."

"Oh lord," chuckled Copper. "He's not another one of these doddery old country clerical types, is he, all bike-clips and mothballs?"

"As it happens, sergeant, she was a very charming woman," replied Constable severely. "And I should say pretty perceptive. But unfortunately she didn't see the murdered man on the day, so couldn't tell me much I didn't know already."

"So nothing learned, really?"

"I don't know." The uncertainty was audible in Constable's voice. "There may be one or two things floating around in my mind, just out of sight, but I've no idea what they are. They'll settle eventually if they actually are anything. How about you?" He looked around. "By the way, where is everybody? Last time I was here you had underlings assiduously labouring away in the background. What's happened to them?"

"Actually, guv, ran out of things for them to do for the

moment. Thought there was no point them sitting around here staring at the walls, so I sent them back to the station. Looks like it's just you and me."

"So how have you got on?"

"Not bad, sir. Come and take a look." Copper led the way over to a large blackboard on an easel. "Miss Stein told me this was stashed away in a cupboard, so I dug it out. And I've done this." He proudly pointed to a large-scale version of the map from the Three Blind Mice, picked out in different colours of chalk, showing the plan of Blaston Dammett and the route of the run. Clearly marked were the starting point of the race, the Sword and Dagger at the bottom end of the village, and the location of Rex Hope's body. Taped to the board alongside the map were several photographs of individuals involved in the case – a shot of a beaming Bob and Penny Farmer holding a trophy, evidently a clipping from the local newspaper taken on the occasion of a previous race, a picture from the same source of Adelaide Knight behind the bar of her pub, three tankards of her house-brewed ales before her as she was presented with some sort of award, with Sam Booker slightly out of focus in the background, and a leaflet from the Blaston Grange Spa and Hydro, open at the page which extolled their fitness regimes and which featured a picture of a smiling lycra-clad Barbara Dwyer. The final item showed a humourless Phyllis Stein gazed grainily straight at the viewer.

"Best enlargement of her driving licence photo I could manage on our copier, sir," explained Copper. "And I've been in touch with Rex Hope's office – their HR people are emailing me a photo of him from a piece in their house journal."

"That just leaves Mark Lowe," observed Constable.

"All in hand, guv," said Copper. "Miss Stein reckons she's got a picture of him from some old school photos somewhere in the library, so she's going to try to dig that out. But if not, I'll just take a shot of him on my phone when he comes in tomorrow morning."

"You seem to have everything under control, sergeant," said Constable.

"That's not all, sir." Copper basked in his superior's approval. "I've just finished typing my notes, so all I've got to do is turn on my wi-fi, push a button, and they'll all come whooshing out of that printer over there."

201

"I'm impressed." Constable did not sound altogether convincing. "This means that I shall have no excuse at all not to spend my evening reading through them. You'd better get on and do it." As Copper returned to his laptop, setting in motion the clatter and whirr of printing from the machine in the corner of the room, Constable remained looking at the contents of the board. Something was nagging at him in the back of his mind – no, he couldn't put his finger on it. Perhaps Copper's notes would strike a chord.

"Here we are, guv." The sergeant handed over a sheaf of papers in a brown folder. "Happy reading."

"Thank you, Copper. Well, if I'm going to be working late at home, I think I'm quite justified in calling it a day." He looked at the wall clock at the end of the room. "Not that it's particularly early. You may as well bunk off as well. But I shall expect you here first thing tomorrow, bright-eyed and bushy-tailed."

"When did you ever know me not to be, sir?" grinned Copper.

"And we can go through whatever this mighty tome of yours throws up. You've got the key, haven't you?" A nod. "Then I shall leave you to lock up."

As he made his way out through the foyer, Constable was hailed by the slightly disapproving tones of Phyllis Stein. "Leaving so soon, inspector?"

"I have things to do elsewhere, Miss Stein," explained the inspector, feeling unaccountably like a chastised schoolboy. "But don't worry, Sergeant Copper will be locking everything up securely."

"Oh, no need," chirped Phyllis. "It's late library hours this evening, so I shall be here until seven. Not that very many people tend to come in, but it gives me a chance to catch up with my paperwork. And I haven't forgotten that I was going to look for something for your sergeant, so I can do that as well. So, I expect I shall see you tomorrow."

*

The two detectives stood looking down at the body, or at least, that portion of it which was not hidden under the range of bookshelves which rested upon it. But enough was visible … the back of a head with its obsessively neat grey bun, a cardiganned arm ending in a hand which clutched a large dusty book … to make it plain that the corpse was that of Phyllis Stein.

"And it was all open when you arrived?" repeated Andy Constable.

"Yes, guv," replied a still shaken Dave Copper. "Like I said, I only got here a couple of minutes ago. And the front door was unlocked, but I just thought Miss Stein must have come in early for some reason. All the lights were on, and the door to the library was open, so I was just going to put my head round it to say 'don't worry, it's only me' ... and there she was. I just checked quickly to see if she was still alive, but nothing, so then I got on the phone straight away and called it in. And then you got here."

"Everyone's on their way, I take it."

"Yes, sir."

"This is not good, sergeant," said Constable grimly. "It looks alarmingly as if someone has taken it into their head to prevent Miss Stein from telling us something."

"You reckon Rex Hope's murderer's got the wind up?"

"With Phyllis Stein's reputation as the village gossip and know-all, it wouldn't be surprising, would it?" Constable sighed. "This is something of a turn-up. Let's not jump to conclusions. We'll wait to see what our medical and forensic people have to say. For the moment, leave everything as it is, lock the door, make us a cup of tea, and we'll go and take another look at what the lady had told us." He led the way back into the incident room and lowered himself wearily into a chair.

As the inspector finished his tea and reached for the folder of notes, the sound of approaching sirens could be heard. "Trust uniform to make a song and dance when the excitement's all over," commented Constable. "You'd better go out and meet them. Get them to tape the whole building off, but you'd better keep them out of the library until the doc and SOCO arrive, just in case the size elevens compromise anything crucial."

Copper departed on his errand, but was back in a very short time with a stout middle-aged man in tow.

"Still determined to keep me busy, I see, Andy," said the newcomer. "Not content with one body in the case, you give me two."

"Sorry about that, doc. I didn't expect to have to call on you so soon."

"Ah well, no rest for the wicked. Or by the wicked,

apparently," chuckled the doctor. "Oh, by the way, since I was coming your way, I thought I might as well deliver this in person and save the squeezed police budget a few pence." He handed over the large manila envelope in his hand. "Post mortem report on your first victim, the late Mr. Hope."

"Anything in particular I should look out for?"

"Depressingly ordinary, I'm afraid," said the doctor. "Time of death you knew anyway, as near as makes no odds, and cause of death as we suspected – single blow to the vital organs with a knife. Not even a very interesting knife, either – probably the sort you'd find in any domestic kitchen. All the details of dimensions and so on are in there. Otherwise, no other wounds, no unsuspected nasty conditions lurking in the depths. In fact, from my point of view, your corpse was singularly dull."

"Evidently somebody thought otherwise, doc," countered Copper. "Otherwise he wouldn't be a corpse."

"Hmmm. True, sergeant. Well, on with the motley. Another day, another dead 'un. So who's gone and got themselves killed this time?"

"Come and take a look." The inspector led the way through into the library, and stood back while the doctor tutted in surprise.

"That, young Andy, is a very nasty case of an excess of heavy literature. Who is she?"

"A lady by the name of Phyllis Stein. Local librarian, and source of information on all aspects of village life, including those aspects which we think some residents would rather keep under wraps. Which is quite enough to make her death suspicious."

"Right. Let me take a look at her." The doctor threw off his jacket and began to climb into a set of blue overalls. "Which is not going to be easy. I'll start with the bits I can get at, and then perhaps you could rustle up a couple of the beefier plods I passed on my way in, to lift this bookcase off her. Which, if I'm any judge, is going to result in an avalanche of books which will mess things up delightfully for SOCO, but needs must."

"Of course. Copper, would you see to that, please? And we'll leave you to it – we'll be next door in the incident room if you need us."

A few moments later, Copper joined Constable as he stood viewing the case board. "That picture of Rex Hope came through yesterday just as you were leaving, sir," he pointed out. "I've pinned it up there with the others."

"Which means there's just Mark Lowe to come."

"Literally and photographically, sir. Especially since Miss Stein is no longer available as a source of information. But I'll do what I said yesterday and take a mugshot on my phone."

"Sir." One of the uniformed officers from the attending patrol cars looked into the room. "There's a chap out here wants to come in. I've told him it's a closed area, but he says he has an appointment with you. A Mr. Lowe."

"He has indeed. You can let him through."

In response to a murmured 'It's just in here, sir', Mark Lowe appeared in the doorway. Somewhat unexpectedly, the teacher was dressed in the same running kit he had been wearing on the day of the murder.

"Come in, Mr. Lowe," said Constable. "Take a seat."

"What's going on, inspector?" asked Mark.

"I'm afraid there's been another death, sir," replied Constable bluntly. "Miss Phyllis Stein."

"What?" Mark appeared utterly nonplussed. "But how … I mean, who …?"

"Those are questions we're in the process of trying to find answers to, sir."

"Phyllis?" There was clear shock in Mark's voice. "Poor woman."

"Were you close friends, sir?"

Mark shifted evasively. "Not exactly, inspector. I mean, I didn't hate her or anything like that, but she … no, we weren't close," he concluded.

"And, of course, I'm sure she would have had no reason to hate you, sir, would she?" enquired Constable genially.

"What? No, of course not," said Mark hotly. "Why on earth would you say that?"

"So she seems to have settled for a more moderate general disapproval then, sir, from what we gather our conversations with her."

Mark's eyes took on a wary look. "I'm not sure I understand what you're getting at, inspector."

Constable leaned forward, and all traces of warmth vanished. "I think you possibly do, Mr. Lowe. You see, we have been made well aware of Miss Stein's self-appointed role as the chief gossip-monger of the village. And among those pieces of gossip, she showed no reluctance at all in telling us about the rumours that had at one time circulated concerning you and one of your pupils."

"But there was never a word of truth in any of that," protested Mark.

"Oh, she was careful to sprinkle her tale with all sorts of 'allegedlies', but it was clear that she felt that such a thing wasn't beyond the realms of possibility. And it doesn't take much in the way of rumour to damage a teacher's career. I seem to remember that she also spoke of your friendship with Mrs. Farmer in similarly disapproving tones. So you can see why we might think that you would not be a prominent member of Miss Stein's fan club. Nor she of yours."

"That's all you know, inspector," came the reply.

"I'm sorry, sir? Could you perhaps explain."

Mark sighed. "Oh god. This is embarrassing."

"We take embarrassment in our stride, sir," said Constable implacably. "So please go on."

"It was last New Year," explained Mark. "There was a do at the Three Blind Mice that evening. Half the village was there … that's the half that wasn't down at the Dagger. Anyway, Phyllis was among them, and like everyone else, she'd had a drink or two. And it was quite late on, coming up to midnight. I'd just been out to the loo, and I was coming back to the bar when Phyllis appeared in the corridor. Nobody else in sight. And suddenly, there she was, wrapping herself around me, telling me what a good-looking boy I was and she wasn't so old, was she, and then she was trying to kiss me. I nearly had a fit. I thought, what the hell's brought this on? Anyway, I did my best to stop her and laugh it off, and all of a sudden she turned nasty. Said I obviously thought she wasn't good enough for me, and that I evidently thought far too much of myself, and if I thought I was going to get anywhere with a married woman, I'd soon find out what she could do. When she'd finished snarling, she suddenly burst into tears and rushed into the ladies'. And after that night, it never got mentioned again …"

"But no doubt there was a certain coolness." Constable nodded. "I can see that. And tell me, how far was Miss Stein from the truth? Were you trying to get anywhere with a married woman? Are you still, for that matter?"

"Penny? Oh for crying out loud!" Mark sounded highly exasperated. "Look, inspector, I'm a regular at the Mice, and I like to think that I'm good friends with both Penny and Bob. Okay, like everybody else, I think she's gorgeous, and we have a laugh, but that's as far as it goes. I wouldn't actually do anything. So don't judge me by Rex Hope's standards, please."

"But in your opinion, Mr. Hope thought he might have better prospects? Is that what you're telling me?"

"I honestly couldn't say. But if you're looking at me as a suspect because you think I'd kill Rex with a view to improving my chances with Penny, you're barking up the wrong tree."

Constable thought for a moment. "And in any event, it appears you would have had no opportunity to do so. You told us that you saw no more of him after you left the Sword and Dagger after your mid-run rest. And it seems your companions have verified that. So, for now, I've no more questions to ask you." Mark stood. "Oh, except for one. Can you, just for the sake of form, account for your movements between yesterday evening and nine this morning?"

"What, you think I've got something to do with Phyllis's death? Oh, this is ridiculous!" Constable continued to regard him in silence. "Okay. I had a parents' evening last night … finished about half past nine … picked up a curry on my way home … ate it … watched some television, went to bed, got up, and came here. And, apart from about a hundred parents and the guy at the Mughal Palace, no witnesses. Sorry. Can I go now?"

"Of course, Mr. Lowe," responded Constable mildly, rising. "Off for another run, are you?"

"Yes, inspector, bizarre as it may seem, I am. You might have forgotten that there's a village race coming up, but I haven't. And I don't intend to let Bob and Penny down. So if you would like to know my further movements, just in case anything else suspicious occurs around here, I'm planning on looking in at the Mice to check Penny's all right and to tell her that I'm still on for the weekend, and then I'm going for a couple of turns round the course to try to get my head back in the right place. If that's all right by you?"

"By all means, sir," said Constable. "Exercise the demons,

207

as it were."

"Or exercise them, sir," put in Copper over his shoulder.

"Thank you, sergeant. That will do. There is a time for linguistic gymnastics, and this isn't it. Mr. Lowe, thank you for coming in. We'll be in touch if we need to." He nodded and turned away from Mark, who made his way out of the room with an uncertain expression on his face.

"Bit of a turn-up for the books, that, isn't it, guv?" remarked Copper. "Phyllis Stein going all cougar on the teacher. I bet that was a bit of gossip she was careful not to spread. Damn!"

"What?"

"I forgot to take that mugshot for the board."

"Well, you could always chase him down the road and get it," suggested Constable. "Alternatively, you could check next door on Miss Stein's desk to see if she'd found it by the time the bookcase landed on her. Actually, I'll come with you. We might as well see if the doc's turned up anything helpful yet."

The doctor was sat back on his haunches surveying the body of Phyllis Stein, which had been turned over to lie on its face in a cleared spot amidst the welter of fallen books which surrounded it.

"Any progress, doc?"

"A little, Andy. More a case of ruling possibilities out than ruling them in."

"And what exactly does that mean?"

"As far as I can tell from a superficial examination, it's pretty clear that she died from crush injuries. Some time over twelve hours ago would be my best guess. Whether the impact itself was fatal, or whether it was a combination of that and asphyxiation from the weight on top of her, is something I can't tell you categorically until I've got her on my slab and opened her up. Not, I suppose, that the difference is that crucial as far as you're concerned."

"You've turned her over. Any special reason?"

"Well, apart from the fact that the face took a certain amount of direct damage which has not improved the lady's looks, I just wanted to check whether there was any sort of similarity with your other body, for instance by way of a stab wound to the back. But as you can see, not a thing. No other obvious injuries that I can detect, but I'm just about to go over things in rather more detail. Let's see if I can find some nice helpful tell-tale blood or skin under her fingernails from defending herself against an attacker. Once I've done that I'll have her hauled away for closer examination, and then I think it's over to you."

As the doctor began issuing orders on his mobile, the two detectives returned to the other room. "So far, so unhelpful, guv," remarked Copper. "That bookcase – it's heavy, but it's tall. Do you reckon it would have needed a man to push it over, or do you think a woman could have done it?"

Constable snapped his fingers. "Thank you, Copper. Suddenly, a light's just come on."

"I'm pleased about that, sir. What kind of a light?"

"We want somebody with a motive to kill Phyllis Stein. Okay, we know about the possibilities surrounding Mark Lowe. But what's just come into focus is what she told us when she was talking about Adelaide Knight."

"What, that business about the lock-ins, sir? But you yourself said that there was nothing illegal about that."

"Nor is there. But in my wanderings yesterday, I paid a little visit to Miss Knight, included in which was a look at her brewing facilities. And I noticed some other equipment in the next room. She passed it off as just spare odds and sods, but I've just realised why it rang a bell. I was stupid not to realise it straight away. The things I saw were some of the elements of a still. No wonder Phyllis Stein was dropping heavy hints about the local authorities taking an interest. Adelaide Knight is making illicit moonshine!"

*

"So do you really think Adelaide Knight is a serious contender, guv?" enquired Dave Copper as he negotiated the car down the main street of Blaston Dammett and around the local bus as it took on its load of elderly pensioners, bus passes in hand and wheeled trolleys in tow, heading for the weekly farmers' market in Dammett Worthy.

"Look at what we know," replied Andy Constable. "She's a woman who, by her own admission, knows how to deal with opponents. She's certainly no stranger to weapons with shiny sharp edges. And we know that she was quite prepared to resort to violence. It's quite possible that Rex Hope went a step too far, on some occasion we don't know about, and she decided to put a stop to him once and for all. Plus, if she suspected that Phyllis Stein was intent on causing trouble for her, she's certainly got the physical strength to tip over that bookcase. I think a few more questions are in order."

The car pulled into the deserted car park of the Sword and Dagger, which showed no signs of life. Curtains were still closed, and the door was firmly shut.

"Bit early in the day for a pub, sir," pointed out Copper. "Mostly they don't open till eleven. Maybe she's having a lie-in."

"We won't let that stop us," said Constable determinedly. "I haven't got time to fiddle about. Roust her out."

Persistent banging on the sturdy ancient oak door of the inn eventually produced a slightly bleary Adelaide Knight, still wrapping a dressing-gown around herself. "Inspector?" she blinked. "What's the problem?"

"Sorry to disturb you at such an early hour, Miss Knight." Irony dripped from the inspector's words. "May we come in?" Without waiting for a reply, he stepped through the low doorway into the darkened bar, as Addy turned and fumbled with light switches. "I did say I might well be back later, didn't I? Well, later is now. And I would like to know if you can account for your movements yesterday evening from around six o'clock onwards."

"Yes, of course I can. I was here."

"Doing what, exactly?"

"Doing what I always do, inspector," retorted Addy with some asperity. "Getting the pub ready for the evening, and then serving my customers."

"You have witnesses?"

"Yes. Anna was here all the time. Plus a pub-full of customers."

"And this was the entire evening?"

"Yes, until we closed at something after eleven."

"You were alone after that?"

A look. "As it happens, no. A few of my friends stayed on after closing time. Probably until about one – could even have been later. We sat and talked. They may have had a top-up or two, but on the house. No harm in that, I suppose?"

"You didn't leave the premises at all during that time?"

"No, inspector, I did not," insisted Addy. "Look, what is this all about?"

"I have to tell you, Miss Knight, that Phyllis Stein was found dead this morning under suspicious circumstances."

"What, and you think I've got something to do with it? You're mad!" snorted Addy.

"Mad or not, the questions had to be asked. And while I'm here, I have another question for you. Do you mind if I show my colleague here your brewing facilities out the back?"

"Why on earth ...?"

"Well, I did tell you he had something of an interest in beer, didn't I? So I wonder if you could possibly indulge me."

Addy sighed. "If you must. Look, I'm not coming out dressed like this." She reached behind the bar for a bunch of keys. "It's this one. I'm sure you can find your way round by yourselves while I go upstairs and get some clothes on." She turned and disappeared through the door behind the bar.

The door of the brewhouse demonstrated its age by creaking slightly as it opened, but the fluorescent lights which sprang into life at the flick of a switch flooded the room with modern light.

"This is all quite impressive, guv," commented Copper admiringly, surveying the installation. "Every home should have one."

"It's not this I wanted you to see, sergeant. Get your phone out – there are some interesting things which I'd like you to photograph, just through here." Constable pushed open the door to the adjoining room, and stood nonplussed. Apart from a bench and a couple of old ladders propped against the wall, the room was empty. "Oh, for ... damn!" The inspector's fury, though muted, was plain to hear.

"Sir?"

"She's moved it all, hasn't she? All the distillation equipment that I caught a glimpse of when I was here before. She knew I'd seen it, and realised that I would probably put two and two together, so she's stashed it all away carefully out of sight."

"So that puts a spoke in that wheel then, guv."

"Not necessarily." Constable thought swiftly. "Right. Here's what I want you to do. First, get things under way to organise a search warrant for this place. If the pub was as busy as she says it was last night, she won't have had time to do anything

211

complicated. Second, check that things did go on here yesterday as she says they did. Don't bother to talk to that girl Anna – for all we know, she's just as involved as Adelaide Knight. Come down here later and have a casual chat with some of the regulars."

"And if that all pans out, sir? What if we find she's got a motive for both murders but an alibi for each of them?"

"Then, sergeant, we may well be back to square one."

"I do hope you've found everything you were looking for, gentlemen." The light in the room dimmed slightly as the figure of Addy Knight darkened the doorway, her expression smug, her tone sarcastic.

Constable whirled and switched a smile on to his face. "Indeed, Miss Knight. Sergeant Copper here was saying how impressed he was. As, indeed, am I ... by your organisational skills."

"I try to keep on top of everything, inspector," replied Addy. "And I hope you don't mind, but I would like to lock up again. I don't like to leave this place open to casual passers-by – there is quite a lot of value tied up here."

"I imagine there would be." Constable tired of the verbal fencing. "Come along, sergeant. We have matters to attend to." His face set, he headed for the car and climbed in.

Back at the library, the doctor was finishing packing his equipment away.

"How goes it, doc?" enquired the inspector.

The doctor shook his head. "I'm not happy, Andy."

"Unusual for you, doc. Normally, nothing cheers you up like a nice mysterious death."

"Not in this case, Andy. I can't so far find anything consistent with an attack. No defence wounds – no sign that her hands were in a protective position. In fact, the only thing they were holding on to was that damn great dusty book."

"I remember, she had that in her hand when we found her, guv," remarked Copper. He picked up the book which lay nearby on the floor and opened it to reveal page upon page of photographs of village life. "Look – it must be that photo album she was going to look out for me – the one she thought might have a picture of Mark Lowe in it."

"That answers a question," said the doctor. He dropped his voice. "Look, Andy, far be it from me to tell you or SOCO how to do your job, but I've got a theory. For a start, look at those shoes of hers. Rubber soles, right? The sort of rubber that tends to leave scuff marks on a wooden floor like this one. See?" It was true. At many places on the library's parquet floor, small black scuff marks could be seen. "Now look here." The doctor drew the detectives' attention to a similar mark on the front edge of the third shelf from the floor of the bookcase which had been lifted off Phyllis Stein. "I think she was standing on that shelf. Now look again here." He pointed to the top surface of the bookcase, thick with dust. A rectangle clear of dust was plainly visible. "You check that photo album against it, but I think you'll find it a perfect fit."

"So what are you saying, doc?" Andy Constable had a feeling that he knew what was coming.

"Your victim wanted to get hold of that book, which was on the top of a large heavy bookcase, and had been for some time. Goodness knows why, and it's probably not relevant. But in order to get it, she decided to clamber up the front of the bookcase – perhaps she thought she could just reach it, instead of having to go and get a ladder from somewhere. But as she did so, her additional weight was the straw that broke the camel's back, so to speak. Basic physics – the principle of moments, or some such thing that you probably have a vague memory of from your schooldays. The bookcase toppled over, crushing her beneath it. I don't think you've got a murder here. It looks to me like an accident."

*

Andy Constable and Dave Copper stood watching the doctor stow his bag in his ancient Volvo.

"That's chucked a spanner in the works, hasn't it, guv?" remarked Copper. "If Mark Lowe is out of it because of his school parents' evening, and Adelaide Knight turns out to be telling the truth about being in the pub all last night, and Phyllis Stein wasn't killed anyway, surely we're back to square one with Rex Hope?"

Constable had no time to reply. As he drew breath to do so, his attention was distracted by the approaching siren of an emergency vehicle. Stepping into the lane, the detectives could see an ambulance, lights flashing, draw to a halt on the forecourt of the Three Blind Mice, and the swift progress of one of its paramedics into the building.

"What the hell ...? Copper, you'd better go and check what

that's all about." As the sergeant trotted round the corner, Constable made his way to where the doctor was just closing the boot of his car. "If I were you, I wouldn't go anywhere just yet, doc. You never know, this might be another instance where your professional skills are needed." The tone was half-jocular, although the inspector was by no means certain that humour was in order. "Let's see what Copper can find out."

He did not have long to wait. After a few minutes, Dave Copper reappeared round the corner and, puffing slightly, approached his superior.

"It's Sam Booker, guv," he reported. "He's been poisoned."

"What?!"

The doctor looked askance at Constable. "And you thought you were joking, Andy. I suppose I'd better get my bag out again."

"No, it's okay, doc," said Copper hastily. "This isn't one for you. At least, not yet. The paramedics reckon they've got it all under control. They're just getting ready to bung him in the ambulance to whip him into hospital."

"So what happened?"

"I've only got the bare bones, guv. Apparently he was working in the bar, going to and fro between there and the cellar. According to what he told the paramedic between groans, he'd made himself a coffee, which he'd left out back in the kitchen and then half-forgotten about. But then he came up from the cellar, remembered it, and went and took a swig. Didn't much like the taste – thought it was a bit off, so he swilled it down the sink. Two minutes later, he's chucking up. Managed to call for help from his kneeling position over the loo, and Bob Farmer phoned for an ambulance."

"And where had Mr. Farmer been all this time?"

"Doing the books in the other bar."

"And Mrs. Farmer?"

"Upstairs on her own."

"So nobody can account for anyone else? Great!" grunted Constable.

"There's worse, sir," said Copper. "The coffee was standing on the worktop by the back door, which was unlocked and open. And there's a cut through from the car park to the lane."

"So anybody could have got to it? Just what we need. Copper, you'd better stay in touch with the hospital. I want to be kept informed of Sam Booker's condition. Most specifically, assuming they pump him out, I want to know what he's taken in."

"Will do, sir."

As the doctor once again prepared to take his leave, there was a sudden flurry of activity, as two officers who had attended in one of the local patrol cars suddenly emerged from the library building, leapt into their vehicle, and accelerated, siren blaring, up School Lane in the direction of Blaise Copse. "Lively round here, Andy, isn't it?" commented the doctor. "Not so much your peaceful rural idyll."

"Probably just crossed wires, with a bit of luck," said Constable hopefully. "I expect somebody in the control room has doubled up on this thing at the Three Blind Mice, and sent them off in the wrong direction into the bargain. They'll be back soon enough, no doubt."

He was swiftly proved wrong, as a young WPC, one of the incident room officers, appeared in the doorway of the building. "I thought you'd want to know, sir. There's just been a call. Someone's discovered a dead body."

Constable sighed. "Well, you can just call them back and tell them we know all about it. And you can tell them he's not dead, fortunately, and that the whole situation at the Three Blind Mice is all in hand."

The WPC shifted uneasily. "Um ... it's not the Three Blind Mice, sir," she said. "This is something else. One of the local farm workers was coming into the village down School Lane. And he found the body of a man, just by the path leading out of Blaise Copse. He phoned 999 straight away."

"Do we know who it is?" Constable's voice was heavy with foreboding.

"Yes, sir. The chap recognised him. It was the man you were interviewing here earlier on, sir. Mark Lowe."

There was a long pause, during which Constable stood, head thrown back, staring blindly at the sky, while Copper and the doctor exchanged mute looks. Eventually the inspector spoke. "Doc," he said quietly, "I wonder if you would be so kind, if you can spare the time, to come and take a look at the body."

"I knew I should have got out of here while the going was good, Andy," rejoined the doctor. "You know, for some reason, I'm reminded of that scene in 'Death On The Nile' – you know, the one

215

where Bette Davis says 'This place is beginning to resemble a mortuary'." The impression was surprisingly accurate. "And I should know. If you rustle up many more customers for me, I shall have them queueing up in the corridor." He opened his car door. "Well, back to the rock face. You lead the way, I'll follow."

Copper parked his car on the verge of School Lane, under the shade of the last trees of Blaise Copse as they overhung the road, while the doctor drew in behind. As Constable approached the scene, he could see the body of Mark Lowe slumped on the stile – to a casual observer, he might have been taking a breather during his run, except for the large and clearly visible bloodstain on the front of his T-shirt. The two officers from the incident room stood flanking the body, while a little way off, standing holding his bicycle alongside the patrol car, was a very shaken-looking young man in overalls.

"So what happened?" asked Constable without preamble.

"Chap over there was cycling into the village," reported one of the officers. "Saw the guy, and called 999. He's stayed here with the body ever since."

"Copper, go and have a word with him," instructed Constable. "Doc, over to you."

At that moment, the doctor's mobile rang. "Hello … Yes, well as it happens, I'm looking at him now … Don't be silly, when did you ever know me to joke? … Is the van on its way to the Old School? … Well, you'd better get in touch with them and tell them to come up here afterwards. We've got a double load for them." He opened the boot of his car and pulled out a bag. "You know, Andy, I don't think my people and I are geared up for the conveyor-belt nature of death in this part of the world. Perhaps we'll all put in for a transfer to a nice quiet war zone." He slammed the boot. "Right … let's take a look at your latest offering."

"At least I don't need to ask you about time of death," remarked Constable, as the doctor stooped over Mark Lowe's lifeless form. "Or the cause of it, by the look of it."

"Probably not," said the doctor, donning a pair of surgical gloves. He pulled up the front of the T-shirt gingerly. "Hmmm. Stabbed. Single blow to the chest – major trauma to heart or lung, I'd say, if not both. And don't quote me, but I shouldn't be surprised if the knife used was the same, or remarkably similar, to the one used on your first victim. So, same method? Same killer?"

"Except," Constable pointed out, "that Rex Hope was stabbed in the back and this one was stabbed from the front. And if he was sitting here, which it appears he was, since he's quite relaxed and there doesn't seem to be any sign of a struggle, then it looks as if he knew the killer and had no reason to fear anything from them." He grunted. "He was probably dead before he knew it."

"Maybe," said the doctor. "But as for the rest of it, that's rather more your department than mine. I'll just carry on doing my usual once-over, if that's all right by you." He produced a pair of overalls.

As Constable turned away, Copper approached. "Not that much to tell, sir," he reported. "Chap's a cowman on the local farm. He was cycling into the village when he noticed Mr. Lowe sitting on the stile. Knows him from the pub, although this guy usually drinks at the Dagger. Just said 'hi' in passing, but no reply. Didn't think anything much of it, but then he looked again and saw the blood. Nearly fell off his bike, he says. But he took a closer look, realised he was dead, and got on his phone straight away."

"Thank goodness for mobiles," commented Constable. "I don't suppose there's the remotest chance that he saw anyone else, is there?"

"Sorry, guv. He says not a soul. I don't think there's much more he can tell us, but I've got all his details, just in case."

Constable took a decision. "Doc, I'm leaving all this to you. We're going back to the library."

"Reports in due course, Andy," replied the doctor absently, busy with his examination. He looked up. "At least there is one good thing about the situation."

"And what would that be?"

"The more bodies we cart away, the fewer suspects you have!"

*

"Guv, I'm a bit confused." Dave Copper's brow was furrowed in thought.

"Only a bit? You're lucky."

"We've got four bodies ... well, no, three, actually, because the paramedics were looking fairly hopeful that they'd got to Sam

217

Booker in time. But let's include the attempt in the reckoning."

"Go on."

"I just think we've got too many motives, and half of them seem to point in the wrong direction. Look at the Farmers – you could say that Bob Farmer might have had a motive to kill Rex, Sam, and Mark because of feelings of jealousy over his wife. Except that nobody seems to think she's the sort of woman to give him any justification. But if he thought there might be anything going on, he could certainly have got at the last two today – it would have taken some doing, but it's possible – but he was at the Three Blind Mice at the time of the training run, so that rules him out as regards Rex Hope. And pretty Penny? I reckon she's up to fending off any attentions she doesn't want, and there's no way she could have killed Rex anyway. Now, just in case the doc is wrong and Phyllis Stein's death wasn't an accident, we've got a couple of decent motives to kill her, which all come down to the fact that she was spreading the dirt. Mark Lowe had a reason because of this rumour about him and a pupil, but he says nothing ever came from that. Adelaide Knight could have been … probably now is … in trouble over this illicit alcohol business. Except that those two are both accounted for when she died. And in fact, you could look at it the other way round … Phyllis could have wanted to murder Mark in some fit of spinsterish humiliation and jealousy over the New Year's Eve party and the fact that he fancied Penny, except that by the time he's killed, she's lying safely dead on the library floor. And Sam? Well, that takes me back to where I started."

"Let me add to your confusion, sergeant," said Andy Constable, leaning back in his chair and taking a sip of the tea which one of the incident room PCs had just brought the detectives. "No pattern. If, lord help us, there's some sort of homicidal maniac stalking the lanes of Blaston Dammett … even to hear myself say it makes it sound ludicrous … then there's no coherence of method. Let's rule out Phyllis Stein for the sake of argument. The doctor is a remarkably clever man, which he mostly succeeds in concealing behind that bluff 'oh look, another dead body, how amusing' exterior, and I'm inclined to take his suggestion seriously. So we'll assume that her death is accidental, to be confirmed once he gives us his full results. That leaves us with two stabbings and a poisoning. Two different stabbings, I should say. One furtive from behind, and one from the front. So did the second victim know and trust his killer, but the first victim not?" Constable shrugged. "At the moment, your guess is as good as mine. And no weapon, so nothing to point us in any direction."

"Are you sure, guv? What about that nice collection of weapons on the wall at the Sword and Dagger? Adelaide Knight said that they'd lost one or two over time."

"So we have to check around all the customers of the Dagger, just to see whether any of them might have abstracted one of Adelaide's trophies at some time, in the hope that it might just be the weapon we're looking for? I don't think so. We may be in farming country, but I don't think I need to go diving into that particular haystack."

"And the poisoning, sir?"

"Well, it doesn't exactly fit with the other murders. And we know that anybody could have got to the drink to spike it."

"Except Mark Lowe, sir. He never got that far. And until we know what it was in the coffee ..." Copper frowned in thought. "Hang on, sir. I've just remembered. Anna, the girl who works at the Dagger ... didn't she say she was studying chemistry?"

Constable laughed. "So let me see if I've got this right. You are advancing the proposition that, for some reason, somebody from the Dagger wishes to put Sam Booker out of the way? Addy and Anna in cahoots, perhaps? So they swiftly dig out the distillation equipment from its hiding place, concoct some foul poisonous witch's brew, and then come sneaking up the back lanes of the village on the off-chance that Sam might be taking his coffee break at that particular moment?"

Copper smiled ruefully. "When you put it like that, sir, it does sound daft."

"No dafter than some theories I've heard peddled in my time."

"So we're back where we started. In fact ... hang on, sir. Maybe we ought to be doing exactly that, and starting all over again with Rex Hope. And I'll tell you one thing we haven't followed up, and that's what Phyllis Stein told us about him losing all Barbara Dwyer's money. Okay, I can't see any sort of link between him, Mark, and Sam, other than that they were all running together, but they were running past her cottage, and she's got a thoroughly plausible reason to hate Rex. Who's to say she didn't see him go running past on that day? Maybe he made some smart remark as he went by. And she could have snapped, nipped into the kitchen, got hold of that veg knife that we saw her doing such a good job with, chased after him, and stuck it in him in revenge."

"Copper," said Constable, getting to his feet, "that is a delightfully melodramatic scenario, but it may have a kernel of truth in it. And it's certainly one aspect we've overlooked." He rubbed his hands together. "Right. Back in the car. We shall go and pay Mrs. Dwyer a little visit."

As the detectives made their way out of the building, the head of the SOCO team poked his head out of the library. "Oh sir, we're finishing up in here. And they've just taken the body out to the van, sir, so I don't know what you want us to do."

"Lock up the room and leave the keys on my desk," replied the inspector. "Then, unless you've been told otherwise, I assume you'll follow the van round to our other scene of crime and see what work there is for you there." With a brief glance at the anonymous black van which now carried the body of Phyllis Stein, the detectives climbed into Copper's car and set off back down towards the bottom of the village.

A knock at Barbara Dwyer's door brought no response. Dave Copper, returning from a fruitless foray into the back garden of the cottage, reported, "No sign of her, guv. I expect she's at work. After all, it is a weekday."

"You're probably right, sergeant. One tends to forget people have ordinary lives." Constable looked at his watch. "You could try ringing, find out what time she's likely to be home. I assume you've got the number of the place she works at."

"Trust me, sir. Got a note of it here." Copper consulted his notebook, and then swiftly dialled the number. "Hello ... this is Sergeant Copper of the County Police. I'm wanting to get in touch with Mrs. Barbara Dwyer. She's one of your instructors there ... Yes, of course you know that. So might it be possible to speak to her? ... Oh. Until what time? ... And when does that one finish? ... Right. Could I just leave a message for her then, please? Could you ask her to call me back on this number, or get in touch with me at the village library as soon as possible? ... That's right – Sergeant Copper. Thanks. Bye." He put the phone back into his pocket. "No luck, sir. She's just started a class, and then she's got another two straight after that, so she's not going to be available until much later on. We might have to leave her until tomorrow." As he finished speaking, the phone rang. "Blimey, that was quick. They must have gone and interrupted her or something. Hello ... speaking. Oh ... It's not her," he mouthed silently to the inspector. "I see. And what are they saying? ... That's good news, at least. Tonight? Wow! Okay, I'll pass that on. Thanks." He hung up again. "Word from the hospital, sir. About Sam Booker. Apparently it's not as bad as they feared. Obviously he didn't ingest as much of the poison as was first thought, and he's much better than expected. They wanted to keep him in overnight for observation, but it seems he wasn't too keen on the idea, so they're holding on to him for a few hours and letting him come home later this evening."

"Something else for tomorrow," said Constable. "Well, at least the potential body count is down by one."

Copper's phone rang yet again. "Suddenly everybody wants me," he quipped. "I never knew I was so popular. Hello? ... Oh, great. That was quick ... Yes, he makes me jump about a bit too. But it's there at the station? Thanks." He disconnected. "The search warrant, sir. It's ready and waiting on your desk."

"Excellent. We'd better go and pick it up hadn't we? Yet another thing for tomorrow's to-do list. By the way, sergeant ... 'jump about'?"

"Oh ... er ... just talking about a mutual friend at the station, sir," replied Copper hastily. "Nobody you know. So, I presume it's back to the library so's you can pick up your car."

*

Andy Constable pulled on to the old school playground, to find Dave Copper standing waiting for him, alongside a patrol car containing three uniformed officers. The inspector wound down the car window.

"Morning, guv," the sergeant greeted him. "I've been calling the station about you. I thought you'd be here yonks ago."

"And so I would have been, if I hadn't made the mistake of leaving the crucial paperwork sitting on my desk yesterday. So, I thought, I'll nip in on my way and pick it up. Won't take a second. Huh!" A derisive snort. "I got collared by the chief superintendent, who wanted a nice casual informal chat about clear-up rates. And you know what he's like when he gets going. Half an hour later, nothing of any value has been said and I'm biting the carpet, but fortunately he got a call from someone even higher up the food chain, and I managed to escape. So now we can actually get on with some proper police work. Hop in, and we'll go and rummage Adelaide Knight."

As the little convoy drove past the Three Blind Mice, Constable caught a glimpse of the pale face of Sam Booker at one of the windows. "I see our invalid appears to be up and about. I must say, he seems rather eager to get back to work. If I'd been him I would have taken some time off to lie around at home."

"Apparently he lives there, sir. Well, I gather he rents one of the flats over what used to be the stables. Lucky, really. It can't be easy, a young chap like that, finding somewhere to live in a place like this. You know how they're always going on about affordable housing on the news."

"And handy for his job. Mind you, he still looked a bit peaky. Oh well, up to him. We have other fish to fry. By the way, anything from Mrs. Dwyer?"

"Rats!" exclaimed Copper. "I knew there was something else. She came into the library just after I arrived, sir. I didn't know how long you'd be, and she said she couldn't wait, because she was expecting one of her private training clients at home, so she left you a note. Something about never being asked about seeing Rex Hope. I meant to pick it up. We could go back for it."

"Leave it for now. I'll take a look when we've finished down here."

On the forecourt of the Sword and Dagger, Anna Prentiss was just laying aside the broom with which she had been sweeping the area, preparatory to picking up a bucket and scrubbing brush with the evident intention of washing down the wooden tables. At the sight of the police vehicles, she cast an uneasy look over her shoulder towards the open door of the pub, before stepping forward.

"Inspector? Is something the matter?"

Constable ignored the question. "Is Miss Knight here, please?"

"Yes. Yes, she is. She's round the back in the brewery."

"Good." Constable took a step towards the door, but was forestalled by Anna as she put a hand on his arm.

"Is it ... is it about Sam?" queried the young woman hesitantly. "We heard last night. Is he ...?"

"Mr. Booker has been discharged from hospital," said Constable, not unkindly. "He's not in any danger. We aren't here to discuss him, at least, not directly. We have a warrant to search these premises." He turned to the uniformed officers emerging from the patrol car. "You three, make a start inside. I assume Sergeant Copper has explained what this is all about?"

"Yes, sir."

"Good. Copper, would you go round and find Miss Knight, please. Tell her I'd be glad of her company."

"Righty-ho, guv." Copper loped off round the end of the building.

It seemed only a matter of seconds before the sergeant reappeared. His former cheery manner had deserted him, and his face was grim. "Sir ..."

"Well? Where is she?" asked Constable testily.

"Round in the old brewhouse, sir. But you'd better come and see ..."

Adelaide's body lay face-down on the floor, half-in and half-out of the room where Constable had first seen the equipment which had roused his suspicions. Her white top was sodden with the blood from the stab wound in her back.

The inspector let out a deep growl of frustration. "O fool, I shall go mad!" he muttered under his breath.

"You what, sir?"

"Sorry, Copper. It's a quote from 'King Lear'. It just about sums up my feelings at present." Constable gave a deep sigh and began to pace up and down. "This is lunatic!" he raged suddenly. "Who, in the name of all that's holy, could possibly have a reason to murder Adelaide Knight? I'll tell you who," he continued, as Copper drew breath to answer, but then thought better of it. "Rex Hope, that's who, to get revenge for when she beat him up and humiliated him. But we aren't really in a position to tackle him about it, are we? On account of the fact that he's not exactly available to answer questions!" He paused, realised that his junior was looking at him quizzically, and abruptly calmed down. "Sorry about that, sergeant. Sometimes this job gets to you."

"You too, guv? I thought it was just me." The two detectives exchanged small smiles of understanding.

223

"Right. I don't need to tell you what to do. Doctor ... SOCO ... get the uniform lads to stop what they're doing and tape the whole place off." He retraced his steps round to the front of the building, where Anna still stood uncertainly.

"Where's Addy?" she asked. "I thought she'd be with you."

"Miss Knight has been killed," said Constable brusquely. Anna's hand went to her mouth, and her eyes widened in shock. "Can you tell me when you last saw her?"

"It was ... it was about half an hour or so ago," stuttered Anna. "Maybe three-quarters. She said she was going to make a start on a new batch of brewing, so I said I'd get on with the cleaning."

"I'm surprised to find you here at all. I thought you said you were a student."

"I am. But I had a free morning, and Addy said she'd pay me if I did some extra work."

"And has there been anyone else on the premises?"

"Not that I've seen, inspector. Since we came down this morning, it's just been Addy and me."

"Came down? So ... are you saying that you live here?"

"Yes."

"With Miss Knight?"

"Yes ... No!" Anna flushed. "No, not together ... nothing like that!" She sounded embarrassed. "I've got my own bedsit at the other end of the building from Addy's flat. It's Sam's old place – I took it over when he moved out."

"Mr. Booker used to live here?"

"Yes, until the trouble."

"What trouble would that be?" enquired Constable carefully.

"When they had the row about the still ..." Anna broke off. "Oh. That's why you've come to search, isn't it? You've found out about that."

"Yes," confirmed Constable. "Tell me about the row."

Anna slumped. "Sam helped to set it up," she explained. "He's good with stuff like that. But then he told Addy that she was making more than her fair share out of it, and he wanted a bigger cut, and she told him that there was no chance of that. Then he threatened to go to the police, but she said he was as deep in it as she was, and she'd have no trouble throwing most of the blame

224

on to him. Then she fired him, and he went and got the job up at the Three Blind Mice."

"But you haven't seen him or anyone else this morning?" persisted Constable.

"No. I thought I heard someone inside, just after I came out here to start work, but when I looked there was nobody. I thought it must have been Addy." Anna gulped. "Inspector, do you mind if I sit down. This is ... this is horrible." She subsided on to a bench.

"Yes, it is," said Constable in kindlier tones. "Would you like some water?"

"No, I'll just sit here for a bit." Anna sat gazing into the distance, clearly bewildered.

Dave Copper emerged from the front door of the Sword and Dagger, closely followed by two uniformed officers. "All in hand, guv," he reported. "I've left one of the chaps on guard out the back. I've called it in to Control, so they've set all the wheels in motion." He made to put his mobile back into his pocket.

"Sergeant, what's the flashing light on your phone?" asked Constable. "Is it supposed to be doing that?"

"Oh." Copper took a look at his screen. "Voice-mail. Something must have come through when I was on the phone, or else I just didn't hear it ring." He tapped the screen and listened. "Actually, sir, it's a message for you. Mrs. Dwyer. Hold on, I'll put it on speaker and start it again." He tapped the screen once more.

"*Sergeant, it's Barbara Dwyer again. Could you give your inspector a message for me?*" came the voice at the other end. "*Could you tell him that I've remembered something. When you came round to see me, you never asked me if I saw Rex on Sunday morning. Well, I did. I looked out of the window, and he went running past with Sam. I don't know if it helps ...*" She broke off at the sound of a doorbell in the background. "*Sorry, got to go. That'll be my morning victim, or should I say client. But if the inspector wants to ask me anything else, I'm in all morning. Bye.*" The message ended.

"She's obviously got some sort of a tale, guv. Shame it got cut short."

"I'm going round there," said Constable. "There are loose ends here. You'd better stay on the spot and wait for the technicals to arrive. With a bit of luck, I shouldn't be long. I hope." He turned and made for the cottage in Church Lane.

225

The door to Number 8 stood open. Barbara Dwyer lay on her back in the hall, her eyes still wide open in surprise, the blood from the wound in her chest staining the obviously extremely expensive oriental rug beneath her. It took only a moment's inspection for Constable to verify that she was dead. He fumbled in his pocket for his own mobile.

"Police, please, quickly. ... This is D.I. Constable in Blaston Dammett. There's been another murder - a Mrs. Dwyer at 8 Church Lane. Look, I know the technical teams are probably on their way to the village – please pass the information through to them. Thank you." The inspector stood for a moment, calculating rapidly, when out of the front door of the cottage he spotted the Rev. Salter in the lane. He ran out to her. "Vicar, I need you."

"Goodness," said the vicar, "everyone seems to be in a rush. If it's not you, it's that young man of Penny Farmer's."

"Sam Booker? The one who works at the Three Blind Mice? You've seen him this morning?"

"Yes, running up the lane a while ago. Not exactly dressed for training, I thought. Not like last Sunday."

"You saw him on Sunday?"

The vicar nodded. "Yes. I thought I'd told you I saw some of the runners. Mind you, I did think it was a bit odd at the time that he should be running the wrong way."

"How do you mean, the wrong way?"

"Well, he was running towards the Sword and Dagger. The others were going in the opposite direction, towards the copse. I just thought he must have left something behind. Why, is it important?"

"I don't really have time to explain," said Constable. "But right now, I need you here. Mrs. Dwyer has been killed."

"Oh dear lord!"

"Yes, and I have to go. Can I ask you to stay here and keep watch over her until my colleagues arrive? She's inside. And please, don't touch anything."

"Of course." The vicar shook her head in sorrow. "Leave her to me, inspector. Coping with death is one of the things I'm here for. Explanations can wait."

With a brief nod of thanks, Constable sprinted back to the Sword and Dagger, where Copper still waited on the forecourt.

"Hello, guv. That was quick. Where's the fire?"

226

The inspector ignored him and addressed the two uniformed officers seated on benches in the background. "You two, on your feet. One of you, stay here and take over from Sergeant Copper until SOCO arrive. The other one, get up to Number 8 Church Lane. There's been another death."

"What?" ejaculated Copper in disbelief. "You mean ... Mrs. Dwyer?"

"No time to explain now," said Constable, climbing into his car. "Get in. We're going back to the Three Blind Mice. I want to talk to Sam Booker." He let in the clutch and, switching on the car's blue lights, set out at breakneck speed up the main street of the village.

As the two detectives scrambled out of the car at the end of their journey, they were aware of the sound of a scream coming from inside the building. Exchanging looks, they instinctively split up, Andy Constable heading for the front door while Dave Copper ran round the side of the inn towards the rear entrance.

When the inspector entered the bar, he was aware of the sound of voices coming from the direction of the kitchen. Cautiously he pushed open the door. Bob Farmer stood there, every muscle in his body tensed, with Sam Booker behind him, a wicked-looking carving knife held at Bob's throat, while Penny Farmer stood, moist-eyed and trembling, alongside one of the large catering fridges.

"But Sam, he's my husband," she pleaded.

"He doesn't love you," snarled Sam. "Not properly. He never will. Not like me."

"Oh Sam, don't you see? It's just infatuation. It's not really serious."

"You don't understand how I feel." A pathetic tone entered Sam's voice. "Nobody does."

"Sam, just let Bob go," Penny entreated. "Please. This isn't doing any good."

"She's right, Mr. Booker," said Constable, entering the room. "Things are bad enough as they are, without you making them any worse. So why don't you just calm down and give me the knife? You know you're never going to get what you wanted." He took a step forward and held out his hand.

"And you know nothing!" Sam suddenly moved out from behind Bob towards Constable and lunged.

227

As Constable looked down and reflected how strange it was that so much blood could appear so swiftly from a relatively small cut, he was dimly aware of the figure of Dave Copper springing through the back door, seizing the knife from Sam, and wrestling him to the ground.

*

"There's a drinks trolley coming around. Do you want another cup of tea, inspector?"

"I think I'm all right, thanks."

"Well, just remember you have to keep your fluid intake high to compensate for the blood loss. How about you, Dave?"

Dave Copper smiled at the pretty nurse holding back the cubicle curtain in Camford General Hospital's Accident and Emergency Department. "Thanks, Molly, but I'm fine."

"Molly?" Andy Constable smiled. "I wonder, would you by any chance be the Molly that this young man has told me about?"

As the sound of loud and meaningful throat-clearing came from the sergeant standing alongside her, Molly blushed in confusion. "Well, I don't know what he's been saying ..."

Constable took pity on her. "Don't worry," he said, "nothing incriminating. And it's very nice to meet you. I would shake hands, but obviously ..." He nodded to his heavily bandaged right arm. "But perhaps you ought to find time to let him tell you all about what he's been up to today. He's been quite the hero. Maybe you could find a free evening. Not now, of course ... you're very busy, I'm sure."

"Yes ... er ... I've got to ..." With a bob of her head, Molly was gone.

"Guv, ..." began Copper reproachfully.

"Sorry, sergeant. Just a little harmless fun. You'll have to forgive me. It's the kind of thing we poor bed-ridden invalids get up to."

"Bedridden invalid my foot!" snorted Copper. "If you'll pardon the expression, sir. Walking wounded at worst, from what I've been told."

"No sympathy to be had here, then," remarked Constable.

"So tell me, guv," said Copper, eager to move the conversation on to safer ground. "We never really got a chance to chat in the back of that ambulance. How did you figure it all out?" He perched on the hard plastic chair alongside the inspector's

228

bed.

"Partly by a process of elimination," replied Constable. "We'd practically run out of suspects anyway, but eventually a pattern emerged. What was confusing us, of course, was the over-supply of motives for each of the individuals involved, but once we'd cleared a few of those out of the way, it came down to a choice between two of the oldest motives of all ... love and hate. And in this case, it turned out to be love. I think somebody once said something clever about more crimes being committed in the cause of love than anything else. Well, they certainly got that right."

"So talk me through it, guv. It's still all a bit of a tangle in my mind."

"There was a time when I seriously thought that Bob Farmer might be in the frame. I mean, slightly older man, pretty younger wife, and three guys drooling over her to a greater or lesser extent. Jealousy can be a pretty powerful motive, and with his military background he could easily have been capable of drastic action. Of course, Phyllis Stein didn't fit into that pattern, but once the suggestion had been made that her death was an accident, and particularly after it looked as if an attempt had been made on Sam Booker while Bob was nearby, then Bob was starting to look increasingly plausible."

"Did you never seriously consider Penny? After all, she might have got just as sick of being pursued."

"There was no way she could have killed Rex Hope, and if she wasn't responsible for that, there was no logic to what followed."

"You said there were three guys drooling over her, but in fact, Sam was the least drooly. He struck me as shy more than anything."

"Yes, that misled us. They say the shy ones are the worst. We should have paid more attention to what Phyllis said. She told us that he was obviously head-over-heels in love with Penny, and we didn't pick it up. And there's another thing I should have picked up right at the start, and I didn't. I blame myself for that."

"What's that, sir?"

"Don't you remember the first time we spoke to the runners on Sunday? Mark said that he and Sam were together all the time, except for when Sam nipped behind a tree to relieve

229

himself. And Sam went on to say that he carried on following Mark, and that he could see him ahead all the way until he caught up with him at the stile. It sounded as if he was giving Mark an alibi. In fact, he was giving himself one. I walked that course. I followed the route through the wood, and it twists and turns all the way. It would have been impossible for Sam to see Mark all the time unless he was hard on his heels. If you look at that big map you drew, you'll see that the runners followed the path which goes round the whole wood in a big loop. But there are forks in the path at several points. It would have been the easiest thing in the world for Sam to take one of those short cuts and catch up with Mark just as he got to the stile."

"Giving him the time he needed."

"Exactly. And I should have realised that."

"So do you reckon Rex was just phase one of a plan, guv?"

"I think he was. I believe that Sam had somehow got it into his head that if he got rid of all the other men in her life, Penny would turn to him for consolation. So first Rex was killed, and then when Mark went into the Three Blind Mice to check how Penny was, prior to setting off on his second run after he called in to see us, Sam saw his chance. While Mark was going the long way round, Sam went out the inn the back way, met Mark as he emerged from the woods, killed him, and was back at the inn within minutes."

"So the poisoning ...?"

"He did it himself, of course, to distract attention. I remember you made some daft suggestion about Anna from the Dagger concocting a poisonous brew, and I laughed at you. I shouldn't have been so quick, because you had the right idea but the wrong person. Don't forget, Sam had been a chemistry student too, and he'd helped to set up the still at the Dagger. If he couldn't identify something in the kitchen cupboard that would produce some pretty effective results without actually being dangerous, then his education had been wasted. All evidence helpfully rinsed down the sink or flushed down the loo. And it had the supplementary effect that, once he was discharged from hospital, he'd very likely have Penny Farmer cooing over him and playing nurse."

"But why the other murders? What did they have to do with this weird scheme?"

230

"Insurance, I think. As I see it, once Mark was out of sight on the run, Sam went back to the Dagger and collected Rex. You can imagine it – 'Come on, you poor old chap. I couldn't leave you on your own. Let's carry on together'. The fact that he told us Mark had cracked a gag to the same effect was something of a subconscious give-away. Then, once safely in the woods, wham! Now obviously Sam had something against Adelaide Knight anyway because she had sacked him, but there was also the possibility that she might have seen him when he went back for Rex, so that's why he decided to kill her. And from what Anna told me, she may have had a lucky escape herself, because she could also have been a witness. The same applied to Barbara Dwyer. She said in that message of hers that she'd glimpsed Sam through her cottage window. It's equally possible that he saw her, and thought that she might provide evidence that he was going back towards the Dagger. As she did, but too late to save herself. And who knows, if he'd had the time, he might even have put an end to the vicar on the same off-chance."

"Which just left Bob."

"Who was the final obstacle in Sam's way, as he saw it. Never mind that by now we were bound to start to realise that there were very few possible killers left for us to consider. And never mind that, when we walked in on that scene, there was never going to be any chance it would end well. By then, I think he'd lost the power of logical thought."

"Too right, guv," said Copper. "You were rather out of it by then, but by the time we got him cuffed and into a car, he was raving. I think from what I've heard that they're going to get the shrinks to take a good look at him before anything goes much further. So who knows how that's going to end up?"

"I'm glad that's not our province. We've done our work and we shall write up our reports, and after that I'm happy to leave the rest of it to the specialists." Constable's face grew momentarily solemn. "By the way, David, I never got to thank you properly for getting that knife away from Sam."

"All down to that course on unarmed combat and dis-arming criminals, guv," said Copper modestly. "Which, if you remember, it was your idea to send me on. And just as well you did. You know, when Sam went for you and I saw the blood, I thought for a minute that it was last orders for you." He guffawed.

231

"Like the old gag about the Swedish barman ... you know, 'Lars Torders'!"

"I've had enough of barmen to last me quite a while, thank you very much," said Constable with a rueful grin. "And the joke is not really that amusing anyway. Whoever thought it was funny to start making a play on words out of people's names should have his head examined."

At that moment, Molly put her head around the curtain again. "We should be able to let you leave any minute, inspector. Doctor Sworder's on his way."

Throughout the hospital's Accident and Emergency Department, patients and staff alike were startled by the sound of sudden and unrestrained male laughter coming from one of the cubicles.

*   *   *   *   *

THE INSPECTOR CONSTABLE MURDER MYSTERIES

MURDERER'S FETE
(First published in paperback as Feted To Die)
Constable and Copper investigate the death of a celebrity clairvoyant at the annual garden fête at Dammett Hall

MURDER UNEARTHED
(First published in paperback as Juan Foot In The Grave)
A lucky win takes Constable and Copper on holiday to Spain, but murder soon rears its head among the British community on the Costa

DEATH SAILS IN THE SUNSET
Our detectives find themselves aboard a brand new cruise liner, but swiftly discover that some guilty secrets refuse to be buried at sea.

MURDER COMES TO CALL
A trio of cases for Constable and Copper to tackle -
in Death By Chocolate, the victim comes to a sticky end at Wally Winker's Chocolate Factory; in The Dead Of Winter, there's first degree murder at Harde-Knox College; and in Set For Murder, there's a grisly shock in store at the Spanner House of Horror film studios.

www.rogerkeevil.co.uk

Printed in Great Britain
by Amazon

17010564R00139